EVERYONE
SAYS THAT
AT THE END
**OF THE
WORLD**

EVERYONE SAYS THAT AT THE END OF THE WORLD

OWEN EGERTON

SOFT SKULL PRESS
AN IMPRINT OF COUNTERPOINT

To Jodi

I wrote a book for you.

This book is a work of fiction. Names, characters, places, and incidents either are products
of the author's imagination or are used fictitiously. Any resemblance to actual events or
locales or persons, living or dead, is entirely coincidental.

Library of Congress Cataloging-in Publication is available.

ISBN 978-1-59376-518-7

Cover design by Elke Barter
Interior design by Neuwirth & Associates

Soft Skull Press
An Imprint of Counterpoint
1919 Fifth Street
Berkeley, CA 94710
www.softskull.com

Printed in the United States of America
Distributed by Publishers Group West

10 9 8 7 6 5 4 3 2 1

Once upon a time,

in one of the time periods,

an explosion of light came.

And ruined the oceans.

And turned the air to lava.

The end.

                    —Arden, age 7

2,732,841

DAYS BEFORE
THE END OF THE
WORLD

POP

9,502
DAYS

Fuck balls

THE FIRST DROPS of rain were the heaviest, falling in broad, solitary beads. Awesomely destructive, if you were an ant. The boy, who had been meditatively lost in the ants' comings and goings for that past hour, looked up to the black clouds, a drop hitting his face like God's spit. It would be a downpour—a rush of water from the hot Texas skies. He looked back down at the pile, the rain puncturing the grainy surface. Already lines of black ants were erupting from out of the hill only to be thumped by fresh drops. He leaned over the pile, blocking the rain.

"Fuck balls!" he said.

It was his father's expression and it felt powerful. Often his father, working through the night on some vague, nonsensical problem involving numbers and frustration and something called quarks, would hurl "fuck balls" up from the basement.

The rain was falling in full now, soaking through the boy's shirt and turning the dusty yard into a rust-colored swamp. Even using his body as an umbrella, the rain was melting the anthill. A fist of panic squeezed the boy.

The boy had no particular affection for ants. His mother considered them enemies—using bleach and store-bought poisons to rid them from the kitchen and cursing their persistent colonization of the backyard. She would grimace to see her son working to actually preserve these pests. His father never noticed the ants. They were too large. His mother asserted that he was blind to anything larger than an atom. "Milton," she had once told her son. "If it *can* be seen, your father can't see it."

On any other day, Milton might have just watched the ants drown, perhaps even cheered their demise. But something about that day—about the weight of the drops, about the singed scent of ozone in the air, about the tone in his mother's voice as she sent him out to play an hour earlier, and how she had touched his face for a long moment before corralling him out the back door—made the boy feel that to abandon these ants would be a crime.

Without a clear plan, Milton dug both his hands into the pile and scooped up as many ants as he could carry. He glanced at the inner caverns of the mound filled with manic ants carrying plump white larva in their pinchers, then rushed for the shelter of the outer awning of the kitchen door.

The ants began biting before he took his second step.

"Fuck balls!" Nasty pin pokes of pain. The ants crawled from his hands up his thin arms, administering stings with a zealous rage. By the door sat an empty water bowl, once belonging to a family cat that had long since forsaken the family. The boy dropped his fists of ants and dirt into the bowl, but hundreds still clung to him. "FUCK BALLS!" the boy yelled, hopping up and down and wiggling his arms frantically.

"Fuck, fuck fuck balls!" he said, itching at his already welting arms.

The kitchen door opened. Milton nearly stumbled back into the rain.

His father stood, silent and staring. He wore the outfit he taught in—white short-sleeve button-down shirt with a navy-blue tie decorated with the emblem of his alma mater, Rice University. He was a thin man—tall with fingers that twitched at the end of his lanky arms. He looked at his son with confusion.

"The ants are biting me," Milton said.

His father stepped back and let the boy slog in. Milton ran to the sink and plunged his arms under the faucet.

I was trying to save you, he thought as the last of the tiny black dots spiraled down the drain. He turned off the water. In the new silence, the house felt strange, a new strange. He turned to see his father standing on the other side of the kitchen staring at him.

"Where's mom?" he asked.

His father walked to the fridge. "I'm going to make eggs for dinner."

"Mom's not here?"

"She left," he said into the innards of the fridge. "Maybe waffles and eggs."

"She left?"

"Hot damn, we don't have any eggs." He closed the fridge, leaning his back against the door. "Not even eggs." He let his body slide down to the floor, sitting with his legs curled into themselves.

Milton watched his father with curiosity, wondering whether the man would cry. He'd never seen him cry.

"Look, she's gone," his father finally said. "Which is bad. But look, I've told you before, this world is one of countless worlds. Okay? Every quantum event creates a new world. Each world a page in a book with a billion pages. Got the image?"

The boy nodded.

"No, you don't. You don't, because if you did, you wouldn't be looking like that, all stunned and beat up." He rapped his knuckle on the lime-green linoleum. "Listen. Okay? Mathematically speaking, every possible outcome is happening right now. Each page a possibility that is not just possible but existing. Countless parallel worlds with slight and drastic differences." He wasn't looking at the boy. Instead his eyes seemed focused on the floor between his legs. "A world where oceans are acid, another world with no oxygen, another where you were never born, and a world—a world right next to us, closer than our skin—a world where she never left." Outside the downpour petered down to occasional drops hitting the kitchen window in a rhythmless series. His father looked up at him, his eyes clear. "So in our world she leaves. But she doesn't always leave. Doesn't that help? It does, doesn't it?"

The boy was watching four ants crawl in from under the back door, black ships on a massive sea of lime green. What drove them? What in the world could they hope to find? Milton hated them with all his heart.

Mysteries

"SEE THE LIGHTS, Rica?" Her father knelt beside her and pointed out across the dark desert scrub. "Just over the mountain."

She watched them move. Small balls of light dashing in zigzags. One slowed, then shot upward. One faded in and out. One glowed an off-white blue, another slightly green.

"They're just headlights," her mother said, holding Rica's younger brother's hand. "I'm taking him to the potty. Meet you at the car."

"Never seen headlights bounce," her father said to Rica once her mother had gone. One light chased another, the two zipping up and down and across the horizon like squirrels in a tree.

"They look happy," she said.

"I told you Texas wasn't so bad," he said with a chuckle.

"What are they?"

"Mysteries," he said. "Mystery lights. People have been seeing them here for more than a century. No one knows what they are."

Two of the lights darted together, circling each other in a bright-blue glow.

"They're dancing," Rica whispered.

8,753

DAYS

Every moment, a universe

HIS FATHER, BREATH bitter with coffee, shook him awake. "Wake up, Milton. I want to show you something. Look out the window."

The boy, still half asleep, tried to sit up, but his father placed a hand on his shoulder and pushed him back down. "I have to tell you something first. Nothing I'll repeat. You ask me about it tomorrow, I'll call you a liar, hear me?"

The boy nodded. His father's sweaty face twitched toward the window.

"I don't know what they are, but they're better than us and they're alive." He nodded to the boy, his eyes wide. "The whole department knows, but no one will talk about it. We make side comments to each other, knowing looks, but we never just say it. It's like a dirty family secret that everyone knows and no one will talk about. Understand?"

"What's outside, Dad?"

"Remember all those worlds? All those countless worlds? They're not just parallel. Not just a near-endless book. That's too small an image. It's more like a sphere, each point an endless book. A ball of endless books! But you understand. No, don't try. But get this. Every moment—each microsecond—is really another world. A new world exactly like the last moment's world but with the changes of the moment. Every moment, a universe."

His father stared down at him for a moment. Milton knew he was waiting for a nod of comprehension. But he didn't comprehend. His father grunted and grabbed a half-filled water glass from the boy's bedside table.

"In one world this glass is falling." He let the glass go. It fell to the floor, shattering. "In the next world the glass is broken on the floor. See? So experiencing time is just moving from one world to the next and to the next and to the next." He grinned at his son, then raised his head, glancing out the window and quickly ducking down. "Jesus!"

"What?"

He stared back at his son. "So we, just by being alive, travel through the many worlds. But we have no control. We move through in one direction, along one path. Just one book, page by page. We're not so much traveling as falling. Falling through the pages. Or maybe we're motionless and the pages fall through us. Is that it?"

He paused, and the boy wondered if he was supposed to answer.

"The thing is, Milton," he said after a beat. "They, those things out there, can move wherever they want. Any direction, any book, any page. They don't fall. They float."

He took a deep breath. "Do you get it?"

Milton nodded.

"Of course you don't get it," his father said. "But you will. You'll see." He glanced toward the window. "Go ahead."

Milton sat up, keeping his eyes on his father.

"Look!"

The boy turned to the window. There was a man in the yard. Near the back, underneath the dead pecan tree. Naked. No hair or genitals. Just skin—tight, smooth, and nearly blue in the moonlight. *Not a man. Something different*, the boy thought. *A non-man.* Under the tree, his body swayed like a corpse moved by the wind.

"What does he want, Milton? What the hell could he want?"

Milton looked back to his father and he could see now that his father did want an answer, but he had nothing.

"They follow me, Milton. They watch me. Like goddamn ghosts."

Milton looked back to the yard and startled back. The Non-Man's face was an inch from the window, staring in at them with unblinking black eyes, his mouth opened in a silent, screaming gasp.

5,476
DAYS

Chlorine and cologne

RICA WAS THIRTEEN years old when she first considered that what *is* could have been otherwise. When she was five, she hadn't questioned her parents' move from L.A. to Plano, a suburban community on the outskirts of Dallas. But as she entered her teens and her body became a pubescent battlefield of bumps and blood, she examined her life and imagined what might have been had her parents raised her by the Pacific Ocean, in the capital of the entertainment world, instead of an outpost on the plains of Texas, whose cultural highlights included Chili's restaurants and a dozen suburban shopping malls.

As that summer had approached and Plano sank into a roasting, sticky suck, Rica found her changing body releasing sweat in ever-creative ways, her pores opening and closing like a chorus of suffocating guppies. She begged her parents to fly her to California to visit her cousin Cece.

The two weeks in Santa Monica were a heady introduction to her teen years—eyeliner experiments, late-night beach concerts, strawberry-banana wine coolers snuck from her aunt's fridge. Cece dismissed Rica's own modest, one-piece swimsuits and replaced them with low-cut bikinis. She instructed Rica on how to revel in the stares, how to meet a boy's eyes with coy confidence, how to enjoy her expanding attributes.

"Shoulders back, girl. Let those puppies lead!"

"I don't want to show them off."

"Yes, Rica. Yes, you do!"

On the last night of her visit, the girls were invited to a pool party at the Malibu home of a game show host's son. The whole day had been a ritual of preparation. New swimsuits were modeled, then discarded; makeup styles were debated; and flirtatious laughter practiced.

They arrived as the sun dipped into the Pacific. It seemed impossible to Rica

that this same sun's light touched Plano. Surely, Plano lived under the reign of
the humid, half-witted brother of this sun.

Rica followed Cece's lead, circling the pool like seasoned dolphin trainers and
laughing as the boys palmed water toward them. Cece was the first girl in the
water, sliding into the shallow end and inviting Rica to follow. Soon the sky was
dark and the pool full. Radio grunge poured from speakers, beach balls bounced,
exposed skin incidentally touched exposed skin, and the pool transformed into a
chlorinated pheromone stew with nubile teens splashing about like eager, effer-
vescent dumplings.

An hour after sunset, a boy strolled into the party wearing jeans and a perfectly wrinkled, button-down shirt. Rica didn't know him but understood from
the naked admiration of some and the willed disdain of others that this boy was
important. He smiled a near-perfect smile—the ratio of lip to teeth a math-
ematical wonder. He walked a near-perfect walk—a gait communicating endless
energy but charming restraint. And though he looked younger than some of the
boys wrestling in the deep end, he surely was more emotionally mature. Too
worldly for such trivialities as swimming and beach balls. Someone handed him
a soda, which he drank with the gratitude and slightly disguised skepticism of a
visiting dignitary sampling a traditional meal in some exotic country.

Rica went warm.

"My gawd, Rica." Cece tickled her midriff. "Don't drool."

"I'm not!" she said, blushing. "I just thought I recognized him."

"Yeah, you do! That's Hayden Brock. The kid from *White Slavery*. He's been
on *Saved by the Bell*."

"Zack's cousin!" Rica gasped. "Ronny?"

"Ronny."

The party rumbled on. A pint of vodka, snuck from some father's freezer, was
tipped into Sprite, Coke, Orange Crush. The party migrated from the pool into
a game room separated from the main house. The teens spread about the ping-
pong table, the vintage pinball machine, the PlayStation set up on the large-
screen television. Noise and play, laughter and illegal sips. Then the game show
host's son locked the door and turned, grinning, to the room.

"Let's play a game."

It was clear the game would not be ping-pong. A new, illicit anticipation
simmered. Boys nodded, girls giggled, vodka urged, hormones cheered. Spin the
Bottle? Truth or Dare? Seven Minutes in Heaven?

Rica's skin prickled. She sipped her Sprite and vodka and stole a glance at Hayden, who leaned against a far wall with an expression of boredom and ease that Rica found exhilarating.

Seven Minutes in Heaven was the game of choice. Two people in a closet, seven minutes, no questions asked.

Boy's names were scribbled on paper and placed in an ice bucket shaped like an L.A. Rams football helmet. The girls were given an oversize sombrero. The game show host's son drew the names. He had inherited some of his father's pizzazz, slowly dipping his hand into the ice bucket, patiently unfolding the slip of paper, reading the name to himself and making rascally eye contact with the onlookers, playing with the crowd's nervous excitement.

As Rica watched, she had a vague sensation that this game was an all-too-accurate metaphor for partnering. Her name was only in the sombrero because she was here that night. If she hadn't moved to Texas, her romantic opportunities would, more or less, comprise the boys in that L.A. Rams ice bucket. She knew another, less impressive ice bucket, probably a Dallas Cowboys helmet, sat waiting for her back in Texas.

Sure, there were exceptions. Lovers who discovered each other in different social circles, different locales, different generations even. But the common narrative involved being paired, with a name from your near world.

This truth sat in Rica's stomach like a spoonful of gasoline, equally equipped to poison her or light a fire of rebellion in her belly. She swallowed more of her drink.

The game show host's son announced a boy Rica didn't know and Cece. Cece looked to Rica, her eyes screaming. Hoots and hollers raged as the two slunk into the closet and the stopwatch was set.

The door clicked closed and the rest of the party slipped into a thoughtful funk. The game show host's son put some music on, threw out a few jokes, but the kids' minds were all centered on one question: What were they doing in there?

Quick images of flesh and hands and lips flashed through Rica's mind. She took a long sip of her drink and pretended to laugh at a joke she hadn't heard.

Hayden retreated to the pinball machine with a few other boys.

Finally, after the longest seven minutes of Rica's life, Cece and the boy emerged.

"What'd you guys do?" a boy screamed.

"No!" demanded the game show host's son. "You can't ask. It's their little secret." He stared at the crowd with the solemnness of a priest. "Of course, in nine months we'll all *know* what happened." The room burst into laughter.

Rica watched Cece closely. She would wait to ask, but it was clear, *something* had happened. Good or bad was nearly impossible to tell from the confused colors in Cece's cheeks. Rica was still studying Cece's face when she heard her own name called. Her lungs refused any air and for a minute Rica thought she might faint.

"And Rica's lucky compadre is"—the host grinned—"Hayden!"

The blood that rushed to Rica's ears prevented her from hearing the jokes, the laughter as she and Hayden were ushered into the closet. She wasn't at all sure what was happening until the door closed and she stood in half darkness a foot away from Hayden.

For a long beat, neither said a word. The rest of the party was a muffled world away. Chlorine and cologne filled her nose and spiked Sprite bubbled her throat.

"My name is Hayden," he said.

She nodded. "I'm Rica." Her voice felt close.

"I don't really like these games, do you?"

She shook her head, though she hadn't considered the question until that moment. But she wondered if Hayden would have preferred the game with another partner. Cece, perhaps. Or the blond girl with the chest of a college grad.

"But if I had to be locked in a closet with someone," Hayden said with a smile that seemed to shine even in the dim light, "I'm glad it was you."

Heat—glowing stove-top heat—rose to her skin. She was sure he could feel it.

"I saw you when I first got here. Truth is, I would have left hours ago if it weren't for you."

"I don't live here," she said, not knowing exactly why, but wanting Hayden to understand she had made it into the night's sombrero under false pretenses.

"Maybe that's what I like about you," Hayden said with a perfectly executed chuckle.

Everything in Rica liquidized. Shake her, and she'd have sounded like a fresh coconut.

"Five minutes!" someone called from outside. Hayden glanced at the door, then his feet, then her eyes. He stared with a fearless certainty that Rica wanted to devour. A bright, clear realization crystallized in Rica's mind. This will be her first kiss! With this boy. This magic, perfect boy. It will stay with her always. This moment will change her everything. Her head pounded and something acidic like old orange juice filled her sinuses.

"Would you mind," Hayden said, "if I kissed you?"

Rica's soul was already puckering as Hayden leaned closer. He was an inch from her face when she uttered, "No."

Hayden paused. "No?"

For an instant her mouth remained closed. She begged her body to obey, begged her stomach to hold down the fort, begged a *yes* to her lips. *Please, please, please don't let this be the way things are!*

"I—" Hayden began to speak when the line of vomit exploded from Rica's mouth. He stumbled back. Rica reached out, futilely trying to wipe the vomit from his shocked face.

"I'm sorry!" she mumbled, hot tears and snot joining the stomach acids dripping from her chin. Hayden shook his head. She wasn't sure if it was he or the host who threw the door open and spilled light—horrible, unforgivable light—into the closet.

As Hayden shoved past the party toward the bathroom, the onlookers stared into the open closet with disgust, with humor, with relief that they were not the ones being stared at. And Rica knew her name would never again grace a West Coast sombrero and the magic of her first kiss was lost forever to the realm of could-have-been.

Everything happens

MILTON PUSHED THROUGH the unlocked door. His father never locked the door. "If they want in, they'll get in," he'd say. "A deadlock is the worst kind of false security. Like wedding rings and yoga."

He stepped inside, still sweating from the mile bike ride from the high school, his denim jeans sticking to his legs in the early spring heat. Thick olive curtains barricaded the front room from the sunlight. The dust and shadow gave the room an otherworldly feel. A soft squeaking—like a mouse filibustering—emanated from somewhere inside the house. Then a soft crack.

"Dad?"

"Kitchen!"

His father was now almost constantly at home. With no more explanation than "Those damn small-minded Bohr-heads!" his father stopped making his daily drive to the physics research department of the University of Texas. He still dressed for work, the same short-sleeved button-down white shirt and navy-blue Rice tie. He still woke each morning before dawn. Milton would leave him sitting at the kitchen table sipping instant coffee and staring into nothing. He'd come home to find him pacing through the rooms of the small house scribbling into notebooks. Milton would throw two frozen dinners into the oven, and he and his father would spend the rest of the evening in front of the television watching rented horror movies. Each strangled, stabbed, drilled, impaled, or defenestrated teenager would send Milton's father into a fit of giggles.

Once, during a rare bloodless spell of film, Milton asked his father what he was working on all day.

"Immortality," he said, then pointed at the TV. "She's getting it next. You just know it."

In the kitchen, Milton found his father scribbling with a permanent marker on the closed freezer door. The lower half of the refrigerator was ajar. His father clenched the marker between his teeth, reached into the fridge and retrieved an egg. He held it up to his face, then let it fall. It smashed on the floor beside the yolks and broken shells of several eggs puddling on the linoleum.

"They say it can be done." He clucked his tongue and shook his head. Taking the marker from his teeth, he made another note on the freezer door. "Just have to drop it at the exact right spot."

"Dad, it's a mess."

"I always wanted to give it a go! Can you imagine an egg landing all in one piece? Maybe balanced on its point. It happens, you know. Everything happens." He turned to Milton. "I'm glad you're finally home. It's been hours."

"Marching band practice."

"Waste of time." He walked past Milton and into the hall. "I've been waiting to do this until you got here. I want you to see."

"See what?"

"How to live forever!" His father pulled open the basement door and nearly stumbled as he started down the dark steps. "It's Everett's idea. He figured it out. Bohr, the bastard, snubbed him. But it's all there and makes a hell of a lot more sense than the babbling of those Copenhagen cronies. I mean, right?"

Milton flipped the light switch at the top of the stairs. His father stood at the bottom, staring back up at him.

"It's pretty fucking clear, yes?" his father said, gesturing to a wall covered with pages of handwritten equations and graphs, the handwriting immaculate.

Milton stepped down the stairs into the damp, low-ceilinged room. Half of the basement was piled with sagging cardboard boxes and broken furniture pieces. One light-blue suitcase sat near the top—a remnant of his mother's presence.

The suitcase had been left in the hallway the afternoon she walked out. For months it remained there, untouched. Though it was never said, Milton knew he and his father shared the same hope. They imagined the day she'd walk back through the door to retrieve her belongings. Then she would see her son and her husband and she would stay. She wouldn't have to apologize or explain. She could just step right back in.

Stumbling to the bathroom in the middle of the night, Milton tripped into the bag and the two learned that the suitcase was empty. She had left nothing behind.

"Tegmark gave me the idea for building one. But he only *speculated*," his father said, walking toward the far wall of the basement. "But what good is a gift if you don't unwrap it! Right? Take a look at this!"

On a sagging card table sat a metal and plastic contraption looking like four carburetors stuck together with duct tape and a series of wires. Linked to the contraption by two more wires was a black, metal lockbox with two drilled holes half an inch apart.

"Two main components. First, a spin-value detector." He patted the contraption. "I borrowed one from the university! Ha! If they come asking, tell them it was my retirement present. Ha! Better than a gold watch!"

"You stole it?"

"It measures a single electron's spin. Clockwise or counterclockwise. Like a quantum flip of the coin. I'm using hydrogen. Just one electron. Easy." He paused and looked up at Milton. "Feynman told everyone there was only one electron, period. Just one little guy popping around the universe appearing in a zillion places at once! Crazy, huh?"

"Yeah, that's pretty crazy," Milton said.

His father returned his focus to the machine, turning one of three black knobs at its base. The machine purred. "So the machine sits here. I stand over there." He pointed to a large X duct-taped near the center of the basement floor. "And you, monsieur, your table is right here." He took on the persona of a snooty French maître d', a game he hadn't played with Milton for over a decade. Chuckling, he gestured Milton toward one of the narrow poles positioned around the basement.

"Maybe I should go upstairs and clean the kitchen."

"No, no," his father said. "I want you to see this. Hell, I might *need* you to see this." He locked on Milton's eyes and stepped close. "Son," he said softly, "I know sometimes I seem a little eccentric, a little off. I know that. But I know what I'm doing." He took a slow breath. "You're going to witness something. And there's a good chance it won't be pleasant." He took Milton's hand in his own. "Can you trust me?"

Milton found himself wordless.

His father smiled. "Don't worry. I understand," he said.

And Milton felt the handcuff click. Instinctively Milton yanked his arm. The other end of the cuffs pulled against the pole.

"Dad!"

His father was already moving toward the duct-taped X.

"I measured it all out. Tested and retested it again and again." He pulled the permanent marker from his shirt pocket, bent down, and circled the *X*. "I go right here." He stood straight, facing the machine as if at military attention. He eyed the machine, raised his marker, and drew a small *X* on his own forehead. "The bullet will go here."

"What bullet, Dad?" Milton pulled harder, but the pole didn't budge. "Stop this, Dad. Let me go."

"Well, the bullet *will* and *won't* go right here." He walked slowly to the whirring machine and lockbox, counting under his breath. He placed his open palm on the lockbox. "I thought getting the guns would be an issue. Turns out it's pretty easy!"

"Dad, stop this."

His father twisted the other two knobs on the machine and returned to the *X* on the floor. He again stood at rigid attention, facing the machine and lockbox. "I've set it for a hundred readings, once every fifteen seconds. If it reads a clockwise spin, it fires a bullet. Bam! Into the old soft, gray stuff. If it reads counterclockwise it—"

Click.

"Ha! It does that. See. I'm still here. But that quantum event has created another world where I'm dead! See, do you get it now?"

"Dad, tell me there's nothing in that box."

"Hot damn, Milton. I'm not playing with myself down here!"

Milton shook the pole violently. He kicked at it, pushing his body back. The cuffs cut into his wrist. "Dad, please."

Click.

"Dad! Stop this! This is stupid." Milton reached out, stretching toward the card table and the lockbox.

"Don't fuck with this, Milton. Do not fuck with this! It needs to be a clean shot! Fatal. If not, I'll be stuck. And it needs to be fast! Immediate!"

"You're not making any sense, Dad!"

"No such thing as sense. It's just a word small minds use to praise their limitations."

Click.

"Please stop this!" Milton pulled at the pole. He felt a slight give where the pole met the ceiling. "I'll call someone. Get some help."

"Don't worry, Milton. This won't kill me. Not everywhere." He grinned and nodded at Milton. Then faced the machine again. "Okay. Look. Consciousness ends when the brain dies. So if I get shot here, my consciousness will just con-tinue in some universe where the brain didn't die. A universe where I make it through all one hundred clicks. Get it! You'll see me die. Numerous yous will see me die. But no matter what, all I'll experience is any world where the guns click a hundred empty rounds. Immor—"

Click.

"Only ninety-six more rounds! At this point, there's 93.75 percent chance that you will see me getting a bullet through the head."

Milton yanked. The top of the pole budged.

"Stop! Don't move!" his father yelled. "You try and save me, and you could leave me a brain-dead fuck for the years to come. So don't touch anything, okay?"

Milton continued pulling at the pole.

"It's going to go again! Click or bang, click or bang. It's exciting, isn't it?"

"Dad, I'm stopping this! Now!"

"This is what the best of us do. We do what others won't do. Because they don't believe their own math, Milton. They believe shit! I believe, Milton! If those fucking Floaters can do it, so can I. I'll spat all existence. I'll spat my way back and forth. Trust me."

The pole snapped from the ceiling. Milton yanked it back, guiding the cuff up and slipping it off the top.

"Stop, Milton! Saving me is a sure way to damn me."

Once the cuff was free, Milton charged his father. He heard the crack of the gunshot the instant before he plowed into him, tackling him to the floor. The sound of the shot reverberated through the room like trapped thunder.

Milton lay on top of his father, cheek to cheek. For a moment he refused to move, refused to examine his father's face. But the blood pooling on the base-ment floor told him what he would find. Finally, Milton lifted himself. His father's open eyes were wide and dilated. On his forehead, a large hole gaped where the black *X* had been.

4,365
DAYS

Like a dog can sense earthquakes

"WHEN YOU SING, my God, it's fire," Hayden said, spinning the ice in his whiskey backstage at the MTV Video Music Awards. "You are a shoo-in!"

The pop starlet smiled, teeth so white they buzzed. Crew members with tiny black headsets and celebrities of every level bustled about them. But Hayden kept his focus on the starlet.

"I see you on that hospital show," she said with a singsong Georgia accent. "You're good."

"Thanks," Hayden shrugged. "I prefer film. But the writing on that show just grabs me. My agent said, 'Don't do it. It's just TV.' I told him I had to do it."

She sipped her fruit juice and giggled. "I'm nervous! Do you already have the envelope?"

"I do," he said, patting his pocket. "But it's sealed."

"Can I convince you to let me peek?" she said. At twenty-one she was four years his senior and she was beautiful, radiating that brief, crumbling innocence America loves so much. But Hayden felt no intimidation.

"Listen, I don't care what this envelope says. Right now, I'm talking with the world's hottest singer with the year's best video."

A crew member patted Hayden's arm. "Mr. Brock, you're on in twenty seconds."

Hayden downed the last of his drink and handed the glass to the crew member.

"By the way," he said to the starlet, as he ruffled his already ruffled hair. "Consider joining me for a midnight dinner after this circus closes up."

"Midnight dinner?"

"Room service goes till 2:00 AM."

She smiled.

Hayden turned toward the stage. He knew if she won, he'd have no chance with her that night. He also knew, thanks to the unsealed envelope in his pocket, that she would not win. Hayden could sense status like a dog can sense earthquakes. Her star was on the decline and his was on the rise. Tonight they momentarily shared an elevation, and he intended to exploit it.

He stepped out onto the stage, the brilliant lights hiding the cheering crowd. He smiled into the cameras and flicked his chin at the unseen audience. He moved toward the podium feeling not so much that he was walking but that he was lifting his feet and the world passed beneath him.

A little over half his height

MILTON WEAVED THROUGH the sprawling University of Texas campus, a cedar-scented maze of stone buildings, bronze-green statues, and looming pecan trees, each branch heavy with black-feathered grackles perched and heckling the students below. Crowds of students squeezed together on the pebbled walkways. Milton—lanky, acne-plagued, and too shy even to talk to himself—avoided any eye contact or verbal interaction. But he couldn't dodge the smell. An olfactory orchestra of perfumes, body sprays, and hygiene levels. The eager sweat of late adolescent boys, the patchouli and morning pot of art students, the sweet apple smell of well-crafted blondes labeled with Greek script and careful smiles.

Milton studied the map, but it was these others—these close bodies—that pinpointed Milton's true location. He was out of place. His too-new shoes, his bang-heavy hair, his dangling arms and thin shoulders. His everything. He tried denying his presence, holding his breath and floating through like a ghost. But it was no use. He *was*, and he was wrong.

Milton had applied to the university and moved into the dorm simply because it was the path of least resistance. When the paperwork asked him to declare a major, he penciled in *Physics* and wondered why. He despised math, had no inclination toward the concepts. He liked astronomy—watching spheres spin a billion miles away. He loved music. But there it was, written in his scrawl: physics. And he did not change it.

He stepped from the sunlight into a high-ceilinged lecture hall, the August heat colliding with the frigid air like two weather fronts ready to birth thunder. He sat quickly, near the back, but not the very back. The back row was making as much of a statement as the front row, and Milton wanted to make no statement at all. To be stateless, that was his aim.

He was early, the hall spotted with only a few other students. Although he had arrived at what was his last class of the day, Milton kept his eyes on the campus map, pretending to study its markings.

Finally a middle-aged Indian man in a cheap suit walked to the front of the hall shuffling papers and beginning a scripted lecture on the Introduction to Physics. Another student might have begrudged the size of the hall, the student-to-professor ratio, the lecture-heavy pedagogy. But Milton took refuge in the anonymity. He breathed easy for the first time that day. That's when the seat next to him was filled. A small man, a little over half his height, plonked down.

"Jesus, this place! I've known D&D worlds with less crannies, huh?" the small man whispered a few decibels above quiet.

He spoke with such a familiarity that Milton glanced to see if he was some forgotten friend. No. A stranger. A loud, short stranger.

"This is Physics, right?" As he whispered, the small man chewed on the end of his pencil as if it were a Slim Jim. "Don't let me waste an hour in Victorian Literature or History of the Turnip or something!"

Milton didn't like him. He was bouncing words, looks, even questions off of Milton, exposing him like flour thrown over the Invisible Man. Milton ignored him.

"I can't understand a thing this guy is saying, it's like—" The man made a funny noise, a gurgled cough.

But Milton refused to look. True, the professor mumbled horribly. Milton hadn't deciphered more than a phrase or two of the lecture. But mocking the professor on his first day of classes was just foolhardy.

Another wet, weird cough. But Milton kept his focus on the professor. Now the little guy was banging a fist against his desk. Really hamming it up. People were turning in their seats, even the professor was faltering in his speech and shooting glances in their direction. Milton could feel the blood rush to his face. A hand grabbed Milton's shoulder. *Shit, the little man is crazy! He's going to shoot me in the head, look at him, all blue and pointing at his throat waving a pencil with no eraser and—*

Oh!

Milton was not wild about touching people. Not at all. But there was no time. He jumped to his feet and wrapped his arms around the small man's waist. The hall of students, the professor, the Greek blondes, all watching as Milton dry-humped the tiny man like a Great Dane asserting dominance over a Lhasa Apso.

Pop. Out of man's mouth shot something that resembled a detached nipple.

The eraser landed four rows in front of Milton in the lap of a pretty brunette. Milton and the little man both sucked in deep breaths. Faces stared, confused and startled. The little man turned to Milton and released a loud, astonished guffaw. He turned to the staring faces of the class and announced in a booming voice, "This man saved my life!" He turned to Milton and stuck out his hand. "My mother died of choking. An apple," he said, grinning. "My name's Roy."

763
DAYS

Too much want

"SOUP," DANTE TOLD her, "knows everything about the person preparing it. You can lie to friends, family, even your lover." He grinned at her. "But you can never lie to soup. Not without ruining it. Hand me the cumin, would you?"

Rica smiled. "Seems a little over-the-top." She handed him the spice.

"If you want your soup to be over-the-top, then your approach must be over-the-top." He threw a dash of cumin into the cauldron.

Dante was known to the people of Austin, Texas, as the Soup Guru. He was a chef at a midsize bistro on South Congress. Each Monday after the restaurant closed, he would cook vats of soup. Tuesday morning he bicycled from house to house, delivering Tupperware containers to friends and willing neighbors.

Soon word of Dante's soup spread. He became something of a folk hero in south Austin. You'd see him bicycling along the shaded streets, pulling an ice-cooler on a cart behind him. People would call out to him, "Keep it up, Soup Guru!" or "The peanut stew was delicious." He would smile and wave, call out a thank-you or a greeting to a friend. But he didn't stop pedaling. Dante was on a mission. He was bringing nourishment to the hungry, hope to the downtrodden, soup to those who have no soup.

Rica became his lover before becoming his student. And in her more honest moments, she had to admit, the attraction was more to the soup than the man. Not that Dante wasn't handsome; he was—bright, laughing eyes; dark, happy curls; and the lean body of a cyclist. The humiliating truth was that Rica could not give her heart to Dante, or anyone. She had left her heart in the hands of a boy she had shared a dark closet with well over a decade before. A boy who, she was sure, remembered her only as a volcano of stomach fluids.

Dante was a friend and mentor whom she occasionally slept with. It was the soup and the process of preparation that moved Rica. She watched him. He watched the soup.

Rica was already becoming an accomplished soup crafter, but Dante was a master. She pursued her craft at Mundi House, a café on the east side of Austin. But Monday nights, she joined Dante in south Austin for his after-hours culinary ventures.

Hours after the busboys and dishwashers left for home, she would stand by Dante's side in the quiet kitchen, handing each ingredient he called for like a nurse handing scalpels to a surgeon. Dante hovered over the stove, adding a dash of this, a spoonful of that, cooking with the intensity of an atomic engineer and the flamboyance of an abstract artist.

"Yes! Yes!" he'd yell, his eyes closed and his nostrils flaring. "Cloves! I need four cloves!" or "Turn on more lights. My soup needs light!"

Tonight—morning, actually, it was nearly 3:00 AM—Rica was helping him create his acclaimed twig-mushroom-beer soup. The South Congress restaurant was dark and still, except for the kitchen glowing white in the heart of the building.

"Don't expect anything *not* to flavor soup. Including spoons and dishware." He poured in another bottle of Bass ale. "Bottles of beer work better than cans. The aluminum adds an unwanted casualness to the flavor." He snapped four long twigs of oak into the near-boiling stew. "And now we wait," he said, stepping back and clapping his hands. "We'll let it simmer for three hours."

"That's all?" Rica asked.

"There is one more step in the recipe. But it's more of a spiritual ingredient," Dante said, locking Rica in his gaze. "Soup is like a plant or a child. It absorbs the energy of its surroundings. A sad man makes a sad soup."

"Are you sad, Dante?" she asked, touching her chin with her fingers.

"No, I'm fine. That was just an example." He stepped closer. "But this kitchen is cold. There is a hollowness here." He placed a hand on Rica's cheek. "Rica, help me make soup." He leaned in and placed his lips to hers, not kissing, just touching. Rica smiled and breathed in the aroma of boiling beer.

Dante made love liked he cooked. An acute attention to detail, carefully adding just the right pinch and touch. Dazzlingly patient, giving heat its transformative time, understanding that it is not only a question of ingredients but how the ingredients are added. An hour of delicate work and Dante had prepared the most succulent orgasm of Rica's life. She dropped into nearly unconscious sleep, nestled into Dante's shoulder.

Two dreamless hours later she opened her eyes to see a naked Dante sipping the twig-mushroom-beer soup and shaking his head.

"Good morning," she said, smiling from the floor.

"No, not good. The soup is not right." He dropped the spoon. It clanged against the metal counter. "It was the lovemaking. Something was wrong with the lovemaking."

Rica stood up and stretched. "It felt right to me." She wrapped her arms around his chest and kissed his neck.

"No. No. Too much want," Dante said, turning to her. "You should leave now."

She stepped back, her skin bristling. "What?"

"It's no good, you and me. You're just too . . . needy."

"Needy?"

Dante turned back to the stove. "It's all in the soup."

Her throat tightened, a dozen retaliations buzzing in her head. But she said nothing. What annoyed her the most was that she didn't love Dante. She admired him, enjoyed him, but she did not love him. And yet here he was breaking her heart.

"Sorry if that was sudden," Dante said, reaching for the salt. "Breakups are hard."

"Someday, Dante," she said in a slow, steady voice, "someday, could be any day, I'm going to find a way to piss in your soup."

He didn't turn to her, but Dante's back tensed and Rica knew that with those simple words she had added a piss-laced drop of doubt to every soup Dante would ever sip. That was revenge enough. She collected her clothes from the kitchen floor and left.

The sun was rising on what she knew would be a long, slow death of a day. Rica had no time to go home after leaving Dante. She finished dressing in the car and sped to work at Mundi House. She gathered plates, prepared food, hardly noticing a thing. People came and went, but she had no words for anyone. She made a pumpkin curry soup that day. It tasted bitter. People left half-filled bowls on their tables.

Jeppy, the ever-smiling owner of Mundi House, offered to let Rica go home early, but Rica found the prospect of an empty apartment too depressing to consider. She passed the day making coffee and yerba matés and lying "Fine" to every customer's "How are you?"

That night Jeppy projected a film on the outside wall of Mundi House. People from the neighborhood arrived at dusk with blankets and children. Conversations paused, customers walked outside to sit on the warm grass and watch. Jeppy passed around roasted pumpkin seeds.

Rica sat a little farther back and tried to watch. It was some old black-and-white film that Rica had never seen. She wanted the film to be louder and larger, to fill her head and crowd everything else out. But the wall was only so big, and people were sleeping not too far away.

The film was a noir mystery. Someone was betraying someone. Someone else was finding out. Someone was angry. Someone was cruel. Rica breathed. She watched, and that was fine. No one was talking to her. No one was looking at her. That was a relief.

Halfway into the film a city switch box blew and all the lights for blocks snapped out. It was dark. No moon. For a moment Rica was worried people would begin moving, talking, leaving. But then stars crept closer and into view. The small crowd lay back and stargazed. It was quiet.

"Some of those stars weren't there yesterday," a child whispered to his father. "They're new."

"They're not new. We just didn't see them," the father answered.

"A star is always new," another voice said. Loud enough to hear, but soft enough to preserve the mood. "It's the nature of stars to be new. A constant generation of energy. Never the same burn twice. That is until the mass falls below .05 solar masses and we lose the star. Tonight the dwarf nova SS Cygni reaches its high magnitude. It spins around a white dwarf. The two will never touch and will never leave each other. Can you see it?"

"The bright one?" someone asked.

"No, that's Venus. Farther east."

Rica watched the sky as he spoke.

Someone asked another question and he answered, his voice quiet and full. "Stars explode and matter is produced. Energy is incarnated. Our planet and our bodies are likely the aftermath of a dead star. And our star will die, too."

Rica held her breath. He spoke of red supergiants and novas and the resident stars of Orion's Belt. Rica knew very little about the sky. For her it was as if the voice were creating the stars as he named them.

"Sirius, Vega, Algol, WR 104. There's seventy sextillion stars. That's ten stars for every grain of sand on Earth. Each one an oven."

Rica could not see his face, just hear his voice as it explained black holes and light years. Children oohed, parents ummed, Rica cried. It was a surprise, those wet cheeks as the voice explained the terrible gravitational pull of black holes and flower petals of a spinning galaxy. She was pulled from herself, from her hurt, and was gratefully lost in the larger wonder.

"We're watching from inside the canvas," he said. "We're a part of someone else's constellation. And the painting isn't finished. You see new brushstrokes every night." And as if the universe were taking its cue from him, a shooting star streaked light across the sky.

For a moment no one said a word. Then the electric lights cracked back on and the crowd sighed. Now the streetlights and electric hum felt inappropriate, even crude. Rica looked to see who had been speaking and for the first time laid eyes on Milton. He was now staring into his maté gourd, his shoulders moving inward. He was shrinking from the light, a slow implosion. Someone patted his back. He nodded and shyly smiled, but returned his eyes to his gourd. Rica bit her lip.

Later she drove the stretch of road between Mundi House and Milton's home, Milton beside her, pointing the way. A nearly wordless drive across the Congress Avenue Bridge, across Barton Springs to South First Street, passing vegetarian cafés and all-night Mexican restaurants, down Annie, with its cracked sidewalks and oak tree awnings and shoe-scarfed telephone wires, passing hundred-year-old shacks with third-generation inhabitants, purple-painted houses with year-round Christmas lights, and day-old hipster mansions. Finally pulling up to an unkempt, one-story home Milton had inherited from his father.

They sat on cheap lawn furniture in Milton's backyard by the dead pecan and shared a bottle of wine and bag of microwave popcorn. She told him stories and he told her facts. She confessed her recent heartbreak with Dante, leaving out some of the steamier kitchen-floor antics. He told her that dark matter made up over three-quarters of the universe.

"So we don't even know what most of the universe is made of?" she asked.

"That's about it."

She hummed and reached for more popcorn. "That answers a lot of questions."

Little Tick Clicky

THE HERMIT CRAB'S shell was shiny blue green. He had one large purple claw and one small brown claw. His shell was smaller than a man's fist but larger than a lump of charcoal. He lived in a plastic aquarium with forty-seven other hermit crabs in a sidewalk tourist store in Fort Lauderdale, Florida. He didn't know he was in Florida. He didn't know he was for sale. He did know that the water dish was empty. It had been for some time. It was hot.

No matter which direction he crawled, the hermit crab soon came to a point across which he could see but could not move. He could not fathom why. In one direction, past an endless, nearly nude parade of young Spring-Breakers, he could see the blue and white of the ocean surf. He crawled in that direction more than any other, scratching at the unseen barrier and wishing for salt and water. He vaguely wondered why he could see what he could never have. What a bizarre way to design a world.

He did not think much. He was thirsty. A thirst so encompassing it left room for little else. Eight of the crabs in the aquarium were dead. He sensed that he might be sharing a similar fate.

Then, from seemingly nowhere, five towers of peach-white flesh surrounded him and closed in. A hand smelling of sunblock and tequila lifted him in a direction he had not formerly been aware of—up. It blew his mind. So much so that he forgot about thirst.

"How much for this blue and green one?"

She was an Evergreen grad school poet who had not written a poem in over a year. Thin and pale and wearing a bikini as if it were punishment.

"Will they let me take him on a plane?" She puckered up at the crab. "You're my new boyfriend, yes, you are." The hermit crab saw her lips. They were a threat. He clicked his purple claw in defense.

"Click, Clicky. Oh, little Tick Clicky," the poet cooed.
Click retreated into his shell, hiding as best as he could.
"Can I get a cage or box? And a water bowl! Hermit crabs like water, right?"
Click had an extraordinary destiny awaiting him. He had no idea.

**4
DAYS**

A hard, heavy dawn

"FATHER."

With each stroke through the cool green waters Milton exhaled the same word. "Father."

Milton was not a strong swimmer. With his sprawling arms and legs he more often than not resembled a drowning giraffe. He swam Barton Springs, an expansive Austin limestone pool bookended on either end by the mild, murky Barton Creek and shaded by ancient live oaks growing from its grassy shores. Milton avoided the slick shallow limestone floor to the west end of the springs and the tug of the east-end overflow chute. Instead he splashed in circles near the south wall.

"Father."

The word had new connotations. Milton had tried to be thrilled, tried to be supportive. Tried to think as he supposed a father-to-be would think. But the act was brittle and beginning to show stress fractures. Behind every crack were questions: Would he have to get a full-time job? Find health insurance? Open a bank account? Shave? The child was still five months from entering the world proper, but Milton could already feel its demanding presence.

"Father."

A smiling face broke the water's surface beside him and took in a large breath.

"My God, I just got buzzed by a bass the size of my arm!" Roy sucked in more air and disappeared again. This was Roy's habit, filling his lungs and diving deep, returning minutes later with stories of shy sunfish and translucent salamanders hiding in a jungle of ten-foot-high water weeds.

Milton swam to the edge and pulled himself up onto the concrete sidewalk lining the pool, his hair and beard matted to his head like an abundant clump of brown seaweed. He sat, legs dangling in the water, and gazed about the grounds.

Who here could be a parent? Not the beauties, their brown perfect bodies too full of sex and sunlight to ever submit to something as mundane as parenting. How about the round man practicing Tae Kwon Do as if in a slow-motion battle with a swarm of wasps, or the homeless woman who came each day at dawn with a pile of out-of-date high school textbooks? Or the petite lesbian couple with complementary back tattoos of flying blackbirds that fit together like a jigsaw puzzle? Would they make a kid's lunch, drop off a child at soccer practice, change a diaper?

No. Milton was convinced that the great majority of reproduction was accomplished by the bored men and women of the world, the lonely cubicle dwellers and lost suburbanites who believed, in some unexamined way, that having a child would give their lives meaning. His father had a child and Milton could honestly say his father's life meant nothing.

Roy suddenly appeared in the waters at Milton's feet. "What's it called when you stick a hand inside a catfish's mouth and pull it to land? Fisting?"

"Noodling."

"I knew *fisting* wasn't right."

As Roy climbed the corroding ladder, a redheaded woman in a hemp bikini bottom and nothing else strolled past. Roy smiled and sat beside Milton.

"Oh, the breasts of this place," Roy said. "The variety! The small ones with all that fierce authority, the round lethargic ones, even the reticent, long-faced ones. All so good!" With both hands, he brushed the water out of his curly hair. "Too many breasts are begging in this world. Pleading for attention, approval, a valid credit card number. But these breasts, the breasts of Barton Springs, ask for nothing. They're not out for me to see, you know? But they don't mind me seeing either. They simply are. Like pairs of plump Buddhas in full lotus position, bouncing along in happy meditation. I could learn a lot from the chests of Austin women."

"I don't want to be a dad, Roy."

"Okay," Roy said with a slow nod. "I'll do it. Rica's always liked me better than you anyway."

"It feels like it's all just happening to me. I didn't ask for this. It's like I didn't do it. I mean, I know I did it. But I didn't mean to do *this*. I'm going to be a horrible dad. I'm not wired for fathering."

Roy smiled. "I can promise you something, Milt. You're going to love this baby. You just will."

Milton pulled his beard and shook his head. He leaned forward and let gravity pull him into the water. The water, usually brisk, felt warm and welcoming. With his awkward strokes, he paddled to the center of the pool and treaded water.

Roy was a friend. Milton's closest. They had been brothers of a kind since the day Milton squeezed the pink end of a pencil from Roy's throat over ten years before.

Milton had been there when Roy had tried to eat fifty Cadbury eggs in a twist on *Cool Hand Luke* and had almost died from sugar shock.

Roy had been there when Milton had been put on university probation for smuggling an industrial-size bag of Golden Grahams from the dorm cafeteria.

Milton had been there when Roy had attempted to launch a rocket with a squirrel inside. The squirrel was unharmed. Roy lost the tip of his left pinky.

Roy had been there when Milton spent half his freshman scholarship on the head of a Bigfoot he'd seen advertised in *Greensheet*. The boys waited four breathless days to receive the package. Finally it arrived and they locked themselves into their dorm room and closed the blinds. In awed silence, they cut the cardboard top, carefully dug through the Styrofoam nuggets, and found a large glass jar. Inside the jar was a hairy, teeth-baring, slightly decomposing head floating in a thick yellow liquid.

"Ah shit," said Roy, kicking the box and spilling the Styrofoam.

"What shit?" Milton said. "Look at that. Bigfoot."

"It's a dog head, Milt."

"Are you kidding? That's Bigfoot. A young one, yes. But most definitely Bigfoot."

"It's a dog head."

"Have you ever seen a Bigfoot?" Milton nearly yelled.

"Have you?"

"I'm looking at one in a jar right now!"

"Well, Bigfoot looks a hell of a lot like a sheepdog. Agreed?"

"Agreed."

Roy was loyal and smart, but Milton knew that today Roy was wrong. Parents don't always love their children.

In the center of the Springs, Milton spit some warm water from his mouth and thought about his mother. More accurately, he thought of her absence. Her empty dresser with bare wire hangers, the gaps on the shelves where her romance paperbacks had been pried from between her husband's physics textbooks like stray bricks from a wall, her rose-scented shampoo—the half-filled bottle remaining in the corner of his father's shower until the day he died.

Milton let his body sink under the surface. A few bubbles skirted past.

Surely, thirty-two years ago some smiling friend had said to his mother and to his father, "You're going to love this baby. You just will."

He let himself sink deeper into the green glow, past the stripes of sunlight, dancing straws of amber. The temperature felt more like a lukewarm bath than a natural pool. The truth, he knew and hated, was that he hoped that Rica would have a miscarriage. A blameless abortion. Then things could remain just as they are. How easy would it be to not have a child on the way? Not have that lifetime of new demands gathering on the immediate horizon like a hard, heavy dawn? He despised the wish even as he acknowledged it. With this one thought he knew he was proving to be as poor a father as his own, and his child had yet to utter a cry.

The weeds and his hair, swaying in half speed, surrounded him. The water was hot now. Milton was just registering this as abnormal when a bubble, the size of a softball, floated from below him. Then another, just as large. Then a herd of bubbles of all sizes raced past him and to the surface. Milton pushed upward and into the air.

The water was more than hot; it was scalding.

He scanned the surface churning with bubbles, the steam rising like escaped souls, and the dissolving plant matter floating in a green-brown froth. Blisters flared to red life up and down his arms. He splashed in panic, a mouthful of water burning his tongue, his throat. He could see Roy standing and staring.

A small girl in a pink bathing suit teetered at the end of the diving board. Why wasn't someone grabbing her, why weren't people screaming, why wasn't she backing away from the dead fish and snakes floating to the bubbling surface? Milton yelled, his voice ragged with pain. "The water is boiling! Stop! St—" Something grabbed his ankle and yanked. His face sank below the water, his throat filling with burn, the water cooking his skin. Down by his feet, clouded by bubbles and mud, was a face he knew. Blank and pale blue. The face from his backyard. The man—the Non-Man—who had stood beneath the pecan tree swaying and staring at him and his father. Now, here below him clutching his ankle. A voice, muted and calm, whispered in Milton's head. *You don't have much time.*

Milton screamed into the water as the hand pulled him down into the boiling black green.

KRST

"THERE'S NO QUESTION that the time has come, the time is more nigh than ever! Remember what Jesus said? You see the figs ripen on the tree and you know the season. I mean those fat figs are about to fall on their own! But they won't fall because the workers are here to pick them! That's us, people! You, the listeners at home. We are his workers. The workers are few, but the harvest is rich!

"Yes, we play some rocking tunes, here. And I'd like to think ol' Van Sturgeon gets you laughing every so often. But more than that, I get you ready. Ready for the day! That's the goal of all of us at KRST.

"Now it's clear that movements in the Middle East are exactly, I mean *exactly*, what John describes in Revelations. It's scary how right he was two thousand years ago. That's God, people!

"Want more prophecy? Facebook. Yep. Do you know how your little Facebook works? Do you? You think you're safe because you put a little 'I love Jesus' thing on that page of yours? You are wrong. Dead wrong. You are not a name on the Internet. You are a number. And Revelations tells us that many will be marked with the number of the Beast. And that only those marked will be able to buy and sell. Can I buy and sell on the Internet? I cannot. I will not. I will not allow Facebook and Amazon and Apple to give me a number! That's how they do it! It's a number! So they can *allow* me to buy and sell! So they can *track* what I buy and sell. The powers of darkness love it, they *love it*, when you buy your Christian music and posters and books on the computer. They love your money. They love you lining up to get your number.

"Did you think it would be obvious? Did you think the Beast would have a red tail and pointy horns? Did you?"

Until what?

"SHIT, MILTON!" ROY was pounding on Milton's back. Milton coughed, expelling green water all over the sidewalk beside the Springs. A small crowd was gathered around him, staring down. His skin was not peeling, his arms not blistering.

"You okay?" Roy was asking. "You got caught in the weeds."

"Four days," Milton coughed out.

"Not even four minutes, dude," a lifeguard said. "Your buddy here dove in and got you."

"We only have four days."

"Four days until what?"

Milton shook his head. He stared past the people to the rippling waters. A man was doing the breaststroke, the girl in the pink bathing suit laughing on his back.

"Something not very good," Milton said.

Sleepy, weepy, sleepy

RICA LOVED THE warm quiet of the kitchen before opening, being alone in the first light sneaking through the windows, preparing spices, slicing vegetables—the muted blade rhythmically kissing the cutting board. She moved slower today. At four months, Rica was well past the queasy mornings of her early pregnancy, but she found that more and more of her energy was being redirected to her ever-expanding belly. Her body was changing, her small frame thickening by the day and making the kitchen a tighter fit each morning.

Mundi House customers started to arrive at seven, asking for coffee and ginger-spiced tea. Some received their drinks and dashed out the door, but most sat and added to the soft morning hum. Rica watched them from her small kitchen. The girl in the corner laughing into Hemingway. The pretty boy arriving red-eyed and asking that Advil be crushed into his coffee. The two old men cutting the corners from postcards. "We're starting our own coaster company," Rica heard them tell Jeppy.

The soup took most of the morning to develop its flavor. Rica knew this. She understood how a tomato tastes when it swims and steams with a single white onion, how a potato lumbering into the water disturbs the privacy and changes the mood. Pepper sneaks in almost unnoticed, then whistles from within, while salt stings the water before disappearing. Everything flavors everything.

The presence of the playwright scribbling by the back wall touches the talk of the carpenter and his two friends. The tone of their conversations makes its way over to the two girls in the corner; the girls move closer and whisper. The way they lean is noticed by the playwright, and it bends his words. All stewed in the soul that bubbles through the floorboards. Soul soup.

Rica believed the richest element of any soup was its cauldron. A cauldron remembers. It allows soups to soak into its iron, and then gives flavors back to each new creation. The café's walls and tables and chairs were the same. They absorbed the souls. Even the coffee mugs remembered words whispered over their chipped rims.

When Rica finished preparing her soup, she let it sit and helped Jeppy collect dishes from the morning rush. In the back garden an old woman sat sipping hot tea and watching the finches scuttle from tree to tree. When a train passed she watched that, too. Rica knew her, she came to Mundi House often. Rica liked the wrinkles of her skin. *Like an unmade bed*, she thought. She noticed the old woman looking up each time someone entered the garden.

"Waiting for somebody?" Rica asked.

"Yes," she said. Her voice was soft, like a wet leaf. "I'm waiting for Death."

"Death?" Rica asked. "As in dying?"

"Just a visit today." The old woman smiled.

Rica smiled back. "Will you know him?" she asked.

"Oh, yes," the old woman said. "Can't help but know him."

Rica carried the dishes inside. More regulars arrived. Kaz, famous for his tattoo-canvased body and the tiny horns protruding from his scalp, rode up on his bicycle.

"Where'd you get the horns, man?" Rica had once heard a fan ask.

"Magic, son. The strong, good kind."

Jules came in shortly after ten. She drank yerba matés with mint and organized sex-toy Tupperware parties on her laptop. She had once told Rica that she could spend hours imagining complete strangers in the throes of orgasm. Nothing made her happier, especially if the stranger seemed sad or overstressed. Rica thought that was one of the most generous things she had ever heard.

Just before eleven, the folksinger arrived. He sat in the garden strumming new songs. Rica asked him how he was.

"Angry," he answered, going on to explain, in impressive detail, all the wrongs the American government and the popular media had committed in the last day.

"There's going to be another war in the Middle East," he said.

"There's always going to be another war."

"This one is big. And the government isn't saying a word. We gobble up their lies like cupcakes. And the media . . ."

Rica listened and nodded. "Too true," she said. "All too true."

The folksinger paused, studied her face for a moment, then laughed and returned to his guitar.

Not long after, the folksinger was joined by the writer. Rica could see them both leaning back in their chairs, tossing thoughts back and forth like a baseball. Rica knew they'd drink coffee till noon, then switch to beer, and by evening they'd be bumming cigarettes from the pretty girls, though neither smoked.

When the soup was ready, Rica brought a bowl out to the old woman and refused the coins offered in return.

"What is he like, Death?" Rica asked her.

"Humble," the old woman said. "And tired. So I told him we would meet here and chat."

"What will you talk about?"

"I'm not sure. Simple things, I suppose." A figure's shadow crossed the garden's stones. The old woman looked up and flinched, then, seeing it was just a tall boy with a book in his hand, relaxed. "I'm a little afraid," she said quietly.

"Don't be."

"It's nice to be a little afraid."

After the rush, Rica stepped outside to take a break. What would have been a smoke break, if she hadn't quit four years before. The old woman was rising to leave.

"Did Death come?" Rica asked.

"Yes."

"Did you enjoy your chat?"

She nodded. "He's coming back tomorrow."

When the old woman left, Rica took her seat. Her body felt tired, more tired and heavier every day. She could feel her body thickening, swelling, and, most of all, changing. The baby squirmed. Rica placed her hand on the belly and whispered a lullaby.

Sleepy, sleepy. Creepy, creepy. Sleepy, weepy, sleepy.

She often whispered to the child. Sometimes lullabies, other times tiny secrets.

I steal individual creamers from restaurants and drink them in traffic.

I don't believe strawberries taste sweet. They taste delicious, but not sweet.

I think my insides are peach-colored. Are they?

The fetus answered with kicks and pokes, like Morse code. Rica knew each kick carried a vast amount of meaning. A certain kick told Rica that the child loved Miles Davis but questioned Charles Mingus. Another poke: the child preferred waffles to pancakes ... Coldplay is overrated ... a hot shower is the perfect way to begin the day ...

Rica had not planned on getting pregnant. In fact, she and Milton worked to avoid a child. She had been on the pill since her late teens and often Milton brought home specialty prophylactics adorned with bumps, ridges, and tentacles. Milton wasn't concerned that the pill would fail them, he just thought the condoms would be a pleasant surprise. Some boyfriends brought home flowers or boxes of chocolate, Milton brought home novelty contraception.

They were using the Nibbler Special on the night the baby was conceived. Milton had been away on a birthday solo camping trip to the cedar woods surrounding Enchanted Rock State Park some seventy miles west of Austin. On the day he was due to return, Rica lit a fire and poured two goblets of port. She greeted him at the door wearing nothing but a wool cap and three strategically placed spoonfuls of Nutella.

Often Milton returned from his solo weekends quiet and distant. But that night he moved with a slow and sweet boldness, like a Chet Baker ballad. He touched slowly, he searched and discovered. Sensation moved across Rica's skin like orange across the glowing coals of the fire. Then came the Nibbler Special, grinning at her like a naughty, eager Muppet.

She was surprised at what a fine lover he was that night. She was even more surprised a month later when the store-bought pregnancy test showed two red lines. "When we saw two, we knew," went the jingle in the television ad.

Rica was sure the test was wrong. Milton couldn't impregnate her. She had always suspected that Milton's sperm, like Milton himself, would be easily distracted and often unmotivated. Sure, they might set out to find the egg, but they would eventually get sidetracked in the fallopian tubes or lose their way and end up north of the bladder.

But she was wrong. His fellas could swim, as the saying goes. More than that, they could swim upstream, through latex, and against odds. These were high-quality sperm. Her own zygotes, in collaborating with Milton's, had equally shocked her.

But the surprise was quickly replaced with a sick nervousness. Rica had never had a child. Neither had Milton. She wasn't sure if Milton should. The thought of him owning a pet seemed ill-advised. Even a fern would be a risk. It was just the way his mind worked. He might be focused and delightful with a child for a good half hour, but then he'd notice an odd cloud formation or a strange insect and wander off.

On one of their early dates two years before, Rica and Milton had thrown a

Frisbee around the open grounds of Zilker Park. Milton was tall, a good three inches over six feet, and each time he leaped for the disc his thick brown hair and beard bounced around his head like a beaten rug. It was a good date. Sunshine and laughter. Then Milton ran to retrieve an overthrown disc near the park road. A car drove by. Milton casually glanced at its bumper, then continued to stare; finally he broke into a run chasing the car. Rica watched him go, his nappy hair flapping behind him. He looked a little like a dog running on its hind legs.

Milton followed the car out of the park and onto Barton Springs Drive, running on the shoulder and staring at the bumper. Eventually he stopped, rubbed his head, and looked around. He saw Rica, gave her a little wave, and walked back, stopping once to slap his calf with the disc.

"What was that all about?" she asked.

"Mosquito."

"No. The car."

Milton looked around.

"The one you were chasing?"

"Oh," he said, nodding his head. "Bumper stickers. Couldn't read them all at first."

She paused for a moment, then asked, "Good read?"

"Not bad," he said. "Want to go get a beer?"

She did, very much so. As they walked from the park she thought to herself, *Okay. Can't see myself staying too long. But I'll stay for a while.*

With that understanding, Rica relaxed. Knowing she would eventually leave allowed her to stay. And to her surprise, she never wanted to leave.

They were a strange match. Rica was a beautiful creature, admired and pursued by many. More than she knew. And in many ways she was a practical woman. But there was nothing practical in her choice of man. Milton was not wealthy or ambitious to be so. He was thirty-one and had no real career. He paid his bills on residuals from his old band, Pearl-Swine. He did own his house, inherited from his father, but it was in bad repair. He enjoyed her soups, but not with the passion of a fellow artist. He was a recluse. A bit of a freak. One of those kids that used to sit on the front lawn of the high school smoking weak joints and arguing about the geography of World of Warcraft. Finding Rica in Milton's embrace was like finding a ballet dancer inside an Elks Lodge.

So why did she stay? Hard to say. Maybe she enjoyed the kinky absurdity of it all. Maybe it was an act of rebellion against her own pragmatic ways. Maybe because he unintentionally surprised her with nearly every word he uttered. Or maybe Rica cared for Milton because Milton needed to be cared for. Perhaps she was drawn to his need as a gardener is drawn to a sick radish. Maybe none of these fully answered the question. It's just one of those mysteries.

Rica had been content with the mystery for two years, but now she was going to have a baby, and mystery seemed too flimsy a foundation to build a family on. But what could she do? What else was there for her to build on? The baby was coming, and with every day Rica felt a little less free, a little more afraid.

She leaned back in her chair and stared up at the blue sky behind the green and brown of the elm tree. The baby kicked. "Calm down," she whispered. "Baby, baby. I love you, I love you. I'm just a little afraid."

Two college girls walked off, leaving a copy of *Entertainment Weekly* on their table. Rica reached over and picked it up. Hayden Brock, star of television's *Saint Rick*, gazed up from the cover. Rica studied him: his bright, almost luminous, blue eyes, his sandy blond hair slightly ruffled as if the perfect breeze from a perfect sea had perfectly blown past. She touched a finger to the crinkles that formed around his eyes when he smiled. And his chin. God must have wept in joy the day he made that chin. Perhaps God, realizing he had created perfection, dropped his chisel and declared he would never make another chin. That would explain Milton.

South of Milton's bottom lip was a simple slope reaching to his neck. Milton wore a beard and shuddered at the very idea of shaving it. Rica thought that was silly, especially in Austin summers. But when she saw his younger clean-shaven face on the Pearl-Swine album cover, Rica agreed. The beard stays.

She looked back at Hayden Brock staring up from his glossy plane. "Now you'd be an excellent father, I know that," she said. "We'd have to get you out of California. Then get the California out of you. But eventually . . ."

Jeppy came out into the garden with her one-year-old son, Carl, balanced on her hip, a chunky big-eyed drool geyser and eater of all things unclean. Jeppy placed a hot cup of thick tea in front of Rica.

"Remember, one cup a day. It's got everything a growing placenta needs."

"Jeppy," Rica asked. "How was pregnancy for you?"

"Best months ever. Loved it. Loved the sick, loved the tireds. Loved it."

"Of course, you were trying to get pregnant."

"Yeah, we were trying," Jeppy said, using one hand to stack yerba maté gourds from a nearby table. "But we didn't know what it meant. We were just as clueless as you. Maybe more because we thought we weren't. Are you feeling freaked out?"

"A little," Rica said. Carl was squeezing his entire fist into his mouth and moaning. "The timing seems bad."

"When a baby decides it's ready to let you be its mother, it comes. That's all." Jeppy chuckled. "Now drink your tea."

Eber you ara

HAYDEN BROCK'S FAVORITE episode of *Saint Rick* is called "The Write Step." In it Saint Rick meets a little deaf girl who desperately wants to be a professional singer and her dyslexic farmer father, who is in danger of losing the farm to the bank. While working as a hired hand on the farm, Rick teaches the little girl to dance, explaining that "dancing is singing for the deaf."

Rick also teaches the father to overcome his dyslexia using a clever metaphor involving chickens and a combine head. In the final scene, the little deaf girl wins a county dance contest while her father and Rick watch from the audience. The cash prize is enough to pay off the farm mortgage. The father runs onto the stage and hugs his daughter. He picks up the trophy and reads the plaque. "First Palace?" he says. The crowd sighs. "Just kidding," he says. "First Place, you betcha!" Everyone laughs and applauds. But Rick's seat is empty.

"The stranger is gone," someone says. "What was his name, anyhow?"

"Rick," the father says, lifting his daughter on to his shoulder. "They call him Rick."

"Gnood nye, Rick," the daughter says. "Where eber you ara."

The final credits roll while Saint Rick walks alone down a dusty road stretching toward an orange-red sunset.

Hayden Brock nearly cried when he won the Emmy for that episode.

It was the morning after the awards ceremony that Hayden, passed out on his room-size water bed, was pulled to near consciousness by the ringing of his phone. He did his best to remain in his dreams. He had been enjoying one of his favorites, a reoccurring one in which he lay entangled with a small woman with almond skin and sharp eyes. But the ringing frightened her away and she disappeared into smoke.

Still mostly asleep, Hayden reached out a hand and answered, if only to stop the ringing. But the screeching voice of his agent was several levels worse.

"Brock, you really fucked up last night, you know that? You really bit a big one."

"Ah, come on, Ted. It was Emmy night. I was letting loose."

"You had sex with a goat."

"I did not."

Hayden clicked a remote and a wall-size screen popped to life.

"Brock, you had sex with a goat at Visions."

Hayden put the heel of his hand to his forehead. He had gone to the night-club Visions, he remembered that, and it had been Shepherd Night. Visions was known for its theme nights. On Belly Dancing Night no patron or staff was allowed to veil their midriff. On Foam Night the dance floor, bar, and bathrooms were filled to the ceiling with a nontoxic foam. On Bum Night homeless men and women were corralled in and the bar's patrons served them sandwiches and hot coffee while the DJ spun techno beats under old Jethro Tull albums. And then of course there was Shepherd Night. Yes, there had been a goat . . .

Hayden was starting to remember.

"Ted, calm down," he said into the phone. "I was joking around on the dance floor. There was no penetration. I'm sure of it."

"Shit, Hayden, it's in the papers. There's a picture, for God's sake!"

The television caught Hayden's attention—an enthusiastic studio audience watched a screen flashing images of earthquakes, forest fires, grainy footage of buildings collapsing, bridges twisting, a bright expanding mushroom cloud.

"Brock, are you listening to me?"

"It was a joke, Ted. The goat was on the dance floor. It was harmless."

"You don't get it," Ted said, his voice tightening like a twisted rope. "You are Saint Rick. Saint Rick can't fuck goats."

"I told you, there was no penetration."

On the television a round man with a sweaty face full of cooper-red hair gesticulated to the studio audience. The screen behind him now showed computer-animated people climbing into bright blue coffins like oversize Advil capsules. Was he selling tombs?

"Listen, Brock, I told the media that the photo was doctored."

"Nice. Good," Hayden said, stretching and ringing for his morning coffee. "In fact I think that's exactly what happened."

"I don't want you talking with anyone. I'm putting out a press release that you're on another spiritual retreat."

"Have I been on one before?"

"Your drinking binge in Aspen."

"Yes. Good. Nice, Ted."

"But the producers aren't stupid, Brock. They'll drop you. Emmy or no Emmy. They're that close. Just get out of town for a while. Lay low."

Hayden's Haitian manservant, Iola, appeared at the door wearing a cream-colored mock turtleneck and balancing a small espresso and an orange juice on a tray. The size of the water bed allowed for only a narrow walkway between it and the wall. The manservant turned sideways and skillfully shuffled to the bed's side.

"Where should I go, Ted?"

"Shit, I don't care. Just go. Get in your car and drive someplace where people don't own cameras."

"Like the Amish?"

Ted hung up.

As the manservant placed the tray on the nightstand, Hayden nodded a thanks and turned up the television's volume.

" ... tsunami, earthquake, bomb, asteroid!" As the red-bearded man spoke, tiny square examples of each disaster popped up on either side of him. "Whatever hits, you'll be safe a mile beneath the Earth's surface in our hidden facility far from any major strike points or geological hot spots. You'll be prepared to outlive the danger." The camera zoomed in on his face. "Lifepods!"

The phone rang again.

"Hello, Mother."

"Your name is all over the chat rooms."

"Yes, Mother. Doctored photo. A fake. I wasn't even there."

"There's a video. They just played it on the news. Wow, that goat looks scared." She sighed. "And you know how your father feels about these kinds of things."

"Was he watching?"

"He was asleep."

"Good."

"So I woke him."

"Mom, come on."

The screen was now showing a smiling bleached blond climbing into one of the ginormous Advil capsules. The studio audience cheered.

"With our patented Lifepod system the guest will sleep peacefully through the disaster in our subterranean shelter. They will wake to a stockpile of dried food, supplies, and all the comforts of a five-star hotel. Spots are limited. Make sure you reserve your Lifepod today!" The bearded man appeared again, staring into Hayden's room with bright-blue eyes. "This is Dr. Kip Warner reminding you, only the best survive the worst."

" . . . so your father is dressed now and we're coming over." His mother's words pulled him from the advertisement. "We'll be there for lunch."

"No can do, Mother. Spiritual retreat."

"Aspen?"

"No, no. Secret location. Can't say. Very special."

"No goats, I hope."

Hayden clicked the phone off.

"Iola, will you ready my car?"

"Which one, sir?"

"Lexus, I think," Hayden said. "And pack a bag for me. I'm going driving. And while I'm away order a couple of Lifepods, will you?"

"Lifepods?"

"Yes, Iola. Dr. Warner. Pods. One for me, one for my wife."

"You're not married, sir."

"I might be by the end of the world."

Pumpy pumpy . . . smiley smiley

CLICK THE HERMIT crab was hiding in his shell, which was hiding in the purse of a poet, who was hiding in the corner of a rave. The rave was hiding in a warehouse in downtown Seattle. The drug molly wasn't hiding at all. It was everywhere. It was passing from hand to hand, surfing on waves of orange juice and Red Bull. Currently it was rushing through the poet's veins like a child at a water park, squealing as it went, alerting nerves that it was time to feel more intensely, yelling at the emotion glands, "Hey, I've great news! I'll give you the details later! For now, just know that everything is great! Really great!"

Pumpy pumpy went the glands. Smiley smiley went the poet. Swingy swingy went the purse. Shit went the crab.

The slow beat and white noise pounded into Click's shell like the distant ocean that he remembered in only the vaguest sense. Rhythm, pounding, noises, all so constant that it became a kind of silence.

The poet overzealously reached to feel the texture of someone's corduroy jacket and as she did the purse escaped her grip and flew up into the smoky air. Click slipped past the zipper and out into the world. Floating, flailing, and splashing into a spotty teenager's grapefruit juice. Like falling into the center of a sunset, all color, texture, taste, and sound changed in an instant. Then the glass was being lifted. Click scurried, but there was nowhere to scurry. Glunk glunk and Click was slipping along the glass toward two pink lips and a set of crooked teeth. Click snapped onto the pink. The sunset fell away and now Click hung at a perilous height, clinging with his larger claw onto the pink, puffy, waggling thing. New noises. High-pitched yelps. But the beat never slowed.

"That is so cool," someone said.

"Get it off! Get it off!" the mouth yelled.

"Dance, dude. Dance."

Click held on for dear life, but the boy swung his head back and forth, running into a bathroom. It was the lip that finally gave way, and Click went flying off with a tiny chunk of pink flesh in his grasp. He flew for a moment and then landed with a *splonk* in the room's open toilet.

Fist-size piece of strength

SHE'S HOME. THANK GOD.

Milton didn't usually thank God for things. He didn't believe in God, not anymore. But by the time Rica arrived home from Mundi House, he had seriously questioned his unbeliefs.

"Rica," he said as she climbed from her car. "I saw something."

Since his experience at Barton Springs that morning, Milton had not left the house. He paced the rooms, counting brushstrokes on the walls and saying aloud, "I'm as crazy as he was. Shit. Shit. Keep it together. Four days until what?"

Finally Rica had pulled into the driveway and he raced out the door, tripping over a dead potted plant and lurching into the yard.

But how could he tell her? What would he tell her?

"I saw stuff."

"Okay, okay," she said in her calmest voice. "Let's go inside and you can tell me what happened."

He followed her into the house, kicking the potted plant off the steps.

"Have a seat, babe. I'll make some tea," she said, disappearing into the kitchen.

Milton plopped down in the papasan and took a deep, slow breath.

"They don't exist, I know that," he said. "Which is making this all very difficult to grasp."

"We've got some new Tibetan lemon herb tea. You'll like it," Rica said from the kitchen. Her voice cooled Milton down. Always did. She could describe the qualities of tea while he ranted and that alone steadied him. Her voice—just a little scratchy and full of hums—was a rope he could grab onto, and the rope led to a solid stone in her soul. His soul, he felt, was mush. When the waves got rough, his soul churned. But Rica had a fist-size piece of strength that was often enough for both of them.

"Now," she said, walking from the kitchen and handing Milton a cup of tea in an old chipped mug. "What did you see?"

"Barton Springs boiling," he said. "And a man."

She nodded and crawled into the papasan and onto Milton's lap. It was a move she had often done, but one that was becoming increasingly more difficult as she expanded. "So there was a man . . . "

"This is crazy, I'm sorry," he said, pulling on his beard. "He wasn't a man. He was like a man, but very much not a man."

"What was he?"

"My father called them Floaters," Milton said. "I'd always presumed it was something I dreamed or made up. It's unbelievable . . . but I was wrong about something, Rica," he said. "Just because something is unbelievable doesn't mean it isn't true."

"Have you talked to Roy?"

"Roy believes everything. I need a skeptic."

"I'm not a skeptic."

"It's not a bad thing. You just tend to believe only what you see."

"I believe in plenty of things. Love, positive thinking. I do that yoga class. I believe in those kinds of things. I just don't buy into Bigfoot or chupacabra."

"Exactly. A skeptic. That's what I need."

Rica frowned and clambered out of the papasan.

"Four days," Milton looked down into his tea. "He said we have four days."

"Four days of what?"

"I don't know." Milton got to his feet and walked to the window. "Rica, are you sure you want this baby?"

"What?"

"I'm just asking."

"What does that have to do with any of this?"

"I don't know. It's just, you know, the world is so backward and—"

"Fuck you, Milton." She turned and walked into the kitchen. "That is such bullshit and you know it."

"It's not bullshit." He followed her. The kitchen table stood between them. "The world is a mess. People are getting more stupid by the second. There's a new war every other day."

"If you don't want a baby, say it! But don't act like it's some mercy choice, okay."

"I didn't say I didn't want the baby."

"Well, do you?"

Milton said nothing.

"Milton," she said, the anger receding into something softer. "Tell me. Do you want this baby?"

She stood, small. A hand resting on her belly. His stomach whined like a bag of chalk chunks.

There I am

HAYDEN BROCK FELT alive and safe driving through Los Angeles. This was his home. He was loved here, admired. He drove slowly, hoping fans would wave. Just before pulling onto the San Bernardino Freeway, Hayden passed a billboard with an enlarged image of his face.

saint rick
a little heaven on earth every tuesday on nbc.

Hayden winked at himself. "Looking good, Saint Rick."

His image smiled down, handsome and kind, holy with just a hint of sexy. Look at those brown eyes filled with compassion . . . wait. Brown eyes?

Hayden pulled down the rearview. He stared into his eyes. Blue. They have always been blue. He circled the block to get a glimpse of the billboard again. The eyes were the wrong color. Not just the color, the whole shape. Another look in the rearview mirror. He had more eye wrinkles. He circled again. Was his hair really that dark? No. His hair had lightened over the last year. And it was clear, when comparing the image in the mirror and the image on the billboard, that the proportional size of his ears was being horribly misrepresented . . . but it was also clear that the man on the billboard was younger, fitter, and much better rested. It was him, yes. But it was him airbrushed to the studio's standard of perfection. And Hayden was appalled at the number of changes they felt perfection demanded. A horn blasted behind Hayden and he realized he had come to a complete stop in front of the billboard. With a jump, he slammed on the gas and sped up the ramp.

"You're no Saint Rick, that's for sure," he said, and pushed the pedal down a little farther.

Part of him had snagged on that billboard, like a sweater on a nail, and the farther he drove east, the more he untangled, stretching down Interstate 10. Finally the thread unraveled completely, grew taut, and snapped, leaving Hayden loose and uncomfortably free two hours outside of L.A.

Hayden liked directors. He liked them to advise or just plain order him how to play a scene. He enjoyed knowing someone was in charge. Someone other than him. He had been told to get out of town. He had done that. Now what? Where should he go?

Hayden knew he was hungry. That was a place to start. He drove into a Flying J truck stop hours into the desert east of Los Angeles. He pulled up to the front door and hopped out, smiling and nodding, half expecting shrieks and camera flashes. But no one seemed to notice. He wanted someone to approach and offer to park his car. But no one came.

Hayden Brock was a fish made for Los Angeles waters. Those were the only waters in which he thrived. Pools of L.A. exist all over the world. You can find them in the ski resorts of Colorado or the dance clubs of New York or the photo galleries of Paris. Hayden had been to all these places, hopping from L.A. pool to L.A. pool. He thought himself well traveled, but in a sense this desert drive was the first time in his adult life that Hayden Brock had left the Los Angeles city limits. He was a fish out of water.

No one in the truck stop recognized him. There weren't many people, just a few large truckers and cow-eyed waitresses, but still he expected something from someone. He sat in a booth and ate a fried egg sandwich. To his surprise, the waitress brought a check for him to pay. To actually pay.

After eating, Hayden walked through the store section of the truck stop, examining car air fresheners and leather steering wheel covers. Next to the sunglasses display, he found the magazine rack.

"There I am," he said, pulling out the latest issue of *Entertainment Weekly*. hayden brock, the cover read. hollywood's holy man. He looked closer. The eyes were blue . . . but the face on the cover was younger, cleaner. The expression was wiser, the chin stronger, the skin smoother. He looked up at the mirror on the sunglasses display. Even the color of his skin was different. Had he ever been that tanned? For a few minutes he tried to match his expression on the cover. He couldn't quite do it. He looked again at the magazine cover. That man would be on the way to a real spiritual retreat. That man would be sober more often than drunk. That man would never inappropriately fondle a goat.

"Hell, you're no Hayden Brock either."

His cell phone rang and Hayden was thankful for the distraction.

"Ted!" Hayden said on answering. "I did what you said. I'm out of town."

"Yeah, well, you can stay out for a while."

"What do you mean?" Hayden felt an uneasy tremor pass through his body.

"The studio called. You're out. No more contract."

"But I'm . . ." Hayden stared at his image on the magazine cover. "I'm Saint Rick."

"Not anymore. Rumor has it they're going to try for Ryan Gosling."

"To play me?"

"No," Ted said with a clap of his teeth. "To play Saint Rick, which you are not."

Hayden said nothing.

"Look," said Ted, a hint of kindness creeping into his voice. "I'm going to work on this. Maybe we get you a farewell episode or something. And who knows, this might be good for your career. Get you back into movies. Though I kind of doubt it. Maybe some commercial work. You like commercials? Don't sweat it. Just lay low a few days. You still there?"

Hayden nodded.

"Brock?"

"I'm here." The new compassion scared Brock more than anything. Ted was not kind. Compassion indicated that things were indeed very, very bad.

"Okay, Brock. I'll call you in a couple of days. Be good."

And that was it.

Hayden walked to the bathroom. He found an empty stall and sat down on the closed seat. His chin lay on his fists. The stall stunk. Not of the smell of excrement, but of the odors we use to cover the smell of excrement. A fake, flowery, wet smell with tints of acidic citrus, like a bouquet of plastic roses doused with half-digested lemonade.

Hayden let his face slide into his open palms. He was not the man on the billboard. Not the man on the magazine. Hayden Brock, not Saint Rick.

Television sainthood was gone. Taken from him. Pulled from his being like a tooth. Fierce and fast and irrevocable. What else could be taken? His face? His chin? His car? His name? The once-solid world was now riddled with cracks and could crumble to dust in a day.

What if he became a has-been? A once-was?

Who the hell am I?

Everyone would forget him. Restaurants wouldn't comp his bill, fan magazines wouldn't send Christmas cards, studio interns wouldn't bang him in on-set prop closets. What if he lost all the money? Lost the houses?

In a panic, he pulled out his cell and dialed Ted. It rang. And rang. And rang. Finally clicking to voice mail. It was already happening.

He tapped his feet frantically on the stained tile floor. He thought about calling his parents, or his ex-wife, or even his therapist. But he couldn't. He would have to tell them he was no longer Saint Rick. He couldn't stomach their reaction, whatever it would be. Any response would confirm that it was true. He was no longer Hayden Brock, star of *Saint Rick*. Soon, very soon, he would no longer be Hayden Brock, celebrity. He was fast on his way to being simply Hayden Brock. And he didn't like Hayden Brock.

For several minutes he stayed right where he was, sitting on the toilet, alone at a Flying J truck stop over two hours from the Los Angeles city limits, the clues to his identity flaking away. Under the layers of fame, of luck, of looks, of money was a dark blob of wants, likes and dislikes, fears and instincts, all hardly distinguishable from a billion others. There was just nothing to being Hayden Brock.

"Well then," he said out loud, "be someone else."

He heard the idea as if it had not been him who had said it.

"Who?" he asked, again out loud, his voice echoing against the stall walls.

"Be someone they can't take from you."

"Okay. Who?" he asked himself.

He stood up fast, tensing with a new energy. He slammed the stall door open as if the answer might be hiding on the other side. Instead he found the smudged mirror running along a row of sinks. He stepped to the counter and stared deep into his own face, perhaps deeper than he ever had before. And for Hayden Brock, who spent many hours before a mirror, that's saying quite a bit.

He watched his own eyes, desperate to see something of value in them.

"Who can I be?" he asked his reflection. His image paused. It seemed to know the answer, but was teasing Hayden, hesitating like a woman withholding a kiss.

Finally his image leaned in with a smile and whispered, "Saint Hayden."

"A saint? A real saint?"

His image nodded. The idea was outlandish, silly even. And Hayden fell in love with it instantly. It was an idea that had the power to change everything in Hayden's world.

"Yes," he said to himself. "I can be a saint. Not a pretend saint, but a real, live saint."

Hadn't he received thousands of letters thanking him for inspiring their faith? Hadn't people requested his prayers? Hadn't a mother approached him at a publicity event and asked that he lay hands on her autistic son? If all those people believed he could be a saint, why couldn't he believe it himself?

His reflection smiled at him.

In ten minutes the roll of the hills tickled his innards, the smell of spruce sweetened the wind, the top was down, the music was loud, and Hayden, untethered, sped farther east.

No more acting, he thought. *No more pretending, no more glitz, and certainly no more goats.*

Hole of light

IN PURE INSTINCTUAL horror, Click threw his crab legs out to either side and clasped to the crusted walls of the pipe. Below him he could sense a warm darkness, a realm of steamy unknown. Above him was one small hole of light with the muffled music of the party somewhere beyond. Click reached one claw upward and slipped an inch before finding a place to cling. He rested for a breath. Then, using his larger claw to hold him in place, he reached with his smaller claw. He pushed, extending his body out and up, pulling his shell behind him. From above came the echo of water and air. Click raised his eyes to see a cascading downpour. He braced himself. The flush tore the smaller claw's hold, but the larger purple claw held strong. After the water passed, Click continued his climb.

Inch. Inch. Flush. Inch. Inch. Flush. Click's muscles burned. His external joints squeaked. He kept his eyes flicking about searching for holds, only occasionally allowing himself an upward glance to see how far he had traveled. He was closer. Bit by bit, closer. The hole of light, brighter, larger, closer. He could do this. He could reach the hole of light. He was making an impressive cross-claw reach when the light was eclipsed. Click looked up. The hole was now a muted red ring. Click was confused. His goal, the light, gone. For a full two minutes the eclipse blotted the light. Then came the flush. For an instant the light returned, but for what it illuminated, Click wished light would disappear forever.

Cruel to the cat

MILTON SAT ALONE on the metal patio furniture in front of a taco trailer watching the sun set behind the buildings and oaks of South Congress. He bit into his third *migas* taco.

Four days? Four days until what? What if more of them were coming? What did they intend to do?

He felt sure there was something to know that he didn't know, and his thoughts complained like an itch in the center of his skull. He ordered another taco from the sleepy woman inside the trailer.

Maybe he'd seen nothing? Maybe he was as mad as his father? Maybe there was nothing to know at all?

You can't trust what you see. He knew that. You can't believe in anything. Physics had taught him that. He hated physics.

Roy loved physics. He adored how fluid, strange, and yet seemingly logical the world was. For Roy, the weirder the idea, the tastier. The arrow of time is not necessarily a constant; his own body is made up primarily of empty space; the shape of the expanding universe demands an infinite amount of matter like rocks weighing down a picnic blanket on a windy day.

Through their first two years of college, Milton watched Roy gobble down lectures, ace exams, chatter theories. But Milton found it all vaguely nauseating. The language of math felt metallic in his mouth, like sucking on loose change.

Quantum Physics was the worst. Twice a week Milton would sit stone-faced as Dr. Asiv Sang chipped away at the observable world in his thick, and slightly bored, Indian accent. Unbending truths like gravity and classical mechanics were discarded with the same patronizing tone an aging child dismisses fairy tales and Santa Claus.

It was Roy who finally revealed to Milton why he suffered through a subject he detested.

"Ten or more dimensions. Maybe time as a dimension, too," Roy said, splashing his beer at the Cactus Café. "It's all wiggling strings!"

"I can't see any strings! I can't feel any strings."

"You feel nothing but strings!" Roy said.

"What use is a law that makes sense in math but has nothing to do with the world I'm looking at?"

"Who cares about what we see?" Roy said. "So we're blind little moles, we'll barely scrape the surface of it all. But we get to scrape the surface! What was that quote Sang read? 'The universe isn't just more fucked up than we ever imagined. It's more fucked up than we ever *can* imagine.'"

"Not sure that was the exact wording." Milton mindlessly slid his pint glass about the table. "If the world is just a collection of subatomic particles randomly bouncing around, then what's the point? Right? Then there's that whole Heisenberg thing. We can't even look at the world without changing it. Nothing is certain. You can't believe anything."

"No, no, no. It's the other way around." Roy grinned. "You can believe everything. Anything!"

"I don't know why I do this. I'm barely passing. I hate the classes."

"I know why you're doing this," Roy said, smiling. "You're trying to figure out what the fuck your father was talking about."

On the Tuesday of the fifth week of class, Dr. Sang scribbled the words *Schrödinger's cat* on the chalkboard.

An icy prickle crawled up Milton's neck. The professor drew a crude drawing that was, presumably, a cat in a box. All Milton could see was Fluffs.

When Milton had been five, his mother had given Milton a fat, furry, brown and white hamster for Christmas. He named it Fluffs. His father named it Schrödinger.

"A cat in a sealed box," Sang began. "Inside the box is radioactive material in the midst of decay. At any moment an electron may or may not be released. There's also a Geiger counter to monitor the release of any electron. If one particle is detected, a vial of poison will be smashed and the cat will die. If no particle is released, the cat lives on. Its life hangs in a quantum balance."

Milton had woken one morning in his tenth year to find his father sitting in the kitchen staring with red, sleepless eyes at a closed wooden box sitting on the kitchen table.

"What's in the box, Dad?"

"A creature existing in the probability cloud between alive and dead."

Milton had shrugged off the comment and headed to school.

"So Schrödinger explained, with intention to mock, that according to the Copenhagen view, the cat is *both* dead and alive until you open the box and view the cat. Only when the cat is *observed* does the particle *decide* its position and the cat's fate is declared."

On returning home that afternoon, Milton found Fluffs's cage sitting atop an overflowing trash can. Just below it was the wooden box, its lid ajar. He stepped closer. A patch of brown fur, an open eye.

He had banged on the locked basement door for fifteen minutes before his father finally unlatched the lock, opened the door, and stared with annoyance.

"You killed my hamster!" Milton yelled.

"Don't blame me," his father had said. "Blame Schrödinger."

"Now this was Schrödinger's way of mocking Bohr's idea," Sang explained. "But many people have taken the thought exercise as an example of . . . Yes?"

Milton had raised his hand—a rare event.

"Isn't that cruel to the cat?"

Dr. Sang stared back with an emotionless pause. A few of the hundred students in the hall snickered.

"It's a thought experiment. Theoretical. No real cat."

"But," Milton continued, unsure what he was about to say, following a thread by instinct more than thought. "What would a cat, a theoretical one, experience inside the box?"

Sang came close to smiling.

"Interesting question. How does the cat experience this? Let's presume the cat can't experience anything after death . . . Yes, I know many of us would argue this point. But for now, let's say there's not kitty heaven or hell and conscious experience ends at death." Sang paused, thinking. "It depends on which theory you subscribe to. There is the agreed-upon math of quantum mechanics and then there are the dozen or so theories explaining the math. Bohr . . ."

"The bastard," Milton whispered. Roy turned, but Milton kept his eyes on Sang.

"Bohr would say the Geiger counter is observation enough to collapse the wave function. But some of his disciples would argue the cat actually experiences the cloud of probability in some way. The objective collapse theorists would say the environment or the cat itself would observe its own state, and again there would be wave function collapse. While people siding with the many worlds theory would say . . . well . . . how to put this?"

Sang coughed. Milton understood. For the first time, the math and theory were clear—so clear and simple that he understood what Sang was explaining before the professor spoke.

"The cat was in a superposition, a quantum moment of both life and death. But it doesn't experience anything after death, so it only experiences surviving the experiment in some other world. No matter how long or how many times you shove the cat in a box, the cat itself only experiences surviving the box. Experiences another world where it lives. While in nearly countless other worlds, we open the box to a dead cat."

Milton stood. Heads turned. Dr. Sang was busy scribbling a happy face on the cat on the board and continuing his explanation. Milton squeezed past Roy's questioning face, past the knees of his classmates.

"Milt?" Roy said. Milton made his way to the door as Sang lectured on.

"Max Tegmark has some ideas about this. He proposed a machine based on particle spin—"

Milton let the metal door snap shut behind him. He took three steps and vomited into a plastic trash can.

His father was the cat. His father was Fluffs. His father was dead and alive.

It was a theory. Not even the leading theory.

He stepped outside into the sunlight with an empty knowledge that he had gotten what he had come for. He would never step into another physics classroom again.

Choose a faith

HAYDEN BROCK HAD two major obstacles preventing him from becoming a saint:

1. He enjoyed doing naughty things.
2. He didn't believe in God.

He didn't see these problems as insurmountable. Merely challenges. After all, he had learned to tap-dance in three days for his first major role as Chimp-O the plucky orphan on the television drama *White Slavery*.

First things first. Choose a faith.

In Blythe, California, Hayden walked out of the dry midday heat and into a two-story, air-conditioned Barnes & Noble. He purchased a double vanilla latte and sought out the spirituality section. He was surprised at the quantity of options: *Christianity for Dummies, Buddhism for Beginners, Understanding Mormonism*.

Christianity was of course the most familiar. Saint Rick lived out a vaguely Christian/Judeo ethical system, or so he had been told. He'd also celebrated both Christmas and Easter. Christianity might work, but it felt too easy. Hayden remembered a fraternity brother back in college telling him the heart of Christianity was accepting Jesus. What's not to accept? Jesus is great.

Islam looked more exotic, but Hayden had seen the news. Too violent. And too much spicy food.

Buddhism wasn't bad. One of the writers for *Saint Rick* was a Buddhist. Nice guy. But dull. Never got angry. Or even really happy. No, Buddhism was like a sweater Hayden could admire but couldn't imagine actually wearing.

Throughout the afternoon Hayden sought and thought, book back cover by book back cover. On his third vanilla latte of the day, Hayden discovered *A Guide to the Saints.* There in crisp detail and alphabetical order was a description of hundreds of saints. A few he had heard of: Francis, Peter, Nicholas. Most were new to him. But what amazed him was that each and every one of them was Catholic.

Catholic. Like Christian, but different.

Hadn't there been a Catholic family on his block when he was a kid? Yes. The Flynns. Serious family. Well dressed. Clean. Never dragging along neighbors on Sunday mornings like the Baptists two doors down. Come to think of it, they mainly went to church on Saturday night. That makes more sense than Sunday. Hayden hardly ever got into trouble on Sunday mornings. What else about the Flynns? They weren't the screamers and shakers? No, that was the poor family who went to the small white church twenty miles away. No. The Flynns did things with style. With tradition. But what was it they did? Hayden did not know.

"Be careful of Papists," his father had once said, jerking a thumb at the Flynn house. "If America ever goes to war with Rome, they'll be tossing grenades in our lawn."

"Are we going to war with Rome?" Hayden asked.

"Nah. I'm just saying."

The Flynns had a boy his age. A thin boy with wide eyes. He was quiet. Not shy, just quiet. He was calm. His entire family was calm. The Flynns were different. Members of a secret society. Mysterious and . . . what was it? *Sure.* That's it. They were *sure.*

Hayden tossed his empty cup, gathered the book on saints plus a Catholic Bible (they have their own Bible!) and *A Guide to the Catholic Calendar.*

He piled his books by the nearest open register and placed his credit card on top.

"Are you a member?" the girl behind the counter asked.

"Not yet," Hayden asked. "Are you?"

"All employees get free membership."

"Get out!" Hayden examined the store with new eyes. Barnes & Noble, a quiet Catholic haven, granting young people membership into their holy society. "I hope someday I can be a member as well."

The girl shrugged and picked up his credit card.

"Wait. Are you . . . ?"

"I am."

"I love . . ."

"Thanks."

You're flying, child. Your tits look great.

AS THE SKY darkened, Rica undressed in her bedroom. She looked down at her round body and touched her belly. It rose up like a bald hill blocking the southern landscape.

Little girl, she thought to her baby, *I can't see my cooch.*

The baby kicked as if to say, "Don't worry, mama, it's still there."

The change of scenery bothered her. It felt too horribly symbolic to watch her sex-realm disappear behind her yet-to-be child. Her breasts were changing, too. Growing in weight and size. This worried her almost more than the hidden nether regions.

Rica's breasts had always been extraordinary. She loved them and they loved her, so seeing Rica alone was like seeing two friends you enjoy as a couple. And they hummed. A sweet, wavering hum, like the flight of a hummingbird. Lovers believed her breasts to be sacred. Milton and Rica had made love three times without him touching her chest. He ran his fingers along her collarbones, he nibbled at her navel, but he only gazed at her breasts. On their fourth night together she took his hand in hers. "It's okay, Milt," she said, and placed his trembling palm on her right breast (the finest of the two). Milton smiled. Slowly he lifted his other hand and placed it on her left breast (some would argue that, in truth, the left was the finest). He knelt there on the bed, eyes and hands on Rica's humming breasts.

"They're warm," he said, his eyes wide with wonder. Rica nodded.

But now things were changing.

"My body's been hijacked," Rica had told Jeppy a few days before. "I was a sex kitten, I really was."

"You still are. Didn't you have any second-trimester urges?" Jeppy was slicing tomatoes in the Mundi House kitchen.

"I was hot and bothered for a few weeks. Surprising Milton in the middle of the day and all, but it felt like a last hurrah, like a dying man getting up to dance one last time." Rica added a pinch of dried lemon peels to her soup. "I thought my body was built for me. Now I find it had this secret agenda the whole time. My tits, Jeppy. I love my tits. I love using them to get better service at restaurants. I love distracting people at bookstores. But tits are really for milk making. They've been waiting for this."

"Rica, Rica, Rica." Jeppy shook her head and placed her knife down. "You have no idea how sexy fertility is. It's one thing to see a butterfly sitting on a leaf, it's another to see it in flight. You're flying, child. Your tits look great."

Rica wrapped a satin robe around, or almost around, her body and strolled down the hall and into the living room, her mouth curling into a secretive smile. From her purse she pulled out a DVD. She placed it in the player, lowered the volume to barely audible, and pressed play. The film was *Night Beat*. It was Hayden Brock's one major film credit. He plays FBI agent Chip Bradley, a spunky new recruit who gets shot with a high-powered crossbow within the first thirty minutes of the film.

Rica had rented the film over a dozen times and had never gotten further than that scene. She tried once, but found that *Night Beat* without Hayden Brock was a poorly written, tedious piece of fluff-crap. But the first half hour was wonderful. Chip's wry humor, his naive excitement, his expertise in martial arts, and, most impressive of all, his generous spirit. When not chasing down drug lords, Chip Bradley volunteers with Big Brothers Big Sisters. Every Saturday he takes a twelve-year-old boy named Rocket to see life outside of the inner-city slums.

"Why do you do it?" his grizzled older partner, played by Emilio Estevez, asks.

"When he grows up there'll be one less drug lord to track," he says. And he smiles. And when he does Rica's naughties throw back the shutters, sweep the porch, and turn on the flashing "Open for Business" sign.

Then comes the horrible ambush in Redwood Park. Chip and his partner are waiting to meet their narc when out of nowhere an arrow rips into Chip's chest. In slow motion, his body flies backward and is pinned to the gigantic trunk of a redwood. A trickle of blood dribbles from his surprised mouth. His partner runs to his side. Chip looks up at him, struggling to breathe.

"Partner, do me a favor. Take Rocket to the rodeo now, huh?"

"I'll take him," his partner says. "I'll even buy him a hot dog."

Chip smiles, sighs loudly, and drops his head.

Rica cries every time. She also inexplicably feels that some kind of justice has been dealt.

Tonight Rica paused the movie the moment before the arrow is launched. Chip Bradley is in midchuckle, reacting to an off-color joke his partner made about his cooking abilities. Chip is turned slightly, looking into the camera, smiling out to Rica. Rica smiled back.

Hayden Brock—his looks, his movements, his voice—stirred something in Rica that no other person did. There he was, frozen on the television screen, like some high-definition version of the ornate icons her grandmother used to pray to. A perfect balance of distance and presence. The image of Hayden Brock was alluringly illusive and undeniably tangible. He was there and he was not there. The perfect man.

"Hayden Brock," she said. "You'd want this baby." She placed both hands on her belly. "I wonder where you are tonight. I wonder if you remember me at all."

Can I help you?

"HEY! YOU!" CALLED the woman from inside the taco trailer. "I'm shutting down. You want any more?"

"No. No, thanks," Milton said with an embarrassed cough. "What time is it?"

"Ten till ten."

"Crap!"

Milton's heart gave a sick hiccup. He was late for work. He jumped up, grabbed his bicycle parked beside him, and aimed himself downhill toward the shine of downtown.

The avenue's boutiques and vintage stores were long since closed and the street artists were packing away their wares, but the restaurants hummed with diners sitting on open decks or crowded around window-side tables. Guitar-driven Texas blues splashed out from the Continental Club each time a customer snuck out to smoke. In an empty lot on the east side of the road, a row of converted Airstream trailers sold gourmet French fries, tacos, and high-priced pastries.

Downtown Austin was home to the Crockett Brew-and-View Movie Theater. The theater, carved out of the innards of an old warehouse, was known to host the most eclectic collection of films of any theater in the country. One night would feature the latest art flick from Paris and the next night would be a marathon of all three *Porky's* films. All this and beer. The Crockett was one of Milton's favorite places in the world. Even in college, Milton was a regular customer of the Crockett. Standing in line for Kung Fu Sunday tickets, arriving naked for free seats to Doris Wishman's *Nude on the Moon*, gawking at Quentin Tarantino, Peter Jackson, and other film celebrities who would drop by the theater unannounced.

After abandoning faith a year after college, the Crockett became Milton's house of worship. Two to three nights a week, one could find Milton sitting in the dark feasting on films. He sat in the rows with a congregation of zealots laughing or screaming in unison, being transported by stories and images, connecting with truths hidden in fictions, and, if only for a couple of hours, believing in the images before him.

After a year or so the staff knew Milton by name. He'd stick around after hours, help bus the dishes and clean the floors, and then sit drinking beer and talking films with the waitstaff and cooks. Even the owners, Dag and Chloe Jones, knew Milton and more than once comped his bill.

One night, after a screening of a documentary about a man who legally married his full-size sex doll, Dag and Milton stayed up talking in the lobby. At first it was small talk. "How'd you like the film?" and "Ever used a sex doll?" As they talked Dag kept refilling both his and Milton's glasses from a bottle of tawny port. The conversation moved from sex documentaries (*Twisted Sex*, *The Lifestyle*), to sexploitation films (*Swinging Secretary*, *99 Women*), to blaxploitation films (*Dr. Black, Mr. Hyde*; *Cotton Comes to Harlem*; *Sweet Sweetback's Baadasssss Song*), white trash–sploitation (*The Preacher*, *The Passing*), and finally on to good old-fashioned horror. H. G. Lewis's low-budget masterpieces, the Italian gore classics, the genius of George A. Romero. By 3:00 AM the bottle was empty and Dag was offering Milton a job.

"I just bought two hundred unmarked prints from a bankrupt drive-in in Kansas. Drove up there, paid cash, drove them back. Killed my truck with the weight, but so worth it Should I open another bottle?"

"No thanks, Dag. I've got to bike home." Milton could feel his tongue stumble. "So what movies?"

"Don't know. Unmarked, mismarked. It's a mess. Drive-in movies. Mainly from the '70s. I want to show a different one every Thursday night. I see you staring at my glass. Come on, I've got a bottle right behind the counter."

"Really, I've had enough." Milton rubbed his head. "So you want me to watch them?"

"Yeah. Help me pick out the ones worth watching. Then introduce them to the audience. You know, say a few words, spill some trivia. It'd be fun," Dag said, ducking behind the bar. "And I'll give you 100 percent of the door."

"Wow."

"But it's free to get in."

"Oh."

"So I'll pay you in beer and food and any movie you want to see. Here, hand me your glass."

Milton had been hosting the Thursday Freak Show ever since.

Milton had never been late for any Thursday show. It was matter of respect—to the audience, to the film, to the Crockett. Milton was speeding toward Riverside, his bike wheels emitting a high whine. Just as he passed a custom-made boot boutique, a flash of pain shot through his eyes. He screeched to a stop and threw both hands over his eyes. The pain was an expanding pressure, as if someone were pumping fluid into each eyeball. For a moment Milton feared they'd both pop. He opened his eyes and the night sky was now day bright. He stared down Congress Avenue and saw suns, a dozen miniature suns bouncing like basketballs. Buildings melting like butter. Birds, bats, insects flying up and blackening the sky above the suns, above the burning.

Milton squeezed his eyes closed and gasped. When he opened his eyes again the vision was gone. Just the dark road, just the city lights. People crossing back and forth, cars wheeling by.

It was surely past ten now. He put his feet to his pedals and aimed for the Congress Avenue Bridge. Each time he blinked he saw the colored shadows of the bouncing suns. *It's all right, it's all right,* he told himself.

As he reached the bridge, the pain pierced his head again, fiercer this time, hotter. Without stopping he slapped his hands over his eyes. The handlebars twisted and Milton lurched over them and onto the road, knocking the air from his lungs. He opened his eyes and the sky was dripping fire like burning plastic. The waters under him bubbling and black. People dancing. Skin falling from their bodies as they moved. Whoosh. A long, hot wind, and all was dust.

The horn knocked the vision from his head. He was kneeling in the road, his hand bleeding.

"Hey, you okay?" someone shouted.

Milton didn't answer. He struggled to his feet, climbed on his bike, and darted on. His ankle ached. His head felt heavy, waterlogged. *But it wasn't real. Just pictures.*

He pedaled up to the front of the Crockett and realized he had left his bike lock at home. *Shit.* He quickly removed his belt, strapped the bike to a parking meter, and ran inside.

"Get your ass in there, Milton. It's 10:09," the manager said as Milton stumbled in. "What the hell happened to you? You're bleeding on the handrail."

"Sorry, sorry." Milton rushed past her and down the aisle to the front of the theater. The visions, the Floaters, the thoughts would all have to wait. He had a job to do. A microphone was waiting for him. Milton picked it up with one hand and used the other to hold up his pants.

He knew a crowd of at least a hundred and fifty was watching him, but he refused to look. He feared the faces. He loved his job, loved sharing whatever he knew about the obscure film featured, but if he saw those faces watching, waiting, judging . . . it would kill him. He didn't close his eyes as he did in the Pearl-Swine days. He had worked out a different method of avoiding eye contact. He found a point or object, anything other than a person, and aimed his words there. Tonight it was a pint of dark beer.

"Hello, everyone, and welcome back to the Thursday Freak Show," he said to the beer. "Tonight's film is the 1973 classic *Invasion of the Bee Girls*, a.k.a. *Graveyard Tramps*." Milton paced in front of the screen, glancing up every few steps to see that the beer was still paying attention. "The plot's as old as Shakespeare. Hot radiated housewives kill off the men of their community by screwing them to death." The beer chuckled at the concept. Milton's head started to ache. Not the expanding-eye pain. This was his whole brain filling up like a water balloon abandoned on a sink's faucet.

Say it. Say it.

"William Smith stars as the FBI agent called in to investigate. You might recognize him from his later role as the Marlboro Man or as the bad-ass Russian commander in *Red Dawn*. The screenplay of *Bee Girls* was written by Nicholas Meyer." Clapping. The beer must know his stuff. Under the smell of popcorn and pizza, Milton noticed a sweet burning smell. "That's right, the writer and director of *Star Trek II* and *VI*, i.e., the good ones." Milton's head was pulsing now.

Say it, Milton.

Say what?

You won't know until you say it.

"There's some nice nudity in this one and lots of whipped cream." The beer hooted. "Apparently the ladies use Cool Whip to radiate—" The beer was rising from his place. Floating up. To a mouth, a nose, a face. Milton made solid eye contact with a complete stranger. Milton froze. His head beating like an elephant's heart. His jaw tightened.

Say it now.

He saw them all now. Hundreds of eyes watching. A fear, like waking up to find yourself standing on the edge of a skyscraper, squeezed Milton. And there, behind the crowd, in the back row of the theater, was the blue screaming expression of the Floater, its thin naked body a foot taller than the people sitting beside it. The same Non-Man. It stared at Milton. No one else moved. No one seemed to notice it.

And Milton knew.

Say it!

"And I should also tell you," he said, stuttering slightly, "that is, I think you should know . . . the world is going to end. Probably Sunday. Monday at the latest. So, you know, be ready for that."

The crowd chuckled.

Milton squeezed his eyes and opened them again. The Floater was gone. A mass of amused, expectant faces. Milton gave the projectionist a nod and the room fell dark. The audience cheered and Milton walked.

"Not staying, Milton?" the manager asked.

"Can't," he said, walking past. "End of the world."

He hadn't understood until the moment he had announced it. The visions, the dread, the message the Floater was telling him.

His bike was gone. So was his belt. Milton started walking south, holding his pants with one hand and tugging on his beard with the other. He walked slowly. Beautiful people with tight clothes and perfect hair brushed past, smelling sugary and strong, laughing, touching each other, disappearing into bars from which music and chatter poured. *In three days you'll all be dead.*

On the sidewalk in front of him, a blond girl stood at an ATM. Her shirt ended just over her navel. Her breasts seemed to float, holding the rest of her up. Milton watched them. Magical, happy orbs. He wanted to hold them, cradle them like orphaned rabbits, tell them it would be okay.

"It's all right, little ones," he said. They nodded back, telling Milton that, yes, it was all right.

"Uh, excuse me?" a voice above the orbs said. "Can I help you?"

Milton looked straight into the deep-blue eyes of the girl. "No," he said. "I'm afraid you can't."

He walked on, out of the noise and crowds. On the steps of city hall, a man in stained jeans and no shirt asked Milton for some change. Milton pulled out his wallet, took out all his cash, and placed it in the man's hand. It was $47.

"Thanks, dude," the man said. "Made my day."

Buttered

HAYDEN BROCK LEANED back against a pile of Hilton suite pillows and studied his new collection of Catholic literature. Page by page, dogma dictum by dogma dictum, a picture of his chosen faith took shape. Faith, Hayden concluded, was the act of believing in unbelievable things. The more unbelievable, the more profound the faith.

Wine becoming blood. Pretty unbelievable. Good.

Bread becoming the flesh of a man. Even better.

The man whose flesh becomes bread actually being God disguised as a human. Excellent.

Hayden now understood why Catholics were so sure of their prayers. Once you bought the bread turning into the flesh of God stuff, believing God hears your prayers was easy.

Hayden ordered some rolls and a bottle of wine from room service.

"Fine, sir," said the voice on the phone. "And what kind of wine would you like?"

"Red. Most definitely red."

"Any particular red?"

Hayden thought for a moment. "What's the most blood-looking?"

There was a pause on the other end of the line. "That would be our malbec, sir. We have a '92 . . ."

"That'll do fine."

When he opened the door a few minutes later, a young woman holding a tray gasped. She had fair skin, dark eyes, and a chin like a scoop of ice cream. Hayden flashed his finest TV-star smile, took the tray, and, without having to be asked, signed a napkin as a tip. The girl blushed and made her way down the hall, glancing back every few steps. As he closed the door, Hayden noticed that the girl walked with a limp. *Sad*, he thought as the door clicked closed.

Hayden sat on the floor with the tray. Then he readjusted himself to a kneeling position. He laid the rolls out on the tray in front of him and picked up the bottle of wine. *A '92 malbec. Not a great year*, he thought. *Of course it doesn't matter. Soon it will be 33 AD. That's a good year.*

He popped the cork and whispered a prayer. "God, make this into Christ, please."

He was quiet for a long moment. Finally he reached for a roll and took a bite. It was buttered. That seemed wrong. It's one thing to eat the body of Jesus. It's another thing to first cover that body with butter.

He poured half a glass of wine and sipped. Nothing tasted different. It was bread and it was wine. It was nice how the bread soaked in the wine. It was pleasant how still the moment was. But nothing supernatural was happening. He closed his eyes and remained still. The room's air-conditioning hummed, and stories below, there was a gentle buzzing of traffic. Hayden listened to the soft noise. He let all his thoughts float past and felt his heart slow. He knew he was experiencing something very near to peace. A quiet sort of feeling, like waking up in the middle of the night and not minding that the lights are out and you're alone.

Hayden remained on his knees for six minutes. Then a knock on the door punctured the stillness. He opened the door to find the pretty girl with the limp.

"I just got off work and thought you might like some company," she said. In her hand was a half-full bottle of Jack Daniel's. For a moment Hayden hesitated. He was trying to be a Catholic saint. As far he could recall, Mr. Daniel had never inspired a saintly act. But the girl smiled, a sort of crooked smile. That was enough. Hayden smiled back and ushered her in. He liked how she limped. It had a certain sexiness to it. It also reminded him of episode 35 in which Saint Rick convinces a recently disabled Olympic gymnast to begin a career in pottery.

The girl stood by the bed. "Mind if I get a little comfy?"

"Be my guest."

She giggled and removed the small, blue Hilton vest and sat on the bed. She shook out her hair and stretched out her arms. With her eyes fixed on Hayden, she unscrewed the Jack Daniel's cap with her teeth and spit the cap across the room. It bounced against the air conditioner. She passed the bottle to Hayden who suavely swiped it from her hand and took a swig. She then rolled up her left pant leg. Something about the color and shape of her leg seemed out of place. Hayden leaned in closer and took another sip.

"This thing has been rubbing on me all day," she sighed. With two fast snaps she disconnected her leg at the midthigh.

Hayden squealed.

"Did you just squeal?" she asked.

"I did."

"You have a problem with prosthetics?" she asked.

"No, no. Not at all," Hayden said, staring at the plastic leg lying on the floor. "I just love whiskey!"

He pushed the bottle back to her. She smiled. "Go fetch a glass or two, will ya?"

Hayden grinned. He swaggered into the bathroom. *I can do this,* he told himself in the mirror. *It's kind of kinky. I like kinky.*

He reemerged with two water glasses and a warm pair of bedroom eyes. He was pretty sure he knew what would be happening next. Hayden Brock had made love to three hundred and eight women. Possibly one goat. He believed himself to be a master of seduction. He took great pleasure in how his eyes and witty remarks wooed the women he desired. The truth that he only suspected in his darkest moments was that it was his fame and not his sexual allure that won women over. The same people who long to rub elbows with the rich and famous are even happier to rub other body parts. In his heart of hearts, Hayden knew, Chris Elliott probably got laid just as much as he did.

But sitting on the bed with Melinda, that was the girl's name, Hayden shoved all doubts from his mind and enjoyed the erotic-ego-adrenaline rush of being wanted by a stranger.

The two were quickly and pleasantly drunk on whiskey and pheromones. A shoe, a leg, and the remains of Hayden Brock's first communion lay scattered on the floor. Melinda downed the last swig of the whiskey and tossed the empty bottle against the wall. It clanked and fell to the floor unbroken.

"So, Saint Rick," she said, pushing him onto his back. "Shall we lay hands on each other?"

"Ohhh," Hayden said with a giggle.

"Or"—she delicately straddled him, her leg nub rubbing on his outer thigh—"do you want to speak in tongues?"

She lowered her face to his, a tongue darting out to wet her lips.

"Wait!" someone said. To his surprise, it was Hayden. "Wait, wait." He pushed Melinda off of him and stood beside the bed. "We can't. I mean, I can't do this."

"Can't?"

"I'm sorry. I'm trying to be a saint. A real one. A Catholic one."

"I'm a Catholic," Melinda said, reaching for his thigh.

"But I'm different. I don't believe in God."

"Neither do I."

Hayden stared into her wide eyes, tree-moss green. "Honest?" he asked.

"Honest to God." She flashed her crooked smile.

The two embraced.

Same source as the wound

CROSSING THE FIRST Street Bridge toward home, Milton kept his eyes on the watery mirror of sky and skyline below him. Milton felt the distinct desire to pray. He fought the urge like an alcoholic refusing a shot.

Years before, only months after Milton had abandoned Dr. Sang's class, Roy presented a bold plan to cover some of their college expenses. A tiny tutoring business.

"We'll aim our advertising at the ladies! Just think, sitting in pink, puffy dorm rooms explaining the mysteries of math to some lost coed! We'll meet girls, Milton! Women!"

True to the plan, the boys stuck fliers to walls of Littlefield women's dorm, Gregory Gym's ladies' locker room, and the World's Best Frozen Yogurt shop on the Drag. Soon enough both boys had a full dance card of eager young women begging to be enlightened to the mysteries of math. Or just to have their homework finished.

In their second week of tutoring, Roy came back to the dorm room he shared with Milton and related what he called "the most magnificent moment of my life!"

That evening he had been tutoring a plump art history junior on the nature of parabolas. Roy, thrilled simply to be in the presence of a woman, was at first unaware of her hungry, predatory expression. When he finished the last equation, she smiled, asked him to sit beside her on the futon, and put on a Morrissey CD. Before the third song, the art historian had straddled Roy and gobbled up his virginity as if it were a leftover tater tot from a Sonic takeout. Her girth and Roy's less-than-stellar stature made for an awkward matching, like a pro wrestler riding a bucking miniature pony. But there were no complaints. Roy was left dazed, delighted, and grateful. He collected his things and readjusted his belt, grinning like a villain. The art history major giggled and scheduled another tutoring session for the following week. On his way out the door, she handed him his tutorial payment in cash.

She was the first of many. It was as if some secret, underground network of adventurous women had put out the word on all channels that Roy was a willing sort. Or perhaps it was something in Roy's newly deflowered demeanor that alerted ladies to his gleeful eagerness to play.

Night after night, he'd return to the dorm room he and Milton shared filled with stories of free-thinking liberal art majors or, even better, theater majors, with a deficiency in math skills but an openness to other arts. Some women were attractive, others less so. But Roy quickly developed an eye for inner beauty.

He'd complete the pages of assigned equations, careful to adorn his numbers with enough bubbles and flair to divert a professor's suspicion. Then he and his client would move to her thin dorm bed or apartment couch and wrestle with geometric formulas of another kind. And still, he got paid.

"There's a name for this kind of work," Milton told him.

"It's a noble profession. As old as farming!"

"I don't know how you do it."

"You just have to let them know that you're willing. If you can communicate that without dousing it all with desperation, you've got it made!"

Milton was desperate. He wore desperation like a neon ski jacket with a turquoise fringe.

Halfway through the semester, Roy was spending three to four nights a week educating the masses one coed at a time. Milton, meanwhile, had found his client base whittled down to one.

Her name was Tess. She wore a perfume that brought to Milton's mind fields of wild strawberries and honeycombs, though he had never seen a field of wild strawberries nor an actual honeycomb. Her eyes, bright as broken glass and twice as sharp, would watch him while he stumbled through explanations. He found it hard to bear so he kept his own eyes to the page. Malice-free but inquisitive, her gaze had a force he could feel. Later, when alone, he would check his cheek for the red burn mark.

Once he made her laugh. Nothing terribly witty. "The worst thing about imaginary numbers is someone took the time to imagine them."

Tess laughed. The sound danced through Milton's soul like carbonated bubbles. He found himself crafting another joke the next week, and the next, soon spending hours on what would hopefully come across as an offhand witticism.

And when she laughed, he thrived.

But no Morrissey played, no futon was shared, and Milton never stayed beyond his allotted hour. In the name of reticence, Milton kept a professional demureness, never broaching any personal subject more intimate than her preference in pocket calculators. And Tess, though friendly, affectionate even, shared little about her life and thoughts outside of math. Until one day late in the spring, she invited Milton to the University of Texas's Fellowship of Christian Athletes Spring Campout.

"I'm not an athlete."

"That's all right. I only play tennis. And I'm pretty bad." She laughed. Oh, that laugh.

"I'm not a Christian."

"That's okay, too." She smiled, those eyes sweetly cutting into him. "Well?"

"Can I bring my roommate?"

"*Can you bring your fucking roommate?*" Roy was horrified when Milton recounted the conversation.

"I was nervous! I didn't know what to say." Milton paced the dorm room, which, considering his wide gait and the limited square footage, didn't amount to much.

"A girl asks you camping and you offer to bring your roommate?"

"It's a Christian campout, not some sex orgy in the woods!"

"We'll see about that."

The next weekend the boys arrived at the grounds of a middle school summer camp in Roy's half-dead VW Bug with sleeping bags, swim trunks, and apprehension.

They wandered into the crowded dining hall—three rows of picnic tables in a wide cedar cabin. Tess waved from across the room. Leaving her conversation with a broad-shouldered baseball player, she jogged through the crowd and gave Milton a hug, an act of intimacy she had never displayed before. Though the embrace was gentle enough, Milton lost his breath.

Tess led them through the hall, smiling and nodding at friends. It was immediately apparent that this was not Roy and Milton's crowd. These people owned matching socks, these people voted in national elections, these people knew more about the University of Texas's football record than they did the Italian cannibal/zombie film genre. But to both Roy and Milton's surprise, these people were kind and welcoming.

The daylight was spent on girl-versus-guy touch football, ultimate Frisbee matches, and swimming in the silt-heavy lake. In the evening the campers gathered in the dining hall with the picnic tables pushed to the sides. They sat on the floor before two seniors with acoustic guitars and the words of hymns, camp songs, and Eagles ballads projected on a white screen. After the sing-along, a speaker was introduced, a former NFL linebacker who, enthusiastically if not all that elegantly, shared the story of his conversion to Christianity.

The rest of the night was pickup basketball games played under the fluorescent lights of the outdoor court and an extended game of capture the flag among the dark pines. The next day's schedule was packed with a similar slew of activities.

Roy, as always, threw himself into everything, exhausting himself in the games and even the singing. Milton followed, his shyness soothed by the occasional smile from Tess from across the field or while passing in the pine-lined paths.

By late Saturday night, Milton sat in a sleepless haze as the crowd of campers listened to the former NFL linebacker's most passionate talk yet.

"Listen, on the football field there's an inbounds and an out-of-bounds. Those lines are defined. Clear as chalk. Life is the same way. You know when you're out-of-bounds, even if you don't get caught. Your heart tells you."

This illustration drew Milton in, not that he had ever played a formal game of football, but he did know the reoccurring sensation of being out-of-bounds.

"I know a lot of those college profs want to tell you that it's all relative, that those lines are something we make up as we go along. I had those same eggheads when I went to school."

The crowd chuckled. Milton could just catch Tess's laughter in the mix.

"Can you imagine playing football with every player making up their own boundaries? Their own rules? It'd be Aggie training week."

More laughter. Milton dared a glance at Tess. She threw her head back in her amusement, showing her white teeth and red mouth.

"But I'm here to tell you there are things that are certain. Things you can count on as solid. Not just now, but forever." He lifted the small, worn Bible. "No matter what anyone says, there's truth that doesn't change."

Roy slumped forward, dozing. Milton leaned closer, drinking in this possibility. The world was not how his father had described it, nor how Dr. Sang had taught it. Could it be that the world consisted of truths?

"God and his word. They don't change. God drew the chalk boundaries in the field of life. And you know who has stepped out-of-bounds? We all have. The play is over." The linebacker nodded slowly in what felt like an overly choreographed pause. "Even worse, each of us has enough penalties racked up to push us back past our own end zone. Left to our own devices, every offensive play we try ends up a safety."

Milton was lost, but something snuck through the football lingo and monotone presentation. A solid world, a clear distinction between right and wrong. A solid something emerging from Sang's probability cloud or his father's endless parallel universes.

"So what do we do? We've been acting like there's no rules, no boundaries, and we find ourselves way back in our own end zone with two seconds on the clock. Well, I'll tell you what happened. The referee—who is also the coach and the owner—he put on a helmet and jersey and joined our team. And, man, can he run! Give him the ball, and he zooms, dodging, cutting, knocking the other team down flat and scoring the ultimate touchdown!"

A couple of guys in the crowd hoot.

"That's Jesus. That's what happened on the cross. Salvation."

Milton tried to follow the connection, but couldn't. In his head was a bleeding man in a robe dancing in an end zone. Somehow that was salvation.

"The question each of us has to answer as we mope in our own end zone is this: Are you going to give Jesus the ball?"

After the talk, a bonfire was set ablaze. The scent of burning marshmallows and the play of light gave the night a feel of fantasy, of fairy tale, of possibility. Roy had met a girl, of course, and lured her away from the fire with promises of constellations and shooting stars. Milton circled the fire in a daze, new ideas finding form. *One truth, not many. Not random. Knowable.* Perhaps the world did have boundaries and a Maker of boundary lines. Perhaps—and this was most tantalizing of all—the world had a point.

Tess touched his arm. "Want to go for a walk?"

After concealing the muscle spasm in his neck with a cough, Milton said yes.

They strolled through the dark woods toward the lake, her strawberry perfume mingling with the smell of pine. She spoke in a soft, melodic tone about how very much she loved Jesus, how real he was, how she knew he would never abandon her.

"My parents divorced when I was three. I've never had the best relationship with my father. But now I have a relationship with my Heavenly Father."

"My father's dead," Milton spit out, unsure why he had shared this.

"Oh gosh," Tess said. She put a hand to her chest. "My grandmother died last summer. I bet you were mad at God for taking him."

"No."

"Oh."

"He took himself. If there's anyone to be angry at, it's him." His throat felt dry and suddenly narrow.

It was quiet by the water, the singing and laughing of the bonfire softened by the pines. She sat on a log overlooking the lake and asked him to sit beside her.

"I've never done anything like this before," she said.

"Me either," Milton said.

And she laughed. She took Milton's hands—her hands so warm Milton nearly swallowed his tongue. She smiled and opened her eyes to him. Milton's body chemistry boiled over, but he forced himself not to look away.

"Milton," she said in a quiet voice. "Would you pray with me?"

Pray? She wants to pray? How do you pray?

"Close your eyes," she said, and bowed her head.

For a moment Milton kept his eyes open and stared at the smooth shine of the top of her head. His stomach wiggled. He closed his eyes and breathed nothing but strawberry perfume.

She whispered that he should accept Jesus into his heart, that the time was now. "Can you feel him? He's here." She squeezed his hands.

"Yes." *Wait, what?*

"Do you want him to come into your heart?"

"Yes," he said. "I do." *I do?* And then he was surprised to hear himself whisper, "Come into my heart."

When he opened his eyes, she was smiling, glowing. Milton had never made anyone but his mother smile with such joy and that was an image just on the edge of his memory. He smiled back, giddy, drunk on perfume and sleepiness.

"Everything is going to change now," she said, giving his hands one last squeeze before releasing them. She jumped to her feet. "We should get back," she said. "My boyfriend will be wondering where I went."

Like stepping on a nail, the pain shocked Milton, filled him with a thick sensation of sudden nausea, and hurt doubly for the fact that it should not have been a surprise.

"Are you coming?"

Milton stood, numb and wordless.

"You know, I knew there was a reason God never gave me a talent for math. It was so I could meet you and you could meet Jesus, right?" She laughed, and the bubbles sent through him burned.

"Tess . . ." he managed to say. She turned, her smile as lyrical as the half-moon peeking through the trees. He could say nothing more. She reached out and took his hand.

"It's okay," she said softly. "I never thought about it this way, but right now you're kind of like a newborn. Born again, right? So I bet things feel a little weird."

She led him back through the pines, the light and shadows of the bonfire moving in the distance. As they walked, quiet now, Milton learned his first lesson of faith. Comfort may come from the same source as the wound.

He watched wood burn, seeming to disappear in the process of transformation, sending out a heat that warned in its warmth. He watched Tess across the flames nuzzle into the chest of the broad-shouldered baseball player. Roy was gone, somewhere, he was sure, happily seducing a young Evangelical. The world, Milton felt, was horribly lonely and on fire.

Milton walked from the fire back toward the still lake waters. He sat on the same bench Tess had led him to and watched as the moon disappeared behind low clouds. Insects hummed, a few small drops of rain tickled the lake's surface, and Milton hurt like never before.

"Please, God, let this mean something."

The next night, back in the normalcy of their dorm room, Roy asked a reticent Milton his thoughts on the weekend.

"I think . . . I'm not sure, but I think I became a Christian," Milton said.

"Yeah?" Roy said, chewing on a pencil. "Well, okay. We'll be Christians."

Milton smiled. Roy stood.

"Want to order a pizza?"

No time for certainty

RICA SLEPT, HER limp body sprawled out on the couch, the remote still resting in her grasp, and the frozen face of Hayden Brock as Chip Bradley gasping from the television.

Milton burst through the front door. Rica jumped, her finger pushed down, and with a *whack* a steel hollow-tipped arrow rammed through Hayden's heart.

"You're home early," she said, dazed. She sat up and clicked the television off as Chip Bradley's partner pried Chip's corpse from the tree and used it to escape a downpour of hollow-tipped arrows.

"Rica." Milton knelt beside her. "The world is ending."

"Please, not that again." Rica pulled her legs underneath her. "Listen, I've been thinking. If you don't want to be responsible for—"

"The world is ending! The Floater told me. Or led *me* to tell me. And a bunch of others. I said it out loud and knew it was true."

Rica paused and studied Milton's face. "Please, Milton."

"They're showing me some horrible stuff. End of the world stuff. It will all be over by Sunday."

"This Sunday?"

"Maybe Monday. I guess it depends on what time zone you're in. That's stupid, I know, but true." Milton shook his head and took Rica's hand in his. "Babe, I thought there'd be time to be better. To, you know, be there for you. But now things are going to get bad. And there's stuff I have to do."

"Slow down," she said. "Couldn't this be another Bigfoot or pyramid power?"

"Of course it could be," he said, plunging his hands into his hair. "But there's no time for certainty. I have to act. Tell people. Be a messenger."

"Why you, Milt? You get hives when the anchorman uses second person."

"I can't figure it out. Can't hear what they're telling me." He paced the living room like a long-haired Groucho Marx. "I need to do something. I've never done anything!"

Rica shook her head. "If you don't want this kid, just say so. Don't blame it on some ghost or alien spouting about the Apocalypse."

"They're interdimensional travelers," Milton mumbled.

"Run away if you want. Really," she said, rising to her knees. "I give you my blessing. Honestly. Go commune with ET and talk Revelations. I'm having a baby in five months. That's what I'm doing."

"That's not enough." Milton stared at his hands. "I don't want to live for a baby just so that baby can grow up and live for another baby. People call that a purpose. It's nothing but survival. Survival is overrated."

"That's such bullshit, Milton," she said. She heard the brittle coldness of her tone. "You're just afraid."

"It's the end of the world. It's a good time to be afraid."

Behind every good saint

ALMOND SKIN AND green eyes. She was close; he could smell her skin and hair. They were together in a house no roads lead to, a house alone.

Hayden woke to glass clinking. The hotel room was dark, it was still night. The air-conditioning droned away. Hayden sat up. On the carpet by the foot of the bed Melinda sat pouring a glass of red wine. She looked up at Hayden.

"Just a little midnight snack," she said through a bite of bread.

"Wait," Hayden said, still less than awake. "That's the body of Christ."

Melinda paused for a moment and examined the roll in one hand and the wine in the other.

"I'm surprised it's not more gamey." She took another bite and followed it with a gulp of wine. "You think vegetarians go to mass? That must be a dilemma." She laughed. A loud full laugh, pieces of Christ's flesh and blood flying from her mouth.

Hayden fell back and blinked his eyes. He dragged himself from the bed and stumbled to the shower.

It was a powerful shower, the kind he liked. He wanted the water to sober him up, clear his head, wash off the events of the last few hours. His first day to sainthood had not gone as expected. He gargled water, trying to get the taste of whiskey and Melinda out of his mouth.

Melinda. He had been led astray so easily. He knew house cats with more discipline.

But maybe this was exactly as it was supposed to happen. God does move in mysterious ways, doesn't he? If God could change wine into blood and bread into flesh, couldn't he also change Hayden into a saint? And would it be that strange if he sent a loose, one-legged whiskey-drinking woman to help him on his quest? Of course. She was a Catholic, after all. God was giving him a partner in pilgrimage. A support for his journey. Behind every good saint lay a good woman. Or at least that's how it should be. Especially in the twenty-first century, now that we understand sex, in a scientific sense. He lathered up his armpits. Maybe he'd fall in love with Melinda. Maybe they'd get married. A beautiful Catholic wedding with a priest and candles.

"So many towels," he cheered as he stepped from the shower. "And each a different size." He wrapped a large one about his waist and a midsize one around his head. Both fit perfectly. "Providence!"

He pranced from the bathroom feeling clean and light. "Melinda," he sang, and leaped onto the bed where she now sat using the remote control to flip through the adult-movie selections. "I'm driving east." He stomped around her like a child on an inflated moonscape. "Why don't you come with me?"

"I can't," she said, laughing.

"Sure you can!"

"No, really, I can't," she said. "What would my husband say?"

Hayden stopped stomping. "You're married?"

"You'd like him. He's a big fan of your show."

"But you slept with me." Hayden stepped from the bed. The flicker of the television on Melinda's face made her look distorted, evil. Hayden searched for his pants. "And you're a Catholic."

"You're Saint Rick. You seduced me."

"I seduced you?" He found his pants under the bed and his boxers wrapped around Melinda's prosthetic leg.

"Don't worry. I have no regrets. It was passion. No one can fault passion," she said, reaching out and touching Hayden's shoulder as he tied his shoes. "Let's order ice cream."

Hayden stared for a long moment. What was this feeling? Disgust. That was it. He was disgusted. And proud to feel so.

Hayden stood. He stared down at Melinda as he buttoned his shirt. "I'm very disappointed in you," he said. He shoved his Catholic books into his traveling bag and stamped out of the room. The door had just clicked shut when, with a swipe of the key card, the door reopened. Hayden marched back in and bent down beside the bed.

"What are you doing?" Melinda asked.

Hayden stood, bouncing the leg against his palm like a batter with his bat.

"Hey wait," Melinda said, lurching forward. "That's mine!"

Hayden shook his head in disappointment and walked from the room with Melinda's leg under his arm.

Baby simply

MILTON WATCHED RICA sleep, how she curled into herself, her hands holding her taut belly.

They had talked for nearly two hours before she had finally yawned and retreated to the bedroom.

"My head hurts," she had said, crawling under the sheets. "The world's not ending this morning, is it?"

"No," Milton said. "Sunday, I think."

"Okay, let's take a break." She smiled. "Don't run off today, all right?"

Now watching her sleep, he thought of the child. His child and hers.

Did the baby know where her food came from? Where the warmth came from? Where the muffled voice and happy hormones came from? Or was her world simply the womb, just what she saw and touched? A world whose edges she could palm. Or did she suspect more? Did the baby believe in the existence of the Mother?

Rica rolled her face deeper into her pillow.

The baby didn't question. Milton knew that. The baby simply lived. A living, unquestioned faith so complete that it appeared effortless. The Mother was where the baby lived, breathed, and had her being. Is that faith or recognition? Do we have faith in gravity? Imagine the gravity-doubter grasping on to handrails and fence posts, leaping from stronghold to stronghold in fear he might float away. Gravity still there, but the man's lack of trust, of faith, preventing him from enjoying it.

So the baby trusts without effort. Then the baby is born, removed from the Mother. Pulled from the state of unquestioned and unrealized faith into a cold new world where the edges are an eternity away and even breathing is new. It must be horrifying. Colors, air on skin, space, and moving blurs. To suddenly be alone and separate. The baby is given a breast. She connects again. And faith grows legs. The baby seeks and finds the Mother seeking her. The baby grows. She is a walking child. She can survive alone. She believes in the actuality of the Mother, but does she know, trust, love her Mother? She leaves the womb to meet the Mother. She leaves the womb to grow, to become a mother herself.

Damn it, Milton, he told himself, *you don't believe in God. Try and remember that.*

Milton crawled into bed beside Rica. He stared at the white ceiling.

Sunday will be a birthday. The amniotic fluid will wash away and all our philosophies will be revealed to be nothing more than the bubbles of fetuses. The outer world will be strange, as incomprehensible as our world is to the newborn. What will Sunday bring? What will Monday be? Utterly strange and somehow recognizable? Will we breast-feed?

He closed his eyes and was asleep in a breath.

Shit Walk

THE MUCK CLUNG to his boots like instant brownie batter, but Kiefer Bran didn't mind. As a rule, he was supposed to dislike the required hikes through the low-ceilinged, ripe-smelling, dark bowels of the city. But Kiefer loved them. An on-site inspection, a "Shit Walk" they called it back in the office, offered solitude, the adventure of the unknown, and the strange unearthly beauty of Seattle's undercity labyrinth. It was the very reason he had taken the job with the Sewage and Wastewater Department eighteen years before.

This night's inspection was not the average Shit Walk. The department had received over fifty calls reporting sinks and toilets backing up with thick, red sludge. One woman's bathtub had filled with red ooze from her drain. A phone call had yanked Kiefer from his bed and sent him hiking below.

He swung his flashlight down tunnel 18, one of the city's oldest. Directly above him, he knew, was Twenty-fifth Avenue where rich women go to buy expensive shoes and tiny lunches. He was below them, and by being below them he felt above them. The walls glistened in the light as Kiefer checked for damage or irregularities in any of the pipes emptying into the flow. Nothing out of the ordinary. Rounding a curve in the sewer, he noticed something moving at the end of pipe 18C. He aimed his flashlight. Hanging onto the edge of the pipe, dangling over the waste, was a blue and green–shelled crab.

"I'll be damned," Kiefer said. He stepped closer and watched the tiny thing try its best to climb back up into the pipe. "Look at you, little fella." As he watched, the crab lost its grip and Kiefer stuck out a gloved hand and caught it before it splashed into the filth. "Got ya."

He placed the crab in a sample jar and tapped on the glass. "I'll find you a good home."

He placed the jar in his pocket and continued examining the pipes. He expected the sludge was due to rust. Some of these pipes were a century old and in need of serious maintenance. But people don't give a shit where their shit goes. Not until it bubbles back into their houses. Then they start yelling.

Kiefer was whistling, the sound echoing back to him from all directions. Right under pipe 18F, he knelt by the thick creek of filth and filled another sample jar. He shone his light into the goo. It was a dark red. He stopped whistling. This didn't look like rust. Hard to say, though, with all that crap in there. He stood up, screwing on the cap. For a second he lost his footing and slipped against the wet wall. He steadied himself and shone the flashlight on his sleeve. It was wet and red. He wiped his gloved hand along the bricks. Sticky. He rubbed the liquid between his thumb and fingers.

Blood? Couldn't be. Too much of it.

He looked at the creek and down the miles of tunnel. *This is all blood. Shit rivers don't just turn into blood.*

Above him something popped. Kiefer looked up just as a dense spray of blood rained down on him. He lurched away, but his feet slipped and Kiefer fell into the creek. The blood continued to pour, gallons of the stuff. Thicker than paint and stinking of salt and copper. He coughed, covering his face with an arm and crawling from the downpour.

He rose to his feet, red and sick, and trudged backward toward the street entrance wishing to God he could burn his mouth clean.

Finger closer

MILTON OPENED HIS eyes. Something was in the room. His muscles tightened. Beside him Rica slept. Milton did not make a noise. He blinked, begging his eyes to adjust to the dark. It was near. Milton scanned the room without moving his head. He saw it standing by the window staring down at him. The Non-Man.

Milton couldn't breathe. He wanted to yell, to grab Rica and run. He couldn't move. Milton strained to move, to scream. Nothing.

Please, God, don't let them hurt her.

"Relax, Milton," a voice spoke. A voice he knew. "He's on your side."

Milton could feel the weight of someone sitting at the end of his bed. He strained, but in the dark and unable to move his head, all Milton could make out was the shadowy outline of a man.

"There's a lot of things to see," said the voice. "They're removing the fetter field. Way up in the magnetosphere. The prison doors are opening. Means you can leave. Anyone can. Everyone should. I'm guessing no one does."

The Non-Man moved closer. It hovered over Milton, staring down like Munch's screaming figure. It lifted a hand, smooth and free of lines, before Milton's face. It folded three fingers and a thumb and directed one digit toward Milton's eye. It moved the finger closer.

"He's going to unlock something in your head," the familiar voice said from the bottom of the bed. "I would like to say it won't hurt. But it will."

Milton's throat spasmed in an attempt to scream.

"Stop breathing so fast. You'll hyperventilate."

Please don't. Please don't.

The Non-Man's pale hand reached toward Milton's face.

"Relax, Milton. And for once in your goddamn life, try and listen," the voice said from the foot of the bed. He patted Milton's shin. "I'm going to tell you what this planet is all about. You think you know. You haven't got a clue. Not the faintest."

The Non-Man extended one long finger toward Milton's unblinking right eye.

Wicks trimmed

"THAT WAS LARRY Norman's 'I Wish We'd All Been Ready.'" Truly a retro classic, but never more appropriate than now. Personally, I prefer his version to DC Talk's, yes? Intern Ami is nodding. Ha!

"Now I know some of you want me to shut up. Want me to stop my yapping and just play the tunes. I get your mail! 'Dear Van Sturgeon. Shut up!' Ha! But I won't. You know who wants me to shut my trap? You know who hated the day we went to satellite radio? Satan. The Prince of Lies hates my truth. It burns his ears. Is it burning yours?

"What can we do? Do we wait? Do we sit in our AC houses all fat and bored and American? No! America is the Whore of Babylon. That's why so many other false prophets have misjudged the day. They thought America was the Jerusalem, American was chosen! I thought it, too! Well, that's just not true. America is a whore, people. I know, it's hard to hear. We are the Whore of Babylon. We are worse than that. We have deceived and seduced the nations. The Antichrist is America!

"I'm so excited! Glory is so close you can just feel it, can't you?

"Intern Ami looks nervous. She's great. Intern Ami, I know you love her. Can you imagine the things to come, the words of John and Daniel, the visions God gave thousands of years ago, now coming to be? He promised. And he shall not fail to fulfill the work he has begun, he will be faithful, he will not be mocked. He is God! And he will call for his own.

"What are we to do? We are the virgins, we must have our wicks trimmed, we must have the feast prepared. Are you going to your job tomorrow? Why? Are you saving for retirement? Are you sending your kids to some public school tomorrow to learn whatever new idea strikes their fancy? There's no time for that! Do you—and I despise this phrase—'Live and let live?' No more! Time to prepare. The owner of the Vineyard is returning. Some in your churches will say I'm wrong, that it's untrue, that the world will continue as it always has. This is a lie, and it comes from the Father of all Lies! They are cold water, and even if you are on fire for God, their chill is making your church lukewarm, and what did Jesus say about the lukewarm? He said spit them out! Spit them out! I'd say it's time for *hot* churches. Churches glowing like coals! Push those ice cubes from your churches. Let them go. Push them out. Purify your houses of worship!

"Okay, okay. I know! More music! Well here's 'Last Breath' by PFR. Love this song!"

Go shower

RICA OPENED HER eyes. It was dark. Milton was standing beside the bed, staring down at her.

"Milt?" she said.

"They've sent fire into my bones."

"Milton? Wake up, babe."

"I know what Earth is. It's an institution. This whole planet is. Earth is the mental asylum for the entire universe. Insane souls, every one of us."

"Milton, just wait."

Milton circled the bed, his eyes bright.

"We are the mentally ill of the universe. Earth is our asylum. Do you realize there hasn't been a murder anywhere else in the universe for the last three million years?" He punched the wall and a framed photo fell to the floor. "All this—countries, religions, families, art, wars—it's all just sand castles in the nuthouse. Our bodies are holding cells for insane souls."

"Sit down, babe."

"We're just patients. Just inmates." He turned to her and his expression made her shiver. "You don't believe me."

She said nothing.

"Go shower," he whispered.

"What?"

"Go shower!" He pulled the sheets off Rica and dropped them to the floor. "You're filthy. You're covered in vomit. Go."

Rica didn't move.

"Go!" He threw his fist down on the mattress. Rica pushed herself back and stood on the other side of the bed.

"What are you doing?" she said, her hands moving to her belly. "You're still asleep."

"I am not asleep. Now get in the shower."

"You calm the fuck down right now, Milton!" Rica yelled.

Milton's expression changed. He looked confused. "I'm trying to help you," he said in a quiet voice. "Don't you feel dirty?" He stepped forward.

"You stay right there," she said, pointing at him with one hand and pulling on her sweatpants with the other. "Something is wrong with you, Milton." She grabbed her purse. As she moved to the door, Milton stepped in front of it.

"Please don't go."

She paused for a moment, studied his eyes, and then maneuvered around him. He didn't try to stop her.

Holy fuck

HAYDEN BROCK WAS lost. He had left the interstate on a whim only a dozen miles after leaving the hotel and quickly found himself swirling around narrow unlit desert roads in the dead of the night. He had no specific place he wanted to drive to, no specific direction he wanted to head. Just vaguely east. You would think a person free from the responsibilities of a destination would have no problem being lost. If you don't care where you're heading, why would you care where you are? But Hayden was panicking. The dark roads had been a thrill for approximately fifteen minutes. Then he started to worry. Where was the interstate? Where were the large green signs shining with information and arrows? Where was he? His heart felt like a shaken hornet's nest.

He was driving fast, speeding to somewhere else. But each somewhere else was as distant and dark as the place before. The road rose and fell in gentle swells and for an hour he saw no other car and no buildings. He turned onto different roads, one after another, randomly hoping this one would lead him back to the bright world. As he sped forward, roadside images caught the headlights and glowed for a passing moment—tractor parts, tires, metal remains of he-did-not-know-what. A lone coyote cowered on the shoulder, its eyes gray-green, its back arched. This stretch of road was pockmarked with potholes and tar-filled scars. Hayden eased on the gas and bounced along. The edges of the road were jagged lines of crumbled pavement. Then the road ended. Hayden slammed on the brakes, and the car skidded along sandy asphalt. He sat in the idling car, staring out the windshield, trying to understand what he was seeing. No barrier, no sign. The road had just faded away, thinned, and vanished. It wasn't that the road changed into an unpaved road. In the splash of headlights he could see no path, no tire tracks, just scrawny shrubs and stone.

Hayden turned off the ignition and stepped from the car. He held his breath and stepped to the uneven edge, like an unmoving lap of surf. He looked out. To his surprise, with the headlights off, he could see more. The moon, nearly full, was low, disappearing behind a rocky hill miles away.

As he released his breath, all the panic left his chest. Hornets flying into the open air. He took several deep breaths. Moments before he had been moving, enclosed in his tiny car, smelling nothing more than conditioned air and seeing only what his headlights showed him. Now he was still and the entire silent world lay before him. The silence was the strangest thing Hayden had ever heard. It filled the air in a way that all the blaring sounds, beats, and screams of Los Angeles never had.

And the stars. He could see worlds and worlds. *I had no idea,* he thought. *This, this I can believe.*

Hayden watched one star glide through the others. Not a shooting star. Just a dot of light slowly moving past the others. *I didn't know stars moved like that.* It looked happy, enjoying its unhurried tour. He followed it across the sky till it was almost directly above him.

"God," Hayden whispered. "Are you here now?"

The star seemed to twinkle, to wink at him. Hayden smiled. It winked again. Grew brighter. Much brighter. Hayden rubbed his eyes. It was larger now, far larger and brighter than any other star, and every moment it was larger still. Hayden stopped smiling.

The star's white was now a glowing red and orange, growing, filling more and more of the sky. Far away, near the horizon, two white streaks burned in the sky. A roar filled Hayden's ears as if all the air had been sucked from the world and was immediately blown back in. Hayden screamed. The star was now a ball of fire rocketing down to the desert like a falling red sun. Hayden saw it hit in the mountains, saw a cloud of rock and sand explode upward. He had one breath before the sound slammed into him like a body-size fist and threw him to the ground.

The sound rumbled away, echoing through the desert behind him. The dark quickly covered the distant cloud. Nothing remained but a dull orange glow somewhere in the mountains. Soon the stillness returned. Hayden stayed on the ground, his hands digging into the sand up to his knuckles.

"Holy fuck," he said.

3
DAYS

The nail won't fail

THE FOUR AND a half years following Milton and Roy's Fellowship of Christian Athletes' weekend retreat were unflinchingly Christocentric. They woke up an hour before class to study the Bible and pray together, they joined Tess's Evangelical church, Roy abstained from his tutorial trysts, and Milton learned all the songs of Michael W. Smith on guitar. They didn't abandon their love for off-kilter horror and sci-fi films. They still forsook sleep in order to devour Art Bell's AM radio updates on the face of Mars, time travel, and the government's secret antigravity technology. But in all things Christ came first.

One evening the two were talking about the Grays: thin, gray-skinned, almond-eyed aliens so often featured in films and *X-Files* episodes.

"You think the Grays know about Jesus?" Roy once asked.

"Hey man, 'Every knee shall bow' means *every* knee."

When Roy failed Advanced Computer Science Programming his junior year, Milton comforted him by saying "Three things eternal, Roy. God, his Word, and people's souls. The rest is fluff."

Milton believed this with all his heart. God was his Holy Father. Jesus was his savior and friend. The Holy Spirit was his counselor. The Bible was a perfect book filled with perfect wisdom. He crafted his life around these truths.

Sure, he had doubts. Sometimes he and Roy would stay up all night wrestling with a difficult passage or concept. But even through the doubts, he trusted. Peter had to walk on water, Abraham had to tie up his son, the children of Israel had to follow the pillar of smoke. Trust, even when doubting, was the root of faith.

In their senior year of college, Milton, Roy, and three other university students led the music for their church's contemporary service. Milton played rhythm guitar. Roy sang, encouraging the congregation to stand, sway, sing along. The worship centered on modern hymns with a few classics thrown in, all with a rock foundation that appealed to the younger attendees. The band was good—tight and competent in execution with just enough flair and personality to keep it interesting.

One night over stacks of raspberry pancakes and black coffee, Milton and Roy wrote a song:

The bread is broken, the words are spoken
I turn away
I sold my soul, for a bag of gold.
I'll lose my life today.
Cut me down. Cut me down. I'm sick of hanging round.

The song was written from the point of view of Judas as he left the last supper to betray Christ. They presented it to the other members of the worship team the next day.

"I love it!" said Stan the bassist. "It's not a worship song. But it's dark and biblical."

"The hanging part's cool," said Pick, lead guitar and seminary student. "Matthew records the hanging. Acts says he fell in a field and burst open. So scholars deduced Judas must have hung himself over a cliff and the rope snapped and he fell into a field. Is there a way to put that in?"

It was Jimmy, the drummer, who came up with the lyric for the song's bridge.

Kill the man, kill the man, kill the man I kiss.

Stan was right in describing the song as not appropriate for a worship service. But they worked out a musical arrangement and practiced it nevertheless. More songs followed, mainly from Milton: "I'm Crossing Over," "New Man," "Blood Brothers." Soon the band had a complete set of original songs and a clever cover of the Doors' "Light My Fire," replacing *baby* with *Jesus.*

Come on, Jesus, light my fire.

It was their pastor who recommended that they play for the church's twenty-somethings' singles mixer. The boys christened their band Pearls before Swine, which they found delightfully biblical and sassy. As the date of the singles mixer approached, Milton found that panic was growing in him like an accelerated tumor.

"But you've played in front of the congregation hundreds of times," Roy told him.

"This is different. In a service I'm playing for God. Doesn't matter who's there. This is a performance!"

"Just play, close your eyes and play."

"Close my eyes?"

"Yeah," Roy said. "You only need them to get on and off the stage."

The show was a wild success. Twentysomethings grooving and moving and mingling, and the boys gleefully blasting away. Roy's vocal energy and frantic jumping thrilled the crowd. Pick's face was stern and sweaty, studying his fingers as they ran up and down the guitar neck. Jimmy's drums and Stan's bass were solid enough to build a house on. For Milton, the most memorable moment of that first show was when, during one of Pick's extended guitar solos, Roy nudged Milton and urged him to glimpse at the crowd.

"See who came."

Milton peeked and saw the people. His stomach rose in his throat as if he had opened his eyes to find himself free-falling onto a quickly approaching mound of thumbtacks. But then he spotted, dancing along with the crowd and yet somehow set apart from it, Tess. Of course, she was a church member, in her twenties and single (the baseball player didn't last the semester), so it only made sense that she would be there, but the possibility had not occurred to Milton. She was smiling up at the stage. Milton reclosed his eyes, grinned and sucked on the moment as if it were heaven's own lozenge.

More gigs followed. Church gatherings, a youth group ski trip, high school weekend retreats. Milton pumped out a slew of new songs. A small local Christian label, CrossRock, signed them, and the boys prepared to record their debut album. There was one hitch. They had to change the name. It turned out that Pearls before Swine was the name of a psychedelic folk band that had enjoyed some success in the late '60s.

The boys considered calling themselves PBS until Pick mentioned the threat of receiving a cease and desist from the Public Broadcasting Service. The band had to vote on which key word to keep: *Pearls* or *Swine*.

"It's gotta be *Swine*," Jimmy said. "*Pearls* sounds gay."

"No, man. *Pearl*," countered Pick. "It's white and pure and hidden inside the oyster like the believer is hidden in the world."

It was Roy who came up with the solution. "Pearl-Swine. Cut *before*."

The compromise held, and the band had a new name.

The self-titled album was released to mediocre reviews and poor sales. Outside of some local Christian radio play, Pearl-Swine was largely ignored.

"Hey, we were never doing this for the money or popularity, right boys?" Pick said when the label informed them that there was little interest in funding a second album. "It was for God. First and foremost."

The Pearl-Swine spin was slowing to a natural conclusion, and without too much drama, the boys discussed the details of disbanding. But a call from the CrossRock label changed all that. It concerned one of their songs: "The Nail Won't Fail."

He took the nail, and the nail won't fail.
He felt the wood, and he did it for my good.
He saw the spear, but he knew no fear.
Now break me, take me, make me more like you . . .

The song was doing moderately well on the contemporary Christian music charts, but that was not why the label was calling. For reasons unclear to CrossRock, "The Nail Won't Fail" was quickly becoming a huge crossover hit in the gay club scene. Pearl-Swine's single was being requested in gay dance clubs and bars all across America and earning significant secular radio play. CrossRock couldn't have been more thrilled and urged Pearl-Swine to embark on a national tour.

Milton questioned the tour, the new fan base, the temptation of material success. He brought his concerns to Tess. The two circled Lady Bird Lake along Austin's Hike and Bike Trail. He explained the single, the opportunity, the label's enthusiasm, and his own worries. She listened carefully, her heather hair falling over the sides of her face.

"Milton, it's amazing!"

"I just don't know."

"He's using you to touch those lost men! Amazing. I know it's not what you planned. But that's God. He has his own plans. Mysterious plans!" She took his hand. "I am just so proud."

Pearl-Swine hit the road that fall.

It was a confusing time for the boys. One night they'd be doing a show for thirty kids at a Methodist lock-in and the next night they'd be performing for six hundred screaming gay men. Then there was the night of the Rainbow Faith Rally in downtown Chicago. Due to vague advertising, both fan bases showed up. It turned out to be one of Pearl-Swine's best performances. There were conversions on both sides.

The band's skills hardened in the furnace of touring. Roy bounced about the stage like a manic gorilla. Pick's solos fondled the scales with the frantic passion of a young lover. Jimmy grew his hair out, letting it fly as he slammed down on the drums. Stan took on the unusual but visually effective habit of marching in place as he knocked out the steady bass lines. And every so often Milton, his eyes still closed, would fall from the stage, accidentally surfing on the crowd. The fans loved it.

But after the shows, the real temptations of tour life stalked the boys. Pick was found making out with a fifteen-year-old Baptist groupie in Saint Louis. Stan got caught smoking marijuana in the band's van in Boston. In Wichita, the band walked in on Jimmy watching pay-per-view gay porn with a Presbyterian youth minister. All these infractions were prayed about and forgiven. Only Roy and Milton seemed to be handling the pressure.

Roy spent his free time on tour searching for used VHS tapes. He had recently learned that only a fraction of films ever made the transition from VHS to DVD. Most were left stranded in a dying format. So he rummaged through thrift stores and curiosity shops for rare copies of such films as *Tales from the Quadead Zone, The Satan Killer, Maniac Cop 2.*

While Roy sought VHS, Milton hunted vinyl, seeking each city's vintage vinyl shops—musty halls of wisdom, each curated by its own hermit music connoisseur. Every town, the same pale face and bright eyes, the same shy exterior underneath which hid a cascade of words. Milton would spend hours listening to their tales coupled with vinyl wonders.

"Feel the grooves under your fingertip," one enthusiast urged. "That's the magic of vinyl. It's got texture to the touch *and* to the ear."

Pink Floyd, Phish, Roky Erickson and the 13th Floor Elevators, the Beatles in mono, Dylan on bootlegs. Album after album, Milton would stare into the extravagant cover art and lose himself in the sounds.

As he listened, wildfire drops of potential made Swiss cheese of his preconceptions. Popular music could be more than verse-chorus-bridge. A song could twist in complicated arrangements like Rush's "2112," or be deceptively playful like Brazil's Os Mutantes' earliest albums, or hide its complexity in a radically simple progression like Hendrix's "Hey Joe."

And an album could be more than a gathering of possible singles and necessary filler. It could be a complete work. A whole that has an effect beyond the simple collection of songs. The Beatles' *Sgt. Pepper's*, the Who's *Tommy*, Pink Floyd's *The Wall*.

One rainy Sunday afternoon in Chicago, a used-record store owner locked the door, lit a joint (which Milton politely refused), and pulled out a stack of Beach Boys albums stretching from 1967 well into the '70s. Song by song the store owner constructed what he firmly believed would have been *Smile* had the legendary album ever been completed and released.

He explained to Milton between puffs that Brian Wilson had nearly worked himself to madness in 1967 before abandoning the project to the vaults.

"Every so often someone puts out a new recording or a collection of studio tapes. But that's not the way to hear it! To hear *Smile*, you have to hunt for it," the store owner said, shuffling through the stack. "You see, they released the songs that *would* have been on *Smile* on all these other albums. Like they hid them. Like if you want to find the album, you have to put it together yourself!"

Milton was awed. A hidden album available only to the seeker with faith enough to believe in an album that didn't actually exist. Like pages of the Bible scattered throughout a dozen paperback novels.

While pulling the records from the sleeves and placing them on the turntable, the store owner threw out strands of opinion and trivia like a one-man ticker tape parade. But once the needle touched the black, he snapped into a reverent silence.

Smile.

Opening in a cappella prayer, diving through fire, earth, water. Laughing its way through a kind of American pop symphony.

Smile burst Milton's concept of pop. He left that record store late in the afternoon, twelve Beach Boys albums under his arm and a new vision growing in his thoughts. Why shouldn't Christian rock aim for the heights of secular pop?

While still on tour, Milton began composing a full concept album based on the book of Revelations.

Although Milton wasn't as familiar with the book as he was with the page-worn gospels of his New Testament, he felt sure Revelations was the right choice. The operatic power of Christ battling the Antichrist, the intensity of Apocalyptic poetry, and the undeniable commercial appeal of end-time scenarios all added up to what Milton envisioned would be nothing less than the finest Christian rock album of all time.

Plus, according to Pick, the Apocalypse was quickly approaching. So the timing was perfect.

Alone in a hotel room, night after night, Milton sucked down cups of instant coffee and pored over Revelations, soaking in the poetry, the imagery, the violent warnings, and frightening condemnation. He began outlining songs: "Break the Seal and Break My Heart," "Devil's Got a Lot of Heads," "Too Lukewarm to Swallow."

But after the first creative outpouring, Milton hit a block. The more he read, the more terrified he became. Jesus was different in this book—harsh and judging and royal. The man who had denied a crown now sat on a throne of judgment, the man who urged the turning of the other cheek now tossed the lost into a lake of fire, the man who spoke of love now inspired fear. The God who was love in "his" very nature, he had been told, now sent seven bowls of wrath to humanity.

He dreamed at night about the Four Horsemen: white with his bow and no arrows, red and his blood-soaked sword, black bringing famine, and finally pale Death with hell at his heels. He dreamed of a pregnant woman running to the desert and the dragon waiting to eat her child. He dreamed of flying bugs with human faces and mountains dissolving into boiling seas. He woke wet with sweat in his chilled hotel room and scribbled his dreams into lyrics.

But in the morning light, those lyrics seemed too dark, too violent for Pearl-Swine.

He tried using actual verses from Revelations for lyrics and found himself writing songs he would never want to perform. More and more, his distaste for the text and his questioning of God paralyzed his pen.

Milton only managed to complete one song for the would-be concept album: "Who's Gonna Park the Car." It fell into the underappreciated genre of Rapture rock.

The trumpet shouts, time's run out. Jesus is arriving.
I'm not dying, more like flying. Wish I wasn't driving.
I'm going up to meet Jesus in the stars
But who, tell me who, not you, but who's gonna park the car.
(bridge)
All those that love the Lord are going to take flight,
So make an unbeliever your designated driver tonight, that's right!

There was a told-you-so pleasure to the song that the rest of the band adored. It was a comforting concept to believe that the universe would pull down the curtains of mystery, point out you and your friends, and say, "Yeah, they're right."

The band quickly added it to their regular set list and even recorded a version that was released as the first single of the forthcoming album.

One cool summer night, Pearl-Swine performed at a church camp in Colorado for two hundred or so dancing teenagers. Toward the end of their set Roy introduced the camp's speaker, Richard Van Sturgeon. Roy handed the microphone to a middle-aged man in a button-down Oxford shirt.

"Here you go, Mr. Van Sturgeon."

"Hey! Call me Rich, okay? I'm not that old! Man, these guys are rocking the place, huh?" The crowd cheered. "Hey, they're going to take a quick break, maybe slam some Gatorade. I want to take a chance to talk to you for a while. Now this whole week we've been talking about the J-man, and last night we talked about the cross. Big stuff. The day God died. And this morning we talked about that empty tomb. The evidence that proves that Jesus was not just some teacher, but exactly who he said he was. That's right, the *S-o-G*. Son of God. Now there's one more act to the story. The last chapter. Someday, maybe today, Jesus is coming back. He said he would, and he keeps his word. But it won't be the same. He won't be coming back mild and kind, no more disguise. This time he'll be on fire, coming out of the sky. God's gonna kick in the door of creation and come rushing in. Now the Bible says there's going to be a trumpet. And it's going to be loud. Heard all over the world. And anyone alive who has given their hearts to Jesus is just going to disappear. Bam! Gone! God's going to teleport all his children into heaven. Now for some of you, that sounds great. Jesus coming back into the picture, calling his family home. Yes! But for others, that sounds kind of scary. Maybe you've got some stuff you haven't dealt with. Maybe you're not right with God. Maybe you've been living in his world, with a body he gave you, and totally ignoring his wishes. Maybe you're one of those goats we talked about yesterday instead of a sheep. Maybe when that trumpet blares you're going to find yourself left behind. Maybe your friends are gone; maybe your parents are gone. But you're still here. It could happen right now. The Rapture. This second. Snap! Some of you will disappear in a flash. You'll blink, and when you open your eyes you'll be standing with Jesus. And some of you will be left here wondering what just happened, but you'll know what happened. And about then things on Earth are going to get pretty ugly. The Bible says Satan will be in charge. Yeah. The people left will be hunted down. Some tortured; some raped. I'm not trying to bum you out; I just want to put it out on the table. Where are you going to be on that day? With Jesus or that place where Jesus isn't?"

Pearl-Swine quietly returned to the stage. While Van Sturgeon talked, they noodled through a long instrumental introduction to their ballad "Heart Gift."

"And what if you just die? What if you die tonight?" Van Sturgeon said, closing his fists and looking as if he might weep. "Is he going to call you home? Or will you go to that other place? Have you opened your heart to God's gift of Jesus? It's not too late to open your heart. You can do it right now as the band plays this next song. Don't let this chance go by."

Van Sturgeon nodded to the band and the song began in earnest.

I know you're low. I know you need a lift.
I lived to die so by and by you could have my Heart Gift.

Teenagers were swaying, crying, arms around each other, singing along.

Milton could smell them. Youthful faith. Youthful fear. It has its own scent, like the air before a rainstorm. Kids were coming to the Lord tonight; his nose told him so. But some wouldn't. Some would be left in that world the speaker described.

As the last chord of "Heart Gift" still vibrated, the band slammed into "Who's Gonna Park the Car."

That night in the bunk room the camp had provided for the band, Milton lay awake penning a new song in his head whose entire lyric consisted of "What the fuck, Jesus?"

The next day, as the band's van curved down the mountains and toward the flatlands of east Colorado, Milton shared his struggles with the band.

"Love it, Milt," Roy said. "Write your questions into songs."

"Dude, we all have doubts, but we don't sing about them," Stan said.

"Why not?" Roy asked.

"You want to be a stumbling block?" Pick said. "We're edifiers. That's our calling."

Roy referenced Job, the Psalms of David, John the Divine's *Dark Night of the Soul*, but to no avail.

Milton said nothing. He couldn't take the argument, the soft stabs of words. Milton felt like a lobster who'd just shed its shell. From the backseat of that van, he watched the mountain give way to the plains and thought of Tess. Thought of sharing his fears with her. She'd hear him. She'd offer to pray. She always offered to pray. And Milton loved her voice in prayer—airy and sublime. She'd end with the customary *amen*, raise her eyes, and smile. That smile would hold no answer, but it would offer comfort.

Milton began composing a long, handwritten letter to Tess sharing all his doubts, all his wants, all his heart. He mailed it from the road.

Four days later, Milton was shuffling through a stack of forwarded mail minutes before a show at the Boy Barn Bar in downtown Pittsburgh. One letter was a single piece of thick cardstock draped in white lace. In the finest calligraphy, it announced the marriage of Tess Peters to an investment banker from Houston.

Milton did not cry or shudder or even share the news. He went onstage ready to perform.

Milton was strumming away, eyes closed. He could hear Roy singing his lyrics with three hundred gay men singing along.

I want to live inside of you. Give inside you. Dwell inside of you.
Inside of you.
I'm coming . . . oh, Lord, I'm coming . . . I'm coming home.

He was imagining the dancing, thinking of the key change, wondering if he needed a haircut, when his Christianity fell away like a dead fingernail.

Milton had often prayed for others, often prayed that God's will be done, but only three times had he made a direct request for himself. Once, as a child in the seconds between the firing of the basement suicide machine and the last twitches of his father's body. Again, on a sleepless night in his senior year of college when he begged God to let Tess be his wife. And lastly on that Boy Barn Bar stage. He asked God to not let his faith die.

Three strikes. You're out.

God allowed him to not believe, and that was evidence enough that he did not exist.

Shortly before going into the studio to record their second album, Milton announced that he was thinking about becoming a Buddhist.

"You can't do that," Pick said.

"I still want to rock for Jesus."

"You can't be both a Christian and a Buddhist."

"Why not?"

"They contradict each other." Pick shook his head. "Buddhists don't believe in God."

"Then I'll be a bad Buddhist."

"No, man. No way. This whole thing has been going on for too long," Stan said. "Milton, you need to make the call. Walk the walk, or leave the band."

"Whoa," Roy said. "Are you kidding? We wouldn't be here without the songs he wrote."

"We've been talking about it, Jimmy, Stan, and me," Pick said.

"You've been talking about it?" Roy bounced out of chair.

"Just talking. And we think maybe it's a good idea for you to take a break, Milton. Maybe sit out for a while."

"Sit out of the band?"

"Sorry, man. Real sorry," Pick said. "But better to get kicked out of a band and *learn* than get kicked out of the kingdom and *burn*."

"Nice, Pick," Stan said.

"Thanks."

Roy was flabbergasted, hopping about and arguing like a crackhead debate champ. Milton did not argue. He did want to "rock for Jesus," but he was also keenly aware, painfully aware, that he no longer believed in Jesus. Not in the way the others did. The Buddhist part turned out to be a transition. All Christians losing their faiths become Buddhist for a little while. Strangely, very few Buddhists become Christians.

Roy joined Milton in leaving Pearl-Swine, claiming "It was more fun when we weren't getting paid." He and Milton tried to form a Buddhist band called the Lotus Motion. They played only two gigs before calling it quits.

The last song Milton attempted to pen was an exploration of his father's philosophy. "The Many *Me*s." He strummed away, thinking of words that rhyme with *quantum*, when he stopped. For an instant he saw a million *hims* scattered across existence strumming the exact same chords, working on the same melody, trying to justify rhyming *Compton* and *quantum*. Some Miltons were married to Tess. Some had unshakable faith. Some were born dead. Some were nearly an exact replica of himself— countless other Miltons doing the exact same thing in the endless worlds that pressed against this world. Nothing was unique. It was hard to see the point.

Milton retired from music, citing exhaustion.

Pearl-Swine went on to record several albums and continued to tour. "The Nail Won't Fail" was still their opening number, and their initial slew of songs still comprised their most popular tunes. So every month Milton received a substantial check in the mail from Pearl-Swine. In this way, Milton was supported by the fruit of a faith he had discarded.

Mingus would approve

RICA ARRIVED AT Mundi House hours before opening. She sat on a bench outside and watched the sky move from black to blue through all the watercolor hues of dawn. The sky looked unhealthy, fragile, like a child that might not last its first year.

She let herself in, turned up Mingus's album *Let My Children Hear Music* on the stereo, and began creating an elaborate soup incorporating as many ingredients as she could lay her hands on—garlic, tea leaves, cilantro, molasses, cucumbers, oatmeal, mushrooms. She turned up the Mingus. It was some of his strangest music. Jazz, it might be called, but the music went beyond jazz. Stranger and fuller. Filled with wild harmonies and unexpected twists and yanks. The music and food, the rhythm and chopping, the spank of the bass and the pop of boiling water all helped crowd out the thoughts of the last two hours. Milton with his confused face and cruel words. The chill that still stuck to her bones. Where was his mind? Too much to hold right now. Too much.

She turned up the volume till her ears hurt. That's how she liked her music, just a little painful. She knew Mingus would approve. Hell, he put the pain in himself. He slammed two notes together that harmonized, but just barely, two notes that had to work at it. They weren't a C and a G, more a C and an A-sharp. That's how she saw her and Milton. No one would choose to put these notes together, no one but a mind like Mingus. And when Mingus did it . . . when he played or wrote or yelled, he said, "Yes, this is how it is supposed to be. These notes belong together." He told the notes, "You can fight, you can twist, but know that you are home. This is where you are supposed to be." And the notes listened. And the notes sang.

But times were strange now. Milton was frightening. He was dangerous. Rica was not afraid for herself. If Milton had pulled this same shit a year ago,

Rica would have pinned him down till he came out of whatever mind-funk-cavern he had fallen into. But now there was someone else to be concerned for.

For years the most important part of Rica's life was herself. Milton had snuck in. He was important, but in truth, she was still higher ranked. If she had to make the choice between his life or hers, she would take the bullet, save his life. But it wouldn't be easy. It would be an act of kindness, not compulsion. Now there was the baby hopping and bopping in her lowers. If the same choice were to arise for her and the child, it would be no choice. As Rica saw it, the child who had yet to take a breath was the most important part of the universe.

That's why she had left. This baby needed strength. Needed a father with compassion and caring eyes.

In one *Saint Rick* Christmas episode, Rick plays Santa for a Mexican orphanage, asking each child what he or she wanted and producing their exact wish from his sack. A toy truck, a kitten, a bag of wildflower seeds. The last child in line sits on Saint Rick's knee and asks, "Santa, I want you to be *mi padre, por favor*."

And Saint Rick, a tear in his eye, says, "I'd like that as well, Pepe. But I'm Father Christmas. That means I have to be everyone's father."

She let the episode replay in her head, from the opening teaser of the orphans in the harsh Mexican heat the day before Christmas to the images behind the closing credits, the same images as every episode, Saint Rick walking toward an ever-sinking sun, alone and holy.

Before being pregnant, *Saint Rick* had been a guilty pleasure. Not just the entertainment or the eye candy of Hayden Brock, the pleasure that caused her guilt was the world the show described. A world where problems have solutions, where redemption can be found in a half hour, where God reaches down and helps us repair our lives.

As she replayed the Christmas episode in her head, Mingus's *Let My Children Hear Music* filled in as a bizarre soundtrack. The music consciously created from embraced frustration, from spectacular failed attempts to reach past what music is supposed to do, was now the backing for what Rica knew was a trite television script where life's questions are satisfied with shallow answers and tidy plots.

When the song "Don't Be Afraid, the Clown's Afraid Too" hit her head, replacing the sentimental strings of the end credits of *Saint Rick*, Rica shivered. The music was strange, filled with time changes and weird chord choices, themes developed, then warped and questioned, the snarling of circus animals played like chaotic instruments. That music over the mental images of Saint Rick walking into the sunset created a strained juxtaposition.

With *Saint Rick*, art answered nature, tied up the loose ends with a bow. But Mingus's music danced with nature, a horn solo with a growling lion. The combination of the two, the frame-bending music and clean world of *Saint Rick*, perfectly fit Rica's restless soul.

In that small kitchen, her baby kicking, her heart hurting, Rica felt she might choose between the two. Did she want Mingus's madness or Saint Rick's salvation? The questions of jazz or the answers of entertainment?

"The Chill of Death" was the second-to-last song on the Mingus album—minor notes and dissonant chords, and Mingus's throaty voice describing death's seduction and a road leading to nowhere but hell. Saint Rick, for all his silliness, triteness, ended each episode walking into a sunset promising life and heaven and another episode the following week. Which road to choose?

And Rica was not walking alone. She carried a passenger. She had glimpsed a little hell in Milton last night, in his uncertain, haunted eyes. If only for her baby's safety, she would choose a shallow heaven over a deep hell. Mingus's music was more real, perhaps more alive. But Saint Rick was safer. With the baby bouncing inside her, she now felt that perhaps she had underestimated the value of safety for most of her life.

With Mingus's "The I of Hurricane Sue" blaring all around her and the aromas of the bubbling soup filling the air of the Mundi House kitchen, Rica touched her belly and yelled out a prayer. "Oh, Saint Rick, be with us in this our hour of need!"

Every feather, every bone

CLICK'S NEW WORLD was glass, curved, and capped. He twisted his shell, just able to turn a circle. He could find no corners, just the close curve and the blurred world beyond.

Everything had been dark for a time. Sometimes still, sometimes rumbling. He tapped his claw against the invisible boundaries. The taste of air was changing and no new air could enter. Click wondered if perhaps this darkness could be a home.

Then his entire cylindrical world had been pulled into the light and placed into two small, pink hands.

"A hemit cwab! A hemit cwab!" a high voice chanted, and a toothy face stared through the glass. The face squealed, and Click yanked himself into his shell. Everything moved and bounced. Someone was dancing. Someone was skipping. He ricocheted off the sides, off the sky and ground. "Thank you, Papa! I love him! I love him!"

"That's what I said," a man's voice echoed from farther away. "How much body waste is one funeral parlor *allowed* to dump? I mean, really! It's a public sewer!"

"Calm down, Kiefer. Don't get all worked up."

"I was covered with blood, Carla! Dead people's blood! It got in my mouth!"

The bouncing stopped. "Whose blood?" the high voice asked. Click peeked out.

"No one's blood. Papa's just joking," a woman said.

Click breathed in. The air was wrong. Thin.

"I want to name hew Patches! Patches di cwab!"

"Five-minute warning. Go get your school clothes on."

The skipping started again, circling the room. Click bounced and rattled, up and down and side to side, clanging against the glass in rhythm with his tiny crab heart. Dizzy and breathless. Breathless. Breathless.

"Okay, okay," the woman was saying. "Did they give any reason? I mean, the parlor?"

"Weight Watchers."

"Weight Watchers?"

Click sucked in through thin crustacean gills, but there was nothing left to breathe.

"The local Weight Watchers had some kind of field trip yesterday. The annual smoothie picnic or something. Anyway, a big passenger van turned over on the 405."

"I heard about that on the news." The woman lowered her voice to a whisper. "Twenty people died."

Hungry for breath. Starving for breath. The crab's thinking twisted like a ribbon. Click could see the ground three feet below. He spiraled about the room. He forgot the toothy girl, forgot the jar. He was simply flying, circling. His black beady eyes narrowed as he zoomed.

"Twenty large people," the man said. "And seventeen of them went to Still Pines Funeral Parlor. They were swamped."

"Mama, who died?"

"A bunch of fat people, Becky," the man said.

"Kiefer!"

Click could fly! He'd find the ocean and air! He'd fly to the coast, above the line of wet and dry. Seagulls crying out! Crying for food! He'd snag the wing of a seagull with his large claw and dangle! He'd jerk the shrieking bird to the sand. With slow snaps and nibbles, Click would kill and devour the seagull! Eat every feather, every bone. Then Click would fly away!

"I've got nothing against fat people. Hell, I'm no petite. Just all that goddamn blood!"

"Becky, ignore your father and go put on some clothes."

"Yes, Mama."

Fly above the ocean, out farther than the waves. Nothing but ocean and sky. Blue and blue and the warm in between. Just warm . . . sleepy warm . . . sleepy warm.

"And hand over that crab. It can't very well live in a jar for the rest of its life." With a quick twist of the sky, air rushed into the world, and Click breathed again. "I'm sure we have a shoe box or something. What do hermit crabs drink? Do I put salt in its water?"

Stiff reality slapped the dreams away. Click no longer believed he could eat a seagull. No longer even desired to. But he wished he did.

"Jesus, I still have that taste in my mouth!"

As Click tumbled into a brown, square world of corners and air, he felt a pang of anguish. What gave him life destroyed his dream.

Something had changed

THE SMELL WOKE him. Like a dentist's office only stronger, sicker. The type of clean smell that is so fierce it becomes its own kind of stench. Milton, his eyes still closed, reached out his hands. He felt something wet and furry. His eyes shot open to find a recently dejarred, pickled Bigfoot head an inch from his face, its eyes pale yellow, its lips purple and bloated. Milton yelped and scrambled to his knees.

He was in the basement. The open door at the top of the stairs cast just enough light to fill the room with shadows. Boxes, bags, the memory of his father's bleeding body.

He tried to recall the night before. A Floater. He remembered that. And Rica leaving, fear in her eyes. She was afraid of him. What happened? Lastly, Milton remembered the world was ending.

He climbed the stairs and walked to the bedroom. Rica was still gone. The memory of her fear was a sick, doughy ball in his stomach. He called her cell but there was no answer. He did not leave a message.

The sharp smell of formaldehyde still clung to his hands and face. Milton turned on the shower. He watched the steam build in a daze, his head reeling like a Doors keyboard solo. He was about to step under the water when the phone rang. Leaving the shower running, Milton sprinted back to the bedroom and grabbed the receiver.

"Rica?"

There was nothing.

"Hello?"

Nothing. No dial tone. No sound.

Milton pulled the phone from his head and noticed something else. Something had changed. He stood rigid. The sound of the shower was different. A change of tone. He recognized the change. The water was no longer hitting the floor of the shower. It was hitting a body. Milton quietly placed the phone down.

He walked out of the bedroom and into the hall. The door to the bathroom was open and a few wisps of steam floated out. Milton stepped closer. A man's voice was humming a melancholy tune. Closer, still in the hall, Milton could see a figure standing behind the frosted door of the shower. Part of Milton wanted to run, but something larger whispered there was no more time for running away.

"Who's there?" he asked. The humming was the only answer. It was a tune he recognized. Something from television. Milton stepped into the bathroom. "I've called the police," he said, and wished to God he had. No response from the shower. Milton was now in front of the door, watching the blurred shadow behind the door. It looked as if he was washing his hair, lathering up. The steam billowed out and wet Milton's face. He reached and grasped the shower door's handle. He paused, swallowed. The humming stopped. The figure dropped his arms to his side. Through the glass, Milton was face-to-face with a figure he couldn't quite see. His hand was still on the shower door handle, but he stood still for several seconds. Finally he yanked the door open and a cloud of steam filled the room.

There stood, naked as Milton, a person Milton had seen before. A famous face. Yes. That was the tune. From the television show. Saint Rick was in his shower.

"Milton," Saint Rick said. "Drive west. Find me."

Steam clouded everything. Milton stumbled back and fell to the floor. Saint Rick stood only feet away, still under the running water. Milton crawled backward toward the bathroom door. The phone rang. Milton looked away for a second. When he looked back the shower was empty.

Name's Jim Edwards

"AGAIN, OUR LEAD story," the radio-voice said through the Lexus's stereo. "NASA reports that six satellites fell from their orbit last night, causing panicked reports all over the world."

"No shit. Satellites," Hayden said to himself.

"Scattered debris made it though the atmosphere, causing spectacular impacts in Arizona, Northern Australia, and parts of the Atlantic Ocean. No injuries have been reported. At this point the cause is still unknown, but some scientists believe a connecti..." The radio-voice bled into static. "...to the rec...sun flares is poss... holes...magnetosphere and the magnetic..." More static. Then a new voice came across the airwaves announcing, "A full hour of the best in soft jazz."

"Ahh, crap," Hayden said. He sighed and stepped on the accelerator. He was back on the interstate now, mindlessly heading east. He was also, unbeknownst to him, on his way to his first act of Catholic compassion. Hayden Brock was going to pick up a hitchhiker.

He didn't consider stopping when he first saw the man. He had never stopped for hitchhikers. Hayden knew from his studies of late-night cable television and *USA Today* articles that hitchhikers ate people and wore their flesh as a loose fitting shawl or do-rag. The only people who picked up hitchhikers were naive sexually active teenagers on their way to secluded cabins, or other serial killers looking for a challenge.

As Hayden drew closer he could make out the man. He looked old and wet. It had rained most of the morning, and judging by the clouds, it would soon start again. The man was sitting on a stuffed green army bag. A large off-white hat covered most of his face, and an arm and thumb extended out from his hunched figure. He didn't look like a cannibal. He looked tired. Something twitched in Hayden's heart. He hesitated for a moment as he passed, but quickly pulled over.

The hesitation, though, caused Hayden to bring the Lexus to a halt forty yards from the man.

Hayden put on his hazards and worked to clear the passenger seat of Catholic books, CDs, and empty bottles of ginseng energy drinks. As he removed the clutter, Hayden found himself excited for company. He had talked to no one since leaving Melinda early that morning. He had continued east, but with no goal in mind. He had just driven straight, filling the hours with little more than miles.

Hayden glanced back and saw that the old man had made it only twenty feet. He had stopped, leaned over, and looked to be catching his breath. As he started walking again, Hayden noticed his legs were severely bowed, as if he were carrying an invisible tree trunk between his thighs. Over one shoulder was the large army sack. The other hand held a black plastic trash bag, the kind Hayden's lawn boy used to collect cut grass. It looked heavy. Leftover body parts from lunch? No, probably not.

Hayden wasn't sure what the proper etiquette was. Should he help the guy with his bags, or was it rude to presume he needed help? He decided it was best to follow the same procedure for being pulled over by the police: stay in the car, both hands on the wheel, make no sudden movements. It took another six minutes for the old man to reach the car. He tapped on the passenger-side window. Hayden stared for a moment. He could still drive away. But already a few new drops of rain were rolling down the window. Hayden stretched over, unlocked the door, and pushed it open. The man stood there wheezing.

Hayden gave his best Saint Rick smile. "Hello. Do you need a lift?"

"What the fuck do you think?"

Hayden blinked.

The man struggled through some more breaths before slowly squeezing his bags into the back of Hayden's Lexus. He then wheezed a few more times, "*Heeweezz* . . . You couldn't have . . . *heeweezz* . . . reversed a little, huh?"

Hayden tried to chuckle. But it came out more like a swallowed cough.

"You got a leg in your backseat," the man said, nodding at the prosthetic.

"Yes, I do."

Finally he sighed and dropped into the passenger bucket seat. Hayden forced himself not to think about the leather upholstery, not to concern himself with the possibility of water damage, not to notice the ripe scent of wet sweat and stale tobacco. He just kept smiling.

"Well," Hayden said, putting the car in gear and pressing on the gas. "Let's hit the road."

"Don't mind if we do," the man said. Then he farted.

Hayden was sure he had made an awful mistake. It was a sensation that would return to him several times over the next three days. In fact, he would grow to enjoy the feeling. Fear of having taken the wrong the step is at least evidence that one is walking.

The man wore blue jeans and a dark denim shirt. He took off his once-white Stetson and laid it on his lap. His mustache was the same shade as the hat, except the bottom ridge, which was tobacco brown. He pulled a red bandana from his shirt pocket and wiped the sweat and rain from his lean, pockmarked face. His eyes were a cloudy blue. *Like an overused hot tub*, Hayden thought.

"I've been out there for an hour. No one even slowing to take a look," the man said. "Thanks for stopping. Feels good to be inside."

Hayden nodded and turned on the heater. They drove for a while with no sound but the soft jazz playing on the radio.

"Yep. Thanks," the man said. "You care if I smoke?"

Hayden had never allowed a lit cigarette within ten feet of his car. He had lost several friends and one lover over the rule. But the idea of telling this old man that he could not smoke seemed impossible. He shook his head.

"You want one?" the man offered. "They're not the best, but it's what I got. Shit, take one."

Hayden, to his own surprise, took one.

"Name's Jim Edwards. You?"

"Hayden. Hayden Brock." Hayden waited for the usual response—"*The Hayden Brock?*" or "Oh my God, Saint Rick!" or "My wife loves you." Jim Edwards did none of these. Just nodded and lit his cigarette. He leaned over and, using one hand to steady the other, held an open flame for Hayden to light his own. Hayden noticed the knuckles, swollen, the skin callused. When Jim Edwards pulled the lighter away, Hayden could see his own soft, well-tanned hands on the steering wheel. He felt a vague shame. Then nearly coughed up every organ above his lower intestine.

"Yep," Jim said with a chuckle. "Not the smoothest, but cheap. I smoke Winstons when I can afford them."

Though Hayden had tried most narcotics, he had never smoked a cigarette. But he had been around cigarettes, knew people who smoked. And even with his car rule, he was sure he had inhaled at least a few packs' worth of second-hand smoke. But this was completely different, like breathing in ground-up glass rolled in nettles. Hayden wasn't sure what to do. The guy didn't have much money and he had gifted the cigarette. But he didn't want any more of it getting inside his body, so he did his best to let the cigarette hang from his lip while he held his breath. But the smoke, seeing the lungs were closed, went for the eyes. Tears welled up to block the path.

"You okay?" Jim Edwards asked.

"Just thinking of an old friend." Hayden took three quick puffs, got the cigarette past halfway down, and smashed it in the car's ashtray. He casually rolled down his window, even though the rain was falling in force again. For a few miles they drove in silence except for the soft jazz and Hayden's occasional hacking throat spasm.

"So," Hayden said, after recovering control of his breathing. "You're heading east?"

"I am now," Jim said.

"Where are you going?" Hayden asked.

"There's a rest stop just east of Las Cruces, New Mexico. I stay there sometimes. I know the custodian."

"You just want a rest stop?"

"I can catch a ride to Houston from there. Gotta get to the VA hospital by Monday. Got some cancer things on my back, they're gonna cut 'em off."

"Wait, New Mexico? That's like another state from here."

"Yep. I really appreciate it," Jim Edwards said. "They cut the stuff off before, but it keeps growing back."

No way, Hayden thought. *I'm not driving this guy all the way to Las Cruces. Sainthood or no sainthood, I'm not crazy.*

"Hey, I'd like to drive you," Hayden said. He was planning on continuing with "but . . ." The problem was nothing came after "but." Mentally, he searched for excuses. *But I can't because . . .* Because what? He had no other appointments, no plans, just a vehicle and time. Besides, Jim Edwards had what Hayden severely desired without even knowing it: a destination. So Hayden just repeated himself. "Yeah. I'd like to drive you."

The radio blurted out another belch of static. " . . . no cause for alarm," the radio-voice said. "In other news, television actor Hayden Brock is being sought by police for questioning in connection with a sexual assault and theft case. Melinda Hawks of Blythe, California, claims that Mr. Brock forced—"

Hayden clicked the radio off. "Huh," Hayden said with a forced chuckle. "No news but bad news."

Jim Edwards looked at Hayden from the corner of his eye and nodded.

Hard to think with all the sirens

MILTON TRIED CALLING Rica three more times, but each attempt ended with her cheerful voice asking him to leave a message. He was just pulling on jeans and a near-clean T-shirt that he had fished from the floor of his closet when the phone rang. He leaped across the bed to pick it up.

"Hello?"

"Hey, Mitt, how are you feeling?" Roy asked.

"The world is ending."

"Which world?"

"This one."

"I'll come right over."

Milton hung up the phone and sat on the bed. His head felt heavy. Too much to handle. Too much strange. And he could still see the fear in Rica's eyes. Fear of him. Where could she be? They didn't have much time. Then it hit him. Of course, she was at work. Everyone was still going about their business. They didn't know. No one seemed to know, except Milton. Milton quickly dialed Mundi House. Rica picked up.

"Rica, it's Milton." There was no response on the other end, but she didn't hang up. That was encouraging. "Rica, something weird is happening."

"Yes, Milton," she said. "You're losing your mind."

"No, that's not it."

"Do you remember last night?"

"Okay," Milton said. "Maybe that's part of it. But something else is happening, too. I've got to leave town."

"Then go. I'm staying. I don't trust you right now. I don't trust that you're safe for this baby."

"Rica, please. Give me some time to figure this all out. All I need—"

"I can't hear you . . . someone's yelling outside," Rica said. Milton could hear the yells through the phone.

"I've got to go west and find—"

"What? Someone's dog is going nuts. What did you say?"

"I've got to find Hayden Brock," Milton said.

Silence for a moment. "The actor?"

"Yeah. On that saint show."

More screams came through the phone.

"Rica?"

"Oh my God. A rat. A big fucking rat! Lots of them."

"Rica?"

Screams.

The phone went dead. Milton tried calling back. A busy tone. Milton called 911 and was immediately put on hold. He stood for a moment. *What do I do? What do I do?* On the floor of his closet he spotted an old aluminum tennis racket. He grabbed it and ran to his bike. Only after a search of the house did he remember that his bike (and belt) had been stolen the night before.

Milton ran from the house and down the street, trying to deduce a way to cross the three miles between his house and Mundi House. He was halfway to Riverside Drive when a voice beside him said, "Hey friend, what's the rush?" It was Roy leaning out the window of his VW Microbus.

"Drive me to Mundi House."

Roy didn't ask and didn't hesitate. "Get in."

Milton jumped in and Roy slammed his foot down on the gas, which doesn't do much in a 1972 VW Microbus. The bus rolled on toward Lady Bird Lake. "We'll be there in three minutes," Roy said.

She'll be fine, Milton thought. *Probably a raccoon. Nothing to worry about. Hard to think with all the sirens.*

The Microbus screeched to a halt.

"Sweet Lord," Roy said. Two cars were burning on the Congress Avenue Bridge. Billows of black smoke filled the air. On the bridge a man was dancing and jumping with something small, gray, and furry clinging onto his back.

"You see this, too?" Milton asked.

"What am I seeing?" Roy asked.

"Beginning of the end."

Oh my God! Nutria!

NO ONE IN Austin was prepared for the nutria to attack. They had been docile for so many years. These possum-like creatures, near rascals, beady-eyed water rodents no bigger than house cats had kept to the lakes and muddy shores, quietly apathetic to the city surrounding them. People watched them slinking and swimming and foolishly believed there was nothing to fear. But on this day the nutria crept from the water, up the north banks, and onto the pathways and roads of downtown Austin.

The first victims were a young woman and her dog running along the Hike and Bike Trail. Her yellow lab started barking at the shrubs; she yanked back on the leash. A small river rat slinked from the foliage.

"See, Rex," the woman said. "It's just a nutria. It's all right—Oh my God!"

The creature leaped at the dog's throat. The woman screamed and dropped the leash. Another nutria fell from a branch above and landed on her head. Other joggers stopped midstride. They didn't offer help at first, just stood gaping, unable to grasp what they were seeing. The woman thrashed her head from side to side. Finally, a man in tight shorts took a branch and smacked the nutria off her. The creature hit the ground, twisted to its feet, and hissed at the man. It turned and scurried down the path. The other nutria abandoned the whining dog and followed.

In the beginning it was just the random one or two nutria being spotted, but within ten minutes of the first attack, the creatures were roving in packs of twenty or more. They marched fearlessly, causing a four-car pileup on Cesar Chavez Street. Metal crunched around them and some were crushed into a pulpy mess, but the other nutria didn't flinch. Their army advanced.

The Austin High School marching band was ambushed while perfecting their rendition of Michael Jackson's "Thriller." The beating drums and feathered hats seemed to enrage the rodents and they attacked with even greater fury. Horns, teenagers, and band directors all squealed together in a horrible harmony. A Duck Tour amphibious vehicle filled with wide-eyed tourists collided with a mass of nutria just past the First Street Bridge. The Duck Tour bus skidded out of control, jumped the curb, and splashed into Lady Bird Lake. Three homeless men rescued a besieged meter maid and carried her down Congress Avenue, pursued each step of the way. Hundreds of nutria swarmed Whole Foods at Sixth and Lamar, biting and scratching, devouring tray-loads of free samples and sucking fresh linguine from the pasta maker. A motor scooter flipped over one of the creatures on Lavaca Street.

"Oh my God!" screamed the toppled scooterist as he struggled to his feet. "Nutria!"

I can't do this

MILTON JUMPED FROM Roy's Microbus and ran toward the bridge, the tennis racket still gripped in his fist. He circled around the burning cars, feeling the heat press against his body, and reached the screaming man. Two other men were trying to peel off the nutria, but the man's thrashing frustrated their attempts. More nutria were approaching from the north, weaving through the unmoving cars filled with frightened faces and muffled screams. An ambulance shrieked on the north side. Milton looked up just as it swerved off the road and into a large oak. *I have to get to Rica.* Milton ran to the attacked man, raising his racket to swipe one of the nutria off his back, but the man spun around and slapped Milton in the face. Milton stumbled backward, hit the railing, and flipped over it.

He was halfway down before he realized he was falling. Quick thoughts of hidden branches and broken necks flashed by, and then he smacked into the water. All the air rushed from his lungs like foam from a shaken beer can. He climbed up through the green water. The surface was just an inch away. No. More water. Just there, just a little farther. Finally air. Milton coughed and sucked. Above him on the bridge he could hear yelling and crashing.

Milton whipped the wet hair from his eyes and paddled in place. He was twenty feet from the south shore, two hundred feet from the north shore. Rica was to the north.

I can't do this. I have weak arms. It's medical. My drowning won't help her. I should go back south and try the cops again. Swimming north is suicide.

While these thoughts ricocheted around Milton's head, his body started swimming north with fast, clumsy strokes.

It was going to

A NUTRIA SQUEALED and lunged for Rica's leg. With a sharp kick, Rica sent it flying from the front counter of Mundi House. It landed on the floor among the dozen other wet rodents. On the counter beside Rica, little Carl clung to Jeppy like a lost monkey. Jeppy was weeping into Carl's shoulder and whispering "It'll be okay, Mama's here. Mama's here." The folksinger and the writer had also squeezed onto the counter, knocking the register and tip jar to the ground. An oversize, off-white nutria pulled itself up a column a foot away from the counter, whipping its pink tail behind it. Rica scanned the room for a weapon. There, next to her foot, was her soup ladle. The nutria was nearly chest level with Rica. It stared at her and hissed. Slowly Rica bent her knees, keeping her eyes on the rat. She reached down without looking and found the ladle. With a sudden swing she smashed the ladle against the nutria's skull. It fell to the floor with a thud.

"That one wasn't attacking," Jeppy said.

"It was going to," the writer said.

"Only strike if they strike first," Jeppy cried.

"Jesus, Jeppy," Rica said.

Fingers of God

HALFWAY ACROSS LADY Bird Lake, Milton decided his body should have listened to his head. But by now, forward was as far from shore as backward, so he swam on, sucking in mouthfuls of mossy water and gasping for air. He had a stitch in his side, as if someone were wringing out his spleen. His head echoed his pounding heart, and his legs floated behind him like lumps of cooked ham. But he still swam forward. He focused only on the next stroke, the next arm lift, stroke, breath, stroke, breath, mouthful of lake water, stroke, breath. He peeked up to see how far the shore was. Not much closer. Stroke, breath, stroke, breath. Over his splashing and sputtering he heard a new noise. A hiss. Milton looked up, and floating before him, its dark-gray nose just above the water, was a black-eyed nutria. Milton jerked back, pushing a spray of water at the thing. The nutria lurched forward and clamped its teeth into the web of Milton's hand. Milton gasped in pain and pulled his hand back, but the nutria held on, short, wet breaths puffing from the sides of its thin, gray lips. With his free hand Milton slapped at the nutria, but it only bit down harder. Milton was trying to yell for help when something under the water snapped onto his crotch. Milton opened his mouth, but no screams were left.

He sank under, his open mouth filling with water. He reached down, grabbed a handful of fur, and yanked the thing off his crotch. It gave way, wriggled free of his grasp, and latched on to his thigh. The pain was pink against the green shadows and bubbles. It was getting darker the deeper he sank, darker and colder. His throat squeezed. He thrashed, but it only seemed to push him farther down. The green was changing. The shadows swarmed before him. Different shadows, slower and more graceful. There was pulling and a struggle, his hand was free. So was his thigh. But his strength was gone. Nothing left. No muscles. He sank deeper and deeper till the shadows blended into the dark. He thought of Rica.

He thought of the baby. He thought of his father in gym shorts and a headband. He thought of the chocolate bar wrappers on his bedroom floor the morning after Halloween. He thought of purple. How dark purple can be. Darker than black. Black was easy. Black was void. Purple was black with personality. The baby would love purple. She'd collect purple pieces of plastic and purple stones and build purple labyrinths in the front yard. His feet hit the bottom. Was he that far down? The ground pushed up against his feet. Pressure pushed up under his armpits as if the fingers of God were cradling him, lifting him. The green grew lighter and lighter.

He dreamingly glanced to his left. There under his arm, paddling four thick legs, was the walnut head and serving-bowl body of a turtle. It craned its head toward Milton and, Milton could swear, nodded. Milton looked to his right. Another turtle labored under that arm. He looked down and found a turtle under each foot. He looked up and saw the blurry white shine of the surface. The sight slapped Milton awake. He reached, crawled, pushed his way upward, his head swelling and his lungs squeezing. He exploded past the surface and into the air. Milton sucked in a violent reverse scream, his head filling with colors and sparks.

In front of him a green-brown head popped above the water, an island of shell appearing behind it. Three others surfaced around Milton, a snatch of gray fur still stuck in one of the turtle's sharp jaws. The turtle immediately in front of Milton opened its mouth so widely Milton could see its black tongue. "Take her with you," it said, and all four turtles sank away.

For a moment Milton floated, his body and thoughts bobbing. He was only fifteen feet from the shore now. He paddled the last stretch and crawled onto the north shore of the lake. Sirens and screams filled the air. And another sound. A chorus of cawing. Milton rolled onto his back. Above him flocks of black, crow-like grackles darted though the sky. Each flock moved as one, zigzagging through the air, landing for seconds on a tree, a power line, a rooftop, and then flurrying into the sky again. They weren't alone in flying. A trail of black emerged from under the Congress Avenue Bridge. Bats, thousands of them, were pouring out. The bats didn't usually hunt till dark. It wasn't even noon yet. As Milton watched, a patch of grackles collided with the train of bats. They fought in mid-air. An inky-black puddle of twisted wings and claws, screaming caws, falling into the lake.

Milton pulled himself to his feet and ran east toward Mundi House.

Chewed

"IN THE SOUP!" Jeppy cried. "Rica, it's in your soup!"

"Fuck the soup!" the folksinger said. "Fuck the fucking soup."

The floor of the coffee shop was now carpeted with nutria. They chewed on the legs of chairs, tore through books and magazines, gnawed on the wires.

"Calm, everyone," Rica said. She double-fisted her ladle like a bat above her shoulder. "We are going to be fine. Stay calm."

One nutria with a wire clenched in its teeth screeched and shook violently. Sparks flew. The lights flickered off. Even with the shreds of daylight coming through the windows, Mundi House was dark. And the smell of singed fur rose to fill the room.

Roll in the dust

MILTON SPRINTED THROUGH downtown. The roads were jammed with unmoving cars. Drivers pounded on their horns, setting off the alarms of the parked cars lining the curb. Milton passed an older man perched on top of a mailbox, screaming at the people around him that there was no more room. A woman in a bright-pink dress twirled around and around, swinging her purse like a mace. People were crawling up the embankment of I-35, waving at unstopping cars. A policeman stood on top of a squad car taking slow aim with his pistol and picking off nutria one by one.

"Roll in the dust, mad men!" Milton yelled as he ran. "The time to be slaughtered has come."

Moldy soccer balls

LIKE VIKINGS OVERWHELMING a walled city, four nutria scaled the counter at once. Rica took aim at one and slammed down her ladle, but the thing inched out of the way and the ladle clanged against the countertop. Another nutria jumped and bit Rica's wrist, a line of blood spraying out. At the sight of blood Jeppy burst into a panicked wail. Rica dropped the ladle and swung her arm and the nutria against the wall. The thing let go and dropped back to the floor. More were reaching the countertop, using the distraction of the first wave. One latched onto the writer's sandaled foot. He yelped and stomped. Four more rushed him while his balance was off and he fell from the counter, landing on his back on the hardwood floor. Rica reached a hand out to the man who was now wriggling under the bites of a dozen gray bodies.

The door flew open. Rica looked up to see Milton, silhouetted against the midmorning sun. With fierce kicks Milton made his way through the nutria. Gray bodies flew across the room like moldy soccer balls. Milton reached the writer and yanked nutria after nutria off of him, pitching each removed rodent against the back wall. The writer's face was streaked with blood and a rip of red stretched along his left arm. Milton helped him stand, and he scrambled back up to the counter.

"We've got to get out of here," Milton yelled.

To his knees

"TAKE THE BABY, Milton!"

Milton stepped to the counter. Rica pulled Carl from Jeppy's arms and shoved him forward to him. Milton took hold of the boy and turned to the door.

"No. Please, no," Jeppy cried, and jumped from the counter. She landed on Milton's back and wrapped her legs around his waist. Milton wavered for a moment, but then started waddling toward the door. The toddler squirmed in his hands and Jeppy's arms tightened around his neck.

He was five feet from the door with both mother and child when he heard a scurrying above him. He looked up just as a nutria fell from a rafter and landed on his face. Carl screeched, Jeppy buried her face into Milton's back and squeezed her arms even tighter. Milton could see nothing but the pink underbelly of the nutria. His mouth was filled with skin and nutria sweat. He pushed out a muffled yell.

Rica was yelling, but Milton couldn't make out the words over Carl's screaming. His throat twitched under Jeppy's arms. He faltered, fell back a step, and then forward onto his knees. Jeppy was only inches from the floor, but still she clung to Milton's back. Milton, still blind, lifted Carl as high as he could. He shook his head back and forth, and with the help of a few well-aimed kicks from Carl, the nutria fell from his face.

On a stool, just in front of him, was the largest nutria he had seen yet. It stared at Milton with red eyes. Milton stared back. It bared its yellow teeth and cocked its head to one side. "Stop struggling," it seemed to be saying. "You belong to us now."

Milton tried to tell the nutria to fuck off, but his neck was squeezed shut. He could see the nutria's claws, see its muscles tense. Milton knew, somehow, that it would aim those claws for his eyes. It wanted him blind. Its throat made a sick gargle and it leaped. In midair, inches from Milton's face, something solid and brown flew in and smacked into the nutria's head. The coffee cup shattered on the floor beside the nutria's unmoving body. Milton glanced up at Rica, who was rearming herself with a new mug.

Outside, tires skidded to a halt. Through the open door, Milton could see Roy jumping from his Microbus. Jeppy dropped to her feet, grabbed Carl, kicked the new nutria corpse, and ran for the bus. Roy reached Milton and pulled him to his feet. Together they battled back to the counter, Rica helping their cause with ceramic projectiles.

When the path was clear enough, Roy and the folksinger carried the writer out to the Microbus. Rica and Milton quickly followed. The bus's wheels spun in the gravel parking lot, caught, and jerked the bus out onto the road and toward south Austin.

A simple arrow

BECKY AND CLICK were friends. She called Click Patches. Click didn't mind. Becky and Patches were friends.

Even in the short hour before school that morning, they had played a lifetime of games. Patches with the cat. Patches drinking hot cocoa. Patches going down the slide. Can a crab wear makeup? Yes, a crab can. Can a crab balance on the handlebars of a bicycle? No, a crab cannot.

Becky's mama told her that Patches would not be able to join her at school. Becky said she agreed that school was no place for a hermit crab and she would not even think of bringing Patches with her. Becky lied.

Becky kept Patches close the whole morning. Reading time, nap time, math time. Patches was hidden in her dress pocket, scratching a little hello every few minutes. Finally during art time, Becky pulled Patches out and placed him on her easel. As Becky painted, Patches scratched at the canvas. Patches was the best crab ever.

Patches turned to Becky and wiggled his antennae. Becky nodded. She picked up a new brush, dipped it in the thickest, reddest paint, and marked a simple arrow on Patches's shell. The arrow pointed forward, from the back of the shell toward the opening.

"Will you visit?"

" . . . "

"Oh. That is a weally long way. Can I visit?"

" . . . "

"I'll wemeba. I pwomise."

Becky gently picked up Patches and carried him to the glass door leading to the playground. She kissed him on the shell, careful to avoid the paint, and placed him down just outside the door.

"Good-bye," she said.

Click crawled away in the direction of the arrow.

What a rat bastard

BEING A SAINT, Hayden concluded, wasn't easy. Jim slept next to him, and Hayden felt he could just as easily hate him as love him. Or easier still, harbor no feelings at all. But saints loved others more than themselves and Hayden loved himself so very much.

Saint Rick wouldn't cringe at Jim's mucus-laden snores, wouldn't begrudge that the previously untouched ashtray was now tainted with ash and stubs, wouldn't mind if a drop of drool stretched from Jim's open mouth down to the leather seat. But Hayden wasn't Saint Rick.

He had received three voice messages that morning. One from the Blythe Police Department asking him to drop by and answer some questions. A second one from his mother, who had left a long tirade including the statement, "We saw this coming . . . except for the leg part." And finally, a message from his agent, Ted: "Hayden Brock, you fuckup, fucking fuckup. You are fucked now." That was all he said. *Cryptic,* Hayden thought.

To make matters worse, a dirty green eighteen-wheeler was now tailgating Hayden. Twice already this same truck had passed, moved into Hayden's lane, and slowed down. Twice Hayden had retaken the lead. Now the truck was on his bumper. Hayden thought about pushing on the gas and making some serious distance from the truck, but considering his current relationship with the authorities, speeding seemed unwise. Now the truck was passing him again. It swerved just inches in front of the Lexus.

"That truck cut me off," Hayden said out loud.

"What a rat bastard," Jim Edwards said, and then opened his eyes.

The truck rattled in front of them. A bumper sticker on the left side read HOW'S MY DRIVING? and listed a phone number.

"That's it. I'm calling," Hayden said, picking up the phone and dialing the number. "Hello? Yes, I'd like to report some poor driving."

"Really?" said the voice on the phone.

"Yes, really. One of your truckers is out here on Interstate 10 driving like a jackass." Hayden looked over at Jim. Jim gave him a thumbs-up.

"Jackass, huh?" the voice said. "What does the truck look like?"

"Kind of beat-up. Green."

"What's he doing now?"

"Swerving back and forth. Shit! He just slammed on his brakes. I almost plowed him."

"What do you think he'll do next?"

"Next? I don't know." Hayden rolled his eyes at Jim. Jim nodded reassuringly.

"You think he might stop the truck and stomp your ass? You think he'll do that?" the voice said. "I mean, you are reporting him."

"He doesn't know—" The truck was slowing.

"And you in your pretty Lexus. I think he *should* stomp your tax-dodging ass," the voice said. "In fact, I'm going eat your throat and shit in your glove box."

"Bad," was all Hayden had time to say. Red brake lights flashed in front of them. Hayden dropped the phone, swerved into the next lane, and slammed on the accelerator. He was close to passing when the truck jerked to the side and clipped the Lexus, sending the car spinning off the side of the road.

"What the hell is happening?" Jim yelled.

Hayden's face was now the color of Jim Edwards's ash pile. The engine of the Lexus was no longer running. The truck pulled off the road in front of the car, and a large, dark man stepped out. His arms, his neck, his face were all hair. In his hand he held something gray and rigid.

"Is that an armadillo?" Jim asked. "It is. It's an armadillo with a beer bottle. I've seen those at the truck stops. How 'bout that."

The trucker gripped the armadillo by the tail. He slammed it onto Hayden's hood; the beer bottle held in the claws shattered.

"Get out, motherfucker. I want you to meet somebody," the trucker said, moving to the driver's-side window and tapping on the glass with the armadillo snout.

"Don't get out, Hay."

"No shit, Jim."

Jim Edwards opened the door and clambered out, using his hands to help lift his legs.

"Jim, what are you doing?"

Jim was reaching into his bag in the backseat, stopping once to scratch his beard.

"Okay, old man, you first," the trucker said, making his way around the car. He lifted the armadillo over his head. Jim Edwards turned and aimed a polished silver pistol at the trucker's face. The trucker froze.

"Drop the armadillo," Jim said in a steady voice. The trucker hesitated. Jim let out an impatient grunt and fired into the ground. The air cracked and dirt spit upward. The trucker dropped the armadillo. "Now get the hell out of here." The trucker galloped back to his truck, climbed in, and sped away. Jim slowly climbed back into the car, placed the pistol on his lap, and rubbed his legs. Hayden stared at the gun.

"It keeps me safe," Jim said.

"I think I peed."

"It happens."

Do you want to miss this?

"I HAVE SOME questions about the end of the world," Roy said. Milton looked away from the live footage of animal control workers clearing nutria from a statue of a Civil War general on the grounds of the Texas Capitol. Jeppy was asleep on the couch, gripping Carl to her body. Carl was wide awake and chewing on her hair. Rica was in the kitchen bandaging her hand. The writer and folksinger had decided to risk the roads and walk to a convenience store for beers.

"Are you sure?" Rica had asked them. "There're still a lot of those things out there."

"We've got to try," the writer said.

Milton stood, turned off the television, and motioned for Roy to join him on the porch. The streets were quieter now. A few sirens still echoed in the near distance.

"When?" Roy asked as soon as the door closed behind them.

"Sunday. Maybe Monday."

"Well, it had to happen sooner or later." Roy sat on the porch couch. "Mayan calendar, pole reversal, the endangered honeybee. The end has been nigh for years. What we should do is get some dinner. Enjoy each other's company. Maybe score some weed."

"Roy, everyone on Earth is going to die."

"That's always been the case," Roy said. "You're just upset that we're all going to die on the same day."

"I should also tell you that Earth is an insane asylum for the universe."

Roy turned his head to Milton. "What now?"

"Our souls are mad," Milton said. "You must have known. All this . . ." he gestured toward the street, the city. "All this is just a hospital."

"Wait. The Grays?" Roy said.

"Hospital staff, basically," Milton said. "The UFOs, the abductions, just nurses doing the rounds."

"Crop circles?"

"A kind of Rorschach inkblot test for us."

"Roswell?"

"Weather balloon."

"Really?"

"Sorry, Roy. I knew you'd hate that." Milton rubbed his face. "All our history, just crazies. They've had some successes, some cures. Buddha, Rumi, Rasputin."

"Rasputin?" Roy asked.

"I have to do something. I have to drive west. I should leave tonight. There was this man, this television actor, in my shower, and now I have to go find him."

"Does Rica know you're showering with men?"

"Should I marry her?"

"Right now?"

"Now is about all we've got." Milton stopped pacing and sat down. "I figured you could do the ceremony."

Years before, Roy had been ordained by a small online church based out of Tulsa, Oklahoma. He sought ordination so he could legally perform the funeral service of his grandfather. He worked on the eulogy for days, ordered the flowers, hired a caterer, taking personal interest in every detail. Roy wanted the service to celebrate his grandfather in a remarkable way. His grandfather wasn't as enthusiastic.

"I'm not dead, Roy."

"But you will be," Roy said. "Do you want to miss this?"

"It's morbid," his grandfather said.

"Come on, Grompy. You're in your eighties."

"I'm seventy-seven."

"Practically in your eighties. I don't want to wait till you're in the ground to honor you."

"Then throw me a roast, for God's sake."

"It's not like you have to die for this."

"Well, that's nice."

"But if you could lay in the coffin for the ceremony."

"A coffin?"

"Don't freak out. It's open casket."

"Does she want to marry you?" Roy asked. From his pocket, Roy pulled a mahogany pipe. To Milton's knowledge, he had never smoked it, but had been clenching it between his teeth since college.

"I'm not sure. I think so."

"You know, most marriages don't survive the first five years."

"We won't survive past Sunday."

"Good point." Roy took the pipe from his mouth, knocked it on his palm. "So when do we head west?"

Milton looked up. "You're coming?"

Roy nodded.

"You believe what I'm saying?"

"I'll tell you on Monday." Roy replaced the pipe between his teeth and looked out on the shady road running in front of the house. A thin woman in a muumuu glided by on roller skates. A potbelly pig jogged beside her. She waved. Roy waved back. "I'm not so worried about the world ending. But Austin ending, that's tragic. This town makes humanity look good."

Austin

ROY WOULD ASK that God bless Austin, but it was clear that God already had. Austin, near the end of the world, was in a golden age. And like all cities in their golden ages, it was claimed that the real golden age was years before. The golden light made even the city's past brighter.

Sweet city. Sweet pockets. Aging east side, wealthy west side, the north slanting right, the south running left, a swelling campus and a pink-domed capitol smack in the middle.

Semiemployed thirty-year-olds and graying hippies claiming bands, watching films, drinking Shiner Bock and espressos and discussing Howard Zinn and Tom Waits. Hip to be poor and forgivable to be wealthy.

Limestone pools filled with children and dogs.

The twenty-four-hour Mexican bakery where at 4:00 AM bleary-eyed hipsters cross paths with early-shift migrant workers.

Poor young couples paying above their means for organic meat.

Bikers and walkers and those that like to watch circling the green waters of Lady Bird Lake.

A dozen kinds of music. A dozen levels of quality. Three city blocks.

Artists and architects, computer madmen and cupcake crafters, midwives and politicians, movie stars and car washers. Every busboy is an artist, every checker has a degree, every tramp writes poetry, and everyone, everyone, is in a band.

Basement jazz, backyard folk, dance-floor country, pop-rock pranksters. Scene wizards with squeezed eyes swaying to B-3 organs, blues mythmakers smoking between sets and singing to disciples in the alleyways.

Films and films built on thrills and debt, breaths of cinematic gore and glory fueled by the passion of white-eyed will-bes.

Makeshift theaters with scriptless plays every night of the week. And they laugh on the stage and they laugh in the seats and they laugh at the lack of border between the two.

A variety pack of politics. Tolerance and racism are no longer segregated.

Liberal women have clandestine affairs with conservative men.

Conservative women have clandestine affairs with liberal women.

The governor could go either way.

The bistros of South Congress, the taco stands of East Eleventh. The brewpub by the hospital. The French jazz spots on East Sixth. The coffee shops everywhere. And in each place you find people you've met somewhere at sometime whose name you can't quite remember. But you'll talk for a while. In this way you have decades-long relationships with people whose names you never recall.

The heat of summer so intense that the day waits for sunset to take its first full breath and no one expects to accomplish too much. The late-arriving fall, pecans and acorns drumming away on the tin roofs and porch awnings. The surprise child winter sending ice puddles that close schools and shut down the government. And spring. A sweet-toothed dragon decorating the city with flowered scales and barbeque, breathing festivals for fire.

Yes, says the city. Yes, say the ever oaks and clogged creeks. Yes, says the smiling guest of a front yard party sneaking a smoke and glancing down the slow hill, up the sidewalked street, over the low roofs. Nod your head. Hold your joy. Austin is.

Four-hundred-gallon vat of puffed wheat

PATRICIA BLEET WAS sitting on a park bench eating a chicken salad on wheat and having amorous fantasies concerning her hair. Patricia adored her hair. It was her art and her child and the lover on which she doted. Each morning she woke hours before having to report to her job as assistant quality control agent at Sammy's Suga Smax Cereal Company so she could craft, curl, or cuddle with her hair.

She had visited a barber only once. A small trim at the age of nine. Thirty years later, she still regrets ever allowing those blade-bearing thieves near her amber locks. Her hair was now four feet long. She wore it in a myriad of styles. Down, up, permed, straightened, and, as of late, beehived. Oh, how Patricia loved her beehive. It was not fashionable. It was not easy. It was not even healthy. But it was her pride and glory. The style stood nearly a foot and a half from her scalp. Though she was only a little over five feet tall, she often had to duck when walking through doorways. She loved it.

"Oh my," she'd say after an impressive duck. "Almost had a ceiling-scraper." She'd then pat her hairdo and giggle.

She had finished her lunch now and would soon have to return to her work examining vats of cereal and answering to Mr. Peterson, the head quality control agent. She didn't like him at all. It would be a long, dull afternoon, she was sure. But for now, outside and alone with her hair, she felt relaxed and at home in the world. She closed her eyes and drifted to sleep in the warm sun.

What Patricia did not know, did not even begin to suspect, was that a shiny hermit crab with a red arrow painted on his shell was hanging from a branch an arm's length above her tower of hair. She had only just closed her eyes when Click lost his grip and plummeted into the do.

Patricia was startled awake. She quickly touched her hair. Click, seeing the hand approaching, burrowed deep into the hair's core.

Patricia checked her watch and waddled back to work, balancing her hair like a queen balancing a crown.

"You're late, Cousin Itt," barked Mr. Peterson. She hated it when he called her that. "Now go check all the B-vats. We ship today. Okay, bubblehead. Ha!"

No, she did not like him at all. They had made love once, just once, years before when she had first started at Sammy's Suga Smax Cereal Company. He had initiated it, buying her after-work margaritas and buffalo wings and then inviting himself into her apartment. Patricia found his company and his technique mediocre at best. Plus, he was balding. But when he left while she slept, when days passed without mention of their exchange, when he never suggested another spree of margaritas, Patricia found herself feeling oddly defeated. Since then, Mr. Peterson held a sick status above her that had little to do with his rank in the company.

Why did she put up with it? Why didn't she tell him what's what? Then she could leave this job, invest her savings into her very own beauty salon. She'd call it Patricia's Hair Palace. She even had a slogan. "No scissors. Just style!" Oh, it would be a beautiful place. Why didn't she leave? She could do it today.

"And double-check the puffed wheat, okay, Chewbacca?" yelled Mr. Peterson.

No, she couldn't leave. She'd fail. Simple as that. She always failed. Then she'd have to come to Mr. Peterson and ask for her job back. He'd gloat. He'd jeer. That would hurt too much.

Patricia stirred the vat of colored marshmallow chunks and glanced over the surprise toy supply, checking off the list on her clipboard as she went. She daydreamed of hair spray and conditioners as she slowly made her way to the four-hundred-gallon vat of puffed wheat. She leaned over the vat and gazed at the mass of sugared puffs ten feet below her.

The hermit crab nestled in the dark safety of her hive slipped from the front of the hairstyle and into the light. He clasped onto a strand of hair, dangling above the vat like Bruce Willis from the roof of a high-rise business building.

What if God sent some kind of sign? Patricia thought. *Some sign that he wanted me to quit. That he thought I could do it.*

"No, no," she said aloud, shaking her head. "God doesn't send signs like—"

From out of nowhere a colorful shell fell from the sky and landed on the mountains of cereal below her. The shell had legs! It scurried about for a moment. On its back was a bright red arrow. Patricia gasped. She followed the arrow's point and it directed her vision straight to the emergency exit. When she looked back, the shell was gone, and there was the slightest movement in a nondescript indentation in the wheat puffs.

Thank you, God.

Patricia set down her clipboard, patted her hair, and walked through the emergency exit never to return again.

The sky declaring war

"WEST?" RICA ASKED. "West where?"

"I'm not sure. Marfa, I think." Milton was pacing through the living room.

"That's over four hundred miles away."

"Roy will drive. You can sleep in the back. He's got that mattress back there."

"That's just creepy," Rica said.

Outside the sky had grown gray, leaving the room shadowy and cool. Jeppy was now awake, sitting beside Rica and breast-feeding Carl. She hummed an old Harry Nilsson song and rocked the child side to side. Rica wanted to do nothing more than sit and listen to Jeppy's humming.

"Milton," Rica said, closing her eyes. "I'm pregnant, I'm exhausted, I've been chewed on by a nutria, I'm not leaving."

"She should stay here, Milton," Jeppy said, her eyes glancing up from Carl. "The fumes in the back of that van can't be healthy."

"We'll crack a window," Milton said to Jeppy. He stopped pacing and stared at Rica. "You have to come. The turtle said."

Rica opened her eyes. "The turtle?"

"There was a whole mess of them, but only one said anything."

Rica looked at Jeppy, who only shrugged. Rica rose to her feet.

"Follow me," she said to Milton, and with fast steps walked into the bathroom. Once Milton was in she closed the door.

"What the fuck is up with you?" she whispered, poking a finger against his chest and backing him into the shower door. The rattle of the door made him jump. "Milton, you're acting crazy."

"I'm seeing things, Rica. Unbelievable things. Except I believe them, so that makes them believable by definition. You saw today. You saw what's happening."

Milton scanned the room, looking beyond Rica as if the perfect argument was hiding somewhere behind her.

Rica turned her head and stared out the small window above the toilet. The sky was darker now and the first few drops of rain were rolling down the glass.

"A few river rats going nuts isn't evidence of the Apocalypse."

"The nutria attack was just a start. Things are going to get much worse. Fire and blood, monster-ass hail the color of coal, all that biblical shit. They've shown me things."

"Who? Your ghost friend?"

"It's not a ghost, and yes. And something else. Something in my head."

"You're hearing voices, Milton," Rica said, whispering from the back of her throat. "That's psychotic."

"I know it sounds crazy, but . . ." Milton's jaw tightened. "I know what I'm supposed to do. At least the next step."

The drumming of the rain against the roof grew louder and Rica raised her voice above the downpour. "What if you're not *supposed* to do anything, Milton? Maybe you don't have some special job. Maybe you're just like the rest of us, huh?"

"But I'm not!" Milton nearly yelled. "Have you ever just known something? I mean, you just *know*."

"No." She leaned back against the sink. "I'm guessing the whole time."

The rain was now a constant white noise.

"Okay, you don't have to know. You don't have to believe any of this. You just have to . . ." Milton looked to the ceiling and took a deep breath through his nose. He brought his head down and met Rica's eyes. "Can you trust me enough to come with me?"

Rica studied his eyes. She slowly shook her head. "No, I can't." She took a deep breath. "Milton, I've got to think about what's best for the ba—"

The bathroom window shattered, spraying glass over both of them. Rica yelped; Milton fell back against the shower door, nearly falling in. On the ground between them lay a fist-size chunk of black stone. For a moment both stared down at it. Milton knelt and touched it with a hesitant finger.

"Ice," he said.

Above them the roof shook as if slammed by the swing of a sledgehammer. First just one smash, then another, followed immediately by another.

"Holy fuck," Rica said.

Soon the impacts were coming fast and overlapping, loud as shotguns. Rica caught Milton's eye for a second, then they both tumbled out of the bathroom.

Jeppy was curled over Carl. "What is that?"

Rica followed Milton through the front door and onto the porch with Roy. The sky above them bubbled gray and black like a boiling pot. A piece of black ice the size of a brick crashed down, shattering the windshield of the neighbor's car, another splintering the branch of the oak in Milton's front yard.

Jeppy, clutching Carl to her chest, appeared at their side.

"We should call someone! Who should we call?"

The writer and the folksinger sprinted down the street, six-packs in hand, dodging black ice-stones the size of apples.

"Run!" Roy yelled.

The writer was laughing as he ran into the yard, lifting the six-pack. "At least we got the —"

A black bowling ball of ice smacked against his skull and he fell to the grass in a lifeless thud. Rica and Jeppy screamed, Carl erupted into a screeching cry. The folksinger, a step from the porch, turned and leaped back to the writer.

"No!" screamed Milton. "Don't!"

The folksinger was just kneeling when another stone knocked him to all fours. He looked to the porch with crazy, pain-filled eyes. Roy jumped toward him an instant before a black ice chunk the size of an oven slammed into the folksinger. Milton yanked Roy back under the porch.

Cannonballs of ice fired from the clouds, the sky declaring war on the earth. Down the block a piece of hail sliced a power line in a shower of sparks. The line fell to the sidewalk, flailing like an injured snake.

Rica couldn't take her eyes from the unmoving bodies in the yard. The fist-size hail that was landing in the soft mud around them. *Bubble tea*, Rica thought. *Black pearls and bubble tea.*

"We have to go," said Milton.

"What?!" Jeppy yelled.

"This house won't stand." Milton turned to the others. "Roy, get the bus."

Without hesitation, Roy dashed from the porch to the bus parked against the curb.

"Rica, Jeppy," Milton said, "We're going to run on the count of three."

"I'm not running anywhere," Jeppy said.

Rica only stared at the bodies.

Roy had reached the bus uninjured and swung the side door open. He had replaced the backseats with a used mattress years before. He sat on the mattress now, waving the others in.

A black ice rock, the size of a refrigerator, smashed into the middle of the street just feet from the bus, shattering into countless pieces and shaking the ground.

"See!" screamed Jeppy. "It's safer here!"

From inside the house came an enormous crash. Looking back through the door, Rica could see a massive boulder sitting where the kitchen once had been.

"Monster-ass hail," Rica almost whispered. Milton reached out and took her hand. She looked into his eyes and nodded.

"One, two, three!" Milton said, and pulled Rica into a run toward the bus.

"Shit! Shit! Shit!" Jeppy yelled as she ran, Carl in her arms, toward the open bus.

Before the door closed, Roy was driving.

Rica stared back at what had been her home for the last two years. A tree branch from an ancient live oak snapped above the porch and crumpled the front section of the roof.

Roy wove the bus through the debris-strewn street as hail continued to rain down around them.

"Give me a phone! Does anyone have a phone?" Jeppy yelled, squeezing Carl to her chest. Roy and Milton exchanged glances and Milton shook his head. "Fucking hippies!" Jeppy yelped.

Roy swerved onto Lamar and headed south. Cars and trucks filled the sides of the roads, some parked beneath trees, other crumpled into each other, clogging the street. Red and orange flames darted out of a pizza parlor and a bar.

"Just make your way west as best you can," Milton said.

"I want to fucking call my boyfriend!" Jeppy yelled.

Roy turned right off Lamar and zigzagged through blocks of residential houses. The downpour of hail was lighter now. The occasional oversize hunk smashed to the street and shattered like black glass, but the heart of the storm had passed, leaving a wet drizzle.

Keeping just west of Lamar, Roy avoided the jammed roads and made it as far south as Highway 71. The whole time Rica sat in the back, staring out at the damaged homes and cars. Loose branches dangled from trees and the gutters rushed like tiny whitewater rapids. Car alarms wailed from miles around. Sparks sprayed out from loose power lines in random spurts.

Roy was cutting through a mall parking lot when Jeppy ordered him to stop.

"I'm getting out here. Right here!" She pointed to a restaurant. "I'm going in there and I'm calling Todd."

"Fuddruckers?" Rica asked. "You're vegan."

"I don't give a fuck. I'm getting out of this bus now." Jeppy pulled at the sliding back door, but it stuck halfway open. Milton climbed out and yanked it the rest of the way. Jeppy, eyeing Milton with suspicion, crawled out holding Carl. She turned to Rica.

"Come with me."

Rica climbed out and stood beside Milton. "I'm going with him."

"Why, because the turtles said so?"

"Only one of them spoke," Milton said.

"I trust him, Jeppy," Rica said. She reached out and touched Carl's wet face. "Be careful, okay?"

Jeppy nodded. "You be even more careful."

Skiing and ice wine

HAYDEN BROCK BROWSED the sunglasses rack and watched Jim Edwards flirt with the teenage girl behind the counter of the Gas 'n' Go.

"I tell you what." Jim leaned against the counter. "We'll trade. I'll take your little pink hat and you can have mine."

"I don't think so," she said, smacking her gum between each word.

"It's a Stetson."

"Do you want a bag for the beer?"

Hayden sighed. Jim was not that talented of a flirt. The trick to seduction, Hayden knew, was to say very little. Just smile and nod. It had worked for him almost every time. Didn't help his marriage much. It only lasted eight months.

His wife at the time, Winter Hass, was a successful model turned failed screenplay writer who was devoting her days to completing a bio-epic script based on the life of Deepak Chopra.

The wedding of Hayden and Winter had been a small affair in Vail, Colorado. *People* magazine had purchased the pictures for over half a million dollars.

The first month of marriage went fine. Skiing and ice wine.

The second month was a breeze. Windsurfing and piña coladas.

In the third month the momentum slowed. Television and skim milk.

It was the fourth month when Hayden came home and Winter noticed he was wearing his wedding band on his right hand. He wasn't trying to fool anyone into thinking he wasn't married. Everyone had seen the pictures in *People*. He wore the ring on the wrong hand to announce that he was both married and available. Chicks dug it. Winter understood this immediately. The tantrum was fantastic, Winter yelling and throwing whatever her hands could find. Hayden was smacked between the eyes with Deepak Chopra's *The Seven Spiritual Laws of Success*. Hardback edition. He was taken to the emergency room and given five stitches. *People* ran the story three days later.

In month five Hayden discovered Winter and the seventeen-year-old star of *Beach Life* snorting cocaine in the house sauna. Winter swore it was only a maternal friendship and that the kid had brought his own coke.

Month six was remodeling. The romance rallied. Small talk and red wine.

Month seven was sexy. Afternoon bedroom bouts and tequila. Hayden had high hopes for the future.

In month eight, Hayden found the seventeen-year-old in the sauna again, this time snorting cocaine from Winter's sweaty nipples while in the corner, holding a camcorder, stood Deepak Chopra wearing nothing but an impressive erection.

That was the end.

Hayden Brock and Jim Edwards sat drinking Old Milwaukee beer at a New Mexico rest stop. They watched a wild orange sun sink into the flat sands.

"I've never seen the sun so large," Hayden said, sipping his warm beer.

"Global warming," said Jim.

"This spot is beautiful. You've been here before?"

"Plenty of times. I've slept at every rest stop on this road. Been living on I-10 for six years now. Back and forth between Arizona and Texas. It's good. You meet folks. You see friends, like Pete over there. He's been the custodian here for two years. Good man. Hell of a ladies' man. Ladies stop here, he lays on the charms, and bam! They're in his mop closet poking away."

"You had many lovers, Jim?"

"Is three many?"

"No."

"Then no," he said, lighting a cigarette. "To be honest, it's more like two and half lovers. The first was a spinster friend of my mother's. I was thirteen. The last was my wife. Met her two days after getting out of the army. Married her within a month. I was faithful to her for thirty-seven years of marriage and six years of widowness, so far."

"What about the half?"

"A dwarf hooker in Korea." Jim dragged on his cigarette.

"A dwarf?"

"All I could afford. But I tell you, she gave me the most passionate night of my life."

"Wow."

"And gonorrhea."

"Oh." Hayden opened another beer. "Aren't you going to ask me how many lovers I've had?"

"No."

"Three hundred and eight. No, wait. Three hundred and nine."

Jim whistled.

"But the best of my life . . ." Hayden shook his head. "Being with her is like, I don't know, like having your penis in a freshly baked loaf of bread."

"That's disgusting."

"I'm just looking for the best image."

"Well, leave food out of it," Jim said. "What's her name?"

"Don't know. Only see her in my dreams." Hayden leaned his chin on his palm. He watched the sky mellow, watched the glow of Jim's cigarette, watched stars pop into view. "She has almond skin," he said.

Two hours later Hayden Brock lay down to sleep on top of a picnic table. All night a train of traffic rumbled by. *All those journeys*, Hayden thought. His mind was warm with sleepiness and beer, thoughts floating like smoke twirls. *Sweet world. Safe world.* He felt very good about all things.

A table over, Jim Edwards slept, his hand under his shirt gripping his pistol.

Night-black skin

THE WORLD WAS dark and close. Click had often buried himself in soft sand and felt cool and safe. But Suga Smax did not possess the comforts of sand. The puffs were clunky and clumsy. Sand moves like thick water; Smax move like sticky boulders.

The world held one hint of light, below him, or above him if he was upside down. The light was a pinprick, so slight that Click wondered if it existed at all. Still, Click was drawn to it. He burrowed through the Smax, maneuvering over and around each puff toward the light. It was a slow, painful crawl. Every inch or so Click would have to stop and remove a piece of Smax that had wedged into his shell. To make things more difficult, often everything would shake and rumble. With nothing unmoving to grip, Click would be rattled to some far corner of his new world. Sometimes he'd land near the edge of the world, where the puffs end and an invisible skin crinkled. Past the skin was a gray, flat sky.

After each shake, Click would shift to reorient himself and search until he again found the one point of light. Then he'd once more begin the slow climb. For a while the world held still. He crawled and crawled, but the light seemed no closer. He became convinced he was only pushing puffs behind him without moving forward at all. Still he crawled. What else could he do? Finally a puff slipped aside and the light shone before him, particles of sugar floating in the pinhole's single ray.

The light changed the world. He could see the puffs of wheat in detail, see his own sugar-coated claws, and something else. He was not alone. A face, black, white, and red, buried in the puffs. It was a small red-lipped seal. He could only see part of her, but she seemed as lost and alone as Click himself. She wasn't moving. Perhaps she was stuck.

Click carefully removed some Smax from her face. She was beautiful.

Night-black skin; wide, thought-filled eyes; and the cutest little whiskers. Click reached out a hesitant claw and touched her whiskers. She didn't retreat from his touch. She locked Click's gaze with an unblinking stare so rich that Click had to look away. His heart pounded like the crashing ocean waves he could no longer fully remember.

The world rumbled again and the seal dove into his embrace. Click gently stroked her, comforting her. She smelled clean and sweet. So close. So alone. Her fear birthed a new courage in his soul. Click squeezed his two claws around her. The seal squeaked. Click melted.

Don't be silly, Rica

POP!

The arrow slams into FBI agent Chip Bradley's chest. He falls back against a tree, his face wrought with pain.

Pop! Pop!

Two more arrows slam into his body, which is now naked. He calls out in pain. He moans.

Pop! Pop! Pop!

"No," Rica yells, and reloads her crossbow.

Rica opened her eyes. It was night-dark and the air smelled of motor oil and cotton. A tinny voice was passionately lecturing from a radio. "But satellites don't just fall. Not half a dozen at once. No. The big story tonight is what the government is not telling us! We're under attack, and I say the French are behind it!"

The floating voice, confident, almost jovial only added to Rica's waking confusion. Where was she? And why?

"Did the muffler wake you?" Roy whispered from the driver's seat. "It's got some rust holes and the inclines are hell." He glanced back with a smile, his mahogany pipe sticking out from his mouth.

The *where* was easy. She was lying on the mattress in the back of Roy's Microbus. They were heading west through the hill country of Texas. But even as she sat up and shook off the sleep, the *why* eluded her. Beside her Milton snored softly in his sleep.

In the front, Roy pressed another button on his radio and a woman's voice came through the speakers. "How do you expect animals to react? We've been encroaching on their habitat, polluting their waters, heating their climate."

"You're saying this was an organized attack?" another voice asked.

"I'm saying we're getting what we deserve."

Rica watched Milton, still sleeping, snort once and smack his lips. She was traveling west, following a man who thought space aliens wanted him to meet up with television star Hayden Brock before the world ended on Sunday.

What was she doing? She tried to retrace the path that had led her to this moment. Not just the black ice, not just the wild nutria. How had her life become so entangled with the gangly, off-kilter Milton Post?

"Any news?" Rica asked.

"Plenty," Roy glanced back. "Death toll in Austin is above fifty. Most of the city has no power or water. And Austin's not alone. Mudslides in Egypt. Goat stampedes in New Zealand. It's nuts!"

"Jesus."

"And Milton's not the only one talking about the end of the world."

Roy switched to another station and turned up the volume. A friendly voice with a slight Southern twang spoke. "Listen, friends! I'm not doing this for profit. It's not like I'm selling airtime by telling my sponsor there won't be air for much longer. And there won't be. We're close! Praise Jesus, we are so close!"

The VW jerked a little as Roy downshifted. Milton rolled onto his side. Rica stared at him for a long minute.

She felt sick.

And knowing Milton, especially with Roy helping, they really would find Hayden Brock. She'd be face-to-face with Hayden Brock after all these years, after all those dreams, all those fantasies. Would he really smell like mountain air? Would his arms have that soft-stone feel? Would the sweat on his stomach taste like sea salt?

Milton rolled onto his back. Still asleep, he attempted to run his hand though his hair. It only made it halfway before getting snagged.

"The only thing I'm selling is truth, and I'm not selling it, I'm giving it away. Because you can't buy it! Come on! This, all of this, had been foretold in the scriptures . . ."

There was Milton. The father of her child. This is the man she'd stay with. She would never know the real taste of Hayden's stomach sweat. In fact, she now felt pretty shitty for even wondering.

It was a familiar guilt. More than once while making love to Milton she had imagined she was actually with Hayden. In those dark moving moments, she pictured another life in which she had not vomited on the teenage Hayden Brock, had not slunk back to Texas in humiliation, had, instead, touched lips in that cramped closet, connected with the young star, began a written correspondence filled with wit and poetry, met up in each other's homes for holidays and school breaks until they both felt at ease in the presence of either set of parents, planned clandestine weekends in Vegas throughout her college career, broken up at the beginning of her grad school studies when a delicious med student courted her with mix CDs and promises of endless security, swept her off her feet when Hayden proposed while accepting an Emmy on national television, married in a discreet ceremony in Rome, and were now making love with the intimacy of lifetime lovers and the recklessness of strangers.

Then she'd remember she was in bed with Milton.

She was not proud of these fantasies and often fought against them. But when her guard was down, as it often was in lovemaking, the visions crept back in.

In fact, the night of Nutella and the Nibbler, the night the baby was conceived, Rica had closed her eyes and for a few brief moments felt Hayden's body in Milton's place. She had quickly shoved the apparition away and refocused on Milton. But the sensation had been intense enough for Rica, in her most honest thoughts, to consider Hayden Brock as the child's other father, the lust-father.

Milton snorted in his sleep.

"The signs are so clear you'd have to work to ignore them. And that's what most of the world does! They work to ignore the truth burning before their eyes! And they've got plenty of burning in their future . . . "

How could she so clearly love and not love the same person? How do so many vague and random moments lead to something as concrete as the present? Why the hell had she vomited in that closet?

Milton tried to move his hand from his hair, but his thick mane put up more resistance than his hand was willing to overcome and Milton's hand fell back to his scalp. Rica thought it might be nice to die. The baby squirmed inside her. *I'm sorry*, she told her baby. *Shhh, now.*

The baby. She held more weight than all Rica's doubts and fears.

"That sound, listeners, that sound you hear is the very sweet intern Ami handing me a Red Bull and a Slim Jim. You know why? I'm not sleeping tonight. Stay awake, Jesus told us. Because he is coming! Soon! And I'm staying on the air until it happens! Right here on KRST 88.6 or online at HarvestChurchTruth. com and now on XFM. We'll keep sharing the truth until that trumpet blares!"

A horn boomed outside the bus. An oversize pickup truck rumbled past.

"I'm going as fast as I can, damn," Roy muttered as the bus shuddered.

Rica did not want the world to end. She wanted to meet her baby. Tears came to her eyes. *Don't be silly, Rica*, she thought. *The world is not ending.* But the tears kept coming.

Milton sat up beside her, pulling his hand from his hair and rubbing his face. "Hey," he said drowsily.

Rica turned her head to the window. She watched the world pass through the double blur of speed and tears.

"Can you pull over, Roy," Milton said through a yawn. "I've got to pee."

Pretty fucking amazing

MILTON STEPPED FROM the van toward the thick brush of cedars and grass beside the road. Insects chirped in chorus. He peed into the darkness and bent his neck to watch the stars. Looking forward again he saw a face. Half hidden in the shadow of cedars was the blue face with its frozen gasp.

Milton could not explain why he did not sprint back to the bus. He was not afraid. It felt more like coming upon a doe in the forest. A sense of luck, a sense that the moment was charmed.

"Hello again," Milton said. With one smooth hand, the Non-Man gestured for Milton to follow. The Non-Man turned and moved farther into the trees, a blue glow revealing his path. Milton stepped over the shallow ditch and into the brush.

"Milton?" he heard Rica call out. "Where are you going?"

The low, thick branches hid the stars and soon the bus as well. Milton was encased by the close feel of night and the scented trees as he walked toward the blue glow, branches scraping his skin and snagging his hair. Pushing through a clump of thorny brush, he came into a clearing. There stood the Non-Man and beside him, illuminated by the blue glow and dim starlight, stood Milton's father.

"Dad?"

"Pretty fucking amazing, am I right?"

His father wore the same black pants and button-down white shirt, the same blue tie and black-rimmed glasses he'd worn most days of his life. And even in the weak light, Milton could make out the black X on his forehead.

"You're dead," Milton mumbled, his lips feeling heavy and numb. "I saw."

"You know better than that," his father said.

"So, it worked? Quantum suicide?"

"Yes. And no. I got a lot wrong." A corner of his father's mouth raised in a crooked grin. As he spoke, he seemed to flicker in the dark like a shadow of a candle.

"Are you here?" Milton asked.

The crooked grin grew. "I'm not *not* here."

"And him?" Milton glanced at the Non-Man. The Non-Man moved his mouth—open and closed—but no sounds came out.

"Listen, Milton, try and ask only quality questions, okay? I'd like to say there's not much time. But, of course, time doesn't work that way. There's always the same amount of time. But if you don't know that, or experience it, well then, right now there really isn't much time to spare."

Something was different, a new stillness. The insects' constant whirring had fallen silent. The wind seemed to have stopped. The low light in the clearing shimmered. Milton could see light as particles, a billion particles, each slowly wiggling, each with a glow bleeding into the others. A single oak leaf hovered midfall three feet above the ground.

"What's happening?"

"Call that a quality question? Jesus, Milton, work with me here. How about this; How about you ask why life on Earth is ending?"

"Why is life on Earth ending?"

"Stupid question," his father said. "Does it matter? Really? What are you going to do? Share with the world the mechanics of their death? What good is that? I'll answer that. No good, Milton." He pointed up to the circle of sky above the clearing. "WR 104. That's what will kill you."

"The star?"

"Former star. It collapsed on itself seven thousand four hundred and eighty-two years, three months, and six days ago. Imploded into a black hole and, like a jelly donut under a car tire, shot out a beam of gamma rays."

"GRB," Milton said. "A gamma-ray burst."

"That burst is due to hit Earth tomorrow evening. Smack! Bye-bye, ozone layer. Smack! Hello, radiation; hello, muons showering into every thin human skull; hello, boiling oceans; hello, acid rain; hello, end times."

"That explains the hail. The animals going nuts."

"Hell no." His father gave the impatient flurry of his arms that Milton remembered so often from his childhood. "Gamma rays travel at the speed of light. It won't hit until it hits. No warning."

"But things are already happening. A nutria bit my face."

"Yeah," his father rubbed his chin. "That would be the Floaters and the fetter field."

"Fetter field. You said that before. In my bedroom. I don't know what that is."

"No, you wouldn't. No shame in that." His father nodded. "You've got the magnetic field, right? Nice little shell surrounding the planet, keeping nasty solar winds out. Well, the fetter field is woven through it like thick yarn. Keeps people on the planet. Like a force field for souls. We can stretch it. That's all NASA ever did . . . stretch the fucking fetter field. Like pushing out the sides of a bag. But you can't stretch it far. No soul can. Otherwise we'd have mad souls wandering the universe! But there are moments when you can escape. Tiny moments like death or the moment of birth. But overall, it's a tight net. Right?" His father looked to the Non-Man, who slowly nodded his blue head.

"What does that have to do with nutria and hail and people in my shower?"

"This morning, your morning, the Floaters removed the field. Just took it out. It left thousands of holes in the magnetic field. So radiation is pouring in, the crust is heating, satellites are failing, hail is falling, animals losing their minds."

Milton pointed at the Non-Man. "They're doing this to us?"

"It's all side effects. Well, not the man in your shower. That's different."

"You're fucking right, it's different!" Milton threw his arms in the air.

"Wait! Wait!" His father put both hands up. "The exciting thing here, Milton, the crucial thing, is that the fetter field is open. Gone!"

"I don't understand," Milton said.

"Yes. Your incredibly blank expression makes that clear. Jesus." His father rubbed his eyes. Milton noted how very little death had changed him. "Let's say you run a prison, a prison for the mentally insane, and it's built on a coastal cliff. Let's say a tsunami is heading directly toward the prison. What do you do? You unlock the doors! You open the cells. Let the prisoners run for their lives."

"So we can go? We can leave Earth?"

"Yes. Anyone can! But no one is, Milton. Nobody."

"Why not?"

"The prisoners don't get it! Have no idea what it means to walk free. No idea. They just stay holed up in their cells staring at the open door. And there's no way to tell them. Because they're crazy and institutionalized. But maybe, maybe just the act of freeing themselves will bring about a cure. If they'd just leave their cell. Maybe finding their freedom will be finding their sanity. What do you do?"

Milton shook his head.

"You set their mattresses on fire!"

"What do you mean?"

"We've been predicting the Apocalypse for millenniums. These guys are just making all our dreams come true."

The Non-Man's mouth moved into what Milton presumed was a smile.

"And what? We'll just fly away?"

"It's not flying," his father said. "It's spatting. It's different."

"Spatting? How do you spat?" Milton said.

"What do you think you're doing right now?" his father said.

The Non-Man reached out his long arm toward Milton. Milton watched in a daze as specks of blue light floated from his skin and smeared against the dark. The Non-Man touched Milton's bare arm. His hand was warm.

"Brace yourself for travel," his father said. "I want to introduce you to some people."

Where the hell?

EVERY HORN OF every eighteen-wheeler in the rest stop blasted at the same moment.

Hayden opened his eyes, nearly rolling off the table.

"My husband's gone. Help!" someone screamed.

Hayden rubbed his eyes and tried to make some sense of the chaos. People ran from truck to truck. A dog was howling.

"Hayden. Hayden." Jim Edwards limped toward him. "Let's get out of here. People are freaking out."

The woman yelled again. "Don't touch me! Where's my husband?" Hayden sat up on the picnic table and looked over to the rest stop restrooms. Under the florescent light a large woman was jumping up and down and screaming at a small group of truckers surrounding her.

"It's Grit's wife," one of them said. "Somebody find him."

"I looked everywhere."

"There's Clement's truck. Wake him. He'll know what to do."

"His truck's empty."

"Where the hell is everybody?"

Hayden rubbed some wakefulness into his face as Jim handed him his bag.

"Should we try and help?" Hayden said through a yawn.

"They've called the police, Hay."

"Oh," Hayden said. "Let's go."

The air was sweet, the world was crunchy

CLICK WAS WITH Seal. Seal was with Click. The air was sweet, the world was crunchy. Click could not remember another world. Nothing existed past the puffs and the smooth gray boundaries. There was Click and Seal. Even their dot of light was gone, leaving them alone in a warm darkness. The world quietly rumbled around them.

Click nibbled on a puff. He touched Seal's red lips with the sweet dust that cover each puff, but Seal was not hungry. Oh, she was beautiful. Even in the dark he could feel her beauty. Click had never been so happy.

Something very else

"**WHERE THE HELL** is he going?" Rica asked as Milton disappeared into the cedars.

"You've been crying," Roy said.

"People are dying, Roy. I'm freaking out here."

Roy nodded.

"And Milton is . . . " Rica swallowed. "Roy, where the hell are we driving to? He's talking insane stuff."

"I wouldn't worry, Rica," Roy said. "Milton's a little too crazy to go mad."

"I just want to be careful, you know?"

Before Roy could answer, the VW door slid open and Milton climbed back in.

"That was fast," Roy said.

Milton sat, his mouth ajar.

Roy pressed on the gas and the VW lumbered back to speed.

"I had a dream," Milton said.

"While peeing?"

"No. It wasn't a dream. It was something else. Something very else." Milton slapped his forehead with both palms. "I traveled. I went with the Floater. And my dad. My dad is alive." Milton stood, crouching over. He paced the five feet of mattress and spoke in rapid bursts. "They showed me things. Hidden things. The universe. We're moles, all blind. So blind, all of us, so blind we don't know we're blind. The space right in front of you isn't empty. It's packed. It's full of life and worlds and doors and timelines. You swallow entire histories with each breath. Rub your chin, and you destroy worlds twice as old as Earth with their own Shakespeares, Buddhas, Holocausts. Don't move! Don't move!" Milton froze in midstride, only his beard still waving. "We're killing the children of other worlds," he whispered. He dropped to the mattress and grabbed Rica's thigh. He stared at his hands on her leg. "What do we do?"

"Calm down, Milton," Rica said. "It was a dream."

"Dreams are real, clouds are illusions, rain really is the tears of gods." Milton coughed. "I'm choking on a Gandhi, on an Athens."

"Keep it coming, friend. What else did you see?" Roy yelled from the front of the bus.

Milton lifted his eyes from his hands and stared at Rica's face. "Rica, you are so very beautiful."

"Milton," she said, softly. "You were gone only a minute. You couldn't have—"

"Oh, oh. I was spatting. So for you it took no time at all."

"I'm sorry, what?"

"Spatting. It's how Floaters travel. My dad was right about that one."

"You're going to have to explain," Roy said.

"Fine, fine. I will. You'll like it, Roy. Right up your alley." Milton pulled his legs under himself. "On the quantum level each moment is simply another world. Every sliver of moment, a separate world. We move in one direction because that's all we're capable of. Like rocks thrown in the ocean, we can't swim or float. We just sink down and think that's the only possible direction. Time doesn't pass, we pass through time."

"So spatting is swimming?" Roy asked.

"Yes!" Milton jumped back to his feet. "There's all these tiny wormholes opening and closing. They just spat through them."

"Milton, are you saying you're the world's first time traveler?" Rica asked.

"Worlds traveler!" he said, slapping the sides of his head. "And not the first. Some people got it. Mystics spat. Musicians spat. Soloists do it all the time. The crowd hears a three-minute jam, but the musician is playing a solo for years across the cosmos. Or playing one note, but in that note . . . or between two notes is a lifetime. Or no time. Just spat." Milton threw his arms out. "People make accidental spats all the time. Like when you fall asleep and it feels like it's been hours, but it's only been two minutes. That's sleeping spats. But even when you're awake people take tiny spats."

"What does it feel like?" Roy said, craning his head back.

"Like . . . like an orgasm. But not an average one. A really spectacular orgasm. When you have one of those, you usually spat a little, too."

"Nice," Roy said.

"But we've been stuck! Stuck here. All this time we've been blinded by the guards, shackled. Shackled like prisoners. That's why we have such a hard time spatting," Milton said, grabbing his hair. "I understand now. Last night when I yelled at you, Rica. I was out of my head. The Non-Man, he unshackled me. Unchained my brain so they could show me things, take me places. No wonder I freaked out. And now the fetter field is gone. Now we can spat wherever, whenever. All of us. If we could just learn how!" Milton bounced up and down, rocking the entire bus. "Don't you see it, Rica? You were closer to the truth of things with your jazz. With your soup. You didn't know it, but you've always been so close to it all. I never tasted it. Half alive. Half alive." He trod in circles around the mattress. "Let's stop and eat!"

"We ate two hours ago."

"But I wasn't tasting all the way. Might as well have been talking about food. I can taste now. Rica, let's make love."

"What, now?"

"Roy, you don't mind, do you?"

"Go ahead," Roy said, smiling into the rearview mirror.

Milton knelt down beside Rica. "Rica, let's make love. Real love."

"Milton, you look tired. Calm down a little."

"No, no, no!"

"Go for it, Rica," Roy said. "I'll turn up the radio." He clicked the dial and a news anchor's voice was belching headlines.

"Milton," Rica whispered, "I'm scared by all this."

"A wave can knock you down only if you're trying to stand."

"I've got a baby in me. I am trying to stand.'

"Babies float," he said. "She floats."

"What do you mean?"

"Hey, guys," Roy said, "you should hear this." He turned up the radio.

"Again, thousands have disappeared and the count continues to grow. The vice president has declared a national state of emergency. The president and the First Lady have been missing for approximately two hours. Four planes have crashed over the United States in the last two hours. Reports from Europe are equally extreme. Terrorism has not been ruled—"

Roy fiddled with the tuner.

A woman's voice crackled through. "I saw him there and then he was gone. He was sitting right there and then, just gone!"

Roy twisted the dial again. Snippets came through the static.

" . . . confirmed that none of the prisoners have been found as of yet, but sources . . ."

" . . . only nine years old. Wearing a blue tank top and last seen . . ."

" . . . no bodies have been found, but searchers are still . . ."

Roy kept turning the dial, listening for a moment and turning. At the end of the dial, 88.6, they heard a familiar sound. Roy's voice coming through the radio. He was singing. Milton's rhythm guitar was playing.

Who's going to park the car tonight. . .

The song played through with no interruption from the three travelers. When it ended, it immediately started playing again.

"Milt?" Roy said, swerving the van a little as he looked back.

"Keep driving."

Wheezing the whole time

THANKS TO THE armadillo-wielding trucker, Hayden Brock's Lexus possessed only one working headlight. That single light cut a thin slice out of the black night as they raced east. At Jim Edwards's suggestion the two had left the interstate for the New Mexican back roads. "Less traffic," Jim had said. "Less authorities."

The armadillo sat between them like a Jurassic lapdog.

For two hours they rolled through the dark landscape, occasionally passing through small, half-built towns. A few trailers, a few cinder block homes, a decrepit store or gas station with one sad outdoor light glowing an anemic reprieve from the surrounding night.

"Why would people stay here?" Hayden asked.

"Where else would they go?"

"I don't know, cities?"

"Have you seen how the poor live in cities?"

They'd leave each place untouched and speed into the empty space between. And the towns would be swallowed up again by the dark. Hayden tried to remember the name of each one, thinking at some point he'd mark the route on a map, but a mile into the empty and the name would be lost to him.

They were sailing; the dark was the waters and these one-light towns were mud islands, uncharted patches of earth. The quiet dark between was the beauty. The same sense of vastness Hayden had experienced while looking out from his balcony onto the Pacific Ocean, knowing that beyond the blue waters he saw was more and more and more. Like the sky and stars the night before. This dark, Hayden sensed, was never ending. Hayden felt safe and small in this knowledge.

The headlight hardly touched the dark, like a single drop of cream in a pot of black coffee. But still, Hayden half wished the remaining headlight would blink off as well and leave them blindly barreling forward. He pressed down on the accelerator with the idea that maybe he could overtake the light and find a pure black. That's where sainthood hid, in the dark. Beside him Jim nodded. Hayden felt Jim must somehow understand. The nod was his approval.

They moved faster and faster, reaching forward to something elusive, something just beyond the headlight's weak beam. They were cresting a hill, doing ninety miles per hour, when something stepped onto the road and into the light. Immediately before them, frozen in midstride, stood a towering, horned brown buck. Its head slightly cocked. Its eyes like puddles of chocolate. Hayden yelled. Jim yelled. The car screeched. The deer did nothing at all. A smack. Metal bending. The car skidded to a stop.

At first Hayden and Jim did not move. Hayden's fingers dug into the steering wheel like roots. Jim's hands were similarly embedded in the dash. Both men were holding their breath. There was a moment of stillness, then a noise. A high-pitched wheezing and scraping, like wood on stone. Jim looked at Hayden.

"Oh God," Hayden said.

Hayden climbed from the car, his insides feeling like a scoop of wet noodles. He stepped to the front of the bent hood and stared at the figure on the shoulder of the road, just outside of the one headlight's beam. The deer, chest heaving, was trying to stand on two broken legs. One of its antlers had been torn off, making its head lopsided. It pushed itself up, but slipped back down, its hooves skidding on the asphalt. It pushed up again, like a baby horse minutes after birth, but full of panic and wheezing the whole time.

"Got to kill it," Jim said.

"Haven't we done enough to it?"

"No choice." Jim held out his pistol to Hayden. "You've got to do it."

"Me?"

"You hurt something so bad that it's kinder to kill it. Now kill it."

"Can't we just let it die?"

The deer fell forward, its jaw hitting the ground.

"Kill it, or I shoot you in the knee."

Hayden turned to Jim. Jim's face was stone. Hayden held out his hand for the gun. It was heavy, much heavier than the prop from *Night Beat*. Its weight was severe.

Hayden gripped the gun and looked at Jim. Jim nodded.

Hayden wanted to do it quickly. He had never seen an animal die, let alone killed one. He aimed at the deer's head and fired. The shot shattered the one antler. The deer stopped trying to stand and stared at Hayden, its eyes egg-size and dark. Hayden aimed lower and squeezed the trigger. This shot went through a cheek and threw back the deer's head. Hayden lowered the gun and sighed. The deer twitched. Hayden raised the gun and fired three fast shots into its body. It stopped moving.

"Makes your hand tingle," he said.

Jim nodded and took the pistol back.

Past Jesus Pick

PEARL-SWINE WAS ROCKING. Tearing their way through a second encore at the Celibate-tion Rally in Boston. Pick had cowritten a song for the night:

Your body is a masterpiece, God crafted every part.
But just like a museum—don't touch that work of art!
Let's wait!

The song slammed into Pick's solo. He was scurrying up and down the neck of his guitar while watching a teenage girl dancing in the front row. She was wearing a tight shirt that read WON'T DO A THING—UNTIL I WEAR A RING. The faster he played, the faster she danced. Her eyes were closed, her body moving like one of those inflatable wiggle-men outside of used car lots. Pick smiled and let his fingers find new notes, new highs.

Crack. Like someone snapped the sky in two. From somewhere a trumpet blared. For a moment Pick thought the keyboardist had accidentally hit a bad chord, but in an instant the crowd was gone, his guitar was gone, the band was gone, and all was light. It was bright enough to blind him, surely, but his eyes didn't hurt. Overwhelming, but he was not overwhelmed. Why weren't his eyes closing? Why was the air so warm? His body floated . . . like that day in Salt Lake City during the Stormin' the Mormons tour. He had soaked for an hour in Salt Lake. Warm, floating, sun pouring down. This was like that, but the light came from not just above, but from everywhere. He was floating in the light.

"I'm going home," Pick thought, and a lump of happiness the size of a small dog squeezed up from his chest and into his throat. "Jesus is taking me home."

His second thought as he floated was, "I do not deserve this." He knew this was an appropriate thought. He had voiced it many times. But never had he felt it more sincerely than that moment. The light was pure gift.

He could feel motion. Was this really his body? Were those his feet? He had read several books describing the Rapture. Most said, yes, you and your body are taken. But some said it was more a "spiritual" journey and your body is left like the shell of a fruit or something. But look, his feet, his thighs, his . . . *Oh, God, I'm naked*, he thought. *Oh, God, I just took God's name in vain. Oh no.* But then he breathed in, breathed in the light. It was more beautiful for his sin. *God's grace and glory is magnified by my depravity. Yes. I should have sinned more! God be praised! Praise his name.* And in the light Pick broke into his backing vocals for Pearl-Swine's finest praise song, "God of My Life and God of my Heart."

God . . . life . . . God . . . heart! Oh, oh, oh.

He could see nothing but the white-gold glow of it all, but he could hear voices.

Then the light cleared like a morning fog and he was there. Heaven.

It was beautiful. A sky more blue than the purest blue, stone arches and towers scattered along the rolling green hills, white-peaked mountains in the far distance spotted with navy-blue lakes. It was just like he had imagined only better, brighter, richer.

People were everywhere. All of them naked. But no one cared. No shame, like the first days in Eden.

Children chased rabbits, an old woman picked flowers, a young woman danced in the grass. It was the girl from the concert! Her shirt was gone, but he recognized her. She had long blond hair and tawny skin that . . . *Oh, goodness*, Pick thought, *not even five minutes and I'm lusting.* He quickly looked back to the old woman bending over a flower bed. *That's better.*

The lust surprised Pick. He had thought that when he finally made it to heaven he'd be leaving his sin nature behind. *Wasn't that what Paul said? Aren't I supposed to be perfect now? I'm not even close. I can feel sin all over. And I'm naked.*

Not too far away Pick could see people donning white robes. *Wonderful.* They were being handed out. *But does everyone get one? Maybe just the really good folks. Oh, I hope I get a robe. Wait. That's so selfish. Surely the selfish don't get a robe. So I don't want one. I want the others to have them. But am I just saying that so I can get one? Oh, God, help.*

Someone handed him a robe. "Here, brother."

Pick took a deep breath and slipped on the robe. *Stop being such a judge, Pick.* The robe was light, soft. Flowing against his naked body. *Don't think like that. Come on.*

Now people were moving. Pick followed. So many faces, but he saw no one he recognized. Yet he *knew* them all. They were family. People were gathering around a stone platform. Pick had to squeeze by some people and push up on his toes to see what everyone was staring at. There, sitting in an oversize throne, was a small, dark-skinned man with a knotted beard and long scruffy hair.

"Jesus!" a little girl near the front yelled.

"Jesus?" Pick said. Pick studied the man. He seemed shorter, darker than Pick had expected. The man's robe was too tight around the shoulders. He kept tugging at it.

"It is Jesus!"

"Praise you, Jesus. Praise your holy name."

Nearby a group broke into "Amazing Grace" but sung to the tune of the Eagles' "Peaceful Easy Feeling." Pick joined in. He'd always loved that version. He opened his palms to the sky, toward heaven . . . but wait . . . he redirected his open palms to the man on the throne. Others were doing the same. All singing, swaying. Some people were singing different melodies, or even the wrong words, but that was okay. Family.

Pick didn't even mind too much when after the last chorus of "Amazing Grace" a group of young men burst into "Love Tree" by the Christian ska band Praiseville. Praiseville had recently knocked Pearl-Swine from the #1 slot on the Christian Top 40.

First will be last, he reminded himself. *First will be last.*

Before the end of the first verse, Jesus jumped to his feet and raised two thick arms above his head. The singing stopped. The man climbed up on his throne and spoke. His voice was rich and compelling, tinged with anger but full of compassion. Pick could not understand a word. It was a language he'd never heard.

The man pointed to his chest and made wild gestures to the sky.

"Yes, Jesus, you're God. Yes!" someone yelled. Several people fell to their knees. Jesus shook his head violently. He jumped from his throne and tried to pull people to his feet.

"Why is Jesus acting that way?"

"How do we know it's Jesus?"

"The Bible says many would claim to be him."

The man spoke on. He tried to mime something. He bent over and picked up imaginary objects from the ground and placed them in an imaginary basket.

"Is he picking up trash?" someone said.

"He's saying we should clean."

"Shouldn't Jesus be able to speak English?"

The man dropped his arms to his side. He looked tired and small. The little girl who had first called his name stepped up to him and touched his hand. Jesus placed a hand on her head.

"Don't touch him, honey. We don't know who he is."

"Check for holes in his hands!"

"No, it's the wrist . . ."

Jesus opened his arms to the crowd. Again he spoke. Pick still didn't understand a word. Maybe it was his fault he couldn't understand, maybe he didn't have ears to hear? Language was a difficult subject for him.

A tall man with thick brown hair jumped up beside Jesus. It was Richard Van Sturgeon. Pearl-Swine had played more than one event where he was the speaker and Pick had read at least two of his books.

Van Sturgeon gave the crowd a warm smile. "Ah yes, friends. Hear the words of the Lord. He is welcoming us to his kingdom."

Jesus said a few more words.

"I believe he says he is so happy to see his holy bride finally in the wedding chamber."

Jesus lifted his shoulders and said something directly to Van Sturgeon.

"Oh, he says, he says, welcome to your reward, good and faithful servants."

The crowd cooed. Van Sturgeon let his voice rise and fall like a sheet in the wind. He moved across the platform, every so often raising his palms toward Jesus as if he were hot. Jesus looked at him without smiling and stepped back.

"I believe he is also saying some of us still have the residue of sin. Yes, yes. Some of us are still unclean. Yes, people. We have carried the filth of the world into heaven like a child tracking mud onto a mother's carpet. Yes. Now tell me, and tell Jesus, who here is saved?"

Hands popped up everywhere. Pick put his up, too.

"But yet we have sin."

Jesus was sitting on the footstep of his throne and watching the crowd with a furrowed brow.

"As a little boy back in Arkansas I'd hear my papa order me to take a bath and I'd run to the sink and splash some water on me. Now was I really clean, people? Was I washed? How many of you have only sink-washed in the blood of the Lamb?" Van Sturgeon gestured to Jesus, who tried to say something, but the man continued. "Yes, yes, Jesus. We have fallen short. But tonight we can be made clean. You can come up here right now. Right now! And be made clean!"

First just one or two stepped forward, then a few more. Soon people poured onto the stone platform. Soon Jesus was lost in the crowd.

Pick turned and walked away from the crowd. He felt dizzy and almost panicked. A strange vibration rumbled between his lungs.

He could pass on the altar call, he knew. He had washed in the blood of the Lamb about as much as one possibly could without drowning. Saved at the age of sixteen, again at age nineteen, baptized by water at age twenty-two, baptized by the Holy Spirit at age twenty-three, seminary classes the same year (though he never got a degree). He gave a quarter of all his earnings to charity and the church. He visited children's hospitals. He had long gospel-sharing conversations with strangers and homeless people. He had never had full intercourse with a woman except for one slip (literally a slip). He had walked the walk. So why did he feel so out of place?

He walked over a hill and through a garden of roses. Soon the roar of the crowd was only a distant hum. A small river ran through some green hills. He followed it upstream, watching the water slide over rocks. A few others were wandering about, but the majority of people were still listening to the man beside Jesus. Pick came up to a boulder on the banks of the stream. He climbed up on to it and watched the water skim by.

Best just to be. Look how pretty it all is. Look at the colors. Things will be okay.

His mother was here somewhere. And his grandfather. And the band, they must be around. Plenty of time to find them. Milton and Roy wouldn't be here. That's sad. He wished they could get in. Roy was a great singer. Dave was a fine replacement, and a really solid believer, but Roy was more fun to watch. He'd jump three feet straight up while rocking out. Pick had made the joke that it was Rapture practice. Those were good days. He wished he could see them, but Lazarus couldn't go from Abraham's bosom to the abyss. That seemed so harsh. But who's the pot and who's the potter? What was it his professor had said? "The question is not, Why doesn't God save everyone from hell? The question is, Why does he save anyone?" Of course, that professor was a Calvinist. And Pick was an Evangelical. Emergent, even. But knowing Milton and Roy and his dad and that old Arab lady who ran the 7-Eleven and his first girlfriend and his sister were all either suffering in hell or in the seven harsh years of earthly tribulation did dampen the beauty of the clear stream and blue sky.

Jesus would explain everything. Maybe Pick would have to learn Aramaic. It had been language studies that had driven him from seminary, that and Pearl-Swine's tour schedule. But now there was time. Jesus would explain. It'd be like coming across a C.S. Lewis quote that perfectly answered some nagging question. It would be just like that.

The water rippled with light. It really was very peaceful here.

From the direction of the throne, Pick could hear yelling. Must be more action. But things would settle. Things always settled. Pick pulled his legs toward him and studied the blue-blue sky. It was so clear. Like the finest morning. But no sun. Soft music was playing. Pick hadn't noticed it before, but now he realized it had been playing since he had arrived. Melodic strings.

Pick heard fast steps coming toward him. He turned around to see the stout figure of Jesus running over the hill at full speed. Jesus jumped behind the boulder Pick was sitting on. Jesus looked up at Pick with serious eyes, shaking his head several times. Pick heard more steps, many more. He turned again to see a crowd of a dozen or so appear over the hill.

"Hey, you," one of them yelled to Pick. "Have you seen Jesus?"

Pick could hear the heavy breathing of Jesus crouching behind him. "Yeah," Pick said.

"Where?"

Picked pointed toward a distant wood of apple blossoms. "He went that way."

"Thanks," the man said. "Let's get him." The crowd ran off over another hill.

When they were gone, Pick leaned over. "The coast is clear," he whispered.

Jesus peeked over the boulder and stood. He smiled and patted Pick's back. That was the finest moment of Pick's life.

Jesus pulled at his robe and started walking in the opposite direction of the pursuing crowd. For a moment Pick just watched. Then he quickly followed, keeping a good fifteen feet behind. Jesus glanced back once and smiled. Pick smiled back. Jesus walked with a strong, fluid stride. His legs were a good deal shorter than Pick's, but he moved with speed.

After an hour or so of rolling hills, the land smoothed into a large field of waist-high yellow flowers. Jesus stepped through, letting his palms brush the top petals. Pick did the same. Past the field was a grove of aspens. Jesus reached out and placed his hands against the trees as he walked. Again, Pick followed his example. The bark was smooth and cool.

They had been walking for several hours but the sky had not changed its hue.

Nor was there any breeze. The branches didn't sway; the leaves didn't rustle. Pick found the stillness eerie.

Pick hoped Jesus would take a break, but he kept walking, stopping only to pick something out of his sandals. Pick was barefoot, but the ground was soft and the temperature mild. Occasionally Jesus whistled. Besides that, everything was quiet.

At the far end of the aspen grove, near a rock cliff, Jesus turned to his right. He picked some berries from a bush growing from the cliff. He ate a few and offered a handful to Pick. They were bitter, but Pick's hunger helped him chew past that. Jesus dropped to his knees and Pick thought he was going to pray, but instead he crawled forward, past a curtain of moss and into a small opening in the stone face of the cliff.

Pick scrambled after him. It was a tight squeeze. Just enough room to crawl. It was dark in the cave. He could see nothing ahead of him, but he could hear Jesus whistling. After a bit of time, he could make out an opening.

Pick emerged into a well-lit hallway running perpendicular to the hole. No grass, no trees, no sky. Just fluorescent lights and hospital-white tiles that seemed to stretch in either direction for miles and miles. It was cold enough for Pick to see his breath. Jesus was already walking down the hall and Pick hurried after him, his bare soles slapping against the floor. Chilled gusts of air cut through his thin robe.

Up ahead Jesus had stopped and was facing the outer wall of the hallway. Wind was blowing his hair back and flakes of white were flurrying around him and sticking to his beard.

"Jesus?" Pick yelled.

Jesus stepped forward and out of sight. Pick sprinted and found an open door. Outside snow and wind whipped through the dusk half-light. Jesus walked into the wind.

"Jesus!" Pick yelled and stepped outside—the outside of an outside. Pick was dizzy and disorientated. The snow felt like broken glass to his feet, but Pick walked on after Jesus. He stepped on something metal and bent to pick it up. It was a crushed aluminum can. The label read MOLSON ICE CANADA'S FINEST.

Pick knew this feeling. Standing on the edge of a canyon, the fall a step away, toes over the lip, the world swaying with horrible possibility. He looked to his left. Stretching out into the distance stood a dozen or more huge gray domes, each larger than any building he had ever seen. Like the Superdome but expanded three times. He looked to his right and saw even more domes. He turned all the way around to see the massive dome he had stepped from. Pick's blood was ice, his heart seizing up like a broken blender.

"Wait, Jesus!" he yelled, and ran a few steps toward him. Past Jesus, Pick could see faint headlights on a distant highway. "Jesus!"

Jesus stopped and turned. With slow steps he walked back to Pick.

"Thank you, thank you," Pick whispered.

Jesus stood before him, spit already freezing into icicles on his mustache and beard. He placed a warm hand on Pick's shivering arm.

"Please," Pick said, "let's go back in. This isn't real. Go back in and I'll follow you."

Jesus smiled and looked down at Pick's shoeless feet. Jesus shook his head and said something quiet and sad.

Pick shook his head, he didn't understand, he couldn't understand.

Jesus looked smaller in the outer world, almost frail, the wind whipping his robe like a broken kite. Pick had the strange thought that he could knock Jesus down if he wanted to. Jesus knelt down before Pick, and now Pick's confusion was complete. Every knee shall bow . . . every knee but his. Never his. Jesus touched Pick's bare feet. He then removed his own sandals and placed them, one by one, on Pick's numb feet. He stood straight and smiled. Pick said nothing. The sandals were too small for his feet. Jesus again began walking to the far lights of the road.

Pick found his voice. "Wait. The ice . . . this is crazy. You can't leave your kingdom." Pick glanced back at the open door behind him and again to Jesus. He watched as the figure blended into the skyline. He could still catch up. He could still follow. He took a step. A gust of frozen air pushed past and stung his eyes. He squinted. It was almost dark now. Jesus was less than a shadow. He could only see the headlights slowly moving miles away. Pick filled his lungs with the cold air.

"Wait," he said softly.

Pick turned and walked back to the door of the dome. He stepped through, immediately thankful for the warmth. Using both arms, Pick pushed the door closed. Even the sound of the wind was gone.

2
DAYS

Kindness

VOLUMES COULD BE filled on the Floaters. References to them are found throughout human history. The Muses from Greek mythology. The angels who visited Sodom before its destruction. Mayan gods, shadow people, forest fairies, aliens, demons, and sprites. All simply Floaters keeping tabs on the sick souls of Earth.

Mainly, the Floaters watched. They watched souls from every race in the universe swimming within human identities.

Symptoms of an insane soul: jealousy, belief in privilege, uncompromising ideals.

Evidence of a sane soul: kindness.

Most of the souls were considered lost causes. Every once in a while there was a cure, and it kept hope going. But overall Earth was seen as an asylum of inmates more than a hospital of patients. It hadn't always been that way.

Life was just wiggling awake on Earth when the Floaters chose it as their prime facility. One by one, they transported the sick souls of the galaxies to the small planet. At first the Floaters developed mitochondria as holding cells for the souls. It relaxed the souls. Being one-celled was very calming. But there was no hope for cures. Mitochondria had few opportunities to be kind.

So Floaters transported the souls from the mitochondria to the more complicated eukaryotes, but the extra cells didn't help. They thought that perhaps sexual reproduction would help the cause and there was great hope in the development of dinoflagellates—but souls squirmed and mated with little progress.

So it continued for millions of years. Floaters tried something a little larger, a little more complicated, a little more brain, some feet. But each try wasn't quite right. Eventually Floaters created dinosaurs to hold the souls. It was fun to watch, but not much of an improvement. So they once again removed the souls and abandoned the species to their own evolutionary path. In this way, Floaters played an indispensable role in the early development of the planet's biological systems. It could be said their intelligence helped design much of what we know of life on Earth.

The problem with all these bodies, from mitochondria to mammoths, was contentment. Once the souls were placed in trilobites, raccoons, or narwhals, they were happy to be just where they were. They were still insane, but they had no desire to heal. An injured bird will never flap its wings without an opportunity to fly.

What the Floaters needed was not so much a locked cell as a tether. Giving the souls a better view but not enough mobility to wander and cause damage. A short leash so the soul could glimpse freedom and hopefully desire a cure.

So the Floaters developed a body and mind from which a soul can taste, but not quite touch, the marvels of all that is. Thus was born humanity. A frustrated breed by design. Souls that sample the sky but cannot freely fly.

At first it seemed a perfect solution. The tension of these hobbled beings led them to create and craft. Some souls made music. Others made pictures. Cave drawings and myths about the stars. The Floaters were fascinated.

There were early signs of kindness as well. Mother to child. Brother to brother. Though the Floaters understood that this was only necessary kindness, one that served the giver and the receiver, one reserved for a soul's immediate circle. It was little more than an extension of self-love and self-protection. A good beginning, but that kindness needed to mature.

Instead that seedling kindness became the very excuse for every shade of horror and violence. In the name of family, tribe, and culture, the souls crafted weapons and hunted down other families, tribes, and cultures. So human history is a record of patients ganging up on other patients, enslaving some, murdering others, all fighting and slaughtering for an extra inch of the madhouse.

Every tool of healing the Floaters provided, every health-inspiring aspect of the planet they had chosen, was twisted by the souls to create more madness. Souls saw the beauty of trees and uses of wood, then destroyed miles of forest. They discovered art, and made advertisements. They were given lovemaking and almost immediately invented rape. They named God, then declared God as vengeful and full of wrath.

The Floaters floated about the world whispering the secrets of the universe to the humans. Hardly a soul listened. Instead the sad mad creatures babbled about the price of grain, who owns what, which sports team will win which game, and what's on television.

There were some success stories. Some salvation. Mostly people no one has heard of. Some were wise, some were half-wits, some were religious hermits, some atheistic capitalists. They were souls who had grown through several lifetimes to be kind and were allowed to rejoin the greater universe. Some successes, but not nearly enough to justify an entire planet. In the history of Earth there have been a total of 807 cures.

Dick-mobile

"THAT'S IT FOR the Lexus," Hayden said, examining the crumpled hood and green puddle forming under the front bumper. Dawn was edging away the dark. Flies were gathering around the deer carcass.

"The car is fine," Jim said from beside the deer. "Just needs some tinkering. I'll get my tools." He hobbled over to the car, his bowlegs popping.

"Jim, the car is dead. I'll call a tow truck."

"Bastards, every one of them. I'll fix your dick-mobile."

"Jim, if you can fix this, it's yours."

"No shit?"

"No shit."

Jim Edwards opened his black trash bag and pulled out a dented red toolbox. He used a hammer to pry open the hood and peered in.

"You know, Hay, you're soft," he said with his head buried in the mangled innards of the engine.

Hayden crossed his arms over his chest. "I'm soft?"

"Yep. All soft. You haven't done anything with your life."

"I've won two Emmys."

"Not a thing." Jim bent down to the toolbox, grabbed some chicken wire and a pair of pliers, and returned to the engine. "You want to be a saint, huh? You should try being a man."

"Now you're just being rude."

"Yeah, I am. Go ahead and turn the key," Jim said.

Hayden dropped into the driver's seat and, leaving the door open, turned the ignition. The engine turned over but immediately died.

"Okay, hold it." Jim stared at the engine and rubbed the back of his neck.

"Now, Hay, I'm not a religious man, but I'd say killing that deer was the most holy thing you've done."

"How's that?" Hayden leaned out of the car.

"Because," Jim said, burying his head under the hood. "You didn't want to do it, didn't get any kind of reward, and you weren't even sure it was the right thing to do. But it was kind. As close as I can tell, that's holy."

"You did threaten to shoot me in the knee."

"Ah, I was just giving you a friendly push. Try it now."

Hayden turned the key and the engine hummed to life. Jim slammed the hood down.

"Fixed. You owe me one fancy, deer-stained dick-mobile."

The edges of the world exploded

CLICK NUZZLED INTO Suga Seal. The point of light shone down on them again. The puffs, now adopted by the couple as children, cuddled near. This was all he knew. Any other life was forgotten. Seal, sweet smells, loving puffs. Click was home, happy. He would live and die here with love and family. This was the world. But the world ended.

The world's very foundations shook, the sky ripped open, and a cruel white light shot through the puffs.

"Pass me a bowl." A growling sound thundered from past the world. Click dug his claws into Suga Seal as the world twisted and every piece of matter tumbled toward the sky. For a brief second Click watched the puffs, their children, fly to what had been up, then he and Seal were falling up as well. Click looked to Seal. Her face was calm. Click, gaining courage from her strength, held her tighter. They fell from the world into the light and space, horrible space. Splash! Into a white, wet swamp. Puffs drowning all around them. With his free claw, Click tried to gather the puffs to him. From above him maddening screams scorched the air. "Holy crap. A crab!" He tried to look up but the unimaginable colors—so different than the black, white, gray, and wheat brown of the world before—were moving. And in the unbelievably high sky above them four blades spun in a slow circle. The swamp was moving, bouncing, and the screaming continued. He peeked over the edge of the swamp and saw the boundaries of the world approaching. *Errrk.* And the boundary swung open! Had it not been for Suga Seal beside him, Click would have fainted. The swamp moved past the boundary and the edges of the world exploded outward once again. Above him was no sky, only forever blue. And a fierce light-point that looked like all the world, and hundreds more, burning.

Click chattered. He still had his claw latched onto the Seal's flipper. He could now see even her stoic face betraying hints of fear. Why hadn't he protected her? Why hadn't he kept the world small, seeable, believable? A force hurtled them from the white swamp and into the space. Click snapped both claws into Seal as they rolled with white and puffs in the open air. He locked her eyes in a fierce stare. Everything, everything was unknown except for her. Click and Seal. A world of two even if all worlds end. Splash! Wet, brown, earthy water. Click and Seal sunk down. Something in Click knew this wet brown, knew it to be sanctuary. He tried to tell Suga Seal as much as they sank down. But Seal slowed her sink and began pulling up. Click tried to crawl up with her, but the pull down was too great. There was a moment of floating balance, Click pulling down, Seal pulling up, the two bobbing in one place. It did not last. The two lovers were being pulled in opposite directions by forces they didn't understand. Was he leaving her or was she leaving him? One of Click's claws slipped from Seal's flipper. Her free flipper reached up, pointing to the place she must go. Click knew she was right. Knew she had to move on. But how could he let go? She was always the stronger one. With a tiny crab nod he opened his other claw's hold. Click sunk down. Suga Seal floated up. Click watched her, keeping his eyes on her sweet face for as long as possible. She slowly left his view, her body blending into the brown, her white eyes disappearing behind the murk, soon it was just her silhouette against the rippling surface, and then she was gone completely.

Click landed in the soft muck. He wished with all his heart that the mud would swallow him whole.

My wife wouldn't kill a roach

THE THREE HAD listened to "Who's Gonna Park the Car" fourteen times before clicking the radio off and driving in silence. Milton sat on the mattress, his legs crossed, his back against the driver's side of the bus. Roy bent over his wheel, wordless and worried.

The one gas station they had passed was in flames and surrounded by fire trucks.

"At least the firefighters are still on duty," Roy had said. "The system hasn't broken down yet."

"It won't take long," Milton said.

"We're going to need gas at some point."

The VW rumbled out of the hills and into the flat of the West Texas desert. A new sun crested to the east, casting a stubby shadow on the road before them.

"There's nothing out here," Roy said. "We're almost dry."

Miles later, Rica spotted a grungy sign reading GAS standing alone in the barren landscape.

"Oh thank God!" Roy exhaled. He steered the bus off the exit. He turned into a small gas station and came to a rattling stop in front of a pump. "We were running on less than fumes."

"Is this place even open?" Rica asked.

"I'll open them myself if I have to." Roy climbed from the bus and headed to the station.

Rica slid open the back door and stepped out. The morning air was cool and dry. She stretched and looked back at Milton, his eyes open but his expression blank. "Milton," she said. "Do you want anything?" He didn't answer.

She slid the door closed behind her and moved to the pump. A large padlock kept a steel rope looped around the handle.

Roy walked out of the store, fast steps, nearly running. "Let's go."

"The pump's locked."

"Forget it. We need to go. Now. Please."

"But we're out of gas. There's nothing for miles," Rica said. "Roy, are you okay? What happened."

"Fine! Fine—"

A yell rang out from behind the gas station. Rica swung her head around. Coming from the side of the station was a middle-aged man in mechanic's overalls carrying a shotgun. "Get the hell away from my gas!"

"We'll pay, sir, we only—" Roy started to say.

"Only the damned are left. Only the damned," the man yelled.

"Sir," Rica said, stepping forward with her palms facing out.

"Goddamn!" He stumbled and leaned against the side of the building.

"Sir," Rica said again. "It's going to be okay. We can help—"

He fired. Rica screamed. From the corner of her eye, she saw Roy's head whip back, saw him fall against the VW.

"Roy!" Rica screamed. Roy had his palm pushed against the side of his face. His back to the VW, Roy slid down to the asphalt. A second shot exploded, hitting the ground between Rica and Roy and sending up a cloud of dirt.

On instinct, Rica ran. She sprinted toward the station office and pushed against the glass door. The door swung open and Rica fell forward. She pushed her arms out, doing her best to break her fall before her belly absorbed her weight. She hit hard. Immediately the muscles in her stomach clenched.

Catching her breath, Rica rolled onto her back. There was blood everywhere, on the ground, on her arms, her hands. "Oh God, oh God." Rica examined herself, checking her belly and underwear. Dry. She searched for a wound, but found nothing. Blood was covering the floor. But it was not her blood. She pushed her back against the counter and looked out the dusty glass door. The man was walking to the VW bus, reloading his shotgun. Roy was still on the ground, pushing himself back behind the bus.

"My wife wouldn't kill a roach," the man was yelling outside. "She'd catch 'em and let 'em go. Shit, even Billy Graham killed roaches."

Somewhere a television reporter was announcing and reannouncing the news, a monotone loop of white noise.

Rica crawled behind the counter hunting for a phone. She threw a hand over her mouth to muffle her scream. A woman's body lay on the floor, a red, wet, coaster-size hole in her head and a handgun two feet away.

Grab the gun. Just grab it. Rica reached and wrapped her palm around the pistol's handle. She crawled back to the door, the blood soaking into her pants and shirt. She again pressed her back to the counter and stared out the door. At first she could see no one, then she saw the man and his shotgun near the rear of the bus.

She made a plan. She'd yell, "Freeze!" If he didn't freeze, she'd aim for his leg.

She rose to her feet. Deep breath. Deep breath. Jump. She pushed herself out the door.

"Freeze!"

The man did not freeze. He swung the shotgun towards her and fired. Rica could hear glass shatter behind her. She fired the pistol at him—*fuck the leg, anywhere.* She missed him completely. The man was taking aim. She fired and missed again.

Then for a moment, hardly a moment, she was glad she had missed. Compassion, like a quick smell. Rica was still clutching her gun. There was no time for the feeling to form a thought or give orders to her muscles. Just an instant of forgiveness. Then a gun blast. The man fell sideways. Rica looked at her gun. Had she fired again? Roy walked out from behind the VW aiming a black pistol at the man's body, his other hand still pressed against the bloody left side of his face.

"Roy?" She ran to him. "You're bleeding."

"No shit. Is he dead?"

Rica turned and looked at the man's unmoving body. A chunk of his head was missing, like a bite from a plum. "Dead," she said.

"I shot him in the head. Why'd I shoot him in the head?"

"Roy, we need to get you to a doctor."

"Is Milton okay?"

The side of the VW was splattered with pea-size holes. Rica ran toward the door and pulled it open. It was empty.

"Milton!" she screamed.

"I'm here," Milton, his hair peppered with gray, stepped from behind the building. "Let's fill the tank and go."

Cruel beliefs

FROM INSIDE THE VW, Milton heard Rica's and Roy's panicked voices just moments before a spray of pellets ripped through the metal. But the spray froze in mid-flight before Milton's face. He lurched forward and pulled the door open. A man aimed a shotgun directly at him. But no one was moving. Nothing was moving. It was as if the world were on pause. Roy's body hovered mid-fling toward the backside of the bus. Pellets had cut into his face and neck, but the blood had yet to flow.

"Oh, Jesus," Milton muttered.

Rica's face was solidified scream.

"She's pretty," his father said, standing beside the man frozen with the shotgun. The Non-Man stood farther back. "Prettier than your mother, even. A little thin in the hips, perhaps."

Milton circled her. He wanted to hold her and carry her and the baby away. The Non-Man walked from behind the bus.

"What the fuck are you doing?" Milton said, stepping toward him. The Non-Man twitched backward.

"Milton," his father barked. "Show some restraint. The Floaters aren't doing anything we didn't ask for, nothing we didn't work to believe. That includes you, Milton! You believed in all this."

"You're blaming me?"

"People expect Raptures, they get it," his father said. "People await a wrathful god, they'll get one. Nirvana, Jahannam, hell, Judgment, Apocalypse. Their faith is coming to be. Every faith. Maybe it's people's best chance at a cure."

Milton cradled Rica's distorted frightened face. "It's just . . . cruel."

"Cruel beliefs lead to cruel actions," his father said. "People should be responsible for the beliefs they hold."

"This is fucking madness!"

"Look, Milton." His father cleared his throat. "She won't die here. Him either." He flicked his chin toward Roy. "You'll all drive away in a few minutes."

Milton looked up at his father. "But then the fucking world ends."

His father nodded.

"Can I stop it?"

"No."

He pushed past his father to the Floater. "There must be something you can do. Nudge the planet or build a force field. Something to protect us!"

The Non-Man stared at Milton, his eyes calm and curious.

"They wouldn't even if they could," his father said. "This is how it is."

Milton swung back to his father. "In *this* universe, right?" He spit out the words. "There's a billion Earths that won't end in two days!"

His father smiled. "So you were listening. Good boy."

"Jesus, Dad!" Milton flung his hands in the air, tracers of color following his movements. "Can I warn them? Can I tell people?"

"Yes," his father said. "But they won't hear you."

"Then why the fuck are you telling me all this? Why are there television actors in my shower and turtles talking to me?"

A warm hand touched Milton's shoulder. The Non-Man's hand rested there. Milton recognized something like compassion on his long face.

"Follow me," his father said, and began walking around the corner of the building.

Milton hesitated, staring at Rica.

"She'll be fine, Milton. He'll keep an eye on them," his father said, nodding to the Non-Man.

Milton followed his father. Fifty feet behind the building, up a slight incline, stood a double-wide trailer. His father moved toward it.

"You know what really fascinates those Floaters? Really just blows their world-hopping minds? Us. Humans. Something about our madness they abhor and love. Do you know that of all the creatures in the entire universe, we are the only ones willing to believe what we know to be untrue?"

"Lies?"

"Stories." His father pulled open the trailer door and stepped inside. Milton followed. It was homey, with thick carpet and large armchairs. Unmoving black smoke hung above a pan on the stove. His father moved the pan from the stove to the sink. "We scream at a monster on the screen. We cry for characters in a book. We allow ourselves to believe what we understand to be not real. It's unique to us. Maybe a consequence of our confinement." With his eyes, his father motioned back to the door. "Some of them want what we have."

"Madness?"

"Stories. Faiths. Suspension of disbelief. All of it. I know, I know. Why? But there you are," his father laughed. "That fella out there. You wouldn't believe this, but that blue fella who has been to all places, been to all times. He's jealous of you. Jealous of your mad, crippled soul. It just cracks me up." His father tapped his foot on the carpeted floor. "You're out of gas. You'll be needing this."

Milton looked down to see a small padlock key by his father's foot.

Jesus-18

JESUS-18 STUMBLED FROM the dome's glow—larger than the temple, larger than Jerusalem itself. The cold bit into his now bare feet. He winced and prayed with each step. The landscape had boulders and dead grass and iced-over snow clumps. The clouds were thick, but Jesus-18 could tell that the sun was low. An hour, maybe less, and it would be night.

He liked night. From the fishermen he had learned to walk at night. They woke hours before the sun's rising. They knew night. God gave us half-light and half-dark. We should know the dark. He hides in darkness. Then, like the sunrise, he is there. And it is nothing like you had remembered or had thought or had described.

Falling every few steps, Jesus-18 trekked on. He reached the road. It was like no road he had ever seen. One long flat stone. Only Rome would build such a road. A cloud of fog rolled onto the road and even more of the world was gone from his sight. Jesus-18 was not anxious. He hardly ever was. He had realized at an early age that not knowing was part of the call. Like Father Abraham who had no law, no book. Only a voice. And that voice said walk.

Jesus-18 walked in the empty road. It was easier than the sharp earth. The sky was darker now. Wind gusts from different directions whipped around his body. He felt the wind was trying to tie him in knots, like the questions of the scribes coming from here and there, with no desire but to confuse and convict. Others had honest questions. They'd sit close and whisper, "Tell us of the King." What could he do? He told stories. God is Father. God is Farmer. God is Mother Bird. Only stories could come close to describing God. And even the stories fell short.

Sometimes he tried to tell more than he knew. Tried to describe what he didn't understand by telling stories they could not understand.

Behind Jesus-18 came a loud rumble. He turned and saw a long beast sprinting down the road. Blazing eyes and a roaring moan. Was it an angel or a demon? Jesus fell to the wet road. The creature shrieked and stopped before him. It was larger than any beast, larger than a house. He could hear its rattling breaths, could smell its smoky stench. Jesus pulled himself to his feet and stared into the demon's white, fiery eyes.

"Leave here, demon. In my Father's name, leave!"

The demon's ears shot out from the side of its head. It was listening.

"Leave here!"

From the demon's head appeared two figures like men. They approached Jesus-18. They were tall, large. They spoke and smiled. Jesus-18 did not know what to do. The two manlike creatures lifted Jesus-18 and carried him into the demon's head. *What are you up to now, Father?* thought Jesus-18.

Poverty sucks as much as wealth

JIM EDWARDS WAS racing his new Lexus through the desert roads of the Davis Mountains. Hayden was riding passenger. It was not his car. Both were incredibly pleased.

"Beautiful day," Jim said, squinting his eyes at the sky.

"Beautiful," Hayden said, watching the blur of orange cliffs out the passenger-side window. He only turned forward when Jim slowed behind a small beaten-up red pickup truck loaded down with boxes of groceries.

"Must be a nice life out there in L.A. Sun and women all day," Jim said.

"Maybe," Hayden said. "I never felt it. Never felt really good. I had plenty of sun, plenty of women, plenty of all the stuff I wanted. It was great in that way, but I'm happier now. I think in L.A. I was too happy to be truly happy."

"Hayden," Jim said, drumming his fingers on the steering wheel. "You are a red, white, and blue pussy." On the incline the pickup slowed to nearly fifteen miles per hour. Jim honked. "And just so you know, poverty sucks as much as wealth. Maybe more. You're just enjoying something new."

"You're wrong, Jim. I'm free now." Hayden could just make out the head of the truck's driver. It made Hayden cringe. A huge bald spot in the center of an otherwise full head of hair. A personal nightmare of Hayden's.

"You're not even free, Hay. You'll go back. You'll tell yourself, 'How could I not go back?' That's how free you are." Jim laid on the horn again. "Damn this guy is slow."

"No fear of that," Hayden said. "Nothing to go back to." An arm in a loose brown sleeve came out of the pickup's driver window and signaled a left turn. Something in the weight of the sleeve was familiar to Hayden.

"What? The fake leg thing? Come on. You'll get an L.A. lawyer to get you a week of charity work. Easy." Jim pressed on the gas to pass the pickup on the right.

"I don't want to go back, Jim. No soul there. How can I be a saint with no soul?" As the Lexus accelerated past, Hayden caught a glimpse of the pickup's driver. Young and pale, he wore a heavy brown frock like some throwback to the Middle Ages, but driving a pickup truck through West Texas. Hayden turned in his seat to see the boy steer the pickup from the road onto an unpaved track.

"Jim, monks are Catholic, right?"

"Never met a Baptist one."

"Pull over."

Jim yanked the Lexus onto the shoulder, kicking up a cloud of brown sand.

"I'm getting out here."

"Hey, Hay, I didn't mean to offend you." Jim turned to Hayden. "There's nothing out here."

"There're Catholics." Hayden patted the armadillo and opened the door.

"They'll think I killed you and stole your car."

Hayden nodded. He took a napkin from the dashboard and pen from the glove box. He scribbled a note:

Jim Edwards did not kill me. He earned this car.
He is my friend.
        Hayden Brock.

He handed it to Jim. Jim smiled and tucked the napkin in his front shirt pocket.

"I'm taking my wallet and the leg. The rest is yours." Hayden climbed from the car and lifted the prosthetic leg from the backseat. "Get yourself to Houston and cut that thing off your back."

"There's more than one."

Hayden reached out his hand. Jim took it in his.

"Good-bye, Jim Edwards."

"Pleasure riding with you, Mr. Brock."

Hayden closed the door and watched what was formerly his Lexus speed up a desert hill and out of sight. Then he turned back to the unpaved road and started walking.

I've been gone for years

RICA WAS DRIVING, her clothes sticky with both Roy's and a stranger's blood, her foot pressing hard on the gas pedal. She could feel panic running through her veins like lighter fluid waiting to ignite.

"You've lost blood, Roy," she said. "Stay awake and we'll find a hospital," Rica said.

"I shouldn't have shot him in the head. I shouldn't," Roy mumbled from the mattress in the back. "I lost my pipe."

She and Milton had cleaned most of the blood from Roy's wound, revealing a sprayed pattern of small holes covering the lower right side of his face. Two holes in his neck, like a vampire's bite, bled ceaselessly. Rica had found an old shirt in the VW and ripped it into strips. As best as she could, she wrapped one strip around the wounds on Roy's face and tied another around his neck. The blood quickly soaked through. Milton knelt beside him, holding a dirty towel against Roy's neck.

"I've got metal in my face. I'm swelling up," Roy muttered.

"Fort Stockton will have something. A clinic. A hospital. That's not far," Rica said, trying her best to sound sure. "You'll be fine."

"We can't stop. Not yet," Milton said. "We need to go farther west."

"Milton," Rica yelled. "Roy's been shot in the face."

"I think the one Floater, the one with my father is a renegade. I don't think he's supposed to be helping us. The Floaters *want* us all dead."

"I don't give a fuck, Milton," Rica said, squeezing the steering wheel. "We're going to the nearest hospital!"

"Maybe our madness is spreading. Spreading to the Floaters. And they don't want it getting off the planet."

"Shut up, Milton. Shut up," Rica said.

"It's spreading?" Roy asked. He tried to sit up but winced and fell back.

"Like a good joke!" Milton said. "It gets into the Floaters' heads. Maybe. Maybe. This one . . . this Non-Man, he wants to become like us. Imagine a nurse checking herself into the mental ward. Ha!"

"Milton, I want you to stop this now. Just stop," Rica said through clenched teeth, staring back in the rearview mirror. "There're no Floaters. Roy's been shot. That's it. That's real."

Milton gazed at her through the mirror. "You don't believe me?"

Rica swallowed. Milton looked different. His hair was more gray than brown now and the skin around his eyes was lined with new, deep wrinkles. "Milton," Rica said, her voice softening. "Baby, we've got to find some help."

Milton ran a hand through his hair and strands of gray came loose in his fingers. She watched him hold the clump of hair in front of his face, examining it like an artifact.

"Baby, what's wrong with you?" Rica said, her voice cracking.

"I'm not the best spatter," Milton sighed. "It cost me some time."

"I don't understand . . ."

"I've been gone for years."

"Milton," Roy said, clutching at Milton's shirt. "I'm in a bad place. I'm going to start screaming soon."

"Okay, okay, Roy," Milton said. "I'll scream with you."

Christian Heaven Domes

JESUS-18 WASN'T THE only Jesus making his way through the cold climes of Western Canada. In all, there were twenty-eight Jesuses. One for each Christian Heaven Dome.

The Floaters had always been intrigued by the religious beliefs of the humans. Sometimes the beliefs seemed to offer hope of cures. But more often they led only deeper into insanity. As the end approached a radical plan was green-lit. Satisfy their beliefs. See what happens if everything a person believes comes true.

They began by building a huge Christian Heaven Dome in the wilderness of Western Canada for the Christian population of North America. But a quick examination of the tension between the different Christian sects led them to conclude that they would, in fact, need several Heaven Domes, one for each major denomination.

As the domes were being completed, the Floaters took a blood sample from the Shroud of Turin and, using the DNA, cloned a Jesus of Nazareth for each dome. Next the Floaters orchestrated a Rapture.

The Baptists took to their dome immediately. The wide-open spaces, the basketball courts and baseball fields, the buffet of summer picnic delights. Upon finding Jesus on a golden throne, they circled up and sang hymns of worship. Jesus, who spoke Aramaic, understood none of it, but he did like the melodies, especially the more upbeat ones. He rose to his feet and danced to the singing. The Baptists stopped singing and gave Jesus a stern look.

"No dancing?" Jesus asked in Aramaic. The Baptists continued staring. Jesus sat back down. The Baptists started singing again. Jesus decided this party needed a helping hand. Not far from his throne was a fast-flowing waterfall. With a quick prayer Jesus turned the waterfall into a fountain of rich, aromatic red wine. Everyone pointed and cheered, until one young man used his hands to sample the wine. He spit it out and yelled something. Now they all looked horribly upset. Jesus was confused. He raised his arms in question. The Baptists shook their heads at him. With a shrug Jesus turned the winefall back into water.

Later that night, while the Baptists were asleep, Jesus crept off his throne and out of the dome.

The Catholics, who had never expected a Rapture, were a little freaked out. But they did like heaven. Their dome was filled with candlelight, Gregorian chanting, the thick smell of incense, and the rich colors of stained glass. It was clean and sublime. Unfortunately there was a small, scruffy, Jewish-looking man sitting on what was obviously the Pope's throne. Not that the Pope was complaining. He stood humbly by waiting for the mix-up to be corrected. Soon enough the Catholics removed the scruffy man and placed the pontiff in his rightful place. The scruffy man didn't seem to mind. He scurried around heaven standing on chairs, rambling on in some foreign tongue, and generally making a nuisance of himself. Heaven had to have order, everyone agreed. After a search, a gate was found and the small scruffy man was asked to leave.

The Unitarians removed the throne from their heaven as soon as they arrived. All that was left were green hills, soft light, and the continuous music of Enya. Jesus liked these people. They all seemed very pleasant.

Jesus pointed to his chest. "Yeshua," he said.

"I'm Yeshua, too," said a short woman with a toothy smile.

"So am I," said a large freckled man.

"So are we! So are we!" chanted a group of children.

Jesus felt dizzy.

In another Heaven Dome the residents tried to lynch Jesus for his dark skin. Another refused to let him leave the throne, even to use the lavatory. Many of the domes were filled with questions.

"Are you one with the Father and the Holy Spirit? Or an individual in a relationship?"

"Why is my neighbor Phil here? He's a bastard."

"What about gays in the military?"

One by one all the Jesuses were either kicked out of or willingly abandoned their Heaven Dome. So during the last days of Earth, twenty-eight Jesuses went wandering across the expanse of North America.

The perfect reward for enlightenment

THE CONCEPT OF a Rapture is unique to a certain section of the Protestant world, but the Floaters found it so effective at giving at least a selection of people a taste of their own versions of an afterlife that they built over a thousand domes across the globe. Tian Domes in rural China. Pure Land Domes in East Asia. A Jewish Heaven Dome in the Middle East with a smaller sister dome in southern Florida.

Domes for Hindus were varied. There were the more concrete Vaikuntha Domes: noiseless escalators connecting a series of levels filled with endless comforts and pleasures and finally culminating with a top-level paradise bursting with song and dance like a high-budget Bollywood spectacular. Other domes attempted to create the experience of *moksha*, the escape from *samsara* and the egoless union with Brahma. The closest the Floaters got to this sensation was a very large hot tub and clouds of vaporized lysergic acid diethylamide. A similar approach was taken with constructing Nirvana Domes for practicing Buddhists. It was a fantastic success. LSD and hot tubs turn out to be the perfect reward for enlightenment.

Zen Nirvana Domes were identical except for the addition of snapping turtles to the hot tub waters.

Several varieties of Islamic Jannah Domes were built. Many centered on a mystical stupor similar to the Nirvana Domes; some were not unlike the Christian Heaven Domes but with better food and more stylish furniture. Other Islamic Domes attempted a more literal interpretation of Jannah descriptions. The concept of Houri, or celestial virgins, was a tad tricky. In one particular Jannah Dome the Floaters did indeed provide seventy-four near-perfect virgins for every deserving man and woman. The problem was the virgins weren't virgins for long. Within fourteen hours of the Rapture, there were only three virgins remaining in the entire dome. Two young, disinterested men and one quick-footed eighteen-year-old girl.

Desire

THE MUD WAS cold, but Click didn't care. Brown creek water surrounded him, murky and full of shadows. He did not move. He did not want to move.

Crab memory is a soft palette. Details disappear easily. Faces, places, and events all drift away. Click didn't recall the details of Suga Seal's white whiskers and black nose. He didn't remember the sticky puffs or the white wet or the sinking from the sky. Click could only feel. It was as if he were sharing his shell with something heavy. Far too heavy to move. He sank a little deeper into the mud.

The mud would soon cover him completely. Click wanted this. He wanted to not see the water and the world. He wanted to forget the slight memories he had. He wanted to be a stone.

Far above him, past the brown, Click could see a bright-yellow shimmer. He had been closer to the yellow, to the light. It had been warm. It was far away now. He understood far away. Distant. Far. Far away meant he could not touch it. Far meant something was gone.

He watched the yellow above. Watched the color dance. It hurt. Loss. But something else as well. He hurt because he wanted the yellow. Loss echoed throughout his shell and came back as desire. He missed what was not there, and then he desired what was not there. He hoped for the yellow. The pain of regret came with the new ability to hope. If one can be moved *away* from what one wanted, can't one move *toward* what one wanted?

Click desired. Click hoped. Click wanted to move. He shifted his claws and pulled, but the muck held him. His shell was so very heavy. He pulled up again and moved the slightest bit, but the mud sucked him back down deeper than before. A fog of mud billowed in the water around him. He squirmed and sank even deeper. Nearly all his shell was now buried. The more he struggled, the deeper he sank. Only his eyes and his one purple claw were above the silt now. He didn't move, afraid that any more attempts would bury him in the dark.

In the murky waters, a shadow darted toward him. Click watched as two wide eyes materialized. Two polished pebbles floating in the murk. He remembered her eyes then, remembered how they held him with unblinking love. Click's heart broke with want. He lunged out a claw to the shadow, all his desire pushing from the mud. He snapped onto something. And with a wild plop he was yanked from the muck. Water rushed by. Click's shell was jerked back and forth, but he did not let go. He looked up, but instead of seeing his Suga Seal, he saw his claw clasped onto the lower fin of a silver and black trout. Below him the ground sped by at a dizzying speed. He was moving. Darting toward his deepest desire, whatever that might be.

Hook in his chest

HAYDEN WALKED. THE ground beneath him was hard and cracked. In all Hayden's years in Los Angeles he had not walked more than two hundred yards in one stretch, unless you count StairMasters and jogging machines. But this day he had already covered miles.

The sun was high. He could feel it burning the skin of his nose. Beside him, down a steep incline, a muddy river curved in and out of sight. Far off, cliffs the color of sunsets rose against the sky. Occasionally a breeze tasting of cedar blew past, but for the most part the air was still and hot.

The opening credits of *Saint Rick* show Hayden walking down a long, dusty road. Slightly more paved, but similar to the one he was walking on now. Hayden's acting in the opening montage is superb. His face tells of a man feeling the pain of the miles but resigned to the burden. A man who has made peace with his blisters.

Hayden had not made peace with his blisters. He cursed them. He considered stopping, tearing off his shoes, and crying. But something dragged him on. A slow pull, a hook in his chest. There was no solution in stopping. No one would come get him. His answer was to walk.

His feet grew heavier with each step. He dragged the rattling prosthetic leg behind him, making a shallow trench the width of a woman's thigh. The grit-filled wind stung his cheeks and the white sun baked his scalp. Hayden felt raw and empty. A green-brown river slithered some fifteen feet below him. He wondered if he could reach it, and, more importantly, if he could return from it. He could climb out on the far side, but where would that leave him? And the current might pull him down long before that. Hayden Brock was not a strong swimmer. He kept to the road.

But where would the road lead? So he had seen a monk and decided to follow.

The truck was most likely miles away. And who says he was really a monk? Hayden wasn't really a saint. And even if he was a monk, that didn't mean he was driving to any kind of sanctuary. Maybe it was just a shortcut to another highway.

Falling forward step by step, his eyes stinging with sand and sweat, Hayden grew confused. The ground beneath his blistered feet might not even be a road anymore. With a panic he had no energy to express, Hayden questioned whether he was not simply walking in circles.

He would die out here, that much seemed clear. Perhaps death was cooler than this heat. He imagined himself lying down on the ground and pulling the earth over him like a blanket. Closing his eyes. He laughed at the thought. The laugh coughed its way into a sob. He didn't want to cry, didn't want to waste the little water his body had left. He wiped the tears from his eyes with his sandy sleeve, sending the landscape into a blur.

He sat down and closed his eyes. He missed Jim Edwards. He missed his parents. He missed his agent Ted and Iola the Haitian manservant. He missed water. He would die, his flesh left for some desert breed of ants, his bones bleaching in the desert sun until they were little more than chalky twigs. He would die here.

He opened his eyes and noticed something in the distance. A gathering of low, mud-brown buildings at the bottom of a shallow depression. He could just make out the red pickup glimmering in the sun. Hayden laughed aloud, his tears momentarily staining the parched desert surface.

Stay awake!

"THE FIRST IN starlight, the second in moonlight, the third in full daylight." Brother Brendan was sitting in the reading room trying to stop the letters from floating from the page. This was often a problem when reading. Vowels were especially buoyant. "The first water, the second wine, the third oil." His best chance was to read rapidly and turn the page before any letter could peel itself from the page and flutter away. But Joachim of Fiore asked to be read slowly, asked that each phrase led the reader to prayer and contemplation. If only the letters would float from the page as full paragraphs, or even words, that would make it easier. Instead they jumbled in the air letter by letter, buzzing around the monk's head like a family of gnats.

Yes, yes, but if he let the letters float, if he could learn patience, perhaps they'd return to the page on their own. Perhaps they'd spell new words, new secrets and poems. Ah, but it would be nice to read a page slowly, as the author wrote it.

Of course, Brendan knew these words of Joachim, knew his three stages of history, his poetry describing the era's end. It will happen! This world will end! Yes! As Joachim said! It will end in 1260! Yes!

But no, no. It was false.

Wonderful.

Easier to trust those who are so clearly wrong. Less chance of trusting simply because you believe them to be trustworthy. What's the honor in trusting someone who can be trusted? Trust a liar! Yes! Or a fool! Yes!

Brendan was pressing a particularly persistent *U* to the page when the stranger stumbled into the room. A thirsty stranger, Brendan could see that immediately. He was also carrying an artificial leg. Brendan closed the book and stood.

"Welcome," he said. "May I fetch you some water?"

The man tried to smile, at least as far as Brendan could tell. Brother Brendan ran from the room and down the hill. He paused at the dining hall and shook the pebbles from his sandals. Then quickly walked through the doors, past the long tables, and into the kitchen. He poured a large glass of water and placed a thick piece of cheese on a plate. Balancing both on a tray, Brendan scampered back up the hill to the reading room. His guest was sitting at the table. Brendan set down the tray and sat across the table from him. As he gulped from the glass, Brendan studied him.

"Would you like some more?" Brendan asked.

The man nodded.

Brendan hopped to his feet, grabbed the glass, and darted back down the hill and to the kitchen. Then sprinted back. He placed the refilled glass in front of Hayden and sat back down.

"You didn't drink from the river, did you?"

The man shook his head.

"Good, good. Poison, you know. Kill you fast. What's your name?"

"Hayden."

"That's a fine name. I'm Brother Brendan." He blinked several times. He could only focus for a few seconds at a time, then the lines combined, changed. In fact, Brendan wasn't positive Hayden was actually there. Often the Akoimetai Brothers were visited by the unreal. It was a blessing. The unreal is a guide to the real within, and the kingdom is within.

They are the Sleepless Monks, following the Lord's command to "Stay awake!" and Paul's advice to "Pray continuously." Yes, indeed, no sleep. Or very little. No, "no sleep" was the wrong way to see it, wrong way to say it. It is wakefulness. Yes, said in the positive. "Stay awake. Watch." Yes. Watchers. Seeing always. Waking is floating. Sleeping is sinking. Each morning a person floats into the skies of enlightenment, but the nightly habit of sleep is a sinking back to Earth. The next day they must begin all over again. But the Sleepless, oh, they float, up and up and up. Yes, but didn't Jesus sleep in the boat, during the storm? He was faking for the benefit of his disciples. He was? He was.

Anyway, Brendan had slept enough as a child, as small arms and legs, as running in the grass, as grass running. Grass running! Run from the grass! No grass. No, this is desert country. Yes. Where is Brother Arnold? Brother Arnold is dead. Yes, but he is also whispering. Oh, yes. And that raccoon! Fearless! The raccoon is watching. Watching those who watch. The raccoon is Christ. All things are Christ. Love the raccoon. Raccoon, love me. The raccoon is a man is a child is small legs running in the grass. The grass is running. Run!

"Are you Catholic?" the man asked.

Brendan blinked quickly. Yes. The man. He's already finished the second glass. And there was an *A* nestled to his neck. Doesn't that tickle? "Catholic? Depends who you ask. We think so. The last pope thought so. We haven't told the current one."

"Haven't told him what?"

"That we exist!" Brendan said, tapping his fingers on his lips. "According to the books the Akoimetai Order disbanded in the 500s. Wrong side of a heresy, you know. But we never went under. We just got very quiet. Not in praise. We always worship. *Laus perennis.* Our chapel is always singing, never sleeping. Yes. We are one of Rome's secrets. And sometimes that means being a secret to Rome. Excuse me."

Brendan closed his eyes and sighed. He whispered a prayer. "Oh God, you carry me into ecstasy, you surprise me and steal me away, like wind catching a falling leaf. I fly because of you. I am nothing but a dead leaf without you. Oh Lord, praise be your name. Watch out for that raccoon." He opened his eyes and exhaled loudly. "Now," he said. "How can I help you?"

A bed?

BROTHER BRENDAN WAS a little mad, Hayden could see that. He chattered along, but Hayden felt that only a scattering of the words were meant for him. The monk was sometimes calm, sometimes agitated. His eyes had a red-yellow glaze and his thin, ashy hair stuck to the sweat of his forehead. His hands twitched, gripping the table as if he were afraid he'd float away.

"More water?" Brendan asked.

Hayden's thirst still burned, but he couldn't bring himself to send the small monk running off again. Brendan had still not caught his breath from his first two trips.

"I know this is strange," Hayden said. "But I'm wiped out. Could I borrow a bed for an hour or so? I'm exhausted and—"

"A bed? A bed? I'm sure we have one somewhere. Wait here." Brendan jolted up. He swayed on his feet for a moment, then scurried through a door in the back of the room.

Hayden could hear the whisperings behind the door.

"A bed?"

"Yes. He wants a bed. Is there one in the basement?"

"We don't have a basement."

"Fetch Brother Andre. Yes, yes."

The door burst open and Brendan scuttled back to his chair at the table. "A room is being prepared," he said. Two other monks, slightly younger than Brendan, came into the room from the same door. As Brendan smiled at Hayden, the two monks moved to either side of the table, lifted it, and carried it through the door.

"So," Brendan asked. "You're a traveler?"

"I'm an actor."

"Oh good. Very good. Are you acting now?"

"No. I really am very tired."

"Yes, of course you are. Unless you're still acting, even now. That would make you a very good actor."

"I'm not a very good actor."

"That's settled." Another monk peeked in the door and nodded at Brendan. Brendan stood. "Your bed is this way."

Hayden followed the monk through the back and into an empty hall lined with other doors. He could sense eyes staring from behind cracked doors. At the end of the hall was a bare room. In the center was the table. The legs had been cut down to a foot or so and brown fabric, the color of the monk's robes, has been spread over the top.

"Your bed," Brother Brendan said, smiling.

Hayden thanked him and yawned. Brendan nodded. Hayden nodded. The two stood facing each other. Hayden wondered if he was expecting a tip.

"Well, I think I'll take a nap," Hayden said. Brendan nodded. Hayden coughed. "So, I'll see you later."

"Oh, yes." Brendan seemed to remember himself and shuffled out of the room.

Hayden crawled onto his bed/table, exhausted and smiling. He had reached a haven, a place of peace. This mad little monk was kind.

He could feel peace like the first sip of an excellent cocktail. Hayden had grown up with nagging and sarcasm. He had moved to a community of false-heart and low-soul. Even Jim Edwards with his constant travels didn't have peace. But this place, mad as it was, had a quality of rest Hayden had never known. He closed his eyes and slept.

No words

TWENTY MILES OUTSIDE of Fort Stockton they began seeing the cars. Lines of them, crammed with people and belongings. Pickup trucks and SUVs piled high with furniture, overstuffed suitcases and mattresses strapped on top like turtle shells. Each vehicle was full of faces, frantic faces. The exodus crawled east along I-10. The orange VW whizzed by in the nearly empty westbound lanes.

"Where can you go to escape the end of the world?" Milton said.

Rica searched the dial for any news, but the only station coming in was 88.6, still playing Pearl-Swine's "Who's Gonna Park the Car."

In the approaching distance they could see towers of black smoke like pillars holding up the low sky.

"I wish we could hear some news," Rica said.

"The news doesn't know what's happening," Milton said.

"What is happening?"

"All our dreams. All our ideas and beliefs," Milton said. "We've chosen the thousand ways to end the world."

Roy groaned.

"Hold on, Roy," Rica said. "We're almost there."

"Don't stop, Rica," Milton said. "The city is burning."

Ignoring Milton, Rica took the exit for the Pecos County Memorial Hospital. Sirens blared and orange flames twisted within the smoke rising from every other building. Pockets of people still remained, some packing up cars, tying down loads. Others smashing in windows of shops, grabbing, and running.

Rica put a hand on her belly. Her body pressed against her dress, the dress that had been loose the day before. Her womb ached, and fears she refused to name screamed in her head. *There'll be doctors at the hospital,* she told herself. *They'll make sure everything is fine.*

White, red, black . . .

ROY WAS EXHALING long, slow breaths. Milton knew what he was doing. Roy was trying to focus his mind by focusing his breath, trying to look past the pain, trying to meditate through the struggle. Long breath in through the nose, long breath out the mouth. He and Roy had written a song highlighting the practice for the short-lived Lotus Motion called "Don't Believe, Just Breathe!"

But despite the breathing, every few minutes Roy's face cringed in pain and he squeezed Milton's hand till the bones creaked.

Rica downshifted and made a quick right. The bus cut the corner and both she and Roy let out a gasp of pain. Milton looked to the front. Rica's knuckles were white around the steering wheel. Milton scrambled to her side, on his knees by her seat. He placed a hand on her belly and gazed up at her. She was sweating, her cheeks flushed.

"Rica?"

"I'm fine," Rica said. "We're almost there."

The bus passed through a spray of water from a tapped hydrant. For a moment the curtain of water covered the windshield, then cleared to reveal a large stone sign announcing PECOS COUNTY MEMORIAL HOSPITAL. Behind the sign a large off-white building was engulfed in flames. Fire licked upward from the roof and white and black smoke poured from the windows and doors.

"Ah crap," she whispered.

"There, drive there." Milton pointed to a gold and black oversize pickup backed nearly into the emergency room entrance. Two men were throwing trash bags into the back. Another was running back into the smoke. "Fast! Block them in."

"Block them in?"

"Do it!" Milton called out. "They're going to help us!"

Rica pressed on the gas and sped through the parking lot, bouncing over speed bumps. Roy yelled from the back. Rica pulled in perpendicular to the truck and slammed the bus to a halt a foot from of the truck's front bumper. The two men dropped their bags. One of them hurtled himself into the double cab of the truck.

Milton crawled past the passenger seat. "Keep it running," he said. He opened the door, knocking the bumper, and stepped from the bus onto the truck's hood. Below his feet, covering the hood like a Roman ceiling, was a fierce white stallion with red eyes and black hooves.

"Get in, Crutch! Let's go!" the man in the cab of the truck yelled. But the other man wasn't moving.

"Cool it, Bones," he said, pulling a pistol from his back pocket. He was staring at Milton. His eyes, shaded by a bent baseball cap, were narrow and mean. He had a wispy blond beard and a toothless smile that turned Milton's stomach like the smell of rot. "Let's see what they want."

"All we want is some Vicodin. We've got an injured man."

"You got a prescription?" the blond said.

His friend, skin black as asphalt, climbed back out of the truck. He was tall, taller than Milton, and so thin Milton thought he might snap as walked. He glanced back and forth from the pistol to Milton in nervous jerks. "Don't shoot him, Crutch. Don't do that."

Milton looked down again at the painting below his feet. The stallion was in midsprint, wind blowing back its mane, an orange and gold sunset, or sunrise, blazing behind it.

"He won't shoot me," Milton said, looking up at the blond. "You can't shoot me."

"Why not, motherfucker?" He cocked the gun. Milton could see the man's finger twitching against the trigger. But Milton spoke calmly, almost a whisper.

"I know who you are."

"Okay, hippie-shit, off the truck."

"The first seal has been broken. You're Pestilence. You ride first and your brothers follow. You carry a bow and no arrows. You have no bullets."

The blond frowned. He smacked his toothless gums and pushed a breath of air from his nose. "Well," he said, "I know how to get some bullets real fast."

"Hey, get the fuck off my truck!" A man was pushing through the glass ER doors, a puff of hot air and smoke following him. He was broad, muscles like veined stones pressing from under his red skin. His hair was pulled into a tight, black silk ponytail. He shook his head at the other two, placed his trash bag in the back of the truck, and pulled a six-inch hunting knife from his belt.

"You're the second rider," Milton pointed and chuckled. "You're War. Look, you've been given a large sword."

"I wasn't given this," he said. "I took it." He stepped closer to the hood.

"Ah Jesus, ah Jesus," Bones said, shifting back and forth on his long, thin legs, looking like a cartoon skeleton with a full bladder.

"And you," Milton turned to him. "Ha, it's all clear. You're the third. You're Famine."

"Come on, man. No, I'm not."

"Yes," Milton said, nodding and grinning. "You're Famine."

"I got a thyroid problem, okay? It's medical."

"White, red, black . . . " Milton squatted down and shuffled off the hood, searching the area. "Pale. Where is he?"

"Where's who?" Pestilence asked.

"Death."

The three men glanced at each other.

"Where is he? The fourth rider."

"Yeah, well," War started, lowering the knife. "He's not doing so good."

"That's why we're here, man," Famine said in a high voice. "We're bringing him penicillin and shit. Taking it back to Alpine."

"They got a triage set up there. A doctor, but not much stuff," War said.

"You said you got a hurt man?" Pestilence asked.

"Yes," Milton looked back to VW. Rica was staring out, her eyes wide, her hands wrapped around the steering wheel as if it might fly away if given half the chance. "And a pregnant woman."

"Shit, man," War said. "Why didn't you say so? We'll take you to Alpine."

Milton looked back to Rica, smiled, and gave her a thumbs-up. She didn't smile back.

"Should we follow you?" Milton asked.

"In that piece of shit? Hell no." Pestilence spit. "We'll drive you. We got room. We'll be in Alpine in fifteen minutes."

"Great!" Milton said. "Thanks." Milton hopped over to the driver's side of the VW and opened the door. "Okay, babe. We're riding with them."

Rica shot a glance back at the three men and leaned into Milton. "Are you sure?"

"Rica," Milton said with a grin. "They're the Riders of the Apocalypse. We can trust them."

Larger Than Life

COLD AIR PUMPED from the truck's air-conditioning. Rica leaned in and pushed her face to the air like a drought victim to water. She hadn't realized the heat until feeling the cold. The bus had no AC and poor ventilation, and her body was pumping more and more hot blood to build this baby.

"So is that guy your dad?" the driver, the one Milton called War, asked. The skinny one, Famine, sat in the center playing with the stereo.

"My boyfriend." She kept her face in the flow of cold air. She could sense their surprise but said nothing.

"He give you that baby?"

Rica nodded.

"So, what, are you guys hippies?"

"I make soup," Rica said, leaning back.

"Cool," War said, staring coldly out the front window. "I cook, too."

"He works at Dairy Queen," the skinny man said.

"Shut the fuck up, Bones," War barked.

"Well, you do, Blade." The skinny man pressed a button on the stereo and "Larger Than Life" by the Backstreet Boys pounded out of the stereos.

"Turn that shit off," War said, shaking his head.

"It's good," the skinny man said, turning the volume down to a low notch. "It's encouraging."

"I cook *and* I work at Dairy Queen," War explained.

"No shame in working at DQ," Famine mumbled to himself. "I wish I worked there."

"Any news about what's happening?" Rica asked.

"Everything's out. No Internet, no cable, no radio except for that one fucking Jesus station," War said. "They say we're under martial law, but I haven't seen no marshals. The rest of the world seems pretty fucked up, too. I heard something about Jerusalem being bombed."

"Who by?"

"Spain, I think. Maybe China. The news was all jumbled. Hell, CNN was like a comedy show. Some giant wolf thing is running around eating people in Asia. The president of Iran gave a press conference and he was glowing. I mean really, giving off light. Someone said it was faked, but I don't know. And the whole thing in England . . ."

"What England thing?" Rica said.

"Some guy in chain mail broke into Buckingham Palace and cut the queen's head off. Says he's king now."

"Holy shit."

"Jesus is coming," Famine said, nodding as if he were agreeing with someone.

"Jesus isn't coming," War said. "It's just a crazy time. Crazy times happen all the time."

Famine's thin shoulders twitched in a shrug. "Jesus *is* coming," he said under his breath. He turned the stereo back up and nodded to the beat.

The two-lane road was long and smooth, empty barbed-wire fields on either side. For some miles there was peace. Nothing to show that a city was burning a short drive away.

"Where you guys from, anyway?" War asked.

"Austin," Rica said. She was gazing out the window watching the patches of green and brown, the low trees, the distant sharp mountains. It was beautiful. She had passed this way once before when her family had moved from California. Driving across half the nation, she and her brother bickering in the backseat as the southwestern quarter of the country passed by their windows. Her memories of that trip were dominated by fast-food diners and stiff hotel sheets. Her brother was stationed in Virginia Beach now, a career military man. He had two children, two little boys. Her parents had moved out there just after the first one had been born. They had been dreaming of being grandparents ever since their children left home. She hadn't talked with any of them in over a month. No real reason, just a hectic few weeks. She wished to God she could talk to them now.

The road climbed a plateau topped with rocky hills and scatterings of cedar and piñon pines.

"Not far now," War said. "They've set up medical aid at a church. That's where our friend is."

As they approached the outskirts of Alpine, they saw the people. Small pockets walking along the road or out toward the hills. Groups of no more than a dozen. Bags weighing down their backs, children pulling on their parents' arms.

"Where are they going?" Rica asked.

"They're climbing," War said, pointing to a few distant figures standing on the towering ridges. "Higher ground, I guess. Going to the caves."

Passing through a series of jagged outcrops of rock, they came upon the town of Alpine.

Squid

VICODIN WAS GOOD. Very good. Roy lay in the back of the pickup on a bed of bulging trash bags. He watched the sky as the painkillers covered his body, seeing the smoke clear to blue as they sped from the hospital. Tiny white clouds floated up there. Happy in the blue. Ducks were flying south in a V formation. In another section of sky a different flock was flying west and still another north. One lone duck, far off in the sky, was flying in erratic circles.

Milton was sitting near, looking old and wild. Across from Milton sat a man in a bent hat with no teeth. He came with the truck, Roy guessed. Things were still unclear. The past hour was murky for Roy. Pain had been the primary sun in the sky, outshining any star or moon. But now the Vicodin was tinting the sky, pacifying the pain, and allowing dulled thoughts. They were driving west, moving fast. He could feel the road smooth beneath him.

He didn't want to dwell on what he had seen and what he had done that day. The gas station man lying in blood, his head half gone. His wife inside. Instead, Roy watched the sky and meditated on the giant squid.

He often thought of the giant squid, pictured the smooth, elongated body gliding a mile below the ocean waves, as far from the air as Roy was from the airless above. A graceful monster with unblinking liquid eyes the size of hubcaps, slowly massaging grasps of ocean. Did these land storms touch her at all? Or was she still spending her hours skirting ocean canyons and picking fights with grumpy gray whales? For the clouds and the squids this was just another day.

That would be a way to die ... giant squid. Swimming along in the middle of the Pacific. You see the bubbles first, the water swirling, then a suction cup the size of a tire latches onto your torso and pulls you down.

Roy had a mental list cataloging the many thousands of ways a person might die. Every morning for the last decade Roy sat still on a rock in his front yard for ten minutes and imagined his own death. Each time a different scenario. This was neither a morbid obsession nor a death wish; it was a meditation. A reminder to not hold too tightly to anything. It was Roy's way of making friends with the inevitable.

He looked to Milton, the wind pushing his hair around his face, whipping like a thousand thin tentacles. The sky was a blue and white sea.

He was talking, yelling words to the other man. Roy couldn't make out the words. The other man didn't look happy to hear whatever it was Milton was saying.

This had once been a sea, all West Texas had been a sea. You can still find shellfish fossils scattered though the sand. A sea miles long, miles deep. That world ended. Dried to desert, all life turning to dust and stone.

Through the hair Roy could see a laugh on Milton's face. Roy found that ridiculously amusing. All this and Milton was laughing. Old and laughing.

No longer labeled

THE PICKUP TRUCK roared into the Texas desert, the flames of Fort Stockton disappearing behind the rising terrain. Milton sat in the corner leaning against the outside of the cab while Pestilence stared out at the passing landscape from the other side of the bed. A recently doped Roy lay between the two on a mattress of bagged pharmaceuticals. Milton placed a hand on his chest and Roy smiled groggily.

The wind churned Milton's hair; he could see the gray streaks overtaking the brown. He could feel the age in his bones and throat. He felt wonderful. The oversize engine and the wind made conversation nearly impossible, and Milton was glad. Had it been quieter, he would have been tempted to explain his exhilaration to Roy. But he would have failed. He knew that. It was all too strange. His visions, the strings of knowledge spiraling into his mind, the images of fire and falling skies . . . he didn't fear them, didn't try to understand them . . . he accepted them. He no longer labeled them, no longer attributed value to the visions or even attempted to distinguish real from unreal. He let each picture, each idea, wash through him. A baby was coming, a world was ending, a wind was blowing, a friend was hurting, a sun was shining. Life was happening. He was not its judge. And now that he was free from judgment, he felt more alive than ever.

"Why you smiling?" Pestilence yelled over the wind.

Milton shrugged. "End of the world as we know it, and I feel fine."

"End of the world, huh?"

"Yep. Days are coming to a close. And you know what they're doing, Pestilence? You know what their last attempt to cure our mad, mad souls is?"

Pestilence shook his head.

"Listening to the patients!" he yelled, throwing his arms into the air. "This is all stuff we made up. Our scriptures, our religions, our Rapture, our fires. We've been prescribing the Apocalypse for ourselves for centuries."

Pestilence stared at him. *If he had teeth,* Milton thought, *he'd be gnashing them.*

"You're fucking nuts," Pestilence spit.

"Yeah!" Milton laughed.

Milton looked down and saw Roy grinning up at him. He leaned down to Roy's ear.

"Roy," he said. "I'm glad you're here."

Roy nodded. "You're a giant squid, Milton."

Milton laughed even louder.

Filled his heart with sawdust

THE BALD MAN was bored. Bored and sad. He was fishing off a low bridge on a country road. He had been there for hours and caught nothing. That wasn't the problem. He usually caught nothing. His boredom was deeper.

For most of his adult life the bored man had been a bored tax accountant. He lived alone. He had no friends. He watched three to six hours of television every day. Like many bored people, he was boring.

Then, at the age of fifty, he received a letter telling him he had inherited an uncle's secluded cabin. That weekend, having nothing at all to do, he visited the cabin. It was old and small but comfortable and warm. And every wall of every room was covered with shelves of books. Novels, histories, poetry, zoology, physics, biographies, self-helps. The bald man saw this as a sign, a chance to change his whole life, his whole person. He quit his job, stocked up on food and whiskey, and moved into the cabin. Each day he read. And read. And read. When his eyes grew tired, he walked down to the bridge and dangled a hook into the river below.

For close to a decade he read. But earlier that very morning, the bald man closed the cover of the last book on the last shelf. Boredom struck him like a wet bag of oats. It wasn't that there weren't more books to buy and read. He knew that. What filled his heart with sawdust was that *he* was there. Himself—hiding behind that last book like a party guest that won't go home. He had hoped that after reading every volume he would find himself a changed man. But he was the same man he had always been. And he wasn't very fond of that man.

"If a thousand books can't change me," he said to his fishing pole, "what can?"

There was a tug on his line. He yanked. The line yanked back. He reeled in. An impressive rainbow trout danced on the end of the line. But it wasn't alone. Clenched onto its lower fin was a blue-green hermit crab.

The bald man removed the hook from the fish. He then gently pried the claw from the fin. The crab quickly retreated into its shell. The bald man studied the crab and called up his reading of *Hermit of the Sea and Shore* by Paula Wallins.

Judging by the large purple claw it was a *Coenobita clypeatus*. Midsize. Gender was hard to tell. Beautiful shell, though someone had painted a thick red arrow on it. The man leaned his pole on the railing and threw the fish back into the river. He placed the crab on the ground and waited. After a minute the purple claw crept out, then the other reddish claw, and finally the two round eyes. The crab looked up at the bald man and made a low chirping noise. *It's stridulating,* the man thought. *I read about this! I know all about it!*

The crab started to crawl, the red arrow clearly designating the direction. The bald man, grinning like a toddler, left his pole, his cabin, and his books, and followed.

Only on Christmas

HAYDEN WAS WITH *her.*

They rolled and rubbed. Her breathing mixed with chanting music from some far-off place. He tried to say her name but only moaned.

"Shhh," she said. "You don't remember my name."

He woke up in a sweat, his arms wrapped around the prosthetic leg. He was alone. A dozen candles gave the room an unearthly glow. He climbed from the table and stretched. From somewhere outside came faint chanting.

Hayden put a hand to his pounding head and prayed these monks drank coffee. He could have slept for hours longer, but Hayden was eager to see the world he had stumbled into. The hike from the highway had nearly killed him, which made this place even more valuable. Every detail—the earth-brown adobe walls, the one wooden cross hanging, the burning candles dripping tears of wax—every little element was something he had nearly died for.

Taking the leg, Hayden walked out the door and down the bare hallway, no eyes peeking out at him. He passed through the book room in which he had first met Brother Brendan and out into the day.

The sun hovered above the western cliffs, sending bright-yellow light across the handful of adobe buildings. Monks in brown robes tottered along dirt pathways and worked away at chores. A handful of monks worked, bent and digging, on a large vegetable garden. Two other monks were leaning a ladder against a far building. Three were working on what looked to be a large bench; another was pruning a tree. In the center of the estate stood a cream-colored chapel. The chanting came from there.

Hayden was no stranger to seeing people at work. He enjoyed rolling into the studio lot and seeing crews set up cameras, rigs, craft services. All working diverse jobs toward one goal: making his show great!

But these monks moved with a different energy. Though they moved quickly, there was no rush. No anxiety. In Los Angeles everything from filming to love-making to sleeping was strapped with anxiety. It was the gravy every meal was doused in, the spike in every sip, the nicotine rush of every breath.

On a large mound nearby, two monks propped up a crude carving of a man, his arms outstretched to the sky.

"Hello," Hayden called out. The two monks looked at Hayden, then at each other, and then returned to the wooden figure. Perhaps they couldn't hear him. Hayden walked over to them. "So, who is that supposed to be?"

"Please, you do it," one monk, a red-eyed young man, whispered to the other.

"No, you," the other monk, with a thick white beard, said.

The younger monk sighed, walked a few steps to Hayden and poked him in the belly.

"Hey!" Hayden said. The younger monk turned to the elder and nodded.

"How nice," the elder said to Hayden. "You're real."

"A saint of God," said the younger monk in a high, soft voice.

"No, no. Not me." Hayden shook his head. "Just on TV."

"Your question," the young monk turned to the wood sculpture. "He may be Saint Francis. But that's a bit overdone."

"Yes, yes. Overexposed, the poor man," said the elder. "Maybe another saint. Or a nameless saint. Or all the saints never sainted!"

"That's it, Brother Luke!" said the younger. "The saint never sainted!"

"The face is uneven," Hayden said. "That left ear is too high and the mouth is all . . ." Hayden trailed off. The two monks were staring at the prosthetic leg under his arm. The younger one licked his lips.

"So you're the sleeper!" said the elder monk.

"Well, I was sleeping, yeah."

"We all *were* sleeping," he chuckled. "No shame! No shame at all!"

The younger monk leaned into the elder and whispered.

The elder nodded and patted the younger on the back. "Yes, yes. Go fetch him!" The young monk raced off and the elder smiled. "Someone has been expecting you."

"I met Brendan earlier."

"He wasn't expecting you. You surprised him," he said. "But everything surprises him. That's his gift. Now Brother Michael, on the other hand, he's been expecting you for weeks."

"Weeks?"

"I said 'on the other hand.' That is funny," the elder said, rubbing his white beard.

"How could anyone be expecting me? It's impossible. I didn't know I was going to be here until . . . until I was here."

"Did you know that a cockroach can survive for up to a week without a head?" Hayden blinked. "I did not know that."

"And you know what finally does it in? What finally kills the decapitated cockroach? Starvation."

"Really?"

So be careful with words like *impossible*," the monk said, ruffling Hayden's hair as if he were a schoolboy. "Ah look! Brother Michael."

The younger monk approached, his arms around a brittle-thin, ancient-looking man. He was gray and small. The younger monk practically carried him up the mound.

"BROTHER MICHAEL!" the young monk yelled at the old man. "THIS IS THE MAN YOU WERE EXPECTING."

The old man beamed a toothless smile at Hayden. Hayden reached out and shook his frail hand.

"I don't understand."

"LOUDER," said the younger.

"I DON'T UNDERSTAND," Hayden yelled. "HOW WERE YOU EXPECTING ME?"

"When you understand your needs, you expect to see them met," the elder said. "SHOW HIM, BROTHER MICHAEL."

The old man reached down with one hand and clutched his brown robe. He lifted the hem to reveal one pale leg and one bandaged stub. Hayden laughed. The old man laughed, too.

"The leg! Would you like this leg?" Hayden asked, patting the prosthetic. "It's a woman's leg? Is that all right?"

The old man nodded eagerly and stuck out his nub toward Hayden. The other two monks flanked the old man and Hayden did his best to fasten the leg into place. It took some tries, but eventually the leg was secure. The old man stood lopsided and happy. The leg was a few inches taller than its partner and stuck out from the robe as if the monk were standing beside a highway using his new limb to hitch a ride. The younger monk stroked the leg, progressing above the knee until the elder monk slapped his hand.

"Sorry, Brother," the younger said.

Brother Michael's face shone. He nodded and chuckled. Hayden nodded back. The two had a brief conversation consisting of nods and quick bursts of laughter. Then the old man surprised Hayden by reaching with his right arm under his left sleeve and removing his left arm with a jerk. He held the prosthetic arm out toward Hayden.

"For me?" Hayden asked. "I don't need it. You do."

"IT'S MORE BLESSED TO GIVE THAN TO RECEIVE," boomed the younger monk. "ISN'T THAT RIGHT, BROTHER MICHAEL?"

"Best take it," the elder whispered to Hayden.

Hayden reached out and took the arm. "THANK YOU. THANK YOU VERY MUCH."

"And look," the elder said, pointing to the chapel. "Sext is ending. Excuse us. Must go and prepare for prayer." With that the two monks started toward one of the adobe buildings with Brother Michael hobbling between them. As they reached the bottom of the hill, the old man turned. Hayden gave a little wave with the fake arm.

"Oh!" Hayden yelled. "I get it! 'On the other hand!' Funny!"

The elder shot him a thumbs-up.

Hayden held the arm with both hands. It was lighter than the leg but similar. The same mannequin-pink plastic, the same waxy smooth texture. Though the arm showed years more wear than the leg. Hayden had never been given a more wonderful gift, something the giver needed more than he. It hurt him in a new way.

Below him a long line of monks were emerging from the chapel, hands clasped and heads bowed. One monk caught sight of Hayden and hopped up and down like a child seeing a puppy. He broke from the others and skipped up the hill to Hayden. Only when he was a few feet away did Hayden recognize him as Brother Brendan.

"Good morning," the monk said. "Or afternoon actually. Yes. How was it?"

"How was what?"

"Sleep. How was sleep?"

"Fine, thanks. How long was I out?"

"Oh, hours and hours. No shame though. No shame. Not our duty to judge. Eye splinters and all that. Your leg shrunk," he said, pointing to the limb in Hayden's hand.

"It's an arm now," Hayden said. "Why is everyone so busy?"

"Oh, lots of work. We're in preparation."

"What for?"

The monk paused. "We don't know. Something in the air. Something big. You can feel it. Or, at least, we can. Maybe it's 1260 after all."

"A bad thing?"

"Yes." Brendan nodded. "Very bad." He sniffed. "Or not. Perhaps wonderful. Hard to say. Best not judge. Judge not lest ye be judged and all." He sniffed again. "Hungry?"

"Famished."

"Good, good," the monk said quickly. He did everything quickly with twitches and hops. "We eat in an hour . . . or some of us do. Some are eating now. The oldest eat first. Yes. Then they praise while we eat. Always someone praising. Novices eat last, if at all. I hope you like squash."

"Do you have any coffee?"

"Only on Christmas," the monk said. "But you're a guest, and a guest is Christ, and if Christ wants coffee, well then, Merry Christmas!"

The monk skipped down a path to a wide, low-roofed building. Hayden followed.

"So," Hayden said, jogging to keep up. "You personally call yourself a Catholic, right?"

"Yes, yes. Big *C* and little *c*."

"I'm trying to be a Catholic, too."

"Wonderful!"

"That's why I'm here," Hayden said. "I'm trying to figure this all out. I want to believe in God, the Trinity, Mass, the incarnation . . ."

"Oh, I stopped believing years ago." The monk stopped in front of a door. He raised a hand to his mouth. "Silence in the dining hall." He opened the door.

The stone-floored room had seven long tables that stretched nearly wall to wall. Against one wall stood an unlit fireplace. Three old monks, as bent and brittle as Brother Michael, sat scattered through the room, each focused on a small plate of squash. One of the monks had a younger monk beside him spooning food into his quivering lips.

Brendan shuffled among the tables, bowing slightly to each monk. Hayden followed and also bowed. At the far end of the room was another door. They passed through into a wide, clean, well-equipped kitchen. Brendan turned to Hayden.

"We can talk now."

"You don't believe?" Hayden asked.

"No. I mean, I didn't say that. I stopped believing. That's not the same as not believing." Brendan moved to a narrow door near a corner of the kitchen. "I have faith. But believing . . . well, a person believes in scientific theories or newspaper articles. We have *faith* in God. We experience God, even if it is experiencing his absence. And we practice! We act! We contemplate! The son who told the mother he would not help is the one who worked the fields. See? Now, where is that thing?" Brendan was digging into the folds of his robe. He pulled out a large key and unlocked the door. "Yes, yes. The coffee closet."

From high on a shelf Brendan lifted a wooden chest and carried it back into the kitchen. He placed the chest on a counter and slowly opened the lid. Inside were a copper kettle, a metal strainer, and a carefully wrapped, hand-size bag of beans. Brendan scattered half the beans on the counter and ground them with a rolling pin. The familiar acidic smell made Hayden smile. Brendan set the water to boil. He grinned as the steam puffed from the spout. "Choo! Choo!" he said.

Hayden was amazed at how deliberate and slow this manic little monk was moving. Every tool, every step of the process was handled with a smiling rever- ence. He seemed to take a moment of appreciation as he dropped each spoonful of grounds into the kettle. Hayden wasn't sure, but he thought he could hear the monk whisper "thank you" to the water and the grounds and the stove. Beside these whispers, Brendan said nothing.

Brendan prepared a tray with two mugs and the kettle. He led Hayden to a table in the back of the kitchen and the two sat. Using the strainer, Brendan poured the dark coffee into the mugs. He handed one mug to Hayden, took the other for himself, bowed his head, and whispered a prayer. When he raised his head, a smile filled his face. He lifted the cup with both hands and took a long sip.

"Ahh," he said. "What a treat."

"Thanks for making it," Hayden said, blowing into his own mug. "Can I ask another question?"

"We usually eat in silence . . . "

"I want to be a saint," Hayden said. "But I don't believe in God."

"Well, you wouldn't be the first."

"A saint who doesn't believe in God?"

"Belief is weaker than action. Do you see? I share a table with a man. I choose to call him brother. Or I choose to call him stranger. Or I choose to ignore his very presence. I dwell in four walls and a roof. I choose to call it a building or a prison or a home." Brendan sipped his coffee. "That is so very tasty!" He sipped again and smiled. "I choose to recognize this world as holy. I choose to recognize life as holy, you as my brother, and all that is and was and will be as God. And so I live! In this way life is holy and you are my brother."

Hayden smirked. "So, having faith suddenly makes God exist?"

Brendan jumped to his feet. "Who can speak of God's existence?" he yelled. "I'm talking of *our* existence!"

Another monk pushed his head in from the dining area. "Brother, please!"

"Sorry, Brother," Brendan said, lowering himself back to his bench. The other monk nodded and retreated back.

"Are you a saint?" Hayden asked after a moment.

"No, no. Not me," Brendan smiled. "Besides, any true saint would never think of himself as a saint." He stopped and scratched his chin. "But I don't think I'm a saint . . . maybe I am a saint?" He paused again. "No. I just thought I might be a saint. So that proves I'm not a saint. Thank God for that. Do you like your coffee?"

"Yes," Hayden took a sip. "It's strong."

"Yes, yes. All things are. Does that thing hurt?"

"What thing?"

"On your face. Right in the middle. Ow." Brendan cringed.

Hayden touched his face. "My nose?"

Brendan paused for a second. Then blinked quickly. "Nose! Yes, that's what it is. I have one, too!"

"Brendan," Hayden said. "Do you really not sleep?"

"Of course I sleep," Brendan said with a chuckle. "Seventeen minutes every other day."

"How do you do it?"

"I sit comfortably and close my eyes."

"No," Hayden said. "How do you stay awake?"

"Prayer," Brendan said with a serious nod. "And thankfulness. See these?" Brendan lifted the rosary hanging from the rope around his robe. "One thank-you for each bead. Wonderful, wonderful. Here, take them. Try it sometime."

"I can't take that."

"Oh, no, yes. Take it." Brendan rubbed the beads in his hands and passed them to Hayden. Hayden touched the glass-smooth beads, worn to a shine.

"Is it your birthday?" Brendan asked.

Hayden looked up and shook his head.

"I had always thought I carved this for someone's birthday gift. Always waited to meet the birthday boy and present it! Ah, but it's for you. I know that!"

"I wish I had something for you." Hayden looked down in his lap at the prosthetic arm. He placed it on the table. "Here."

Brendan stared at the arm for a long moment. Hayden was beginning to wonder if he'd committed some kind of monastic faux pas. Then he saw the tears racing down Brendan's cheeks and into his beard. Brendan reached forward and touched the arm as if it were a king's scepter.

"It really is Christmas," he said in a quiet, awed voice. "Shall I make more coffee?"

"I'm okay."

"Good, good." Brendan looked into Hayden's eyes and smiled. Hayden smiled back. A moment passed. And another. Hayden felt that the monk should stop smiling and staring and do something else. But Brendan didn't look away. Hayden's cheek twitched. He looked back down at the beads and back again. Brendan was still staring. Hayden had been stared at all his life: the Twix candy bar commercial at age two, the *Wiggles Surf Special* at age six, his role as Chimp-O at seven, his appearance on *Matlock* at nine, as Zack's rebellious cousin Ronny on *Saved by the Bell*, his brief stint as intern Roddin on *ER*, his lead role on *Earthquake: The Series*, on and on to his current stardom. Always a camera, always eyes. There were stares of admiration, awe, lust, intrigue, fascination, even disapproval. But this stare was different. *Because he's crazy,* Hayden thought. But that thought didn't hold. Brendan was more than just crazy. He was holy.

Hayden had the impression that Brendan was seeing something no one else had seen, not just sleepless hallucinations. Hayden felt that this half-mad monk was gazing at a tiny, pebble-size chunk deep inside of him. A part of him that could not be called Hayden Brock the television star, or Hayden Brock the celebrity, or even Hayden Brock. Something deeper and closer to whomever Hayden really was. Hayden felt soul-naked in the gaze. Brendan kept smiling. Kept staring. Hayden took another sip of coffee and scratched his cheek. Still, Brendan smiled and stared.

After several minutes Brendan said in a voice just above a whisper, "Would you like to know the key to being a saint?"

Hayden nodded.

"The key is mystery."

"A mystery?"

"No. Not *a* mystery. The key *is* mystery." He stood, cradling the prosthetic arm. "You know who will absolutely love this? Brother Michael. He'll be thrilled!"

This place will kill us

THE FIRST BAPTIST Church consisted of two buildings: a steepled sanctuary and a less impressive, long, one-story building. The truck skidded into the parking lot, dodging the dozen or so people sorting piles of clothes and groceries. War's fist held firm against the horn as the truck hopped the curve and slammed to a halt on the grass beside a children's swing set.

"They've set up in the basement. You can get help there." War jumped from the cab.

"Hope to see you in heaven," Famine said, and clambered after his friend.

Rica eased herself down from the cab, her belly feeling as tight and heavy as a bag of wet sand. War and Famine joined their third, the one Milton called Pestilence, in grabbing trash bags from the back.

"Can you cool it with the horn?" A tired-looking man with mussed charcoal hair and wrinkled blue scrubs approached them from a door in the side of the one-story building.

"We got medicine, Doc," War said, grabbing a third bag. "Penicillin and shit."

"Okay, okay," he said, holding his palms in surrender. "Just bring it down." The men hitched the bags over their shoulders and ran through the door.

"Roy," Rica said. He was sitting up, almost clear-eyed. The left side of his face was purple with bruises and the shirt he was using on his neck wound was now soaked through with maroon blood, but he was awake. Milton was helping him out of the truck bed, a hand held against his back. "How do you feel?"

"Apart from the face wounds and bleeding neck, I feel pretty good." Roy said. "It's amazing how you can forget pain when you don't feel it."

"Gunshot?" the doctor asked.

"Minor," Roy said.

"You look like shit," the doctor said. "Can you walk?"

"Like a pro."

"Good. Find a cot downstairs and I'll check you out."

The side door opened to a narrow stairwell leading down to a low-ceilinged basement. Two dozen cots filled most of the space. From somewhere a generator whirred, powering the basement's few lights.

Bandaged patients. Head, hands, chests hidden beneath white bandages. Some moaned; some slept. A few others seemed to be helping, sitting by beds, holding shaking hands. One woman with her black hair in a bun sat on the edge of a little boy's cot. She had made a puppet with her hand and was quacking to the boy's amusement.

The woman looked over and smiled at Rica, quacking all the while.

In one corner the three men from the truck stood around a cot, anxiously bobbing on their feet. They were angry, speaking to the charcoal-haired doctor in fierce whispers.

"We can't stay," Milton said. "This place is dangerous. We're supposed to be farther west. Near Marfa."

Rica was too tired to say anything. They found some free cots and helped Roy lie down. Then Rica dropped on the closest cot, turned on her side. The whole place was quiet, muffled. Her body felt drained, every part of her empty.

"Potato chips," she murmured.

"What?" Milton asked.

"I need potato chips right now."

Milton nodded and wandered off through the maze of cots. The hunger had hit her fast. There was a wriggling panic to the hunger, an instinctual urge. Her body needed food and needed it now. For the baby. Rica closed her eyes and experienced something like sleep.

When she blinked her eyes half-open she could see the doctor, his back to Rica, bent over Roy.

"You've lost a lot of blood. But if we keep you rested up, you should be okay."

"Any news? Do you know what's happening?" Roy asked.

"Besides hail the size of easy chairs? Besides a pack of coyotes attacking the high school? Besides half the city disappearing? No. No news."

"Glad to see you've maintained your sarcasm, Doc."

"I'm just trying to keep my head above water here. I've got a load of injured people, low supplies, and the Four Stooges trying to run the place." He gestured over to War and the others from the truck. He rubbed his eyes with his thumb and finger. "We've heard nothing that makes any sense. Lots of rumors, that's all." He spun around to Rica. "Okay, let's see how the baby's doing."

He looked exhausted. His face was drawn, his eyes dark and worn. He placed his hands on Rica's belly. Immediately, tears filled Rica's eyes. She had not realized how very frightened she was for her baby. Now, with the doctor's palms pressing against her, the fear came strong. She closed her eyes, trying to control her concern of what he might find, what he might tell her. But even as she tried, the tears betrayed her.

"I don't feel right," she said.

"Hey, Doc," one of the truck crew called from across the room. "He still looks bad. He's getting paler."

"Okay, hold on." The doctor returned his attention to Rica. He didn't acknowledge her tears. With cool professionalism, he continued the examination. "Hey, I felt a kick. He's got some power legs."

"She's a girl." Rica said, opening her eyes.

"You've had an ultrasound?"

"I just know."

"Everyone thinks they know," he said, pushing against the side of her abdomen. "Any bleeding? Anything unusual?"

"She's pregnant." Milton was standing behind the doctor, his arms filled with bags of barbecue Ruffles.

"Yes," the doctor said. "I can see that."

Without thinking, Rica reached up and grabbed a bag of Ruffles. She ripped it open and was two handfuls in before she realized what she was doing.

"Hungry?" the doctor asked. She nodded, a third handful poised for consumption.

"Doc, come on! He's looking bad!" the blond from the truck was yelling.

The doctor rose to his feet with a weary sigh. "Well, as far as I can tell, you're fine." He smiled at Rica. The first smile she had seen on his face. "Rest up. Don't strain yourself. In a month you'll have a beautiful baby." He turned to leave.

"A month?" Rica said through a mouthful. "I'm only four months pregnant."

The doctor stopped. "Four months?" The worry in his voice sent stabs into Rica. "Are you sure?"

Rica shook her head. "Four months, two weeks."

"Could you be wrong?"

"Hey, Doc, we need you now!" War was yelling.

"Okay. I'll be right back. Just rest here. We'll help you out and get you to a hospital ASAP."

The doctor jogged over to the men. As soon as he was out of earshot, Milton bent down to Rica.

"We have to leave."

"Milton, did you hear him? The baby . . ."

"The baby is fine. She's beautiful."

"What are you saying?"

"She spats, Rica. That's why she's growing."

"Milton, please . . ."

"She's better at it than I am. She ages weeks while I age years."

"Something's wrong. I shouldn't be this big."

"We have to go. This place will kill us."

"Okay then," Roy said, sitting up with a groan and starting to button his shirt. "Let's go."

"No. I am not leaving," Rica said, her voice cracking.

"Death is going to happen here." Milton reached out and took her arm.

"Don't touch me!"

Milton flinched as if he'd been slapped. "Rica, the baby will die unless we leave."

"This is crazy. I need a doctor. The baby needs a doctor. I am staying."

His face, stone gray. Milton jumped to his feet and looked down at her. He was tall, gray, and towering like a winter oak. In that moment, Rica could see the years in his eyes, see the distances he claimed to have traveled. "Please," he said.

But she was already shaking her head.

He lifted his face to the room and raised his arms. "Death is coming to this place," he yelled, spit flying from his lips. "You will all die here."

"Shut the fuck up, man," War yelled back.

Milton screamed and ran through the cots and up the stairs.

"Well, crap," Roy said, and quickly followed.

Rica closed her eyes and tried to breathe.

Yelling, pacing, preaching

ROY CAUGHT MILTON at the top of the stairs, standing at the door and glaring out at the people piling supplies in the parking lot.

"Milton," Roy said, already out of breath. "What are you doing?"

"Roy, I know who I am," he said. "I am called to tell those who will not listen." He put a hand on Roy's shoulder and laughed. "Ever hearing but never understanding!"

Milton rushed away into the small crowd of people. Roy chased after him. He wasn't hard to track with his height and the gray mane flying behind him. But Roy's legs felt like boiling water. The Vicodin was wearing off and the pain was stubbing out its cigarette and returning to work.

"Milton, wait!" Roy yelled.

Milton jumped on a picnic table. "Repent! Repent! Learn kindness if only for a day!" Volunteers stopped sorting for a moment and stared. "Your souls will have no home tomorrow. They will be sent begging."

An older woman approached the table. "Sir, can we help . . ."

But Milton screamed at her like a monkey and jumped from the table. He ran for the sanctuary. Roy stumbled after him mumbling an apology to the older woman. A man with a grocery cart full of canned food pushed in front of him. Roy stumbled and plowed into the cart, sending a hail of cans falling.

"Sorry, sorry," Roy said, clambering to his feet and limping toward the church.

Inside it was cool and dark, lit only by the altar's candles and the muted sunlight straining through the stained glass windows. Scattered in the pews were red-eyed mourners and petitioners. They gaped at the thin old man with wild gray hair and beard who had just sprung to the front of the sanctuary. Milton was yelling, pacing, preaching.

"And all this will be gone. All these bodies. Everything but your souls. Your souls are mad. Can you let go of the madness?" A few faces stared back. Some looked away. "Do not mourn your death," Milton shouted at them. "Mourn your sad lives!"

Roy was breathing hard, warm wet pouring from his neck. He made his way forward.

"These prayers, these books of hymns," Milton was yelling, his voice filled with anger and gravel. "They're nothing more than rocks for drowning men. You have filled your pockets with rocks as the waters approach."

Halfway to the altar, Roy summoned all his energy and rushed forward, sprinting the last steps and throwing himself into Milton's stomach. With a thud, both fell to the floor, a vase of flowers shattering beside them. Roy pinned Milton's shoulders down. Milton was squirming, his eyes wet and furious.

"Let me go!"

"Leave them alone, Milton," Roy croaked out. "Let them be."

"I have to tell them. I'm trying to help them."

"You're pissing on them, that's all. Leave them alone."

Milton stopped struggling and stared into Roy's face. "And you! I see your future!"

"Come on, now, Milt," Roy said slowly.

"You. You . . ." Milton stuttered in rage. For a moment Roy thought Milton would try to bite him. Then the tide changed and Milton's eyes grew calm, his jaw relaxed. Roy recognized his friend once again. "Roy . . . I'm sorry."

Roy nodded. "Let's get you out of here."

But as they stood to their feet, the floor shifted violently and a rumble from somewhere miles below echoed through the hall.

Facts every time

"YOU OKAY?" THE doctor knelt by the cot. "Was that your father?"

"The baby's father." Rica tried to wipe away the tears and potato chip crumbs; they stuck to her skin like grainy sweat. The doctor placed a cool hand on her forehead.

"People respond in different ways when disasters strike. Some revert to religion, some shut down completely, some . . . "

"Some scream that everyone in the room is going to die?"

"Yes. That, too." He brushed back his hair and again rubbed his eyes. He glanced over to the truck crew who seemed to be arguing with one of the volunteers. "Some get damn pushy." He looked back at Rica and half smiled. "Let's see what we can do for you. Four months?"

"And two weeks."

"I hope you're mistaken. In truth, I think you are mistaken." He paused and sucked his cheeks in. "You're showing about thirty-three weeks. If you've been pregnant only eighteen weeks, then something is seriously wrong, but I could feel that baby kicking. Big kicks. I could make out the baby's back. There's no way he's a—"

"She."

He nodded. "There's no way she's an eighteen-week-old fetus."

"I know my body," Rica said.

"I know my profession."

"Doctor! He needs something," Pestilence yelled from the corner, his toothless mouth sending a spray of spit with each word.

Rica sat up on her cot and faced the doctor. "You don't believe me?"

"Look, I can believe a person or I can believe the observable facts. I choose the facts every time."

Rica paused. She looked down at her belly pushing tight against her dress. The world of facts is a world of systems. What doesn't fit into the system is rejected. What would a world of facts do to this baby?

She looked up at the doctor. There was no madness in him, not even the good kind.

"You don't listen to jazz, do you?" she asked.

"What?" He was holding her wrist, taking her pulse.

"Jazz."

"My wife likes Kenny G." He could feel her blood pump; he could count the pumps per minute. Just blood to him, she could see that. Blood moved, blood carried oxygen, blood never burned.

"I should go," she said.

His face scowled. "No. Not a chance. You need—"

"Doc!" Pestilence stomped over. "You've got to give him another pill. Hell, we're the ones who stole them. You're giving 'em out like candy to everybody else. Give him another!"

The doctor stood and crossed his arms. "They don't work that way. They're antibiotics."

"Well, what if we just take those antibiotics back?" Pestilence pushed the greasy blond hair from his eyes.

"I'm doing everything I can here," the doctor said.

"You can do more." Pestilence pulled out his gun and aimed it at the doctor's head. The doctor's arms shot up.

"Whoa, now. Hang on," the doctor stammered.

"It's not loaded," Rica said.

"Shut up, bitch."

"It's not."

"Maybe I loaded it. You don't know."

Rica felt her cot vibrate. The ground rippled. For a second she thought it was in her head, but she saw the others sway on their feet. The stillness. For a second no one moved.

"What was that?" someone whispered.

A loud rumble, like a crashing wave, filled the basement. Pestilence stumbled to the side. The doctor jumped at him, pushing him back over an empty cot. As he fell the pistol fired and the doctor jerked back. He hit the floor, a dark red splotch expanding on his chest.

Pestilence pulled himself to his feet and stared at the motionless body. He turned to Rica. "You said it wasn't loaded!"

Rica stood. The floor undulated like a water bed in the back of a dune buggy. Pieces of the ceiling fell around her and the low lights flickered like mute lightning.

"Crutch, come on!" War yelled. They were picking their friend up from the cot. They hefted his thick body to his feet. For the first time, Rica saw the fourth man's face. Yellow, the yellow of spoiled cream. His eyes tire-tread dark. From where Rica sat she could see no white at all. For a moment she could not look away. He was Death.

A chunk of wall crashed to the ground and someone grabbed her arm. It was Pestilence.

"You got a baby in you. Come on!" He dragged her from the cot. People were shoving and screaming. Pestilence was throwing people back, making a path to the stairs.

"Stop it! Stop it!" Rica yelled. She yanked her arm free.

"Come on, lady!"

The room went dark. Panic filled the space like a stench. The people coughed on panic. The people choked on panic. Lines of light shot from the top of the stairwell down through the crush. Hellish shrieks bounced off the walls, threats and protests and animal fear. Like rats, the people squeezed into the stairwell and clogged the path. Rica backed away. There was a madness in the basement, a whirlpool of desperate fear. The desire to survive was killing them. She moved farther and farther back into the dark and away from the swirling. The ground shifted again. Above the chaos, a pipe burst and sprayed down hot water. Eventually the crowd moved upward, the stairwell began to empty. Rica, a hand on her kicking baby, was preparing to follow when she heard the weeping.

She scanned the basement in the dim light coming from the clearing stairwell. In the back, a figure was kneeling by the doctor's body. It was the woman with the bunned hair, the one who had been helping a child laugh with a quacking hand. The ground shook again and the entire ceiling dropped a foot.

"Hello?" Rica called to the woman. "Can you move?" The woman only cried. Rica crept back, carefully navigating overturned cots and scattered debris. The floor was slick with water and more continued to pour down.

Rica reached the woman and knelt beside her. Gripping the limp hand of the doctor and shaking with sobs, she seemed unaware that Rica was there. Rica placed a hand on her shoulder. "We have to go. We have to go right now." She pulled on the arm, but the woman was unmovable. Rica glanced back at the stairwell, thirty feet away. Was there time to go for help? The baby kicked inside her. *Please God* . . . Perhaps she could run, find someone to carry this woman out.

Then it hit. The hardest tremor yet. The room shifted like a birthday present shaken by a child. Stone screeched against stone, falling, the ceiling stuttering down. Rica was still gripping the woman's arm when she saw the light of the stairwell disappear behind rock and wood.

In a day. In a decade.

HAYDEN FOLLOWED BRENDAN through the last hours of the day. He sat while Brendan studied, listened as he prayed, watched as he spooned hot soup into the mouths of the monastery's oldest residents, and now as the sun sank low he knelt with the monk in the cemetery. A simple collection of several dozen modest stones on a hill overlooking the chapel. Hayden, Brendan, and a handful of other monks were yanking weeds from between the graves.

The work, to his surprise, agreed with Hayden. There was something distinctly solid about the task. Grab, yank. The sticky green stem and blades followed by the soft, white roots. Sweat in his mouth and eyes. He didn't even mind the fact that it was a graveyard, a location he would normally avoid at all costs. He wiped his brow and glanced at one of the markers. It was blank. So was the one next to it. They were all blank. Just rough, dark granite monoliths without a name or date.

"Where are the names?" Hayden asked Brendan, who was digging a few feet away.

"My goodness." Brendan laughed, a fistful of green weeds in his hand. "You work a lifetime to separate yourself from ego, why would you want to carry it to your grave? Ha!" Brendan yanked another fistful of weeds from the ground and held it to his nose, inhaling as if it were a bouquet of roses. He sighed. "All this life popping from death. Wonderful."

Hayden returned to his own work, glancing occasionally at a nameless grave just before him. For him it was a nightmare, a cold horror, to be deprived of one's name. He understood a name was not one's value. That much he had come to discover. But a name *held* one's value, much as a wallet held one's credit cards and cash. Losing your name was essentially losing your wallet. But for these men, these strange, robed, smiling, sleepless men, it was the goal. The ideal. He glanced back and saw Brendan was watching him.

"Hayden," he said. "There is a you beyond you. And possibly one beyond that." Brendan hopped to his feet, ran to Hayden, and dropped down beside him. "May I ask you a question, Hayden. Did you dream?"

"When?"

"When you slept? Did you dream?"

"Sure."

"Dreams! I remember dreams. I miss those. Even the nightmares I miss. What did you dream?"

"I dream of a woman I've never met. All the time now. Amazing woman."

"Oh, women! I miss them, too." Brendan's eyes disappeared behind a long blink. His eyes flew open. "Do you love her?"

"She's a dream. What's not to love?"

Brendan jumped to his feet, dropping his weeds. He raised his voice to a near yell. "Start with that! Yes? Water that! Tend your weedy heart!" Hayden looked, but the other monks continued their work without so much as a pause. Brendan leaned down and pushed Hayden's shoulder. "Tell me, who in this world or any world do you love?"

"Ah. My mom? I like my mom and dad."

"Fine. Good. And . . ."

"Ah . . ."

Brendan didn't wait. He ran a few feet away, fell to his knees, and grabbed handfuls of the sandy soil. "Here! Here in this earth lies my first spiritual mentor. Wisdom in every word. And also the novice who taught me the finest way to boil an egg!" He scooped more dirt. "The scholar who taught me Latin and the brother who sang with such beauty I would lower my voice in choir so I might better hear his, another brother who could have you laugh for a year with a raise of his eyebrow. Oh, he was a wonder!" He weighed the soil in his hands. "All these skills and traits and gifts. But without love they have nothing!" He threw the dirt toward Hayden. Hayden covered his eyes. "They are dead. They are gone. I love them still. If any part of them still exists, it is the part that loved me and God and the world. Even you, Hayden. They love you. You see? You see? That is *what* we are! You and I will die, too! In a day. In a decade." Brendan turned away and stared at the long shadows filling the canyon. "Without love a man is dust long before he dies."

Bacon

THE TWO TRUCKERS, one lean and one fat, covered the small, dark man with a thick blanket and let him sleep on the mat behind their seats. They rolled through the cold Canadian wilds, bypassing towns and cities, mountains and frozen lakes, down across the border into the United States just as the sun was rising.

"Should we tell immigration?" said the thin one, downshifting as they approached the crossing.

"Nah," said the fat one, glancing back at the sleeping figure. He had only been wearing some kind of robe. He had no wallet, no passport. "They'd lock him up in Cuba or something."

"But he looks pretty Arab. Could be a terrorist. Could be smuggling bombs?"

"Where? Up his ass?" said the fat one. "Hell, with all the crazy shit happening, the least we can do is give this sad bastard a hand."

Once stateside they rumbled southward past farms and billboards and Cracker Barrel restaurants. The two truckers whispered pleasantly, occasionally checking on the sleeping passenger and sharing smiles like a couple with a newborn. Just after 10:00 AM the man bolted upright and stared straight out the windshield.

"Hey, look who's up," said the fat one. "We thought maybe you'd died back there." Both truckers laughed. The man looked at both of them and laughed as well. He stared forward again, gripping the back of the seats.

The truck crested a hill and before them the land spread out, an ocean of wheat-gold fields rippling in the morning wind.

The man grinned like a child. "*Tetha malkoothak.*"

The thin trucker shot the fat trucker a look. "Told you he was Arab."

An hour later they pulled into a truck stop for breakfast. The thin one grabbed a booth and ordered, while the fat one led their passenger to a rack of clothes in the shopping section of the stop.

"Let's get you out of that dress," he said. "And I don't mean it in *that* way. Ha!"

The man laughed also.

"You don't understand a thing I'm saying, do you?"

He laughed even harder.

The fat man picked out blue jeans, a red and white flannel shirt, some tennis shoes, and a hat that read GOD BLESS THE U.S. OF A.

"Let's see. These should fit. You're short but big in the shoulders. My brother's got the same build. Shortest kid on the football team, but damn it all if he didn't knock some asses to the ground. You know what I mean?"

The man nodded.

The trucker waited outside the bathroom while the man tried on the clothes. He leaned against the wall and crossed his arms. Why was he helping this guy? He wasn't a naturally kind man. Not that he was a cruel man. Average, he'd say. But picking up a stranger, buying him clothes and food, well, it was out of the ordinary. But something about this guy, something about his grin. He was confused, no doubt. But he was happy, too. Probably a little retarded.

The man walked out of the bathroom. The jeans were on backward, the shirt was draped over his shoulders like a shawl with his chest, thick with hair, uncovered. He was still holding the shoes and hat.

Yep. A little retarded.

"Jesus Christ, boy," the trucker laughed. "Okay, let me help you."

Back at the booth three plates of bacon, eggs, and grits were laid out. The man gobbled down his plate.

"Boy," said the thin trucker, "you sure like your bacon, now don't you?"

The fat trucker smiled at his thin friend. The thin trucker smiled back. They both watched their passenger slurp down another fried egg. It was a good day.

After the meal the three wandered back to the truck. The man stopped before climbing in. He looked to the sky, looked to the sun.

"Don't stare too long," the fat trucker said. "You'll go blind."

The man looked south and pointed.

"Nope. Gotta head east. We're due in Chicago tomorrow."

The man still pointed south.

"Noooo," the fat trucker said with an exaggerated shake of his head. He pointed east. "We gotta go that way."

The man nodded. He stepped up to the thin trucker and hugged him hard.

"Whoa," the trucker said.

The man did the same to the fat trucker. "Okay now," the trucker said, his cheeks turning a low shade of red.

Then their passenger turned south and walked away.

"Good-bye, fella," the thin one said. The big one just waved.

The two truckers watched him walk for a while and then climbed into their truck. They drove east in silence. After some miles, one of them spoke.

"You know, Earl. I'm gonna miss that guy."

"Yeah, me too."

"Think he'll die out here?"

"I'm guessing he will."

Jesuses

NORTH AMERICA WAS crawling with Jesuses. Jesus-12 joined an organic farm commune in Oregon. Another Jesus (Jesus-27) made his way to the Pacific Ocean and walked out onto it. He was last seen by the residents of Seattle skipping over waves and giggling. Jesus-19 walked to Winnipeg, where he was taken in by a homeless shelter, given clothes and food, and taught how to use the Internet.

Jesus-7 wandered into a dress rehearsal of the Havant Church of Christ mime ministry team as they prepared a reprisal of their Easter play *Silent Passion*. Jesus-7 found the plot confusing and the mime clumsy, but he got the basic idea. Someone very nice and holy was being hurt. Jesus-7 was deeply moved and by the end of the performance had given his heart to the tall mime with the red spots on his wrists.

Jesus-10 made it all the way to New York City and stumbled into a scholarly bookstore near NYU. It was quiet and nearly empty. He liked the smell of old paper. On a shelf near the back, he found a copy of the New Testament written in ancient Aramaic. Jesus sat on the floor of the bookstore and read it from cover to cover. Sometimes he sighed, sometimes he chuckled. Other times, especially toward the end, his brow wrinkled into deep troubled trenches. After reading the last page, he stood up and clutched the book to his chest. Using crude hand signs, he asked the bookseller if this was the only book. The seller, thinking the man meant the only copy in the store, answered yes. Jesus-10 sprinted from the store and raced down the busy street ripping pages out as he went.

The Floaters observed all this with great interest and tried to come up with a plan to repopulate their heavens with Jesuses for the last day and a half of Earth. One solution was to gather up all the wandering Jesuses and give them a good talking-to. But it was doubtful whether that would work. Another idea was to clone more Jesuses. This plan also appeared flawed, as the Floaters had no reason to expect the next batch of Jesuses to perform any more obediently than the first. Finally the Floaters came up with the perfect solution. After some work and ingenuity, the Floaters made several clones of the tall mime artist who had played the leading role in the Havant Church of Christ performance of *Silent Passion*.

The plan worked smashingly. Jesus was silent and the heavens were happy.

Well, almost.

Hell in North Dakota

THE JESUS DEBACLE was not the only issue of the Heaven Domes. The Floaters were surprised to discover that many of the residents of the domes, in almost all the faiths of the world, did not think they belonged in heaven. Many believed they should be in hell. So the Floaters built a hell in North Dakota. It was a nasty place.

Hell had no light. No sound. Hell was an itchy soul feeling. A restlessness coupled with a certainty that no rest exists. An aimless anger. A soul-deep ennui.

But (and this floored the Floaters) the occupants of hell all seemed incredibly content. A little research revealed that these people had experienced the itchy soul syndrome their entire lives. But now, in hell, the feeling was understood as punishment. Finally their misery had meaning. There was a point to an existence they, in their heart of hearts, felt to be pointless. The Floaters took note.

He's dead. We're not.

COMPLETE DARK. BREATHING. Fast, shallow breaths echoing off the surrounding stone and wood, only inches away. She could sense her breath bouncing back. Sense that the world was too close. The air, thick with dust and wet, continued to tremor moments after the ground stilled. Water dripped on Rica's face and let her know she was alive. The breathing she heard was not hers alone; the woman with the bun was huddled next to her. Rica reached out a hand and felt a slab of concrete slanting just above her head. The woman's breaths grew faster, shallower. Rica placed her arms around her. "Shhh. It's all right. Shhh."

"We're dead. We're dead," the woman mumbled. "I can't see anything!"

"Take some breaths." She could feel the woman's panic twitch like an animal ready to thrash.

The woman tried to stand and smacked her head against the stone slab. "Oh God. Oh God."

Rica reached through the dark and took both her hands. "Calm down. Quiet." She said it with authority, like a scolding mother. "You could cave us in. I need your cell phone. Give it to me."

"What? What? There's no reception. Hasn't been for a day."

"Give it to me."

The woman fumbled around and placed a thin cell phone in Rica's hand. Rica touched the screen, shedding a low green light on the space. The rubble surrounded them, closing them in a tight cell no larger than the trunk of a car, though tall enough to kneel. The woman's face, a hand's breadth from Rica, was green and black in the dim light. Behind her Rica could make out the doctor's unmoving arm protruding from the debris. Rica faced the woman.

"Look at me. Keep looking at me." Rica could see the panic churning in her wide pupils. "What's your name?"

The woman didn't answer, her gaze darting from the low roof to the close walls, her face trembling. "He's my husband. My husband . . ."

Rica squeezed her hands. "Tell me your name," she ordered.

The woman looked at Rica. "Bethany. I'm Bethany."

"Bethany. I'm Rica." Rica nodded, her face nearly touching the woman's. The woman mirrored her nods. "I'm going to try and find a way out."

Rica quickly studied the walls, searching for a hole, a crawl space. Chunks of ceiling and tiles of what must have been the floor above were stacked on all sides like a confused game of Jenga. Rica didn't dare shift anything that might bring the rest of the wreckage down on them. She could feel the weight of the building teetering just above them. Something to her left caught her eye. Movement of some kind. Rica turned on her knees, guarding her belly carefully. One of the cots lay on its side. The ripped fabric bellowed slightly. Rica held an open palm by the hole and felt just a hint of breeze. She set down the cell phone and used both hands to widen the rip. She grabbed the phone and pushed it past the rip. She could make out the first few feet of a narrow hole, only as high the cot's width.

"Bethany, I need you to listen to me. You need to follow me."

"It's too tight. We can't."

"We can."

"We should wait here. We should stay here." The slab above them squeaked and the jigsaw walls shuddered.

"Bethany, it's time to go."

Rica bent to her hands and knees, her belly hovering a few inches from the ground. She pushed past the cot's fabric and into the passage, gripping the open cell phone. Rica cleared as she crawled, pushing debris behind her and instructing Bethany to do the same. It was slow moving, the sides narrowed, scratching against Rica's skin. The air tasted stale and thick with grit. Behind her Bethany's short gasps kept almost perfect rhythm.

"Hello!" Rica called out every few minutes. "Anyone?"

They crawled for what seemed an hour, pushing stone and sheetrock behind them, inching along. Occasionally a creak emanated from somewhere in the rubble and twice a snap and crash froze Rica's blood. The cell phone lit only a few feet ahead, going dark every few minutes until Rica pressed the screen and it lit green once again.

"Hello?" she called out.

No answer but the close echo of her own voice and Bethany's breathing. *Maybe they're all gone? Maybe Milton left? Maybe they think I'm dead? Maybe I am?*

The movement was slow. A foot of crawling for minutes of clearing. The debris seemed to be repeating itself, the same tile, the same broken cinder block. Rica shoveled them back. In the green darkness her mind wandered. She remembered high school loves, Dante, Hayden, a dozen letters she never wrote. What if she had sent one? What if she had reached out to him? Laughed at the silly moment in the closet. Tried to meet him again. This baby could have been his. She could be with him now, safe, happy. That life, that parallel path of what could have been shone like a distant lit city. If she stared, she could just make out details. The feel of Sunday mornings, the joy of waking up and knowing you are safe. Her hands were still clearing a path, inching forward. But her mind was drifting far away, living a life of different choices. Another life, finer and fuller. She was happier there. Blessed.

But she was here in the cramped ruins, surrounded by wet rubble and the sick green light of the cell phone.

Regret, like a phantom raven beside her, clawed at her head and heart. Regret pointed to the distant lights of that city that could've been and mocked what was. It was feeding off her. Growing fat off of her doubts, her self-hate. Every detail of her life was a morsel it devoured. It called itself hope or hindsight or wisdom, but it was regret.

"I want to go back," Bethany whimpered, her voice childlike and frightened.

"No. No. You're not going back."

"I should stay with him."

"Bethany, he's dead. We're not."

"I want to go back," she whimpered.

"No. No going back." Rica wished she could turn and face the other woman, but there was no room. "Bethany, can you see my ass?"

"Yes?"

"Have you seen the size of it? I mean, it's gotten big."

"Yes. It's big." The woman coughed a small laugh.

"It wasn't always that big. But it is now. Here's what you do, Bethany. Follow it. Don't think, just follow my ass. As long as you see it, you're okay."

Rica crawled on, listening for Bethany's movement. For a moment there was nothing, then Rica heard a shuffling. She was following. She was still there.

They moved slowly. Piece by piece. Stone by stone. Some bricks could be shoved only an inch to the side. Others wouldn't budge. More than once it seemed they could move no farther, and Rica would pause.

"Why are you stopping? What's wrong?"

"It's okay, Bethany. Eyes on the ass."

Eventually a brick would budge or a tile shift and Rica could clear some more space. She wasn't at all sure they weren't moving in circles. But stopping wasn't an option. There was too much fear in Bethany's breathing to stop. Rica muzzled her own panic. She had to. Her heart punched against her chest, but she refused to let fear win any ground. If Rica faltered, Bethany would tip into hysteria. She was too exhausted to fight for herself; Rica now survived for Bethany and her baby. The baby. The treasure in the box, jewel in the cushion. After an hour Rica discovered they were crawling upward. More and more they were on top of the debris, feeling pieces shift below them.

"Hello!" she yelled. This time she heard a reply. A faint voice behind feet of stone and wood. The voice came from ahead, so faint that Rica wasn't sure if it was only her imagination. But even if the voice was an illusion, she knew she needed it, at least for now. "Did you hear that, Bethany? We're close."

The passage ahead narrowed into a hole less than two feet wide. Rica stopped and caught her breath. In the faint light of the cell phone she couldn't make out if there was enough room to crawl with her belly. She would be stuck. Squeezed in. The rubble strained around her, sprinkling dust down. The baby would be stuck. Crushed inside of her. *God,* she thought, *I can't do this. Please don't ask me to do this.*

"You're stopping again. What's wrong?" Bethany said from behind, her voice high and brittle.

"Nothing. We're almost there." Rica bent low, her belly pressing against debris. She shimmied forward, doing her best to slow her breathing. She maneuvered from side to side, keeping the pressure on her hips. Bethany was close behind, both of them squeezed into a passage the size of a coffin. The phone went dark. Rica pressed the screen but nothing. She pressed all the buttons, but the phone was dead.

"Why's it dark? It's too dark."

"Bethany, we are so close. A little farther."

Rica tried to swallow the scream in her throat. She wanted to move, to shift forward, but she felt like stone. In the darkness the fear clenched each muscle, each bone. She felt the scream coming; she felt her legs trembling to kick. Hysteria like rising water filled the passage. Rica held her breath, but it was too much. She was breaking.

Then the light returned. A blue glow. Rica gasped in relief. She let her heart slow again and kissed the phone. But the phone was still blank. The light was coming from somewhere else.

"I see light!" Rica yelled. "Bethany, I can see light!"

The two crawled on, wriggling through a two-foot gap, upward and forward. The blue light grew brighter. It filled the passage. Rica used her feet to push forward, finding new footholds as she progressed.

"Hello? Hello?" she yelled out. More muffled voices called back, she couldn't tell from where. Ahead of her the passage stopped. The blues shone around the cracks of rock.

Rica pounded on the boards, pulling bits and pieces back, hearing the shifting of rubble on the other side. Tiny streams of new air touched her face and teased her lungs. She was close. Very close. A large cinder block with iron barbs refused to budge. Rica pushed, grunted, her whole body shoving against the cement. It moved. Rica froze. It moved again.

At first it seemed the iron barbs were moving, bending. But that wasn't it. Reaching around the block on either side were two pale hands. They gripped on the block and lifted it away. For a moment all Rica saw was blue. Then she saw a face filling the space where the block had been. A soft, wide face, ghostly blank like the expression of a drowned man still in the water. It stared for an instant and was gone. The blue was gone as well. Taking its place were the oranges and yellows of a Texas sunset. Rica pushed her head through the opening and sucked in the air.

"Bethany," Rica yelled. "We're here."

It was a tight squeeze. Rica moved onto her side, dipping her shoulder to fit through. She pushed with her feet and slid out onto the gravel and rock. She rolled over and gulped breaths, her last sip of energy swallowed and gone.

She could hear footsteps approaching, voices calling out. "Over on this side. I see someone." She could feel Bethany emerging. Rica watched the sky, watched the warm hues. A face appeared above her, old with a dirty gray beard and hair, but with eyes clear and blue. And real. Undeniably real. The sun was only minutes below the horizon, the sky like warm coals, the wind moving. All real. Regret, that phantom, could never promise anything as wonderful as real. The city of lights it pointed to could never be reached. It would always remain a lie shining in the distance. But Milton was a truth, a truth now touching her face.

"Oh, Rica, oh my sweet God," Milton said. He reached his arms around her. Rica wept.

If you're going to go bear, go grizzly

MILTON AND ROY had raced from the sanctuary after the first rumble and saw the crowd pushing out of the basement door. Then the collapse. Two of the walls of the one-story building buckled and the roof sank in like a deflating soufflé.

Milton searched the crowd for Rica, screaming her name. He found Blade, the one he called War, and grabbed him by the collar.

"Is she in there?"

"Man, I don't know."

"She went back," said Pestilence. "She went back for some lady and then it all fell in. I tried to get her out."

The digging was frantic. Milton, Roy, and a handful of the strongest volunteers started immediately. They dug on the far side of the building, estimating the spot Rica was last seen. Three of the Horsemen joined in. The other, the one Milton called Death, sat in the back of War's pickup truck, watching them all with dark, hollow eyes. The group worked fast, removing bricks and sheetrock, careful not to step on the debris and cause another cave-in.

Most had helped, but no one had dug and searched like Milton. Roy, working slowly at his side, saw the sweat expand over his back. Milton's palms ripped against the cinder blocks and he bled on all that he lifted, his fingernails, old from his new age, split and chipped as he worked. No matter how much they moved, more rubble was there.

After an hour of digging, they had developed a system, a passing of the heavier rocks, a careful discussion of what to move next. They were below ground level now, reaching and pulling out rubble.

Roy stepped away as Milton and the others argued over what to move. The wound on his neck pulsed against the bandage and his strength was tapped. He sat on one of the children's swings facing the ruins and popped another Vicodin, swallowing it with spit.

Pestilence came and sat by him, wiping sweat from his brow.

"I don't know why we keep digging," he said, his toothless gums smacking.

"These basements were built as bomb shelters. She could still be fine."

"Your friend, the old guy, he thinks the world is ending. You believe that?"

"It's got to end sometime." The Vicodin was coating his throat, easing everything.

"Yeah, sure. I've read the Bible." The man nodded. "You believe in hell?"

Roy looked at him, his pocked face and half beard. "Why do you ask?"

He shrugged. "I don't know. Just asking." He spit on the sand. "I shot a man down there, before everything fell down. It was an accident, but I was aiming the gun at him. You know what I mean?"

Roy was quiet for a moment. "I shot a man yesterday."

"The guy who shot you? That doesn't seem unreasonable."

"I didn't have to shoot him in the head."

"Well, if you're going to go bear, go grizzly." He rose to his feet and rubbed his hands down his filthy jeans. "I sure hope there's no hell."

"You said it, brother."

Someone yelled and everyone ran to find Rica crawling from her hole.

Pestilence and Roy scrambled, too. They watched as Milton ran to Rica and she sobbed with an intensity that made onlookers blush or cry themselves. Milton held her, his arms so tight it seemed he was afraid she'd float away or fall back under the rubble. Milton looked out to Roy.

"Car," he said. And Roy understood.

He turned for the parking lot as another woman was pulled from the hole, her body shaking.

"Is he here? Did he get away?" she was asking through her sobs.

"Who?" people were asking, wrapping a blanket around her.

She cried herself into chest-shaking coughs.

"Can I take one of these?" Roy asked one of the volunteers stuffing grocery bags. She was watching nothing but the scene in the rubble. "Thank you," Roy said as he grabbed a bag.

Roy found a late-model green Volvo wagon parked on the far side of the lot in a spot reserved for the pastor. He picked up a fist-size rock. For a moment he hesitated, but then caught sight of the bumper sticker reading IN CASE OF

RAPTURE THIS CAR WILL BE VACATED. Roy shrugged and smashed in the driver's side window. He reached in and unlocked the door. He tossed the grocery bag onto the passenger seat, cleared the driver's seat of glass with a sweep of his arm, and ducked a head under the steering column. His shoulder ached in protest, but he had no time for complaints. With a few pulls of wire, a click or two and a spark, the engine came to life. The radio was on, too.

"So make an unbeliever your designated driver tonight, all right!"

"Hey!" someone yelled.

Roy shot up, smacking his head against the steering wheel.

Pestilence stood by the door. "You leavin'?" he asked, rubbing his jeans with nervous hands.

Roy nodded.

Pestilence glanced around and then back at Roy. "So, let me ask you. If the world is ending and everything, what do I do? Like, you know, to get saved."

Roy shook his head.

"Come on, man. You must have something."

Behind him Roy could see Milton helping a nearly limp Rica toward the car.

"Milton," Roy called out. "He wants to know what to do now."

Milton kept moving toward the car. "Some will have no idea something like freedom exists. They will die inside an open cell. Some will leave and bring their cruelty with them. Insane souls begging through the stars." He reached the Volvo. "And some will pop and become who they are already. Alive and kind. Free souls."

"Stop fucking around and tell me what to do," Pestilence said, helping to lift Rica into the backseat of the car.

Milton paused by the back door with a confused look. "Be kind."

Pestilence nodded. He looked at Roy. "Okay."

"Broncos!" War called out. "Let's go." The truck's engine roared twenty feet away. Pestilence gave a childish wave and a toothless grin, then ran to join his friends. He leaped into the cab with War behind the wheel. Famine sat in the truck's bed beside his pale friend. The truck spit grass and soil as it growled off of the lawn and back onto the road. Roy watched the red taillights, a burning pair like the holes in his neck. And the sick friend sat high, unmoving and unmoved by the frantic escape. He stared back, he stared at Roy, dark unblinking eyes quickly disappearing in the dusk, passing sentence without judgment. The eyes said nothing of guilt or innocence, but they most certainly spoke of death.

Milton climbed in the back with Rica and slammed the door.

"Where to, Captain?" Roy asked as they pulled away from the church.

"Take us there," Milton said, pointing at a billboard hovering just ahead. It read

88.6 krst marfa, texas

west texas's #1 christian rock station

all christian all the time!

Wrinkle in the soul

EACH PERSON CARRIES the scar of their birth, the button on their belly, the souvenir from a time of utter reliance. Our navels were the parting gift as we were thrust from a safe haven, marking the moment when the pipes were cut, food and blood flowed no more, and we cried and crawled for a nipple. When after ten lunar months of simply receiving, we had to seek and suck.

We also carry the scar of our next birth, the death birth. You'd never know it. Of course you'd never know what a belly button was if no one had told you. But if you examine your soul carefully you'll find a bump. A sweet wrinkle in the soul. This is the soul-navel. The scar of a birth into death that is yet to happen. How can one have a scar for something that hasn't happened yet? Silly question. As if the soul wears a watch.

Worlds have belly buttons. We often call ours Eden. There was no prayer in Eden. Only conversation. But those fruit-filled bites severed our cord and we learned to seek, to suck, and to pray.

Worlds also have soul-navels. A future death scar. Marfa, Texas, is the soul-navel of this world.

Don't look so surprised.

Marfa, jewel of the West Texas desert. The air is no cooler, the soil no more fertile, there is no water. But Marfa lives. An eruption of life in the middle of quiet desert. Marfa. Sweet Marfa. Brilliant Marfa. Named for one of Dostoevsky's loves, refuge to homeless hipsters, haven to desert readers, host to music and art and film. The population is less than three thousand. The elevation is less than three hundred. The average rainfall is less than three inches. Yet Marfa is the most important spot on our planet. The desert Eden. She is the scar commemorating our world's transition from womb to open existence.

Giggle giggle

"ALL THE WAY to the city?" asked the bald man who was no longer bored.

"..."

"It's crowded there."

"..."

"Okay. We can take my truck."

The two of them drove to the city. The bald man driving, the crab sitting beside him. They parked downtown near a fountain and left the keys in the ignition. Click walked in front. The bald man followed.

Next came a lawyer about to race into a mid-morning meeting. The world might be going nuts, but he was sure as hell going to save his firm. He was jumping from a cab toward the glass doors of his office building. And he saw Click on the sidewalk.

He paused.

He saw the arrow.

He saw his next step.

And the next, and the next.

Just to the end of the block, he told himself.

Then came another block, and another. He found he was pressing for the crosswalk so that the crab might pass unscathed. The tall bald man caught his eye. They shared a smile.

Just ten more feet, then I must be on my way. Ten hours later and the lawyer still believed that at any moment he would scurry back to his mid-morning meeting.

The next follower was a movie rental store clerk, then an ER doctor, then an auto mechanic, then a teenage girl who saw Click the moment before her first kiss. The boy's lips were approaching and it meant everything. She would kiss this boy. She would love this boy. She would marry this boy and bear his children. She would . . . Crab. Follow.

All day, one by one, people caught sight of Click and stepped into his entourage. Poor, rich, old, young, black, white. As someone new joined, all the followers smiled at one another, as if to agree how silly it was to be walking (and walking slowly) behind a blue-green hermit crab. And how it was sillier still that they had spent so much time doing anything else. They followed Click down city streets, through open parks, onto a bus, down a highway, off a bus, through a parking lot, down a trail, onto another road.

Occasionally the crab allowed the teenage girl or the bald man to carry him in the palm of their hands, his arrow leading the way. But more often, they walked behind his crawl. Each felt protective of the crab. There was something electric, magic, flamboyant, neon, statically shocking about him.

Sometimes the followers sang. Often Beatles songs because everyone knew the lyrics, even the teenage girl. "With a Little Help from My Friends," "I Want to Hold Your Hand," "Yellow Submarine."

The sun moved, the wind brushed the trees, the road stretched on, others joined. Rain sprinkled. Clouds passed. The people had never known such purpose, such joy, such trust. Lead on, Arrow-Crab.

The day was filled with silent *whys*.

Why was I a lawyer for so long? Why have I never forgiven my brother? Why do I own so many pairs of shoes? Why do I detest waking in the morning? Why do I avoid thinking about death? Why do I hate quiet?

The *whys* were so numerous that they may never have reached the question, *Why am I following this hermit crab?* Then, in the late afternoon, they stopped asking questions. Instead they watched the clouds and grass and road cracks and bird shadows and tree bark. Slow walking. Three hours to a mile.

Family and friends tried to save the walkers.

"It's a dangerous time right now. You need to come home."

"No, I don't."

"Your children miss you."

"Yes. Tell them I send my love."

"You're going to lose your job."

Giggle, giggle.

Click liked his new friends. He never quite saw himself as leading them as much as being on the same path. And what was that path? He didn't know. He knew the next inch. That was always sure. And once he had covered that inch, then the next inch was sure. Almost glowing with certainty. But he also sensed that the final goal was many thousands of inches away.

Something far and rich. More than he could grasp. So he didn't try. He let the unknown shine on him like a warm, distant sun.

Shining, shining, even as the night fell.

The sky rolled dark. Stars appeared. Click and the walkers traveled on.

All Christian, all the time

AMI JAMES WAS huddled in a dark corner of the KRST studio. She was shaking. She was alone. She had been alone for over twenty hours. Music was blaring. She was chanting.

"All Christian, all the time. All Christian, all the time."

Oh God, why hadn't she believed harder?

Two days before she had been so happy. She was a radio-television-film major at Sul Ross State University in Alpine by day and an intern at KRST assisting Rich Van Sturgeon by night.

She loved the job. Filling out notice sheets, fetching CDs and news updates for Mr. Van Sturgeon, even occasionally answering the call lines. Not since helping to build that house in Mexico two spring breaks back had she felt so needed, so on track.

Working for KRST was a dream. Richard Van Sturgeon's voice was silk, his shoulders could lift a small car, he smelled of a woodsy musk, and he had a heart for Jesus. Every song he played was perfect. He knew the classics like an artist knows colors. Every night he crafted a masterpiece from the songs of Keith Green, Jars of Clay, Michael W. Smith, early Amy Grant (before her sexy secular phase, please), and, of course, Pearl-Swine.

Friday night there had been four people at the KRST studio. Van Sturgeon, Ami, Susan from marketing, and Pedro, Susan's boyfriend. Susan and Pedro were working overtime on an upcoming Easter food drive. A basket of food for each needy family and chocolate bunnies for the children. They were in the office searching for the perfect verse for the giveaway bumper stickers they'd include in the baskets. Ami shared a smile with the two of them as she passed through carrying a cold Red Bull for Van Sturgeon.

"Know any good chocolate verses?" Susan asked.

"Gosh, no," Ami said. "But thank God it's not a sin or I'd never be forgiven."

"Amen, sister," Pedro said, laughing. Ami hurried on. She loved making the folks at KRST laugh. That was her spiritual gift, she thought. Lightheartedness. She made her professors laugh in Alpine, she made her youth group laugh, she even got laughs out of the tattooed sculptors and musicians who hung out in Marfa coffee shops, though less frequently.

"Ah, yes. Intern Ami is bringing me a chilled Red Bull to keep the night going," Van Sturgeon said into the microphone in a low melodic whisper. She loved it when he mentioned her by name. He reached out for the can, winking at Ami. "Because, friends," he told KRST's hundreds of listeners, "the time is so close. Any minute. I wouldn't worry about next month's bills, or taking that blood pressure medicine."

He'd been pushing the end times message for a while now. Ami preferred his grace kick or his "life to the fullest" stories. The Judgment and Apocalypse talk all landed heavy and cruel.

"Listen, people. It is time to say good-bye to time. It is time to prepare for eternity. Right now! Because the end could happen before I end this sentence, before I complete the thought, in the blink of an— "

A blast, like hearing a car horn with your head trapped under the hood. Van Sturgeon vanished. Simply gone. The Red Bull can fell to the floor and rolled under the control board, trailing yellow liquid.

Ami screamed. She ran to the office. "Rich disa—" The office was empty. Nothing of Susan and Pedro but a half-filled Easter basket. Ami screamed again. A salmon-pink Bible lay open on Susan's desk. Ami knew. She knew immediately. They had been taken and she had been left. She ran back to the studio. And again, back to the office. Oh, God, why hadn't she believed more? Why hadn't she tried? God had left her. She vomited onto Susan's desk.

All those shoes she owned. So many shoes when so many were shoeless. Or the way she treated her sister. Or that one night with the boy in Mexico. That wasn't working for the kingdom. And pride. Always pride. Oh, God was right to leave her. Oh.

She grabbed Susan's Bible. It was worn and heavy. She squeezed it to her chest and walked back into the studio. She paced back and forth, her head filled with sick slugs of guilt, crawling and sucking.

The red sign reading ON THE AIR was still lit. Ami sat in Van Sturgeon's empty chair. She could still smell his aftershave. With a shaking hand she shuffled through the CDs lined up for the next hour of play. She found Pearl-Swine's *Pearl-Swine* and placed the disc in the player. She selected the last song and hit repeat, sending "Who's Gonna Park the Car" out onto the airwaves.

She let her body fall from the chair onto the floor. The room seemed too large. Dangerous. She pushed herself back into a corner and pulled her knees to her, sandwiching the Bible between her thighs and chest. She rocked back and forth to the rhythm of the song.

All those that love the Lord are going to take flight . . .

Over the music she heard cars pass. She heard voices. She never left her corner. It was a test, she was sure. *Jesus loves me, this I know.*

She slept in fits. She dreamed in shadows. No narrative. No sense. The sun rose, rays of light cutting through the open blinds. More cars, a police siren, some yelling. Then quiet. At noon she crawled to the toilet. She peed and drank palmfuls of water from the sink, still clinging to the Bible. She found a pack of Tic Tacs in Susan's purse and poured them into her mouth. *This is stealing. You are a thief.* She crawled back to her corner.

"All Christian, all the time. All Christian, all the time," she chanted.

Night came again. Ami was sure her mind would not survive it. She tried to close her eyes, tried to sleep. But no sleep came.

She heard a rumble outside. A car close. It was pulling into the KRST parking lot, making her insides spin. *Oh God,* she thought. *UN Peacekeepers. They're going to shoot me.* She crept to the window and peeked through the blinds. A green Volvo station wagon was parking in front of the studio. A very pregnant woman was climbing out, followed by an old man with long, gray hair and a beard to match. *Oh no. Hippies.*

A short younger man walked from the driver's side. His face. She knew that face. She jumped to the pile of CDs, tripping over Van Sturgeon's chair as she did.

There. Look. There. She peered through the blinds again. "Who's Gonna Park the Car" swung into its bridge.

"Oh God," Ami cried out. "Jesus sent Pearl-Swine to save me!"

Are you live?

AMI STOOD AND tried unsuccessfully to smooth her wrinkled skirt. The door that led to the main office was closed. Pearl-Swine would be walking right through that door. She could just hear them call out over the music. She wanted to call back. She tried, but a choked breath was all that came out. She stepped back and knocked a clipboard to the ground.

"Hello?" a woman's voice called. Ami saw the dark shadows of feet beneath the door. Panic grabbed her by the ears and kissed her full on the mouth. "Anyone in there?"

Ami watched the door. She did not want it to open. But she desperately did not want to be left alone again. Couldn't they just stay close? Could they stay in the office and slip her notes and pancakes under the door? The doorknob was turning. Everything else, the walls, the music, her hunger, the pink Bible blurred into a distant background. The door opened with a slow squeak. Ami felt the squeak unwind like a ribbon and fly around her neck, tightening with each inch of open door.

"Hello?" Roy Clamp's face was peeking around the door. "Are you okay?"

Ami's eyes filled. She gasped and the Bible fell from her arms.

"Are you alone in here?"

Roy Clamp's eyes. Ami opened her mouth to answer. A high, quivering voice came out. She was singing.

I lived to die so by and by you could have my Heart Gift . . .

"Oh, poor girl," said the pregnant woman. She stepped forward and put her arms around Ami. Strong arms. Ami felt she could fall if needed. "You're okay now."

The old man moved past them and was staring at the control board. "Are you live?" he asked.

"*I know you're low. I know you need a lift . . .*" Ami kept her eyes on Roy Clamp. He had a bandage on his neck. He was hurt!

"Milton, we have to get her out of here," the warm pregnant woman said.

"Which button to work the mic?" the old man asked.

Ami turned to him. His eyes and gray hair were exploding. He was frightening and wonderful. *Elijah was going on the air. Elijah.*

"Blue button," she said.

Elijah nodded. "Take her to the car. I'll be right out."

Pregnant Woman and Roy Clamp took her arms and led her through the office and out through the glass door. It was cool outside. Good air. *What is he saying? What is Elijah saying to the KRST listening family?*

"Would you like an M&M?" Pregnant Woman asked her. Ami ate a yellow one. It was delicious. She ate a red one. Just as tasty.

In less than two minutes, Elijah walked out the glass door. "All done. Let's go."

"What about the TV actor?" Roy Clamp asked.

"Don't worry," Elijah said. "He's near."

Brendan's blood

SO MY SPIRIT trembles within me,
my heart turns to stone.

Compline. Night Prayer. Brother Brendan had Hayden beside him.

I remind myself of the days of old,
I reflect on all your works,

Brother Brendan had chanted these same chants before, countless times before. He loved them as a man loves a brother.

I meditate once more on the work of your hands.
I stretch out my arms to you,

The Psalms. Praise poems and songs that cry to God. Bright, burning words.

I stretch out my soul, like a land without water.

They were Brendan's blood, they ran through him and his days, through his veins and the veins of his day, carrying life. Chanting is the pounding heart muscle that powers the Psalms though the veins. Each day, each night, seven times in the passing of the sun, always worship, beating in this chapel, beating here before the Host. These voices all seeking more than salvation, more than heaven, more than sanctification, seeking God. Seeking only God.

Same words he read, until the reading was no longer needed, for the words were written on his chest and eyes and tongue. Same words he heard from all the brothers, each voice a man alone, each voice together; sometimes he heard just one monk, one brother, and felt his life. Sometimes all the voices were one voice, one buzz hum, a thick cloud rising from the desert, from this hidden church, up to the sky, to God.

They soaked the walls with chant and words. Leaned against the wall and stained a robe with mud and Psalm.

Same words he chanted too loudly on his first day here a decade and more ago, hoping to impress (foolishness), the same words his mind used to see flowers and towers and trees. Same words he had whispered before he came here, walking the streets after teaching children, finding parks, lying under day-sky night-sky. Using these words to pop clouds and bring rain. The words with the rain and the wet soil he lay on.

Same words, though mumbled and mixed from a child's tongue, he stuttered in the water well his sisters lowered him into, leaving him there as a game. Clinging to a bucket, cold water wetting his pants and shoes, damp brick walls, the circle of sun and silhouetted heads above. He chanted there dangling alone, too long, too long, and as his father pulled him up, the dark running off him and falling below, and as he reached the sun and sky and father's arms, he knew he would be a monk, before he knew what a monk was, he knew.

These words.

Same words mother mouthed while father lay dying in the wheat. Same heard as a child, his grandfather's spittle on his hymnal, his sister covering her laugh. Yes. The same words. They hold those years and the years before, before years, buildings unbuilt taken back stone from stone, unmaking of the bricks themselves, returning to dirt and water. No building. Meeting under tents, under tree branches, on boat decks crossing a salt-sick Atlantic, in hidden caves in English hills, these words whispered, half an ear listening for protestants passing who also read these words and also kill. Yes, and back. Francis spoke these, and Benedict as his monks served him poison and pushed him from the church and the glorious heretics chanted these words. Pelagius, you rolled and rolled from Wales to Rome and home again. And farther, and farther, desert fathers, and women, too. Alone. Chanting in huts and caves as the devils came as seducers, children, false Christs. They chanted and the devils dissolved. These words melted them like saltwater on slugs. Fathers and mothers alone but not alone. He knew he was there as well because he spoke these words and these words were said by them. Communion of the saints. And Jesus. You said these words. And your father said them and your blessed mother and brothers and your cousin John. You disappeared to lonely places to pray and chant and be. You still disappear to lonely places. We still seek

you and tell you of hungry crowds asking for you. You bless bread and hand us baskets, nibbled only after followers, all followers, carried the bread to the people. He
was there, carrying the basket from Christ to the people, chanting as he worked.
The bread in his arms is heavy, the day is heat, his mouth waters seeing the eating,
but he will wait to eat, hoping the miracle is large enough. Psalms, these words,
soak up the saliva from his mouth, absorbing the want. You said these words on
the cross. *Father? Father? Why* ... These words became the language of God's broken heart, and they pierced your heart, and blood flowed and water flowed, wetting the soldiers' feet ... *Surely this man ... surely* ... Yes. And back and back. The
words stinking of burning fat and sticky with lamb blood, covenant blood. The
words said on the shores of the Nile. Exile calls, mothers beating their children
so they might remember a stone temple that no longer stands. Know the words.
Cry the words. Mix the words with tears. Make mud, shape cups. Let them dry
in the pagan world heat. Drink from them. Make temple bricks, save them for
the return, for return. And the rape of the concubine, she said these words, cried
out. Was she heard? *Father, Father? Why* ... And back again to the king who
wrote these words, a holy demon of a man with a blood-soaked throne and bird's
eye view of waiting wives. Waiting and waiting. Why weren't you at war, David?
And back before the words were sung or said, they rattled about, ghosts waiting
for a body. Moses could hear them in a fire's crackle, in his own stutter, mourning
mothers of Egypt cradling dead babies. Words fell from heaven but would last
a day. Try to save them for the next day, and they would rot in your mouth. And
the sons, and Ishmael, and the stolen blessing, and midnight wrestling. Words
dropped with flood rain, these words covered the land and drowned the women
and children and men and animals. All made into mud that dried into dirt that
became a desert. A tower built with human words reaching up to steal the dew
of heaven. God let one drop fall and wet the stones back into mud and sent the
children running with no words they all knew. No words to build with. Further.
Eden, when sin was not a sin and humans walked with God and these words
needed no words. And before. Father. The words used to shape, carve, and craft.
God-spit and God-dust making mortar and building.

The world was soft then, like new gold. God pressed his hands against the
soft. And yes, before. The words in God's silence. Before there was God because
when there was nothing but God, no names were needed. And the words were
God. And the words were not heard, not spoken.

And here now. Same words. Speak them. Chant them. Each holding all.

I have touched fire

"THESE WORDS BUG me," Hayden said in a low whisper. Brother Brendan didn't seem to hear. His eyes were closed and his mouth opened in chant. Hayden turned to the other monk on his right. "Don't these words bug you?" The other monk growled at Hayden.

Who hath placed peace in thy borders and filleth thee with the fat of corn.

Hayden was sitting in the wooden pews of the chapel among thirty of the brothers. Each brother held a book with the words of the chants. One had been loaned to Hayden. Occasionally, seemingly at random, all the monks would stand, cross themselves, and bow low toward the altar. At first Hayden had tried to keep up, follow the words, stand and bow. But after half an hour he grew restless.

Who sendeth forth his speech to the earth. His word runneth swiftly.

It was warm in the chapel. Too warm. And the chanting never stopped.

He scattereth mists like ashes . . . He sendeth hail like crumbs . . .

Hayden's lungs tightened. The smell of sweat-soaked wool filled his chest.

Who shall stand before the face of his cold?

The chanting burrowed into his head.

He shall send out his word . . . and shall melt them . . .

Too hot. Too close in here. Too many words.

He shall breathe and the waters shall run . . .

Hayden rose to his feet to leave. As he stood, so did all the monks. They crossed themselves and bowed as Hayden shuffled past and out the door.

The desert air felt cool and clean. He took deep breaths. The first stars of the night were appearing above the monastery. Hayden paced back and forth in front of the chapel doors. He could still hear the sounds of chanting, but not the words.

Was this why these men were here? Living mad lives on the banks of a poison river? Words they've chosen to believe?

Hayden was an actor, and like all actors he did not trust words.

The more he stood waiting, the more stars he watched shimmer into view, the angrier he became. The sky was filled with stars when Brendan finally walked from the chapel. On seeing Hayden, Brendan smiled but said nothing. He started walking across the yard. Hayden followed and moved to his side.

"Do you know what I know?" Hayden asked. The monk shrugged. Hayden continued, "I know that writers control the world. Always have and always will. It's slow, because they have to wait for things to sink in. TV writers are faster. TV, movies, blogs, Twitter. Before that it was novels, before that plays, before that songs, before that Bibles. All writers. I've met them, Brendan. Stay the hell away from them. They'll make you cry. Or laugh. Laugh out loud. Or make you think something or another thing. But they don't actually think it. They don't actually believe it. They're not crying."

Brendan said nothing. Hayden went on.

"Once at a charity event, I read these lines from a teleprompter all about humanity overcoming the greatest challenges, all about shining in our darkest hours. I got weepy reading it. On a commercial break I found the writer by the coffee stand. He had poured out all the sweeteners. A pile of Sweet'N Low, a pile of Splenda, a pile of Equal. He was adding them in pinches to his coffee. I told him I loved his words. He smirked. He smirked at me. He said to me, 'It's a job, huh? Nice tears, though. Nice touch. That'll get 'em.'"

They arrived at the long building where Hayden had first met Brother Brendan. Brendan opened the door and walked in. Hayden followed.

"See? He lied. He didn't believe it, but he knew how to make me believe it."

Brendan sat in one of the chairs that had once surrounded the table. "But you wanted to believe it," he said.

"So?" Hayden said, walking in circles around the room. "I want to believe I'm not an asshole. Doesn't make it true."

Hayden plunked down across from the monk. Brendan reached out and touched Hayden's nose.

"Friend," Brendan said. "I have seen whales crash through the desert floor from the ocean beneath. I have come eye to eye with sage grasshoppers. I have touched fire, held it in my hand, and hid it in my heart. I have shared riddles with angels. I have tasted dew gathered from the first tree on the third day."

"Yes, but Brendan, you're crazy." Hayden paused a second to see if this had offended him. It didn't seem to, so he went on. "None of that was real. I want reality."

"The real world hides under reality. You have to lose all of it to get a taste of any of it."

"I can't believe that—"

"Stop trying to believe. Just have faith."

"I don't know how," Hayden said.

"Right now, stand up, and walk out. Go into the desert. You'll meet Jesus. Follow him."

"It's dark."

Brendan nodded.

"I'll get lost."

Brendan nodded again.

"And I'll find Jesus?"

"Yes."

"I don't believe you."

"Do it anyway."

Hayden swallowed. He stood up and walked to the door. He'd rather stay. He'd rather drink more coffee and talk in the warmth. He looked back at Brendan swatting at invisible things flying around his head. Hayden took a deep breath and stepped outside.

Fooled by time

RICA USED A can of Campbell's vegetable soup as her base. She added black pepper from four single-serving pepper packets, a sprig of sage, and lastly, with a flash of inspiration, she sliced an apple into the soup. She mixed it all in the hubcap of the late-model Volvo and balanced it on two stones above the campfire Milton had built from scrub and cedar branches.

She and Milton sat watching the new flames lick the bottom of the hubcap while Roy sat in the Volvo, the girl re-dressing his wounds.

Wind whistled through telephone lines. A sad, high-pitched mourning. They had traveled only twenty miles west before Milton, seeing the Marfa Mystery Lights Observation Site, asked Roy to pull over. It was basically a rest stop. A bathroom, a few picnic tables, and a paved platform facing the southwest desert.

Beside the road, the Observation Site, and a few barbed-wire fences, nothing man-made could be seen. The four set up camp near a concrete picnic table. The sun had been below the horizon for over an hour now. The mountains in the distance loomed like whale shadows against the sea-blue sky.

Just a little more time, she thought, slowly stirring the contents of the hubcap with a dried branch. She smiled at the phrase. Time. As if she knew anything about time. Time was a prankster, not to be trusted. She patted her belly. Look how time had folded in on itself, squeezed months into days. She knew the baby would come soon. It was as inevitable as a sunrise.

When she was still, when she let the panic evaporate like sweat from her skin, she could feel her body prepare with the tightening of muscles, the softening of chambers and an excited peace that played in her chest like song. The dance was coming and the hall was being decorated. Her body had never questioned the abrupt jump from four months to seven-plus, never rebelled against time's trick. Her body simply giggled at the change of date and rearranged its plans. Her mind had not yet caught up. Her mind still clung to panic and reason. *How could this be? If time is no longer trustworthy, what's left to trust?*

She was stirring the soup with the branch and with the other hand slowly rubbing circles on her belly.

"How's that baby cooking?" Milton asked from the far side of the fire.

"Fast," she said. Milton was warming his hands near the flames, his shoulders curling inward like a fallen leaf. She could see it; he was also approaching the inevitable. Had also been fooled by time.

"How are you feeling?" she asked.

"Tired," he said, smiling and revealing whitening gums. "And old."

"You're still younger than you'll ever be."

Milton laughed a little. She studied his eyes. Sad but still bright.

"I'm so sorry, Rica."

"You didn't make this happen."

"I thought I had years. More time to do things right."

"Everyone says that at the end of the world." She pushed herself to her feet and walked to Milton. She sat beside him, leaning into his shoulder. She took his hand, cut and bruised from digging through rubble.

"Why save me?" she asked. He looked to her. "Why dig me out of that basement if we're all going to die?"

"You know, I think the Floaters have it all wrong. Our problem isn't madness. It's our sick dedication to sanity."

She frowned. He smiled.

"Rica, the best things I've done have made no sense at all."

She smiled and pushed her head to his chest. "I claim you, Milton Post. I claim you as mine."

She could feel his chest fill with a deep breath. Feel his body curve into hers.

"And you, Rica, are mine."

Most wonderful man alive

ROY HAD HIS shirt off. The girl was close, cleaning his wounds with bottled water. The grocery bag had held a small first aid kit. Not much more than some Neosporin and a few gauzes. He had popped two more Vicodin and felt fine.

She was close and he could smell her. Vanilla and sweat.

"You're good at this," he said.

She nodded.

He turned a little to see her face.

"Head up, please," she said.

"Sorry." He kept his eyes on the Volvo's dome light. "What's your name?"

"Ami," she said to his shoulder.

"I'm Roy."

"I know," she said. "I have your poster above my bed."

"Must be an old poster."

She was cleaning his neck now, the sting causing Roy to flinch. She pressed gauze against him.

"That one is still bleeding."

"It'll stop," he said, though he wasn't sure that was true. He felt like a cracked cup, life slowly but surely leaking out.

Ami leaned back and rubbed her knees. Roy could see her face now, though hair hid her eyes.

"Thank you, Doctor," he said, clapping his hands together. "What do I owe you?"

"I think you're wonderful," Ami said, eyes on her feet.

Roy kept his hands palm to palm and smiled. "Because I called you Doctor?" he asked.

"I've always thought you were wonderful." She looked up at Roy, her eyes peeking from behind her bangs. "Most wonderful man alive."

"Well, there's been a Rapture," he said. "All the good men are taken."

Ami laughed, a young, unafraid laugh. It happened to be the most wonderful noise Roy had ever heard.

Old-fashioned prayer

THE FOUR GATHERED around the small fire, gulping soup from used cans. They ate quickly at first, then slowed as the hunger pangs eased. Above them the sky changed to darker blues, and clouds floated by like shadow continents. In the gaps between clouds, the moonless sky was alive with starlight.

"The soup is perfect," Roy said, slurping another swallow. "It tastes like something. Like Earth."

"Yeah, that's it. I couldn't place it. But that is it. The way Earth should taste." Milton said.

"You might be tasting actual dirt," Rica said. "But I'm glad you like it."

For a few moments, they ate in silence.

"It's quiet," Ami said.

"No insects," Milton said, poking at the fire with a stick. "They've left."

"Left?" Roy asked.

"They worked for the Floaters. Janitorial mainly. Cockroaches, it turns out, are the clean freaks on Earth. We've had clean all wrong. We've had most things wrong." He threw the stick into the fire. He looked at his hand in the light. It was spotted and loose. "Most of the bacteria has left, too. Some stayed. Things will still rot, just more slowly."

"What are Floaters?" Ami asked.

The others hesitated. Finally Roy answered. "Caretakers, Ami," he said. "A bit like angels."

She nodded. "My mother was obsessed with angels," she said. "Had them hanging all over the house, on her keychain, on checks." She laughed a little and paused. "She's gone, I imagine. Dad, too."

Once again the group fell silent.

"I wonder how my parents are," Rica said into the flames.

"I'm older than my father ever was now," Milton mumbled to himself. "That's weird."

"How about you, Roy?" Rica asked. "Any family out there?"

"Nobody," Roy said. "My grandfather died shortly after I offered to throw him a funeral. Haven't seen my father in years."

The four sat in silence for a long while, gazing at the failing flames. Rica palmed her belly, feeling a tiny foot pressing upward.

It grew cooler, the sage-scented wind carrying hints of mountain air. Above them clouds dissolved to reveal more stars than she could remember seeing. With a sky that large and the warm earth below her, Rica found it hard to believe the world would end tomorrow, or ever. She watched the coals grow cooler and wondered if worlds grew cool as well. If existence faded like heat.

Roy tossed another branch onto the fire, sending sparks flying.

Rica looked up, off into the desert. She saw the lights first. Three off-white lights, like headlights, but fuzzier, appeared miles to the west. A fourth joined.

"Look at that."

The lights skipped along the horizon, playfully darting around each other. Sometimes zipping vertically and other times slowly bouncing up and down.

"What are they?" Rica asked.

"The mystery lights," Ami said. "People see them all the time. Drive out here just to watch them. They say they're ghosts or UFOs or something. No one knows."

"I've seen them before," Rica, remembering as she spoke. "When my family moved to Texas. I was a kid. I remember standing with my dad. It must have been around here."

"They look friendly, don't they?" Roy said.

"They look kind," Milton said.

They bumped and jumped, like children with flashlights.

"I like them," Rica said.

Milton reached and touched Rica's back. She sighed and nuzzled into him. She breathed in as much of him as her lungs could hold. She felt tired and strangely content. He reached a hand around her and let it rest on her belly. Swirl, swirl, swirl went the lights, went the baby. All her fears and worries had no place in this moment. She watched the lights, watched them dance.

"Milt," Roy said, a hand on his bandaged neck. "Can't we just spat away? Can't you show us?"

"I don't know how to show you," Milton said. "I'm always a passenger, never the driver."

"Does anyone survive?" Roy whispered, his eyes reflecting the red flames.

Milton said nothing.

"Do you mind if we, I don't know, pray a little?" Ami asked, her voice quiet. "I know he left us, but still . . ."

"I want to pray, too," Rica said, sitting up.

"You do?" Milton asked.

"And I want an old-fashioned prayer," Rica said. "I want *Dear God* and *amen* and closed eyes, okay?"

"Sure," Roy said, straightening up and putting one hand out for Rica and another for Ami. Rica took Milton's and kept one hand on the baby. They closed their eyes. For a minute no one said a word. Then Rica spoke.

"Dear God," Rica said. "Thank you for all these things. Thank you for babies and friends." She paused. "We like being alive." She paused again, longer this time. "Amen."

They stayed still for a few more moments, hand in hand, eyes closed.

White light beamed through Rica's closed eyes. She opened them and quickly turned her head with a cry. Low in the horizon in the direction of the mystery lights was a dazzling light—stationary and painfully brilliant, as bright as ten stars. It sizzled, as if a hole had been burned in the firmament.

"What the fuck is that?" Roy said, shielding his eyes. Like a minute sun, it outshone the other stars and filled the sky with a dusky blue hue.

"It's Jesus!" Ami squealed.

"It's WR 104," Milton said.

"No way," Roy said. He crawled forward onto his knees. "Are you sure, Milt?"

"What's WR 104?" Rica said. Already the light was fading. She could look directly at the large white ball.

"It's a star!" Roy said. "Or, at this point, it *was* a star. It just collapsed."

"It collapsed over seven thousand years ago. Just took a while for the light to reach us," Milton said quietly. "And the gamma rays."

"It's beautiful," Ami said.

"It's the death of all of us," Milton said.

Exploded with white

JIM EDWARDS WAS driving with the top down and singing any Hank Williams song he could remember. He'd searched the radio, a fancy satellite unit. Nothing for hours, and even then just one station playing the same goddamn song over and over.

The night was clear and the air warm. The headlights of approaching cars on the two-lane highway whizzed by and Jim savored how nice it was to not need a ride. He was thinking ahead to a late-night breakfast, to bacon and grits and eggs so hot they burned the tongue. That's how he liked it. Hot! Not too far ahead blazed the sign and lights of a highway truck stop. He'd eat there.

He downshifted into fourth just to feel the engine. It felt good. Not a bad car. Not American, but not bad.

A chirp, like a mechanical bird, rang out. On the floorboards by his feet a cell phone rattled.

"Shit," Jim said aloud.

He reached down between his legs, his fingertips just brushing the phone. The Lexus skirted the shoulder, kicking up a spray of gravel.

"Shit!" He yanked the wheel and straightened the car. The phone continued to chirp.

He reached down again and grasped the phone.

"Hayden? That you?" Jim Edwards barked over the wind. An unfamiliar voice gabbled through the line. "What? Who is this? Iola who? Wait." The man on the phone wouldn't pause. And with the wind and the man's accent, Jim Edwards could hardly understand a word.

"Disaster? What disaster? Wait! Wait! Slow down, son. I'm not Hayden Brock." Jim Edwards paused, then added, "And I did not kill him. I have a note—oh my God!"

The dark sky exploded with white light. Just above the horizon in front of Jim shone a new star—a huge star, beaming down on the highway like God's own flashlight.

The man on the phone was still jabbering.

"Oh my God!" Jim yelled. "So bright. So bright."

The phone went quiet. Then the car, the engine, the lights, all clicked off. The truck stop up ahead went dark, every light out in a snap. The red brake lights of the truck ahead disappeared, as did the headlights of the cars moving toward him. An oncoming car swerved into Jim's lane. Jim twisted the wheel, but there was no time. In the light of the new star, Jim could see the face of the other driver screaming behind her windshield the moment before they collided.

Pissant town

"SOMEBODY! ANYBODY!"

"Shut the fuck up, man. No one is coming."

"They can't just leave us locked up. There're rules."

"Shit, man. Not in this pissant town. What, a population of ten? Man, they are gone!"

"I got drunk! I peed in an alley. Big deal! I didn't even get my one phone call! I've got family waiting at home."

"You can bet your ass they're all gone. It's like Katrina. When the shit goes down anyone with legs to run gets the fuck out of town. They'll leave old people and sick kids and sure as hell leave a drunk ass like you."

"That can't be true."

"Shit, are you crying over there? You lame-ass motherfucker. Man, if I wasn't locked in, I'd abandon you, too."

"No, you wouldn't."

"Sure the fuck would. I don't know you."

"Why does that matter? I'm a human being! I'm a—wait. Did you hear that?"

"Hear what?"

"Shut up. Someone's coming," he hissed. "Hey! We're in here!"

The heavy door creaked open. Steps echoed against the cement floor. A crowd, over a dozen men and women, stopped in front of the cells, humming a slow melody.

"Can you help us? Find the key."

A teenage girl near the front raised her hand. In her palm sat a hermit crab with a red arrow painted on his shell. She brought her hand up to the cell's lock. The crab crept closer and reached a purple claw into the keyhole.

"I don't think that's going to wor—"

Click.

Dot in the dirt

HAYDEN WAS AFRAID. He had walked from the monastery into a darkness thicker than Los Angeles had known for a hundred years. He stepped carefully, slowly, trying to whistle away the fear. Madmen in masks from every slasher film he'd seen, bullies from his sixth grade class, rabid old women with evil powers all seemed to be hiding just past the shadows. How much fear was shoved down in his soul?

"You're safe, aren't you?" he said to himself. "What's to fear?"

"Death," he answered himself.

"Well, I'll die someday anyway."

"Pain," he replied.

"Good point," he said. "I don't like pain."

He glanced up. The stars, even that ridiculously bright one, all seemed too far away, too apathetic. He'd be horrendously tortured and those stars would observe in silence, their beauty untouched. Even at their brightest, they did little to touch the darkness.

When Hayden was a boy he had played inside his grandfather's closet. It was filled with canes and tweed coats and the close smell of leather. That was a good dark. This dark was wide and horrible and cold.

"It's fine. You're fine. Just keep walking."

Hayden extended his stride. A wind pushed by and Hayden shoved his hands into his pockets. His fingers touched the smooth beads of Brendan's rosary. He pulled them out and rolled them between his thumb and forefinger.

Thank-yous, he thought. *Okay.*

He was thankful for bourbon, his water bed, his parents, his lack of scars, Jim Edwards, hot showers . . . He got a little stuck. Could those be the only things he was thankful for? What else? When straight women make out with each other, his fifth semester of college . . . blood oranges, Advil, bread smells, the movement of his hands, stars, his chin . . . Ms. Tosh, his third grade teacher, balloon squeaks, harmonicas, his big toes, his pinky toes, all the toes in between . . . Something loosened inside of him. Each step was a bead. Each bead was a breath. Each breath was a thank-you. Chocolate milk, tequila, eyesight, the sound of applause, driving, strong coffee, skin, hair, snow, hot tubs, ultrathin condoms, John Woo films, Christmas, house-trained puppies, grapefruit, new car smell, women laughing, women breathing, women yelling, TV cop dramas, the Olympics, stunt kites . . .

A shadow moved. Hayden stopped in his tracks. Barely ten feet from him someone was sitting on the ground. Hayden stared until the image formed from the shadow. He was sitting with his back to Hayden. A smallish man wearing a trucker hat.

Hayden watched him for a few minutes before finally clearing his throat. The man startled and turned. He had a round, beard-covered face. He seemed to recognize Hayden, a look Hayden was familiar with. The man smiled and gestured to Hayden to come closer. Hayden carefully returned his beads to his pocket and walked over to the man.

"Hello, I was just—" he started, but the stranger raised a hand and indicated that Hayden should sit beside him. Hayden swallowed and sat. The man smelled of sweat and diesel. But Hayden didn't mind. He nodded at Hayden and then toward the horizon as if they were the audience for a spectacular show in the distant black. Hayden joined him in watching the sky.

The show began. First, a soft change of light, as if a fire were burning a hundred miles away. Pine trees on a slope glowed warm, the sky seemed to heat, and then cresting over the low cliffs came the first tip of the moon. But instead of the off-white glow of a billion other nights, the moon was rust red. Hayden heard the man beside him muffle a giggle. Hayden looked at him, his face reflecting the red, his eyes bright and alive. Even behind the thick beard, Hayden could tell the grin was stretching even larger.

Slowly the moon rose over the cliffs and floated into the sky, illuminating and dominating the night.

"Why is it red?" Hayden asked.

The man shrugged.

"Does it mean something?"

Another shrug.

"I want to be a saint." The words just came out. For some reason, this person seemed the right one to tell. It was clear he wasn't Jesus. Jesus doesn't wear a trucker hat. But Hayden had grown to expect wise words from unlikely mouths. This small, hairy trucker in the middle of the desert might be the most unlikely thus far.

The man nodded to Hayden's question and with his index finger made a dot in the dirt.

Hayden looked up at the man. He was smiling. He was missing teeth. Hayden looked back to the ground and added his own dot.

The stranger added a third dot.

Hayden added a curved line.

The stranger laughed out loud. He pulled his knees to his chest, took a deep breath, and began talking. The words were foreign to Hayden, but the tone was confident, warm, wise. The best kind of radio voice. The kind of voice that you could believe even if you had no idea what it was saying. The man kept talking, pointing out stars, or nearby shrubs, chuckling, then whispering, then nearly yelling. Hayden listened intently, nodding along, laughing when the man laughed, saying *si* every now and then in hopes that the man was speaking Spanish.

Hayden was relaxed, calm. He leaned back and watched the rising red moon as the man continued. He was sure the man was telling a story of some kind. A good story. One with a fast plot and lots of action and romance. He closed his eyes and tried to follow the narrative. Someone losing a lover, having to walk and search. Fighting villains. But finding the lover, embracing. Singing together.

Hayden lost the story after that. The man spoke quietly now. Tone upon tone upon tone. Like a nursery song his mother had whispered. Had his mother ever whispered a song to him? But it was like that. Some old soul-memory.

A new story rolled into the old like a dream. Hayden could see the images in his mind's eye. There was a child now. She had brown hair and eyes that Hayden knew. She was happy. Always singing. She runs, with friends, across a sandy yard. She's laughing. She runs up the steps to her classroom, she's tripping, Hayden cannot stop her falling. She falls on the steps of her school, hitting her face. Her mouth is full of blood. She cries and he runs and he cradles her, blood staining his shirt. He holds her and rocks her, and her cries slow and quiet. She is not heavy. She is no burden. He could carry her down the highway, across rivers. She yawns. He rocks her. She sleeps. Her small hand curled on his chest.

Someone near is still speaking, still tones with no words he knows. Hayden hums along, hums to the sleeping child in his arms. One word hiding among the tones: "Hay-din. Hay-din."

Hayden smiled.

"Hay-din. Oh, Hay-din."

Hayden opened his eyes to the rose-colored night. The bearded man was standing a few feet away and beside him stood a tall, pale-blue man with a sad, gaping face.

"An angel," Hayden said.

Her daughter's hair

WITHIN AN HOUR of the moon's rising, Rica had stretched out beside Milton on the rocky desert ground. She closed her eyes, watching the clouds below the stars. The wind, stronger now, pushing and full of scents. Her first dreams were of sailing.

A small white boat on a blue sea. Wind pushing the white sail outward and forward. She sits at the helm, a newborn in her arms. Gurgles and bright eyes. Then there are trees and a forest floor of leaves and a child crawling. Fat legs and arms pushing down the soft earth. Rica hears herself laugh. Now she's home in Austin, walking in the early evening and singing her daughter to sleep. *Brother John, where are you sleeping?* And the child's sleepy eyes look past her face to the new night sky. *What's that, mama?* Rica looks and sees the moon. Now the child is older with a doll she pretends to breast-feed and a block of wood she uses to telephone Rica from the next room. Rica is cooking for her daughter, the steam rising to her face; she is searching for tastes the child will love. Swimming in Deep Eddy, cold and clear. Climbing out. Rica and her five-year-old daughter drying in the summer sun. She is six and has broken a tooth on the steps at school. Rica holds her for an hour, waiting for a doctor. *Shhhh.* In a bath now, Rica washes her daughter's hair. She smells her daughter. Her hair, strong and dark, like Rica's. Rica feels her daughter's scalp, rubbing the shampoo into the roots, her daughter's head bobbing along. Her daughter pushing the islands of bubbles across the surface of the bath water, singing. Rica pours water from a cup over her daughter's hair, careful to keep soap from her eyes. The hair shines. The skin shines. The child smells soapy, clean. The child looks up to Rica. *Mommy. None of this will ever happen.*

Diluted . . . eternal

MILTON WOKE IN the dark of night. Beside him Rica was tossing, touching her belly, and making sad moans. He lay on his side and watched her, wondering where she walked, what she was seeing. On another day he might have woken her, but on this last night it seemed dreams, even nightmares, were too valuable to shatter.

Then she froze. So did the air. Nothing moved. Milton sat up. Sitting across the unmoving remains of the fire sat his father, tall and calm. Milton was not surprised.

"Hi, Dad."

"You've aged," his father said. He poked at the fire with a long cedar branch.

"Happens to the best of us." Milton rubbed his cold knuckles. "You told me you got a lot wrong. About your death."

"I did. Got some right, too. But plenty wrong."

"What parts?"

He looked up at Milton, his dark-rimmed glasses catching the shine of the coals. "When you think about an infinite number of yourself, how does it make you feel?"

"Diluted."

"Bingo! Me too. And I liked it. It was a comfort to think that the existence of every possible possibility made a single possibility trivial." He rubbed the X on his forehead. "But you see, by the same math a single electron's spin creates worlds!" He flickered in the glow.

"Milton, I was a basketball floating in the ocean. I thought the water's surface was all there was. So I believed I was the shape of a plate, unaware of 99 percent of my actual being."

"And now?"

"All those worlds I told you about? All those separate realities? Separate yous? They're not separate. You are composed of countless yous spread across countless realities. You are not one them. You are all of them. You are not diluted. You're eternal." His father took his glasses off and began cleaning them with the corner of his shirt. "And you are nothing at all."

"How do I save my daughter?"

"Infinite worlds, like infinite pages of a book. We are not the words. We are the ideas that pop to life when the words are read aloud. That's the poetry of it."

"How do I save my daughter?"

"I hate poetry. Always have. Why don't you come with me? Check out of all this crap."

"Dad, how do I save my baby?"

His father placed the glasses back on his face and met Milton's eyes. "It could be, may very well be, that your baby is the reason for all of this."

"The end of the world?"

"The world."

Milton felt a touch on his hand. He looked to see a young child sitting beside him. She had brown hair the color of morning tea and eyes brighter than the coals before them. Her small hand wrapped around two of his fingers.

"Hello," Milton said. "Look how much you've grown."

She smiled.

"What do I do?" he asked her.

She raised her arm and pointed west where the mystery lights danced on the edge of the sky.

Right

ZARATHUSTRA, FOUNDER OF Zoroastrianism, teaches that in the last days, the God of light, Ahura Mazda, will defeat the powers of darkness. He will then cleanse the world with liquid metal and holy fire. Each soul will be judged. The righteous will be welcomed into paradise. The sinners will endure three days of punishment, and then also be welcomed into paradise. He's right.

The Mayan people believe the world will conclude its fifth cycle and end in fire on December 21, 2012. They are right.

Norse mythology describes an end times battle of the Norse gods that covers the world in mayhem and fire and concludes with all the lands of Earth sinking into the oceans, killing off the onlooking humans. Right again.

Hilary of Poitiers believes the world ends in 365 CE. Correct.

Islam teaches "the Beast" will emerge from an earthquake on Mount Safa in Makkah. He will speak to the people, separating believers and nonbelievers. A plague and fire will scour the earth. Right.

Hindus believe the world has been created and destroyed countless times. And will be created and destroyed countless times to come. So very true.

On Pentecost of 1000 CE, the long-dead body of the emperor Charlemagne is exhumed. It is understood that as the Apocalypse rages the emperor will rise and battle the Antichrist. He does.

After a long examination of the movements of the planets, John of Toledo concludes the world ends in 1186. Right again.

Pope Innocent III adds 666 to the year he understands Islam to have been founded and announces the world will end in 1284. Yes.

In the late 1660s thousands of Russia's Old Believers burn themselves and their children alive to avoid the coming Apocalypse. Perfect.

Sir Isaac Newton makes a detailed study of the Christian and Jewish scriptures and determines that the world ends in 2060. Also right.

Charles Wesley, the founder of Methodism, predicts the end to arrive in 1794. Souls will be separated by Jesus. Goats and sheep. Saved and unsaved. Blessed and burned. Yep.

Pastor Charles Taze Russell predicts Armageddon will rage and God will wipe out all non-Jehovah's Witnesses in 1914. Then 1915. And again in 1918. Right on all three accounts.

William Miller and tens of thousands of Americans wait for the world to end on March 21, 1843. They are not disappointed.

Meteorologist Albert Porta concludes that an alignment of six planets will cause an enormous magnetic current and the Earth will explode in 1919. It's fantastic.

Harold Camping convinces thousands that Christ will return and the world will meet final Judgment on May 21, 2011. Those who accept the gift of salvation by way of the cross of Christ will be saved. Others must face the wrath of a just God for all eternity. He's right.

Be careful what you believe. You're right.

Death and change

CLICK AND HIS followers were not walking.

Hours after the new star had burned in the low horizon, the crab wandered from the country road they were traveling and crawled into a stony field. He paused for a moment, scratching at the pebbles. Then using his two front claws, covered himself with soil and stone.

The followers circled and stared.

Click pulled himself into his dark shell home. He felt pressure, a swelling within his being as if every organ were trying to escape. The pressure built, squeezing Click until he could not move, could not think. Like a scream growing louder and louder, beyond what you believed you could endure.

Surely this was death. He could not survive this.

Finally, he heard his body crack. The seams burst. It was release and a new pain. All he wanted was to push his body from him. From him? What was *him* if not his body?

Click's claws twitched. His body felt alien, the tight embrace of an unwelcome stranger. He pushed his skin away, wriggling free into a soft newness. From a vantage point he could not understand, he saw his body—his claws, his legs, his eyes—slowly creep away from him.

The followers leaned close, studying the crab by the red glow of the moon. For over an hour he had remained buried. But now the soil shifted.

"My God," someone gasped.

The crab's elongated, lifeless body hung from the shell.

"He's dead," the lawyer said.

But as they watched, the crab emerged from behind the body, pushing his discarded exoskeleton forward.

"He's molting," said the bald man. "It's how they grow."

"Death and change," said the auto mechanic. "Difficult to tell the two apart."

To Click the red moon dazzled, the wind rushed like chilled water through his shell, the sharp ground pushed upward, cutting into his claws. He was malleable, vulnerable, sensing the world through a skin beneath the skin. He should wait to harden, wait until his new outer layer solidified around him. But he would not. He crawled and felt everything.

THE
LAST DAY

I won't meet your baby

MILTON WOKE RICA in the cool pale hour before dawn. She opened her eyes to his old face, even older now. He smiled and whispered her name, his voice filled with crack and vibrato. She stared at his face outlined by the half-lit sky.

"Milton, you've seen her?"

He nodded.

"What is she like?"

"She is like her mother and she is like no one who has ever been." He brushed some hair from her forehead. "It's time to go."

She moved and felt her belly tight and round. All her muscles ached. Slowly, with Milton's help, she lifted her weight to standing.

Ami was awake, sitting cross-legged by the ashes of the fire, Roy's head cradled in her lap. She was breathing out tears. "He's wet," she said. "He's bleeding."

Milton stepped toward him and knelt. "Roy?"

Rica followed. She awkwardly sat and put a hand to Roy's cheek. It was cool. The sand around his neck was a red mush. Roy blinked and smiled at her. "I'm sorry I won't meet your baby."

"Shhhh," Rica said. "We can drive you somewhere. We can find help."

"The car won't work," Ami said. "Won't do anything."

"We'll figure something out," Rica said to Roy. "You'll be all right."

Roy winked at Rica. "Thanks, Rica." He turned his head to Milton. "Where will you go?"

"The lights," Milton said.

Roy nodded. "I need to stay here, okay?"

Milton nodded.

"You should go now."

Milton nodded.

"Good. Good." Roy blinked his eyes.

"Hey," Milton said, touching his friend's chest. "As far as spatting goes, you're a natural."

Roy grinned.

Milton leaned in close, running both his hands through Roy's hair and gripping his head. He touched his forehead to Roy's and stayed still. A sob, like a hiccup, bubbled up from Milton's throat.

Rica looked up to Ami. Ami's wet eyes catching all the sad promise of the predawn light. Her eyes were asking Rica, and Rica had no answer for her.

Milton stood. "We have to go."

"I'm staying," Ami said.

"Ami," Roy said. "Come on now."

"Why? Why would I walk out there? Away from you?"

Roy laughed. "You got me stumped."

Milton held out a hand to Rica. She took it and stood. Milton moved his head to the west. The lights still drifted above the far horizon. Milton and Rica stepped away from Roy and Ami and the wet, red sand. They stepped toward the lights spinning like renegade stars. Rica stopped and looked back. Ami was stroking Roy's face.

"Milton," Rica whispered. "He'll die."

Milton squeezed her hand and pulled west. "Everyone dies today."

Better than coffee

MORNING FROST GLITTERED under his feet like ground stars.

Hayden had walked all night, following at first the blue, sad-faced man. But when the sky to the east was just beginning to pale, he discovered he was walking alone. He stopped and watched the sun peel over the desert floor. Startled to think this happened every day.

All his limbs ached and his head felt like a punctured tennis ball. But he was smiling. Hayden was surprised to be alive and it felt very good.

"I should be surprised to be alive more often," he said aloud. "It's better than coffee."

Save for a few tufts of trees and grass, the landscape was wide and empty. Hayden noticed a far-off cloud catching the early sunlight, he noticed the frost melting to drops of wet, he noticed the changing smell of a warming Earth.

He came to a two-lane highway and walked along the white stripes with the new sun to his left. The road led into the small town of Marfa.

Marfa sat all but empty in the clear morning light. No cars drove down its wide streets. No lights shone from the old houses, store windows, or the stone courthouse. Hayden passed only a scattering of people: two old men rolling cigarettes on a porch and a young, bearded man in sunglasses and a stocking cap sitting on the sidewalk outside a closed coffee shop.

"You got the key?" he asked as Hayden approached.

"Afraid not."

"This is bad," the man said. "I bet the Iron and Wine show is canceled, too."

"Where is everybody?" Hayden asked.

"Vaporized or something. Other people just drove away."

"Vaporized?"

"*Pop*. Like, turned to dust or beamed up or something." The young man studied Hayden's face for a moment. "Hey. You're that guy from that show."

"Yeah." Hayden nodded. "That's me."

"I hate that show."

Hayden shrugged. "It's a living," he said. "Or it was." He started off down the empty street.

"Hey, you want to get high?" the man called.

"Maybe later," Hayden said without slowing.

Hayden moved south through the town and over a set of train tracks stretching east and west. He navigated poorly paved roads past small houses and trailers. Then there were no more houses or streets, paved or otherwise. The town ended abruptly, like some back lot set with just enough town to fill the background and beyond that nothing.

Hayden found himself again in the rocky desert. He continued south. The only sounds heard were his shoes against the hard sand and the warbling wind. His mind fell quiet as well, trying to keep a loose grip on the near emptiness of the view. He slowed his breath. *This is what they mean by holy.*

Less than a mile away from the last homes of Marfa, Hayden came upon a wooden cabin. It stood at a slant, the roof sinking slightly near the center. Gray-brown logs and mud made the four walls. A chimney of stones was crumbling from the roof. No road, not even a dirt one, led to the house. Neither telephone wires, nor tire tracks. No path at all. No sign of connection. The house stood alone, facing a landscape with no visible life aside from desert scrub.

A hundred yards or so in front of the house stood a sand-brown metal shed, a much more recent construction than the crumbling house.

Hayden paused. No lights could be seen through the small windows, no smoke from the falling chimney, but Hayden was sure the cabin was not empty. He wanted to walk on, leave the ruin behind him, but something urged him toward the porch steps.

He touched the doorknob and the door swung open a few inches.

"Hello?" Hayden peeked his head around the door. The air smelled old, musty. A shadowed hallway lay before him. "Anybody here?" From somewhere in the house came the echo of a strained breath.

"Hello," he spoke. "I was just, you know, passing by."

The moan answered, and in it a word: "Come."

Hayden wanted to run, but he stepped forward and into the house.

"Do you . . . need some help? Should I go—"

"Come," the moan said.

He walked a few steps down the hall into the shadows. Two voices in his head: one begging him to run, the other, quieter by far, asking him to stay. He walked a few more steps. Framed photos hung on the hallway's walls, but Hayden saw them only from the corner of his eyes. His focus was on the door to the left at the end of the hall.

He still felt the sensation of holiness that had come upon him while walking, but it was now laced with horror. He was walking toward something holy, a terrible holy.

"Please," the voice wheezed. The sound froze Hayden's blood. He stopped before the closed door. He could hear the breathing on the other side.

The two voices still wrestled inside Hayden. To run or to stay. To survive or to serve. The choice was new to Hayden. Most likely, the same two voices had argued every day, but Hayden had never considered following the quiet voice as an option. Survive always. Only give away what you do not need, or, more honestly, what you do not want. He had done some charity work, visited sick kids in the hospital. It was part of the role of Saint Rick, but he had enjoyed it as well. He wouldn't have done it otherwise. In fact, Hayden realized, he had only served when he desired the experience of serving.

"Please."

He would not like what he found on the other side of the door. He was sure of that.

"Please."

He opened the door and stepped inside. It was a small room with a chair and against the far wall, a narrow bed clumped with white sheets. A warm breeze blew in through an open window. At first he thought the room was empty, that perhaps he had only heard the wind. He was sighing in relief when the sheets on the bed moved and Hayden saw her. She was old, so thin she was almost not there at all. Her face was sunken, her skin paper.

Beside the bed was a table with a pitcher of water and a glass. The figure in the bed reached out one thin hand and gestured toward the glass. Hayden stepped forward without a thought. He took the glass and filled it. He knelt by the woman and moved his hand behind her head, gently lifting and placing the glass to her chapped lips. Her mouth opened to the water. Her eyes blinked open. Her eyes, a pale blue, stared up into Hayden's.

"You came," she said. "I thought you were dead."

"I . . ." Hayden hesitated. Improvisation was never his strength. "I'm not dead."

"Oh, I'm so glad." She smiled. "Are you sure you weren't dead? I was sure you were."

"I got better."

"Oh. All right then."

She closed her eyes and reached out a thin hand, like a bare elm branch with white bark. He placed his hand in hers. Her skin loose, tissue, warm.

"The mystery lights. Can you see them?" she said. "All around now."

Hayden squeezed her hand. He knew this moment. He recognized what it was. This was the reason he had come so far.

Now would be the time

RICA ARCHED HER spine, using her palms as support for her strained lower back. Milton stooped forward, his back forming the partner parenthesis to hers. They walked west, their dawn shadows stretching before them on the packed, dry earth. The mystery lights still bounced in the distance. Across the sands, standing in the line of their pointing shadows, stood a small cabin solid in the soft morning sun.

"There," Milton said. "That's where we need to be."

"Milton, there's something I want to tell you," she said.

"Now would be the time."

She stopped and turned toward him. "I love you more than I knew I loved you," she said. "I love you so much I can walk into the desert and feel . . ." she thought for a moment. "Not safe. I don't feel safe. But I feel all right not feeling not safe." She took his hands in hers. His hands were soft, like her grandfather's. "If today is the day everything ends, I'm glad I'm with you." She looked up into his face. "I've also loved Hayden Brock since I was fourteen years old."

Milton touched her cheek and smiled, a hundred wrinkles spreading from the corners of his eyes. "Rica, I had a dream come true. I got to grow old with you."

She smiled. He squeezed her hand and led her toward the cabin.

"There's something I haven't told you, too," he said.

"Now would be the time."

"I don't know what it is, yet."

Home-desire

JESUS-18 WAS TIRED. His feet ached. The desert ground, though cooler in the predawn dark, was still hard. He had taken off the heavy shoes the men had given him and left them by a sleeping woman in a doorway. He still wore the warm shirt and strange hat. He had been traveling such distances, passing crowds and noises and miracles. There were miracles everywhere. Polished stones the size of homes moving like chariots, but with no horse. He had ridden in more than one, racing faster than a body falls. Stone and glass towers stretched higher than the Temple by five times. Chunks of sun in jars of ice hanging on the walls, the ceilings, the ends of sticks.

And still with all these marvels Jesus-18 recognized the misery. The rich still looked sick. The poor still forgotten.

In the city he had seen horrible statues. Stone images of dying men, cleanly crucified. They were hung on the outside of ornate buildings. At first, Jesus-18 kept his distance from these places. Were they prisons? Were they houses of execution? Curiosity worked against his fear. He peeked inside one of the buildings, prying the door and pushing his head in. Another crucified statue with a painted contorted face hung before empty rows and rows. Is this where they sit and watch the long death? So much wealth, so much cruelty. Like Rome. A black-robed man approached the door. A holder of nails, Jesus-18 guessed. Jesus-18 let the door fall closed and ran.

He had left the city and sought the desert, walking into the night on the hard silent sands, talking with strange pilgrims, making up stories about red moons and fierce stars.

He didn't mind confusion. He was used to it. As a child the confusion would come in waves. Confusion and sadness. A home-desire sadness. Jesus-18 believed this home-desire was the primary emotion of all people. Home, he also felt, had very little to do with where one was born or raised. Home was the urge of what might be. What *could* and *should* be. Home was the kingdom rising up within the empire, the flower growing in the rock wall, the kind want emerging in the cool heart. He saw homesick souls in all he passed, no matter how foreign, how crippled, how cruel. He saw this home-desire even in the dead.

Like a seed, that's what he liked to say. See the seed grow, transform from small to large, stone to tree. Mystery. Since there is no way to understand a seed, why worry about understanding God? Once he saw that understanding was not the way to know God, he was free. Wine may come from water, waves can be stilled, quiet hearts can once again beat. All things can be if you surrender the need to understand.

Last night he slept in the ruins of a desert farm. He dreamed of his mother. She had the face of every woman he had known. She was holding James as a baby to her chest and singing. Her voice was soft rain.

He woke at dawn and greeted the sun.

Abba, he prayed, *are you here?*

He wept. And wept. As he walked toward nothing but more solitude. The sun peeked over the horizon, sending his shadow long before him. He turned, looking back toward the new sun. In the shine he could see silhouettes walking toward him. Angels? Was he going to be taken home? Was this salvation? They crept closer. Jesus-18 shielded his eyes, but he could still see only outlines against an orange sky. Then a cloud passed behind them, smearing the morning colors. Jesus saw a crowd, twenty, maybe more, walking slowly. They were singing.

He remembered walking, arguing with Peter, laughing with James, flirting with Mary. And talking, ideas popping to life like morning flowers. They were bringing the kingdom. A kind kingdom. No more slavery and riches. Find the abandoned, feed the hungry. All things can be.

The walkers were moving closer, the singing clearer.

Ah, how John would whistle, how Thomas would trip over his robe, how the people listened or yelled, how *fun* it all was.

Slowly, slowly, the walkers approached. The sun rose slightly over their heads. How many miles had they walked? How many had he? He looked at his feet, the dust and blisters, the black nails. Remember how she had washed them, how he hurt for her, how he wanted her, how the hurt and want were one and the same? How he knew that to wash his feet was love, how he wanted to share this. Ah, his feet, bent from many, many steps. Strong from many steps. As he watched, a blue-green shell crawled to the side of his foot. It reached out a large purple claw and gave Jesus-18 a tiny nip on his big toe.

Moments from a family

MILTON AND RICA stepped past the light-brown shed toward the house.

The gate was open. Spits of dust blew through the yard. Rica raised her hand to shield her eyes. The steps up to the porch were worn. Rica could feel them bend under her weight. The front door was open, swinging on its hinges.

"Hello," Milton called out, his voice full of crackles. "Is anyone there?"

There was a breath of silence and then a voice, a voice as familiar to Rica as her own. "We're in the bedroom on the left."

Drips of sweat rolled from under her arms. Milton walked in first. Rica two steps behind him. The walls were lined with framed photos. Some yellowing, the edges curling under the glass. Portraits of a small family. A young woman with thin lips and kind eyes. Other photos were more recent. A woman and a man holding a child on his shoulders. They're laughing. A woman and a boy in the sunlight. The boy now older, wearing blue graduation robes, the woman, also older, beside him smiling. Another photo, black and white, an unsmiling couple against a white backdrop. As far as Rica could tell, the scenes were in no order. Years and generations were scattered, moments from a family. Near the end of the hall was a photo of the kind-eyed woman. She is standing in front of this same house, her belly tight against a red dress. One hand shades her face, the other rests on the belly. Below the shadow of her hand. The woman is not smiling. Rica felt a kick.

"Rica?" Milton said. He was standing by the open door, a hand held out to her. She walked to him, wiping her face. She took his hand and together they entered the bedroom.

Inside the small room a man sat on a chair with his back to the door. Rica's heart made small popping sounds she was sure the whole room could hear.

"Hello, Mr. Brock," Milton said.

"She's gone," he said. On the bed lay a woman. She was much older, her cheeks sunken and her hair a few wisps of gray, but Rica recognized her as the woman from many of the photos. Hayden was holding her hand. With the fingers of his free hand he slid through the beads of a rosary. "That's all. Just gone."

"Who is she?" Milton asked.

He shook his head, took a breath, and set the woman's hand down. When he turned to them, Rica was struck by how much older he looked than on television. But better. Hayden was staring at Rica, his mouth slowly falling open. "Hey," he said. "I know you."

"Mr. Brock," Milton said, "We were sent to find you."

"Yes," Hayden said, his eyes still on Rica. "You're the one. Almond skin."

Milton looked at Rica. Rica blushed.

"This is crazy, I'm sure," Hayden said, shaking his head and standing. "Do you know me?"

"My name is Rica." Rica rubbed her arms and stepped closer. "We met once. A long time ago."

"But you know me, don't you? I mean, we know each other," he said.

Rica nodded. "We do."

Rica's legs buckled. Something moved and changed and water, hot as tears, poured from her and splashed to the floor. Hayden reached out and caught her.

"Outside," she whispered. "I want to be outside."

On the last day

IN THE NINE seconds that WR 104 blazed most brilliantly in the sky, one-third of Earth's population was struck with a fatal dose of radiation. Those living on the western half of the Southern Hemisphere woke on the last day with vomiting, diarrhea, and extreme fatigue: all the early symptoms of radiation sickness.

The gamma-ray burst from WR 104 wiped out the little that remained of Earth's shell. Subatomic particles, muons and electrons, from that distant dying star and our younger sun pelted the planet, spinning like tiny drills into the Earth and heating the molten blood of our crust and mantle. Scientists rushed to understand the situation, to measure the radiations, to explain the catastrophe, but they could do nothing to slow the process.

Churches, synagogues, mosques, and temples filled to the brim with new replacements for those swept away by the Raptures. Bars and national parks and hospitals also filled to capacity.

Though it seemed clear, most people would not accept that the world was ending. It had never ended before, why now? Many claimed the worst had happened. Millions had disappeared, millions more dying. But now things would improve. How couldn't they?

People made plans for the future. People looted computers and televisions, people locked doors before running from their homes, and many people—many—arrived on time for work.

On that last day, the morning rain smelled of sulfur and the sun shone white. The ground trembled, a low humming vibration that covered the world. Still lakes rippled and birds refused to land. People across the globe felt the earth beneath them tense like an angry child holding her breath before a massive tantrum.

Fire taking her body

"WE NEED A hospital," Hayden said, holding Rica beneath one of her arms. "Don't we need a hospital?"

"I'm going to that rock," Rica said. She nodded to a flat stone the size of a dinner table sitting in the midst of the desert scrub. She kicked off her shoes and walked to the stone, aware of each step warm beneath her feet. At the stone she stood, steadied her legs and gazed at the landscape. Her body tightened. She squeezed her fists, closed her eyes, and saw the color of sunsets swirl on the inside of her eyelids. The rush pushed in, then receded. She opened her eyes to see Hayden on one side of her and the age-worn face of Milton on the other. They eased her down. She nodded. Yes. This was exactly how things should be. She smiled at both. Hayden was unsure, afraid, but holding her hand. Milton was strong-faced, his aged eyes fierce and present. She loved them both and there was no shame.

"I love you," she said. Both nodded.

Another contraction grabbed her body. The squeezing, the opening, the softening. Is this like Milton's spatting? This timelessness? This pain? These colors? She opened her mouth and sang a long minor note, sending her pain up to the sky.

The sky seemed to respond, the clouds swirling in on themselves like creamer in coffee.

Again the squeezing, a fire taking her body. Panic offered itself like a drink to her thirst. But Rica understood it was only saltwater. She pushed the pain in breaths and howls.

"Push on my back, Brock!" she grunted through gritted teeth, rolling onto her side. "Lower and harder."

Pain crashed in on her. Nothing—not Hayden, not Milton, not the ending of the world was as thunderous as the pain. It was the truest thing Rica had ever known. She tensed her entire body. Then she opened to the pain, she held it, knew it, released it. And the pain left tidal pools of such joy that Rica laughed out loud.

"That last one felt like an earthquake," she said to Milton.

"It was an earthquake. But don't worry."

Rica looked up at the curdling clouds, burning with bursts of ball lightning. The earth shook again.

Stay, she thought. *Let the Earth do her work and you do yours.*

Sky to touch

WHY ARE THEY screaming? Richard Van Sturgeon thought. *If God is for us, who can be against us?*

He stood on the throne platform preaching. He'd been doing so for most of the last fifty hours, stirring up the coals of faith, keeping heaven warm with devotion. It had not been easy.

First there had been the imposter. The small, dark man sitting on the throne. But that had led to the revelation! That man with his yelping and hiding, that man was the abomination of desolation as prophesied by scripture. And Van Sturgeon came across a new truth. Prophesy doesn't end in paradise! The truth of scripture continues! He explained to the frightened masses how even now the foretold events of the last days were overlapping with the promised gift of eternity.

"He will come to his bride!"

And he came! Jesus came to them, tall, quiet, sitting virtuously on his throne. He said nothing, but he didn't need to. Scripture was complete. He had said all that need be said. And Van Sturgeon could quote scripture, he could be the voice of the Son. Hadn't he been that all his life? Hadn't he given voice to the unchanging truths of God? He called on the residents of heaven to praise in hymns and tears.

Then a chunk of sky fell down upon them.

An octagonal panel of sky blue, fluttering down like a wounded kite. Followed by another and another. Soon more than a dozen holes spotted the perfect sky, revealing swirling gray clouds behind them. Dark raindrops streaked the clear glass where the sky had been.

For a moment, Van had to admit, he was shaken. What was this? What meaning? Like the crowd before him, he was silent. All of heaven held its breath and looked to Jesus on his throne. For a moment Jesus stared up at the imperfect sky. Then he faced his followers.

"I don't know!" Jesus cried, his voice reedy and basted in a thick Minnesota accent. "I'm just as confused as you!" He leaped from his throne and off toward a patch of maple trees. Some pursued him, but most just stood in shock. It was the second messiah they'd lost in less than a week.

Some shook their heads and wandered off to find food or a place to be alone. Others refused to look up at all, and when someone mentioned the gaps, they'd hum hymns as loudly as possible. One man with a face Van Sturgeon recognized from some album he had kept in rotation ripped off his robe and darted toward the waterfall, crying out, "Sorry, everyone! Sorry!"

Van Sturgeon threw his arms open to the murmuring masses. "Listen, friends. Did you think we'd be without doubt? Without sin? We are without sin in the eyes of God only because of the blood of Jesus. But we still have sin! Sanctification continues, friends! We continue to grow toward perfection. And our faith will be tested, honed. Let these signs drive the halfhearted away. Let them scatter. But brothers, sisters, let *us* remain. Let the faithful stay true. We are his remnant! He will preserve us. He has said so and his word is true!"

He took fallen panels and broke them into pieces. They snapped like Styrofoam. He passed the pieces around and urged others to do the same. "Do not be afraid to touch the sky, children! He has given us the sky to touch!"

He spoke for an hour, soothing the crowd like he might a colicky baby, speaking words more for their tone than their meaning. *Shhh, shhh*, his words said. *You are loved. You are cared for. You will live forever.*

Then came the wind. A single gush ripped through heaven and peeled the remaining panels from the sky. The people cowered as the blue came down in an oversize flurry. Then they stood and gazed up to what had been their sky.

"My God," said Van S.

Faces. They saw faces. Blue, long faces with dark eyes and open mouths. They peered in, a thousand or more.

That's when the screaming really took off.

Men and women raced through the grounds of heaven, desperate to hide but finding no place the staring eyes couldn't find them. People cried out, screaming confessions to the gaunt faces who watched without word or gesture. Others flung stones at the blue faces watching. The stones fell pitifully short, raining back down on others. From the platform, Van Sturgeon saw a woman burrow into the earth and pull dirt over her head and body.

Though his throat was dry and his chest ached, Van Sturgeon preached on.

"The witnesses of heaven look upon us. Peter tells us the angels long to look into these mysteries. And they are! They are watching us! Jealous of our fall because we know the glory of redemption."

Dozens, perhaps a hundred, listened. After an hour of enduring the stares from above, the whistling began. A low whine, like air escaping a balloon. And Van Sturgeon's ears popped. Still, he preached.

"This is our blessing!" he called to the dozen or so remaining listeners. "Our Pentecost!"

Someone giggled. The giggler was joined by another giggler. People stumbled, drunk. The Holy Spirit descends on the disciples and they appear drunk to the onlookers. Yes! Yes!

"This is the Spirit! The Holy Spirit!"

Van Sturgeon watched people, their faces pale, falling to their knees, collapsing to the ground, confused and laughing. He sucked in and found the air thin. His chest empty, his head drunk. He gazed up at the watching faces and knew.

They're taking the oxygen. They're suffocating us.

He thought the words, but now the words made little sense. They bounced and rearranged in his mind.

More people fell. Some just lay down in the soft grass as if they were taking a nap.

"Father! Father! We are your faithful!" Van Sturgeon slurred. He swayed where he stood. "We are your chosen! I claim my adoption into your family in the name of Jesus. In the name of his blood."

He stumbled back, the world a haze, and fell into the throne. Sucking in uselessly, he gazed out from his seat at the last ones choking and falling. His hands gripped the sides of the throne. It felt good under his palms, solid. Though he could feel his lungs shrink inside him, he grinned. There was no pain, now. No panic. Black spots filled his eyes. He knocked his knuckles against the throne and whispered into the chaos, "I always knew it would end like this."

Whole life pushing

SOMETIMES IN THE hours of labor, Rica fell into a quietness, almost a sleeping. Other times she moaned like a whale or yelped like a coyote. After one contraction she sent Hayden inside the cabin to find a pillow or a cushion. When he was gone she closed her eyes and pulled Milton's head to hers.

"Milton," Rica said. "I see things."

"I know."

"Hayden is also a father to her."

"I know."

"How?" She opened her eyes and stared into his.

"She told me," he said, brushing Rica's forehead. "Years from here."

Rica began to smile, but a new sensation struck her. A new contraction more fierce than any before. "My God, my God, she's coming!"

Hayden ran back, his arms full of quilted pillows. "Grab my leg, Brock!" She ordered.

Rica had never wanted to do anything as much as she now wanted to push. She shifted onto her side, her head in Milton's lap, Hayden holding a leg. She pushed with a yell that shook the sand. An impossible welling up inside, begging to be out. When it passed, she sucked in breaths. Another push. Her body carrying her forward, telling her what to do. How did her body know? Push! She rolled onto her back and reached above her head to take both Milton's hands. When the next push came she squeezed his hands till his knuckles cracked. Then breaths, a brief rest. Another push, her whole body, her whole life pushing. Milton was yelling with her, howling. Push! The air was filled with complex smells and the pillows wet with every fluid her body could squeeze out. Hayden was still close, but his eyes were wide, horrified. Good. Let him see. She was bringing life. Push! Push! Fierce, like a planet wedged inside her threatening to split her open. Push!

Lightning wiped the sky, dark clouds like a charging army crossed above her. The wind thrashed like a panicked animal. In the near distance, the roof of the decrepit cabin peeled off like the top of a can of fruit cocktail and the walls fell in on themselves.

She pushed, crying out into the wind. How many hours? How many days? The baby seemed no closer to being born. Push! Why wasn't the baby moving? What was wrong? Fear sat as close as Milton and Hayden. *You're going to fail,* fear yelled.

"Milton, Hayden," Rica said, squeezing Milton's hand and breathing hard. "She's not moving."

"Okay, okay," Milton said.

"She doesn't want to come."

Lightning and thunder nearly simultaneously slapped the sky.

"Would you?" Hayden said.

"I don't want to do this," Rica said. "I'm afraid. I'm afraid."

Volcanoes

SOMETHING DEEP IN the mantle of Earth gave, like a planetary aneurysm setting the final phase of Earth into motion. Pressure spots and air pockets across the globe popped in an arrhythmic chorus, as if the crust were bubble wrap heated in a microwave oven. *Pop! Pop! Pop!* Volcanoes linked by hidden belts of molten rock burst in quick succession, sending poison air and liquid fire straight up and over the Earth's surface. People living in any proximity to an active volcanic chain melted in the lava downpour. Rivers of molten rock sliced through their cities and dissolved all they touched. The world hissed a high-pitch sizzle.

Glaciers melted, revealing frozen fresh carcasses of mammoths and extinct tigers. The redwood giants of Northern California burned like colossal birthday candles. Lava pouring from underwater vents built new lands in the world's shallower seas, as if Atlantis were rising.

The waters churned and swelled, crashing over the coasts. Soon, the oceans boiled, sending continent-size billows of steam floating across the globe, smelling of simmering fish, salt, and kelp. Rica would never know it, but on the last day, three-quarters of the world was covered with soup.

He wasn't he

SO THIS IS dying, Roy thought. He didn't feel pain or fear. Just sleepy.

Ami had ripped up a section of her own shirt to bandage his neck and slow the bleeding. Roy admired her midriff. It made him smile, to be dying and still moved by a woman's waist.

She lay beside him, curled against his chest, humming old Pearl-Swine songs and stroking his sweaty hair. The sky above them was a shaken swirl of gray and yellow, clouds and lightning.

In all his morning meditations on death, all the death scenarios he led his mind through, he had never pictured this scene. Bleeding to death? Yes, that he had imagined several times. But Ami was something entirely new. She made dying horribly difficult.

"I hate to die, now," he said, smiling from the corner of his mouth.

"Shh," she said. "You'll be fine."

"I would have loved a few more days. A few more hours."

"Won't there be eternity?" she asked, looking up to him, her eyes wet and shining.

Roy, for the first time in his life, wanted to lie. Wanted to take her small face in his hands and promise heaven and angels, white wine and doughnuts, each day, unending. She would smile. He could give her that smile. That hope. The lie hung before him like a ripe apple heavy on the branch. And she, and he as well, was starving. But Roy knew what comes of biting apples.

"I don't know," Roy said. "I have no idea."

Ami exhaled. She'd been holding her breath, perhaps for years. She nodded.

"I can trust that." She sat up and gazed down at Roy. Then leaning in close, she placed her lips on his. She stayed there for a long wait, sand-wind cutting by, but leaving the kiss intact.

She pulled back just an inch, keeping her face so close to Roy that he could not focus on her features. "Can I tell you something? Something that is maybe bad?" she asked.

Roy nodded.

"I'm glad Jesus didn't take me. I'm glad I'm here."

Roy smiled. "Ah, Ami. The world is ending, I'm dying, my best friend grew old overnight, but the most extraordinary thing about today is you here with me."

The sky behind Ami's face was mad and moving. Burning drops fell like tiny specks of wet fire. Roy was swirling inside. How do you die? He had presumed death would do most of the work. His job was not to fight it. But death was not prying his fingers from life. He had to let life go. He had to lose his life. Let go of hearing, let go of taste, even the taste of sand. Let go of what you see. Not just closing your eyes, that's not the same. See it and don't hold it. Open hand. Open palm. Let it all rest on top. Give. Let go of Milton and Rica and Ami. Her sweet face. Let it go. Let them be. Let go of Roy. Let go of I. Float. He wasn't Roy. He wasn't want. He wasn't his history. He wasn't he. He was the sand as much as he. The Ami as much. The air. The space between the air. Float. He was not he. He would not be coming back. This was going. Being. It was not work. It was unwork. The most important action, he realized, was this nonaction. He let go of realizing. Float.

I actually get it

"I CAN'T DO this," Rica said in a quiet voice Hayden could just hear over the wind. "She won't come!"

The old man put a hand to her head. "This baby will be born today." He was calm, sure. Hayden wished he would reach out and comfort him, too.

"Don't let her die in me, okay? Don't let that happen, Milton."

Hayden stood, feeling an acidic bubble in his throat. He threw a hand over his mouth and turned from Rica. He walked in the direction of the maroon shed. *Too much.*

As Saint Rick, Hayden had once delivered a baby in a grain elevator, but that had been clean and quick. A few minutes of loud breaths and a plump, pink, fourteen-pound baby was in his arms. This was different. The yelling, the smells, the fluids. And she was afraid.

He walked farther, breathing in and out, trying to clean the smells from his lungs. *Too much,* he thought. *You're asking too much of me.*

But he didn't leave. He didn't walk to the town and thumb a ride. He could, but he would not. He was supposed to be here. He had found the girl from the dreams. Or she had found him. She needed him. No wait, she did not need him. He was not needed.

Hayden put his hands to his face and looked up at the twisting, steel sky. No one needed him. This was the world, and he was not the star.

He looked back to Rica. Beautiful, birthing, sickening, existing Rica. She was slowly sitting up, hands on her belly, the old man behind her. He could run. But he did not want to. He wanted to go back to them. To be near them. It hurt, the want, it hurt like a cracked rib cage.

So, this is love, he thought. That's what he was feeling. Love for her, for him, for whatever was squeezing to get out. And for more, for sand, for the few drops of rain just starting to spit down, and the heavy scent of ozone each carried, for his own, stupid, arrogant, God-blessed self.

My God, he thought. *I actually get it.*

He could hear music, singing. It was a song he knew. The Beatles' "Hey Jude."

The singing was coming from behind him. He turned. In the distance a crowd was walking. Their steps slow and their voices full. Some held hands, some shuffled dance steps. In front of them it looked as if a small stone was walking. Hayden watched it, wondering if his mind had melted into delusion.

It was no stone. It was a crab. A hermit crab and it crawled directly to Hayden, proceeding under his legs. The crowd, over thirty deep, flowed past him, smiling and singing.

Hayden recognized two of the faces. One was the bearded man in flannel whom he had sat with for so many hours the night before. He grinned and walked past Hayden. Behind him came a wrinkled, leathery face half-hidden under an off-white Stetson.

"Jim Edwards?"

"Hey, Hay! What the hell are you doing here?"

"Where's my car?"

"Got into a little fender bender." Jim rubbed the back of his head. "Ah, who the hell needs a car? I'm following him." Jim pointed to the crawling crab. "How the hell are you, TV star?"

Hayden stared back at Rica crying out on the stone. "I think she's dying, Jim."

Jim stared in Rica's direction for a moment, then patted Hayden's back. "Nah. Just having a baby," he said. "Dying's a lot quieter."

As each claw

CLICK COULD SMELL Rica. He could smell her joy, her fear, her strength, and it drew him near. He was here. His goal. This was home. He crawled toward her.

The ground shook beneath Click. He had no fear. He was near now. He could see and see and see. Each sight was all things. Each grain of sand was as miraculous as each claw as each eye as each sunrise.

He crawled up the stone and up onto her rising chest, skin wet with puddles of salt that again said home, home, home. He moved toward her face, stopping in a warm valley. He could see her eyes. Breaths poured from her mouth. He sent his own gill breaths back.

To be born

RICA STARED DOWN her body. The crab stood between her breasts watching her. She smiled. The crab raised a purple claw and snapped it in the air. He turned and climbed the hill of her belly, stopping near the peak and scratching at her skin. She knew her child was listening. The crab was calling her to be born.

Her insides tensed and wriggled. A new push was coming. The crab pulled his body into his shell and rolled off her belly. Rica watched him go as the tension in her belly built. He crawled through the crowd and into the waiting hands of the short, bearded man.

Above them a storm cloud ruptured and the rain that had only teased fell in full force. Rica bent her legs beneath her and stood to her feet with a yell. Milton grabbed an arm, Hayden ran to her and grabbed the other. Rica pushed.

The women moved close, making a tight circle around her, every face urging her own, sharing her pain, giving their strength. The rain pushed down, carrying sand and mountain smells. Wetting and washing the ground, making the world mud. The other men formed an outer circle. They joined hands and sang "Strawberry Fields Forever." And behind all this, peeking above the men's heads, a face—blue tone, kind eyes, a constant state of awe.

Push!

The sky burned purple and red and the wind blew in three directions, kicking up stones and water and swirling them around in a whirlpool of air and earth.

Push!

Above her three balls of white light swarmed about like burning gnats. The lights, the mystery lights. So near she could feel their warmth. They zoomed back and forth in wide arches, bringing a white glow to the party circling Rica.

Push!

She could feel the head now dropping down lower, the baby urging herself down. Oh God, she wanted to hold this baby.

Push! Bear down and push!

The wind ripped chunks of earth from the ground and propelled them like roadside trash. The sky now a black rippling sheet streaked with red-orange veins, but below the mystery lights the air glowed white. The light balls floated around Rica, dancing before her. They hummed. Rica's near-perfect and full breasts answered in harmony.

Push!

Rica reached a hand down between her legs and felt the wet hair of her baby's head.

She saw no one now. The world was nowhere, nothing but the welling within her. With a deep, endless moan—the moan of a blue whale, of a widow, of a planet slowing to a halt—Rica pushed and the child, the last child, squeezed from her in a rush and cradled itself in Rica's cupped and waiting hands. For a beat between heartbeats, the child mutely gasped at the world and then, above the storm's howl, sang her high-pitched birth cry.

Austin died

AS RICA LABORED, Austin died. The air caught fire and a circle of transparent flames closed in on the city. Trees and houses dissolved into smoke and dust and heat. Birds with feathers turning to ash screeched through the sky. The people circled inward, wrangled by invisible fire. Highways of unmoving traffic, horns yelling worthless protests, panes of glass bursting, sending showers of hot glass down to the crammed streets and sidewalks. Rain turned to steam before hitting the ground. The air singed lungs and bent light. Barton Springs boiled itself dry.

Jeppy sat drawing circles with Carl on their tile kitchen floor, the crayons melting in their hands. Her boyfriend raced around the house, yelling into a phone that no longer worked. He was crying. The air was heating fast, the walls creaking as they expanded. Carl swirled green crayon wax with his finger.

Out the kitchen window, Jeppy caught a glimpse of blue through the smoke. Perfect sky blue. Her boyfriend ran in squeezing the phone. She caught his eye and smiled.

"Above the smoke, the sky is blue," she said.

He paused. Then dropped down, sitting cross-legged on the floor.

She put a hand on Carl's curly head. "My baby is going to die and the universe doesn't give a high-flying fuck."

Shelter

THE SKY WAS streaked with the color of birth, and the baby cried in her arms.

"Is she okay? It's a she, right?" Hayden knelt beside her.

"We have to find shelter," she said.

"There's nothing. It's all gone."

"Then build something!"

"Hey, Hayden," the old man with bent legs said. "What about that shed? We could at least squeeze her and the baby in there."

Hayden jumped to his feet.

The old man smiled at Rica and tipped his rain-soaked hat. "Congratulations," he said, and hobbled after Hayden.

Someone was touching her hair. Rica turned to find Milton, his wet eyes ancient, his touch warm.

"We have to get her inside," she told him.

He nodded and touched the baby's toes. "She's wonderful."

We won't miss the show

THE HARD RAIN pelted down on Hayden. He yanked at the shed's handle, but it didn't budge.

"Come on!"

"Try the number pad," Jim Edwards yelled as he approached.

"And type in what, exactly?"

"Shit, Hayden," he said, pushing Hayden aside and typing random numbers on the LCD panel. "Just because you're probably wrong doesn't mean you shouldn't try."

The display only flashed a red error.

"Might as well keep trying." Jim Edwards punched more numbers. Chunks of earth flew past, one smacking into Jim's head.

"Jim!" Hayden grabbed him as Jim toppled sideways.

"Damn!" Jim threw a hand to his head. Blood dripped past his fingers.

Hayden pulled Jim closer to the shed door and threw his fist against the panel.

"What the hell is this?" Hayden slammed on the door, solid and unmoving.

"Well, at least we won't miss the show," Jim said. Hayden turned. The sky was a dark rainbow of purples and reds.

Something behind Hayden clicked, a shift in the shed's door. Hayden and Jim turned. The door pushed open and a small Haitian man in a cream-colored mock turtleneck gazed out.

"Iola?" Hayden gasped.

Iola gasped.

"Mr. Brock!" A round man with a copper-red beard emerged from the darkness behind Iola. "You made it!"

For a moment, Hayden was lost. The bearded man stuck out his hand.

"Dr. Kip Warner," he said. "Innovator of the Lifepod."

"Hold on," Hayden said, stepping inside the shelter of the shed and grabbing Dr. Warner's shoulders. "You actually made Lifepods?"

"Sure as hell, I did," Dr. Warner said, sweating and smiling. "You should know, you bought three!"

"I thought it was just a fun scam." Hayden glanced down the steep metal staircase that led down farther than he could see. "Wait. I bought three?"

"You, your wife and Iola here."

Hayden glanced at Iola, who shrugged.

"You're my best customer," Dr. Warner continued. "Truth be told, you're my only customer."

Thunder, like a forest of trees snapping in unison, echoed from the sky. Hayden jumped back outside into the wind and rain. The people with the crab had closed in over Rica and shielded her and the baby with their bodies.

Hayden turned back to Dr. Warner. "How many spots have you got?"

"Let's see, not counting your spots and mine, about thirty-eight."

Hayden grinned at Jim. Jim nodded and stuck his head out the door. "Hey Crabites! We got a spot to lay our heads!"

"Wait, no," said Dr. Warner. "I'm a businessman. I sank near $10 million into this baby. No free rides."

Hayden already had his wallet out. He shoved it in the doctor's hands. "Charge me and add a good tip."

Dr. Warner opened his mouth, but Hayden was already through the door.

Baby mewed

THE BABY MEWED in Rica's arms. The people formed a tent over them, humming the melody of "Julia" and blocking some of the roaring storm. The crab sat in the palm of a teenage girl swaying to the song.

"Milton," Rica said softly. "I'm so tired . . ."

"I know," he said, brushing the hair from her forehead.

"I don't want her to die, Milton," she said.

Milton nodded.

Hayden pushed through the people.

"We've got to go, okay?" He knelt at their side, yelling over the wind. "Can you stand? No, don't stand. We'll carry you. Can we carry you?"

"I'm so tired," Rica said. "I can't seem to move."

She held out the child to Milton and he took the baby in his arms. Hayden lifted Rica from the stone. The wind cried.

"We have a place to go," Hayden said. "A safe place to go."

To hide away

THE GROUND BUCKLED, bubbled in places. Lightning shot upward from cracks in the soil, colliding in the sky and bursting into sparks of white and yellow. People moved, leaning on each other as the wind pushed and squealed. Hayden carried Rica in his arms and Milton followed, holding the baby to his chest.

Dr. Warner stood at the open door, waving them through and pulling the heavy door shut. The din of the storm vanished.

"Iola, would you scoot ahead. Get them into the showers. I don't think we have much time."

Iola nodded, then turned to Hayden. "I tried to reach you, Mr. Brock. I tried as soon as the doctor called."

"Thank you, Iola."

He nodded again and darted down the steps.

"What is this place?" Rica asked as Dr. Warner double-latched the door.

"Bit of this, a bit of that. The initial construction was done by the Air Force back in the '40s. Built a bomb shelter here in '46. Abandoned it in '47 when they closed the base. An old woman lives on the land. Been using it as a fruit cellar, if you can believe that."

"She's dead," Hayden said.

Dr. Warner paused. "Well, a lot of people are." He maneuvered around them and started down the steps. "I offered her a pod of her own. Flat-out refused. No one believes it's safe."

"Is it?" Hayden asked.

"Safer than up there," Dr. Warner said. "The spot is near perfect. No significant volcanic activity, no ocean to drown us. No major cities nearby, so fewer zombies to deal with."

"Zombies?" Milton asked.

"Just taking every possibility into consideration. Overall, this place is as safe as it gets." A sound like thunder vibrated through the metal walls and the stairs shuddered. "A little less seismically stable than I'd hoped, but what can you do?"

"And the Lifepods?" Hayden asked.

"Designed them myself," he said. "Simple, really. Temperature and pressure controlled. Each pod will have just enough hydrogen sulfide pumped in to induce short-term hibernation. We wake up in six weeks. Plenty of food, water, and medical supplies to keep us happy for over a year."

Rica hushed and hummed in Hayden's arms, her eyes dropping. The singing of "Yesterday" rang up through the stairwell.

"I can walk now," Rica said at the base of the stairs. Hayden lowered her feet to the ground and Rica leaned against the railing. "Really, I'm all right."

The stairs led to a short hallway ending at a thick door like something from a submarine. A pile of discarded clothes lay just outside the door. Carefully placed a few feet from the clothes was an off-white, well-worn Stetson hat.

"Good, good," Dr. Warner said. "Undress here. That should be fine."

Hayden and Milton shared a look. Dr. Warner rolled his eyes.

"We didn't get the brunt of that gamma-ray burst. That was farther south. But we got some of it. Can't be bringing all that radiation in. Now, strip down and shower off."

He hopped through the door, clapping his hands.

"Where'd you find this guy?" Milton asked.

"Television commercial."

Rica lifted what was left of her dress above her head. Milton held the baby out to Hayden.

"I've never held one before," Hayden said.

"Funny," Milton said. "Neither had I."

Hayden took the baby and Milton helped Rica.

The baby was warm, tiny. Hayden watched her face, sleeping but moving, as if it were experimenting with expressions.

How can this be? he thought. *How can any of this be?*

He looked up to Rica's outstretched hands.

"You made a beautiful baby," he said, handing the child to her. She smiled and pulled the baby to her bare body.

Hayden quickly undressed as well. Strange to feel the familiar vulnerability of nudity even as the world ended. As he removed his pants, something fell from his pocket.

"I guess we can't bring this in either." He picked up the worn string of beads carved by Brother Brendan. He turned to Rica. "But this is for your daughter when she comes out. A birthday gift."

Rica smiled. "Thank you, Hayden Brock."

He placed the rosary down beside Jim's hat and the three walked through the heavy door together. Inside was a long room lit with fluorescent lights and lined with showerheads. The Crabites, including Jim Edwards, were finishing up, standing naked and wet.

Still fully dressed, Dr. Warner moved through the crowd handing out brown capsules.

"One a person. Helps with radiation sickness."

"Potassium iodide or diethylenetriamine pentaacetic acid?" a bald man asked.

"Yes, yes." Dr. Warner said. "Just take it."

On the far side of the room, the doctor joined Iola in yanking open a hatch on the floor. Dr. Warner faced the naked crowd. "No towels, I'm afraid. Just, you know, wipe off any excess moisture, if you can. I'll prepare the pods." With that he lowered himself down the hatch followed by Iola.

"You know," Jim Edwards said, shaking the water from his arms. "If this guy is some kind of pervert serial killer, he's got it made."

Hayden only half heard. He was watching Rica, her face a puzzle. She and Milton stood beneath one shower. An ancient one, a new one, and Rica between them.

"Mr. Brock," Iola popped his head from the hatch. "The doctor would like to see you right now, please."

Hayden glanced once again at Milton, Rica, and the child and made his way to the hatch.

A narrow ladder brought him to a wide, white room furnished with blue and white pill-shaped pods. It was not as glamorous or as well lit as the television ad, but Hayden recognized it nonetheless.

"Impressive," Hayden said.

"We have a problem," Dr. Warner said from the center of the room. "Did a quick count and we're a little short."

"How many?" Hayden asked, moving away from the ladder and earshot of the others.

"Well, your wife should keep the baby with her. Better that way. But outside of that, it's one person to one pod. By my count, we have one pod too few."

The first of the Crabites' naked legs appeared on the ladder. Hayden turned to Dr. Warner. "Not a word to anyone."

In this case it's true

THE SHOWER WATER cooled Rica's feverish skin. She felt alert and awake, but weak. Milton gently washed the blood and sweat from her as she palmed water over the newborn.

"What are we doing?" she asked, her voice hoarse and tired. "We're going to bury ourselves alive in the hopes of what? Nothing will be left."

She faced Milton, his gray beard dripping.

"If I told you the worst was to come," he said. "If I told you you'd suffer. If I told you asking you to live was harder than asking you to die, but your baby, our baby, will live. What would you say?"

"What do you know, Milton?"

Milton shook his head, then bent down and kissed the waking child.

"She is the best humanity has done," Milton whispered. "A new soul. She is a miracle."

"Ah, Milton," Rica sighed. "Every father thinks his daughter is the best thing to ever happen."

"Yes," Milton said. "But in this case it's true."

Space coffins

"QUICKLY NOW," DR. Warner shouted, adjusting a series of knobs along the wall. One by one they came down the ladder and moved to open pods, staring in and sharing questioning glances.

"Once you're in and the lid is closed, simply breathe naturally. Your system will slow down and you'll slip into hibernation," Dr. Warner explained. "I'll remove the oxygen from the room itself. Even if the world burns, we'll be fine. We'll be sleeping. The pods are hermetically sealed and pressure controlled. Perfectly safe."

"Are you sure about this, Doctor?" the teenage Crabite asked, tapping on the blue lid of her pod.

"I tried it on dogs and monkeys with some very promising results."

"Holy crap." Jim Edwards stood with his hands on his hips. "You're asking me to climb butt-naked into your space coffin and you're not even sure it'll work?"

Dr. Warner turned with a growl. "Look, you're standing in the hull of a space shuttle prototype. One that's been doubly reinforced for stress. Cost me a bundle. Now, by my calculations, 80 percent of the world's population is dead already. And the rest will be following soon. These 'space coffins' are your best and only chance. But if you don't want it, fine. Get the hell out."

Jim Edwards nodded. "Doc, you have my apologies. Let's do this."

Physics, faith, and love

RICA AND MILTON were last down the ladder. Hayden helped as Rica climbed, then Milton lowered the baby down. He followed, his legs uncertain on the rungs.

"Your pods are over here," Hayden said, and led them through the rows of Crabites climbing into their spots.

"Pleasant dreams," an older man waved at Hayden.

"You too, Jim."

On the side wall at the end of the room, next to Dr. Warner's controls, stood the last two Lifepods. Hayden helped Rica climb into hers as Milton cradled the baby.

Her eyes blinked at him, round and dark. She reached up her tiny hands and tangled her pink fingers in his gray beard. She gave a soft cry.

Dr. Warner flipped three switches and something in the walls hummed to life.

"Rica's lost some blood," Milton said to Dr. Warner. "Do you think she'll be okay?"

"How would I know?" he said, twisting knobs. "I studied engineering. Never even got my degree, truth be told." He flipped two more switches and the white lights snapped off. Dim yellow emergency lights tinted the room. "And we are ready to go."

Milton stepped forward and placed the wriggling newborn against Rica's chest. She moved the baby's asking mouth to her breast and looked up at Milton.

"Are you sure it's not better for us, all of us, to just die today?"

"I'm not," he said. He touched the baby's soft back. "Do you remember that I had something to tell you?"

Rica nodded.

"She wants to stay," he said.

Rica's eyes shone in the low light. "Why?"

Milton shook his head. "Because," he said, his voice quiet. "Things don't end, only change." Milton touched the baby. "Physics, faith, and love," he said to her. "The best things make no sense at all. Not to me, at least."

"Okay," Rica whispered. "Okay." She reached up and touched his wrinkled face. Milton nodded and lowered the lid.

Nothing at all

HAYDEN WATCHED RICA'S lid close, his chest squeezing into his throat. Milton turned to him.

"I can count," Milton said with a crooked grin. "Not enough pods. I can't let you do this."

"Look," Hayden said. "I'm not a real pro at this self-sacrifice stuff. This is my first time. So, don't screw it up for me."

"Mr. Brock, it was a pleasure to meet you," said Dr. Warner, turning from his controls with a clap of his hands. "I am going to set the automated system and plug myself in. Good luck up there."

"If it's all right, Doctor," Milton said, "I'll walk him up and latch the door."

"I can let myself out," Hayden said.

"I want that door latched from the inside," Milton said.

"Yes, yes. That would be best." Warner nodded. "Five minutes and the only air in this room will be in those pods, okay? And make sure you seal every door and hatch behind you, for God's sake."

Milton and Hayden moved past the pods. The room was quiet now, still in the yellow half-light. He followed Hayden up the steps, his legs growing numb, his breath stuttered.

He was glad to be old. Something about the weak body, the failing skin and hair, the struggling lungs. Something about it felt natural.

He watched the back of Hayden's head and listened to their echoing steps.

"Hayden," Milton wheezed, "I was sent to find you and did not know why."

Hayden motioned to the stairwell. "Looks like you have your reason."

"Would you like to know what I know?"

"Yes."

"Nothing at all."

Hayden chuckled.

They reached the door. The wind, a dull cry behind the steel.

"You know what I'm going to ask," Milton said.

"Yes. And the answer is no."

"You're willing to die for me. I'm asking you to do one more. I'm running on empty here. I need you to stay and love Rica and love that baby."

"No."

Milton smiled. "Listen, don't be a movie star. Don't be a saint. Just love those given to you to love."

Hayden stared for a long while. Finally he nodded and Milton smiled.

"It will be lonely," Milton said.

Milton unlatched the door, opened it to the red roar of sand and wind. He turned and nodded at Hayden. Milton stepped out and was swallowed by the sand.

Hayden watched the swirl of reds and black for a moment before pushing the door closed.

Floated and blurred

RICA LAY IN the compact dark of the pod, the only sound a faint hum and her daughter nursing. She breathed slowly, deeply, the air tasting of cinnamon. She opened and closed her eyes, but the darkness was too complete to change. She could feel the sleep coming, moving through her lungs and blood.

Quietly, she sang Mingus's dissonant lullaby "Eclipse" to her baby.

Eclipse, when the moon meets the sun.

Her voice echoed strange. Not her own and yet clearly her own.

Sleep moved through her. Milk flowed from her and into the child, into the body her body had made. She shared her body, as they shared breath, as they had shared blood. Where did she end and her child begin?

Eclipse, these bodies have become one.

The sleep sent her floating. Past skin, past blood, and into these other nearby sleepers. As human as she. As alive. Where did she end and they begin? In the black, they floated and blurred into one another. Her, them, she, Earth.

Sleeping floating. And into the dark she whispered.

"We are soup."

Giant orange head

WE'RE VERY NEAR the end now. You might want to know what Milton said back at the KRST studios.

KRST was linked to a burgeoning satellite radio company, U-Sat Radio. In fact, by the second-to-last day of planet Earth, U-Sat Radio possessed the only working communication satellite orbiting Earth. The others, like the one Hayden witnessed, had fallen to Earth in impressive fireballs. Because of this Milton was heard not just by a few, but by billions. Billions searching the airwaves for some kind of news, some word of hope.

He said this: "A man walks into a bar. He sees a guy sitting at the bar with a giant orange head."

As he spoke into the microphone, Milton imagined his father as a young man, sitting in his Austin kitchen, listening to a radio on the table. He's sipping instant coffee and waiting for the next song.

"The man walks up to the guy and says, 'Hey, how'd you get that giant orange head?' 'Funny story,' the guy says. 'I found this genie lamp, rubbed it, and out came this genie. He gave me three wishes.'"

Milton could see his father nod a little and smile.

"'My first wish was to be rich. And bam! Bags of gold appeared all around me. It was great.'"

His father chuckled a little, enjoying the buildup.

"'My second wish was true love. Again, bam! And a beautiful woman was standing by my side and we instantly fell in love.'"

His father's smile grew and he leaned closer to the radio. Milton paused for effect. His dad's eyebrows raised. Milton waited. He could feel his father whispering, "Come on. Come on." Just one second more. Then Milton finished the joke.

"'For my third wish, I asked for a giant orange head.'"

Milton paused and smiled.

"Ha!" his father said and clapped his hands.

"By the way," Milton added into the microphone. "The world's last sunrise is happening right now and it is amazing."

He thought to explain that actually as long as the Earth was spinning the sun is constantly "rising" somewhere. But Milton decided that would take too long.

Ameyn

MILTON TOOK ONLY three steps through the hot rain and biting sand before falling to the ground.

He lay there with no fear, no dread. Just a sense of curiosity and slight amusement.

A hand touched his. The winds died away and the red scratch of sand was replaced by a pale, white glow. He looked up to see the dark, bearded man in the trucker's hat sitting beside him. The mystery lights surrounded them, buzzing in fast arcs, forming a dome of low, white light that repelled the wind and rain.

On the other side of the glow mountain-size hunks of earth slipped from the ground and scattered upward. The stars were hidden in the rush of red soil.

Milton felt a scratching and saw the hermit crab crawling on his leg. He lowered his hand and allowed it to crawl onto his palm.

Outside the wind stopped, as if all the Earth had inhaled and held a final breath. The debris fell, colliding against the surface. All was quiet and brilliant. Then in a rush, the Earth exhaled and a new wind melted the land into a soft, rolling, cream-colored ocean.

"*Ameyn*," the bearded man whispered.

Milton turned to him. He was smiling.

All this, all this was how it was supposed to be.

Or at least how it actually is, he thought.

And the difference between the two meant nothing at all.

One by one, the lights slowed their spin. One by one, they blinked to darkness and the dome faded.

No air. No sound.

For an instant Milton was floating in the stars. For an instant he was with his father, his daughter, his lover. For an instant he was the darkness and one dot among an infinite spray of light.

acknowledgments

MUCH THANKS GOES to my editor Liz Parker for helping me shape this novel. Thanks to Jack Shoemaker, Julia Kent, Kelly Winton, Elke Barter and the entire Counbterpoint/Soft Skull family. Also thanks to Matthew Bialer and Lindsay Ribar of Sanford J. Greenburger Associates. A huge debt is owed to my dear, talented friends who read and reread these pages: Michael Noll, Stephanie Noll, Matt Stuart, Mike Yang, Angie Beshara, Stacey Swann, Mark Barr, Zach Carlson, my big brother Gareth Egerton and others. I owe you backrubs and cocktails. Thanks to my parents for example and encouragement, my brother Gwyn for inspiration and my sister Annwen for teaching me how hermit crabs molt. Love and thanks to Arden and Oscar for emboldening me with hermit crab art and irreverent songs. And a heart-popping thanks goes to the outstanding population of Austin. You fill this book. Finally, thanks to Jodi—my best reader, my best friend.